To Roger Bygott

h

August 2001

IN THE SHADOW OF CAESAR

IN THE SHADOW
OF CAESAR

Anthony Horne

Book Guild Publishing
Sussex, England

First published in Great Britain in 2007 by
The Book Guild Ltd
Pavilion View
19 New Road
Brighton, BN1 1UF

Typesetting in Baskerville by
SetSystems Ltd, Saffron Walden, Essex

Printed in Great Britain by
CPI Antony Rowe

A catalogue record for this book is
available from the British Library

ISBN 978 1 84624 148 2

Author's Note

This is a historical novel, not history. It is set during the latter years of the Roman Republic culminating in the outbreak of civil war and the battle of Pharsalus. The Cottas were a real family of the Roman nobility and related to that of Julius Caesar. Lucius himself, however, his immediate family and a few minor figures appearing in the text are imaginary. The story is told through the eyes of Lucius and via his personal experiences. The rest is based on fact and any student of the period will recognise the events which took place and the people who took part. For those not familiar with these, I have appended a list of major dates and maps of Italy, Asia, Gaul and the relevant part of Greece together with a list of Principal Names.

I should like to record my thanks to Lydia Lindley, Pam Maplethorpe, David Morris, my wife Anne and my daughter Louise, all of whom, in their different ways, have helped me greatly in the production of this book.

A.J.H.

Chronology

ITALY

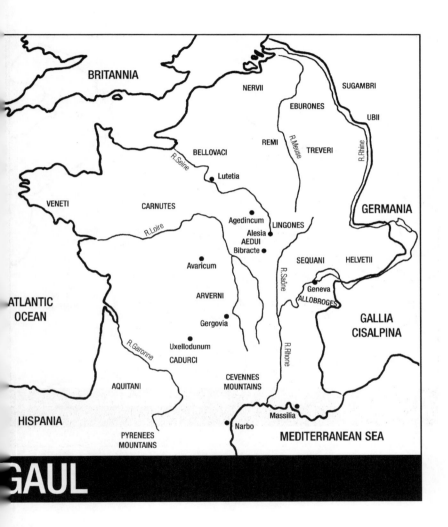

BRITANNIA

NERVII

SUGAMBRI

EBURONES

UBII

REMI

R.Meuse

TREVERI

R.Rhine

BELLOVACI

R.Seine

Lutetia

GERMANIA

VENETI

CARNUTES

R.Loire

Agedincum

LINGONES

Alesia

AEDUI

Bibracte

Avaricum

SEQUANI

HELVETII

ARVERNI

Geneva

ALLOBROGES

ATLANTIC
OCEAN

Gergovia

GALLIA
CISALPINA

R.Saône

Uxellodunum

R.Garonne

CADURCI

R.Rhone

AQUITANI

CEVENNES
MOUNTAINS

HISPANIA

Massilia

Narbo

MEDITERRANEAN SEA

PYRENEES
MOUNTAINS

GAUL

ix

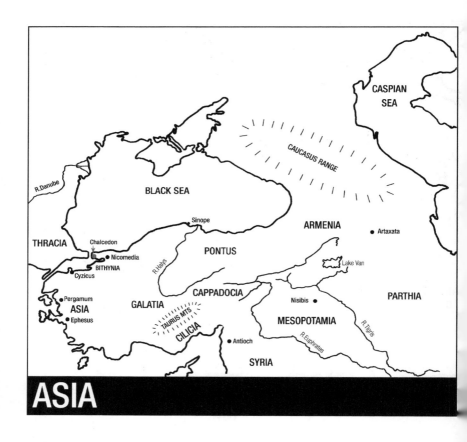

ASIA

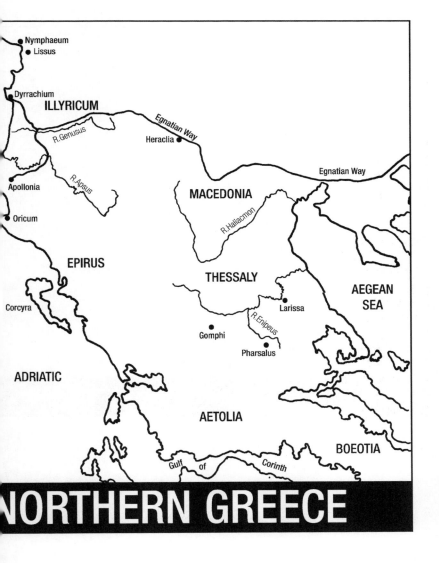

Nymphaeum
Lissus

Dyrrachium
ILLYRICUM
R.Genusus
Egnatian Way
Heraclia

Apollonia
R.Apsus

Oricum

Egnatian Way

MACEDONIA
R.Haliacmon

EPIRUS

THESSALY

Corcyra
AEGEAN
SEA

Larissa
R.Enipeus

Gomphi

Pharsalus

ADRIATIC

AETOLIA

BOEOTIA

Gulf of Corinth

NORTHERN GREECE

Index of Principal Names

Cicero, Quintus	Brother of orator, fought with Caesar in Gaul
Cinna, L. Cornelius	Consul 87 BC, enemy of Sulla, father of Caesar's first wife, Cornelia
Claudius, Appius	Brother of Clodius, consul 54 BC
Clodius, Publius	Caesar's supporter in Rome, tribune in 58 BC, murdered by Milo in 52 BC
Cornelia	Daughter of Cinna, Caesar's first wife
Cotta, C. Aurelius	Consul in 75 BC
Cotta, M. Aurelius	Consul in 74 BC
Cotta, Lucius Valerius*	The Narrator
Cotta, Publius Valerius*	Brother of Lucius Cotta
Crassus, M. Licinius	Financier, member of first Triumvirate with Caesar and Pompeius. Killed at Carrhae in 53 BC
Crassus, Publius	Son of financier, fought with Caesar in Gaul, killed with his father at Carrhae
Curio, C. Scribonius	Became supporter of Caesar, tribune in 50 BC
Curius, Quintus	Catilinarian conspirator, friend of Fulvia
Domitia*	Friend of Lucius Cotta, sister of L Domitius Ahenobarbus
Domitius Calvinus, C:	One of Caesar's generals, consul in 53 BC
Domitius Ahenobarbus, L	Consul in 54 BC, enemy of Caesar
Fulvia	Friend of Curius, the Catilinarian conspirator
Fulvia	Widow of Clodius, married Curio and then Marcus Antonius
Hirtius, Aulus	One of Caesar's officers
Hortensius, Quintus	Advocate, opponent of Pompeius, died 50 BC
Julia	Caesar's daughter by Cornelia, wife of Pompeius, died 54 BC
Labienus, Titus	One of Caesar's generals in Gaul, defected to Pompeius at beginning of Civil War
Laeca, M. Porcius	Catilinarian conspirator

Longinus, L. Cassius	Catilinarian conspirator
Lucullus, L. Licinius	General, campaigned against Mithridates of Pontus
Mamurra	Caesar's adjutant
Marcellus, C. Claudius	Consul in 49 BC, brother of M. Claudius Marcellus
Marcellus, Gaius	Consul in 50 BC
Marcellus, M. Claudius	Consul 51 BC
Marius, Gaius	General, Consul seven times, enemy of Sulla, died 87 BC
Matius, Gaius	Friend of Caesar
Metellus Celer, Q. Caecilius	Consul in 60 BC, governor designate of Narbonese Gaul, died 59 BC
Metellus Nepos, Q. Caecilius	Consul in 57 BC
Milo, Titus Annius	Supporter of Pompeius, rival of Clodius, gang leader
Mithridates	King of Pontus, enemy of Rome
Mucia	Wife of Pompeius before Julia
Murena, L. Licinius	Consul in 62 BC, lieutenant of Lucullus against Mithridates
Nero, Tiberius Claudius	Senator
Octavius, Gaius	Caesar's great nephew, later the Emperor Augustus
Oppius, C	Roman Knight, ran Caesar's office in Rome with Balbus
Paetus, P. Autronius	Catilinarian conspirator
Piso, L. Calpurnius	Consul in 58 BC, became Caesar's father-in-law
Pompeia	Caesar's second wife
Pompeius, Cnaeus	Pompey the Great, General, member of First Triumvirate with Caesar and Crassus, murdered in Egypt after Pharsalus
Scipio, Q. Caecilius Metellus	Consul in 52 BC, father-in-law of Pompeius after his marriage to Cornelia, fought at Pharsalus, committed suicide after Thapsus in 46 BC

Sempronia*	Wife of Publius Valerius Cotta
Servilia	Married secondly Decimus Junius Silanus, mother of M. Brutus, mistress of Caesar
Sulla, L. Cornelius	General, Consul 88 BC, afterwards Dictator, died 78 BC
Sulla, P. Cornelius	Nephew of the Dictator, served with Caesar at Dyrrachium and Pharsalus
Sura, P. Cornelius Lentulus	Praetor in 63 BC, Catilinarian conspirator
Varro, M. Terentius	Man of learning, writer on many subjects, born at Reate in 116 BC, died in 27 BC
Vatinius, Publius	Supporter of Caesar, tribune in 59 BC
Ventidius, Publius	Manager of supplies for Caesar's army

* *Indicates fictitious character*

Chapter I

I sit by my pool. Though it is still spring the sun shines from a cloudless sky, the colour of white marble. At my feet lies my wolfhound, grey round the muzzle and asleep. The two umbrella pines close by offer shade and there is no need of the parasol which my freedman, Theon, has brought out. Even the cicadas have fallen silent in the sultry heat and the only sound is that of the water from the pool as it trickles over the rim at the far end and down the slope to the valley below. The pool was built about a hundred years ago by my grandfather, Quintus Valerius Cotta. He had found a spring on this promontory near Baiae within sight of the Lucrine Lake and decided to build a villa here, knowing that despite its elevated position the house would always have a supply of water. Until the proscriptions of Sulla, of which I will tell later, our family had a house on the Caelian Hill in Rome, a mansion befitting one of the leading families of the city. The house was comfortable and spacious, removed from the hustle and bustle of the streets near the Forum and in the Suburra where blocks of flats rose precariously over the foul smelling alleyways and open drains. Even so, in the summer our house was oppressive and stifling in the heat and my grandfather, like many others, sought refuge where the air was cooler around the coast of Campania.

The pool is rectangular and lined with blocks of dressed stone. Because it is fed by the spring the water is clear and

1

in it carp swim lazily, occasionally flapping to the surface and accepting with negroid lips morsels of food which I or the slaves may toss to them. Today they linger at the bottom to keep cool. Behind me rises the villa built originally round a courtyard to which my father and I have added over the years. When I came to live here permanently after Pharsalus I built a terrace and covered portico looking out over the bay towards Puteoli and the busy harbour there. A path leads down to the sea but it is steep and rocky. Sometimes, on good days, I can manage the descent and I swim off the rocks at the bottom with Theon holding onto me by means of a rope tied round my waist. Nowadays I do not swim well but I enjoy the gentle massage of the warm water which seems to relieve the ache in my foot. Afterwards Theon towels me down and applies unguents to my scars before he helps me back up the path, shading my head from the sun with the parasol. Then I may sit and perhaps doze on the terrace or write laboriously with my left hand a few more lines of my memoirs. In the distance I can just see the small towns round the bay, Neapolis, Herculaneum and Stabiae. Above Herculaneum rises the cone of Vesuvius. On clear days I can make out a thin column of smoke struggling up into the sky from its summit.

When I was a boy I remember that my father told me of a prophecy that one day all the citizens of a city named after the Greek hero Hercules would be killed in a single day by fire and smoke. Apparently Hercules had murdered his guest Iphitus after a banquet, as a result of which he began to suffer from evil dreams and went to consult the Delphic Oracle to ask how he might be rid of them. The Pythoness Xenoclea refused to answer him, saying that she had no oracles for those who murdered their guests. In a rage Hercules plundered the shrine and made off with the votive offerings, saying that he would build his own oracle. The Pythoness then pronounced the prophecy to her attendants by way of revenge for Hercules' behaviour. I suppose there are several towns and cities named after Hercules, but sometimes as I gaze across the bay towards that smoking mountain I wonder what might happen to the little town below. Today nothing disturbs the stillness apart from two cargo ships making their way almost imperceptibly across the sound towards Puteoli. Their square sails attempt to catch what breeze there is and I can just make out the motion of oars. They are probably bringing corn from Africa or Sicily destined to feed the city mob in Rome.

Ajax stirs and licks my leg. I suspect he wants a drink from the little stream at the bottom of the gardens and I follow him as he pads along the side of the pool. We walk down the broad, gravel path lined with box and plane trees. At intervals on each side stand marble statues of Greek heroes and gods. Here Aegeus gazes out to sea in search of the white sail which he had instructed Theseus to hoist. A little lower down Poseidon rises from the waves on horseback and Perseus carries the head of Medusa in one hand with his polished shield in the other. Next we pass Athene as she springs fully armed from the skull of her father Zeus. Gradually the ground opens out to reveal an orchard of apple, pear, quince and cherry trees, the latter given to me by Lucullus when we came back from the campaigns against Mithridates in Pontus. Lucullus also had a villa near here which he bought from Sulla's daughter. I do not seek to emulate the eastern paradises of his gardens with their fountains, secluded pavilions and shrubs trimmed into the shapes of exotic animals. I prefer a more natural look and take pleasure in the wild flowers growing at random between the fruit trees. Here I can pluck a fig or reach down for a wild strawberry. Theon and the slaves have cut irrigation channels which fan out from the pool at the top of the slope and protect the trees from drought. Lower down the ground gives way to myrtle, laurel, oak and cypress. Here beside the

3

stream I have placed a semicircular seat carved from the finest white marble and nearby stands a small pavilion of the same material. If I stay quiet I shall probably catch sight of the kingfisher keeping watch over the little pool a few yards upstream. He often sits in a twisted oak tree bent over the water which is so still that he must sometimes catch his own image. I cannot spot him yet but at my approach a snake which has been basking on the bank slithers noiselessly away into the grass. Ajax laps the water and then slumps down again by my seat. The marble is cool against my skin. Here I am completely alone. The activity of other men does not impinge. I reflect on what I have been, what I have done and what I have become.

I have been a soldier for virtually all of my life. As a young man I went with Lucullus and my uncle Marcus Cotta, his colleague in command, to fight in the war against Mithridates. There I learnt the profession of soldier with the legions. I learnt how to wield the gladius, to stab a man in the belly and without a second look to push forward with my shield seeking another man to kill. Soon, befitting my status as the scion of one of Rome's leading noble families, I was on horseback in command of a legion. Returning to the city I was elected aedile before going with Caesar to Spain as his legate during his governorship of the Further Province. Gaius Caesar had been my friend since we were small boys. We were both born in the sixth consulship of Marius and indeed our families are related. Together we grew up in Rome, though his home was in the Suburra whereas mine was on the slopes of the Caelian Hill. We assumed the toga of a man on the same day. We learnt to use weapons together on the Campus Martius, to throw a javelin and to ride a horse. Then our skin was not hardened by exposure to snow, rain and sleet. The calluses had not yet formed on our shoulders where the straps of the breastplate rub against the skin. This came later during the long campaigns in Gaul.

By the time we crossed the Rubicon to precipitate the civil war I had personally killed perhaps a hundred men, ordered the death of many more and observed the removal of the hands of thousands at Uxellodunum.

None of this gave me a moment's pause. The army of Gaul was engaged upon its conquest with the approval of the Senate and the people of Rome, provided the gold and other spoils came to adorn the city and the houses of already rich men. I was fifty years of age when we crossed that little stream from Cisalpine Gaul into Italy. Physically I was fit and strong from years of campaigning. My muscles were still hard and I had learnt to endure hunger and cold, to stay in the saddle for days on end, even to sleep in it on occasion. Like most Romans, the sight of blood and the infliction of physical pain meant nothing to me. These were merely facts of a soldier's life which I had chosen in preference to a political career, except for my year as an aedile. Looking back I realise that I had become immune to violence; it was not a concept that I understood. Apart from a spell in Rome after returning from the war against Mithridates and before departing for Spain with Caesar, I had known the company of few women. Of course, like any young man I took my pleasure where I could find it. I was tall and well built. I came of a noble family who had money and influence. After exercise and the baths we would go out into the taverns of the Suburra, drink and find girls who for a denarius would do everything you wanted. But you took care to put a dagger in your belt. After dusk the taverns and the alleys were dark and dingy, lit only by infrequent brands. The smoke from cooking fires in the shops drifted into the streets so that sometimes you could see only a few paces in front of you. Often we used to take off our fine tunics and go into the town dressed in clothes taken from our slaves. That way one was less conspicuous. Even so the people would know by the manner of our speech that we were not of their kind. One night my friend Sextus Piso insisted on leaving a dinner that a number of us young men were attending at a mansion on the Capitoline belonging to the Metelli. He said he was going to look for a girl he had met the night before somewhere near the Forum Boarium, the fairground not far from the Aemilian Bridge. We urged him not to go by himself. He seemed to agree but later in the evening when I rose from my couch to seek out Cnaeus Carbo who had gone to speak to the ladies dining in the adjoining room, he told me that Sextus had slipped away an hour before. A freedman of the family found him the following morning floating in the Tiber with his own dagger in his back. It was rumoured that the girl was the daughter of a fuller who had discovered them making love in a room behind a tavern, but though the family of Piso tried to identify the killer the people of the district would say nothing.

When I was just sixteen I met a girl called Domitia, the daughter of Cnaeus Domitius Ahenobarbus. She was the same age as I, with long straight hair which her mother made her gather in a bun and secure with ribbons. Domitia was gay and carefree in contrast to her brother Lucius, a cruel and stupid man who many years later had to surrender ignominiously to us at Corfinium. Domitia had a friend called Cossutia of whom Caesar became fond. For a year or so we went around together as a happy foursome. Sometimes we would go to a play or perhaps to the circus to see the gladiatorial contests and the strange beasts brought from Africa. We enjoyed watching lions pitted against panthers or a solitary bear fighting off half a dozen wolves which had been deliberately starved before going into the arena. Chariot races were also exciting and I remember we were all supporters of the blues. Sometimes we took the girls on horseback out of the city through the Esquiline Gate and along the Via Praenestina towards the hills. One day I arranged to take Domitia alone, as I had made up my mind to seduce her at a spot on the banks of a small stream where the four of us had often been to swim and afterwards drink wine as we lay in the sun. I ordered a slave to have ready a horse at the gate where we met in the middle of the day. Soon we were trotting along the road with Domitia clasping me round the waist. The rhythmic motion of the horse, the sensation of Domitia's firm breasts pressed against my back and her legs entwined round mine combined to produce in me such a burning desire for her that I urged the horse to go faster and faster. I could sense the excitement in Domitia too as she laughed in my ear and clung on even more tightly. After a couple of miles we turned off the road into oak woods which led gently upwards to the hills and the stream which was my objective. The sun blazed down but we were protected now by the leaves which brushed our bodies as we passed through them. At the stream I tethered the horse and unhitched the flask of wine which I then hung in the water to chill. Domitia laughed for my thin summer tunic revealed all too readily my high state of excitement and she told me to cool off in the stream. I jumped in and splashed about for a few minutes, trying not to think about what I wanted to do with the beautiful girl sitting on the bank. Then it happened in a flash. I heard the horse whinny sharply, there was a noise of undergrowth and twigs being broken by swift movement and a large boar was charging at Domitia. I shouted, 'jump!' and she half slithered and half scrambled down the bank before dropping into my arms as I stood in the water. The boar stopped in a flurry of earth and grass before turning and trotting away into the trees behind. We held each other and laughed, although it had been a narrow escape. An angry boar can kill a man with his tusks. Domitia had to wash her dress which had been soiled in the slide down the bank. Together we squeezed and rubbed it in the clear water before scrambling out on the other side from which the boar had appeared. She hung the

7

dress to dry on a bush and side by side we lay naked, she the nymph and I the faun. I kissed her on the lips and breasts, the wine flask lay forgotten in the water. She accepted me half smiling and half giggling. We were both supremely happy that afternoon in the sun by the stream. Our lives had not then been touched by the suffering which she was to know all too soon and which I came to experience in a different way much later. I must have fallen asleep for when I awoke I found that Domitia had plaited a wreath of oak leaves and placed it on my head as a reward for saving the life of a Roman citizen. I pointed out that the civic crown could only be awarded in battle and that anyway she had saved herself from the charging boar. She just laughed and kissed me. We drank some wine and rode back to the city, both looking forward to a life together.

Later that summer Domitia became ill. Her doctors, summoned by her father from Athens and Rhodes as well as from the city, could find no cure. She grew thin until the bones of her arms and legs were visible through the skin. She tried to eat but vomited most of the food. Her father offered sacrifices to the household gods. On the advice of the Flamen Dialis he sacrificed to Capitoline Jupiter a white bull from which drops of blood were mixed with wine and given to the patient. It was all to no avail. Every day I visited her in the family home which was not far from ours, close to the Forum at the foot of the Palatine. Domitia lay on a couch at the side of the atrium in the shade of a colonnade looking out into a courtyard where a fountain played sometimes in a raised pool. A slave girl sat with her whenever her mother Livia was called away to attend to family business. The red and yellow pillars of the colonnade rose gracefully to Corinthian capitals decorated with vines and acanthus leaves. Behind on the walls were murals depicting views of gardens or the countryside. Here peacocks perched on the steps of a villa; a school of dolphins swam alongside a pleasure boat; brightly coloured birds fluttered among trees whose leaves rustled from an unfelt breeze. It was as if the walls were windows onto an idyllic world outside. I loved the place but hated the circumstances of my visits. I watched helplessly as my dearest Domitia withered away. The slave girl would retire at my arrival and I would kneel by the couch to hold the hands which had once been clothed with flesh the colour of apple blossoms and were now reduced to the skin and bones of a scrawny chicken. I wept and in a whisper she would tell me not to weep – that we had been happy once and that was the same as being happy for ever; time had no significance. In the last few days she could not speak and when I squeezed her hand there was no response. Now her parents were with her all the time. Her father sat in a chair dressed in his toga with the broad purple stripe of a senator. Livia crouched by Domitia talking quietly to her and occasionally holding to her lips a bowl of water. Two or three of the household slaves stood respectfully in the background waiting to fulfil any commands that might be given. The clamour of the Forum was nearby but in that enclosed courtyard there was silence as we waited for the end.

One day when I went to the house the slave girl who had sat with Domitia opened the main door and motioned me in. She did not raise her head and I could see that she was weeping. Silently she led me to the tablinum where I found Livia sitting with Domitia's body laid upon a table. Neither of us spoke but I bent down and kissed Domitia's lips; they were white and cold. I placed my arms round Livia's shoulders and stood there for a moment shaking. It was my first experience of death. I had not even seen a dead body before. Soon afterwards I left the house. I went for a long walk by the banks of the Tiber. I was filled with a desire to get away from the city. It seemed the only way to ease the pain. I needed to escape from the places where we had been

9

happy together, from the people who had been our friends. I think it was then I decided to be a soldier.

Now as my life enters its last phase I have many things for which to be thankful. I have a beautiful home decorated with trophies from military campaigns. The masks of my ancestors hang from the walls, together with jewelled swords seized from Gallic chieftains, including the one placed by Vercingetorix on the ground before Caesar in token of surrender after the siege of Alesia. I have furniture of polished cedar brought from Pontus and silk hangings from Armenia. Couches of inlaid ivory adorn my dining rooms and the columns of the peristyle gleam with golden capitals. The floors of every room are decorated with finely-worked mosaics; here fishes swim in a clear blue sea, there a lion springs to catch an antelope or peacocks strut in an ornamental garden. Along the terrace pink roses entwine themselves around the white marble pillars of the balustrade. At intervals are busts of great men: Scipio Africanus stares fixedly south towards Carthage and Quintus Fabius the Delayer is there too. In the middle stands my old friend and leader, Gaius Julius Caesar carved from his death mask, but with hair on his head, as I prefer to remember him.

Apart from my freedman Theon, who acts as my body servant, I have as many slaves as I want to tend the house and gardens. There is also my estate in Picenum, part of Pompeius' property before it was seized at the end of the civil war. My factor Crispinus is in charge there with about fifty slaves to tend the vines and olives. I used to go regularly to visit the property either by carriage or on horseback. Now I no longer trust myself on a horse and the journey by carriage takes three days along bumpy roads. Instead I receive regular reports and accounts from Crispinus. My old friend Gaius Sempronius, who owns the adjoining estate, also writes, each year, to tell me the prices which oil from the area is fetching and the prospects for the grape harvest.

After the war in Gaul I estimated that I had ten million sesterces worth of gold and other booty including slaves, some of which went to the market on Delos and others I gave as presents to friends. When my mother Aemilia died she bequeathed to me the old home of her family, the Aurelii. The house, once rented by Cicero when he was building his own nearby, stands on the slope which is called the Clivus Victoriae, leading from the Forum to the Palatine. I have never lived there and they tell me that Octavius wants to pull it and several other houses down so that a temple in his honour can be built in their place. I do not need the money but I shall ask for half a million sesterces all the same. From my father I inherited warehouses at Puteoli which he built when he saw that the harbour was growing with the ever increasing imports from Egypt, Africa, Sicily, Spain and Sardinia. For these I draw good rent from the grain merchants and importers of wild animals on their way to the arenas in Rome and Capua.

Not only am I a rich man but I have been fortunate to take part in great events, some of which I shall set down in this memoir. A soldier is lucky to fight for as long as I did, not to be maimed or killed, at least in my case until the battle when I killed for the last time and received at the same moment the wounds to my leg and arm. And yet I do not rest content on this marble seat by the stream. The events of the last few years have brought doubts where previously I had none. When we were fighting, conquering and slaying, raping and stealing in Pontus, in Spain and in Gaul, it was for the greater glory of Rome, to extend the influence of the city, to earn honour amongst our peers, to bring in wealth and tribute. Behind us we had the traditions of the Republic, a democracy which had grown out of the ancient kings to produce the great offices of state, the consuls and praetors of whom my family has provided many, the inviolate tribunes of the plebs, the censors and the aediles. The Senate advised and influenced, the assembly of the people passed the laws by which our society was regulated. The system was not perfect but the people were able to vote freely, even if that vote might be influenced by bribery. If a man was wrongly accused he could invoke the protection of the tribunes. A magistrate who abused his power could be prosecuted for his wrongs. This applied not only to the citizens of Rome, but to the provinces whose representatives might bring proceedings to recover sums extorted from a colony by the proconsul or pro-praetor, as witness the prosecution of Verres by Cicero on behalf of the Sicilians. Caesar once accused Gnaeus Dolabella of a similar offence against the Macedonians, though the prosecution failed.

But I am wandering from the point. I mourn the passing of the Republic. When I was young the rule of law more or less prevailed. The city had its own identity and the classes each knew their place in the social order. The Senate met regularly at the behest of the consuls who would listen to the advice of former magistrates and act in the best interests of the State. The people had not degenerated into the rabble which now passes for a population, whose men spend their days in idleness, waiting for the next distribution of free bread or lavish games to distract them from their boredom. Perhaps it was Marius who started the process when he turned a people's militia into a professional army. In the old days, men would return from military service to their land or perhaps to their craft. With the extension of the State boundaries, campaigns became longer and the citizen soldier had to give way to the professional. Then Sulla demonstrated the power of a general in command of his army when he returned from Asia after the peace treaty with Mithridates and enforced his will upon the city. The concept of loyalty to an imperator instead of to the State formed itself in the minds of the legionaries and from that moment the Republic was doomed. It is said that when Marcellus was consul at the height of the crisis before we crossed into Italy he went to Pompeius' villa in the Alban Hills outside Rome and there, before a number of other senators, he presented Pompeius with a sword and asked him to save the Republic. What nonsense! The Republic had already died in the violence and disorder of the previous thirty years. Caesar did not fight against Pompeius and the obstinate clique in the Senate, headed by the likes of Cato and Ahenobarbus, in order to destroy the Republic; he fought because he had no choice. Did they expect him to surrender to his political enemies and be prosecuted to perdition after all he had achieved and the wealth he had brought to the State? Caesar did not wish to rule Rome as a king. He sought to bring order out of the chaos of the preceding years. Who knows, if they had not struck him down, perhaps he would have restored the old institutions and reinvigorated them? Certainly the conspirators achieved the opposite effect to that which they intended. Now, instead of a restored democracy, we have Octavius in the west and Antonius in the east. Effectively Rome is governed by one man with the connivance of a subservient Senate, many of whose members are not even Roman, but from Spain, Gaul and other provinces. The Senate and the people of Rome have gone forever and I for one regret their passing. But I am an old man with old-fashioned views. Perhaps Octavius will rule well and preside over a new society where different values will obtain.

Ala comes down the slope bearing a flagon of watered wine and my fluorspar cup. Silently she sits down beside me, pours the wine and hands the cup to me. I hold it up in the light of the evening sun. The bands of dark red, orange, yellow and green glisten translucently in my hand and I smell the resin as I sip. The last man before me to drink from this cup was Pompeius. He probably obtained it from Parthia during his campaigns in the East, for it was part of the dinner service found in his tent at Pharsalus. After the battle they carried me in to see Caesar, who was eating the meal which had been prepared for Pompeius and his generals. Caesar had me placed on his own couch and gave me wine to drink from this cup. Afterwards he insisted that I keep it as a memento of the battle. Fluorspar is rare and they say that men will pay many thousands of sesterces for a cup such as mine, but I should not sell it for all the gold in the temple of Saturn.

Ala strokes the scar on my arm and soothes my disordered mutterings about the past. Over the years she has learnt to speak very well, though the accent of her native country is still noticeable. Her hair is grey now and the folds of her dress hide a plump figure. When I first saw her at Uxellodunum she had the flaxen hair of the Germanic peoples and bright blue eyes which burned with hatred for the Romans. Her first act was to spit at me. How our relationship has changed as she helps me up the slope to the villa with Ajax padding along behind us.

Chapter II

82 BC

My story begins under the dictatorship of Sulla when I was eighteen. I had spent the afternoon with my friends on the Campus Martius. We had competed to see who could throw a javelin the furthest and also at foot races. I was strong in the shoulders and threw the javelin over a hundred paces, further than anybody else. In the foot races I came second behind Gaius Matius. Afterwards we went as usual to the baths, scraped our bodies with strigils and sweated in the steam. As the sun began to go down I made my way home along the Via Lata towards the Forum. There had been rumours in the city that the dictator would take revenge against those who had collaborated with Cinna while he was away in the East and who had opposed him after he landed at Brundisium. Many feared assassination by Sulla's veterans who roamed the city and were ready to do violence at a nod from their old leader. Such was the atmosphere of apprehension that a senator had pleaded with Sulla to let the people know whom he regarded as the guilty men. 'Certainly,' the dictator had replied, 'I shall be happy to comply with your request.'

As I walked down into the Forum I saw a gathering of people round the foot of the Rostra, the platform from which magistrates habitually address the citizens. They seemed to be reading a notice which had been nailed onto the wall. I approached to ask a man what it was. 'It is a list

15

of the proscribed,' he replied. 'The men whom Sulla has designated as outlaws to be murdered with impunity.' So this was how the dictator proposed to deal with his enemies. I pushed through to the front of the crowd and saw a list of about eighty names. I scanned it with a sickening fear in my stomach. Before I found it I knew that the name of my father, Marcus Valerius Cotta, would be there. Towards the bottom of the second column it was scratched in crude but unmistakeable letters. I later discovered that many friends and political allies of my father had also appeared on the list but I had no eyes for these. Trying to keep myself under control and with my head down I edged back through the throng of people. As soon as I was clear I began to run along the Via Sacra, stumbling in the ruts and once knocking over a slave who was carrying a dish of food into a house. In a few minutes I had reached home. The main door was barred and I had to shout to a slave to let me in.

By this time it was dusk and oil lamps glowed in the brackets on the walls of the hall. Without waiting for the door slave to wash the dust from my feet I made my way quickly to the atrium. There I found my father seated in his curule chair with my mother and brother Publius standing beside him. I began to blurt out what I had seen in the Forum, but my father raised his hand to silence me.

'We already know that Sulla has decreed that I am to die,' he said calmly. 'I fought on the Marian side when he invaded Italy with his army at the end of the campaign in Greece. You know that I opposed Sulla then because he was using the force of arms to secure his political ends. He was acting unlawfully and I made speeches in the Senate and on the Rostra to that effect. But we lost the battles to stop Sulla.' He paused and then continued, 'One of his centurions came here this afternoon to inform me that my name would be on the list you have just seen. I offered my throat to him there and then and invited him to slit it with his

16

sword. The centurion only sneered and said that there would be plenty of others to do it once the list was published.' My mother swayed a little and put her arm around my brother's shoulder to steady herself. Publius was only fourteen but he looked unflinchingly at my father as he spoke. We had been brought up in the traditional way which required the sternest discipline in the face of a crisis. It was not done to betray one's feelings.

My father rose from his chair. 'I am not afraid to die but I must make arrangements now for you and the family,' he said, turning to my mother and taking her hands. 'You and Publius must go to the villa at Baiae. Stay there until it is safe to return to the city. Lucius, you must go into hiding for the time being. As my elder son you too are in danger. I do not believe that Sulla will stop at this first list of names. There will be others and I doubt that those veterans of his will be fussy about who they kill.'

'Could we not all leave Rome tonight?' I asked, knowing all too well what my father's reaction would be. 'The gates of the city are not guarded. By dawn we should be well away. In a few weeks we could be across the Adriatic. We might have to live in hiding for a while but sooner or later Sulla will be gone and then we could return.'

My father shook his head. 'I have no intention of giving Sulla the pleasure of seeing me run like a frightened rabbit. I shall die here in my own house by my own hand like a proper Roman. Tomorrow you must burn my body and place the ashes in the family mausoleum. Once that it is done, you must all leave the city immediately. In any event this house has been forfeited by Sulla together with my other property in Rome. But he has allowed the family to retain the villa at Baiae. Your mother's aunt, Faustina, pleaded with him for this concession.'

And so it was that within the space of an hour my father had decided to die by his own hand and the rest of us had

17

been thrown into an abyss of fear and sorrow. Two of the household slaves were ordered to prepare a bath of hot water. My father took his leave of my mother. He asked her to forgive him for what he was about to do. As a lady of noble birth she knew that honour was more important to him than life. She clasped him round the waist but said nothing. Her body shook uncontrollably and tears fell on his tunic. He kissed her face many times but I noticed that his own betrayed no emotion. It was as if he were afraid to make it worse by showing his love for her. After a few minutes he motioned to me and Publius. 'Take your mother now to her rooms. You, Publius, will remain with her until after this is done.' He gently released her hands from his body, stroked her hair and said, 'There, this is better than some ugly stabbing in the street by hired thugs. I shall feel no pain. You have two fine sons to look after you. Be brave and all will be well.' My mother nodded and even smiled. Then Publius took her hand and led her from the room.

A slave appeared to say that the bath was ready. 'Come, Lucius. I see you have your dagger in your belt. Is it sharp?' I nodded and followed him to the bath-house. We walked across the central courtyard with the slave carrying a lamp before us to light the way. Neither of us spoke. In any case I could not have done so. My whole body felt constricted by the horror of what was happening. When we entered the room I saw that my father's freedman, old Diocles, was already there. He seemed to have been waiting and I realised that my father had already spoken to him.

'Now Diocles, you have my instructions. Make sure that the lady Aemilia and Publius have all they need for the journey to Baiae. Take what you can in the carts. I have freed some slaves today. Others you will take with you to the villa – they will be needed to run the house and gardens. Lucius will give you what help he can, but he too must leave the city without delay. There is gold in the safe. Sempronius will come tomorrow; entrust it to him. He will keep it until it can be taken to the villa and hidden there.'

Diocles stood before his patron, his head bowed. For many years he had been my father's slave. He was a Greek who knew Latin and had some understanding of mathematics. Gradually he had worked his way up the ranks of the household until he became my father's clerk, helping with his correspondence and accounts. He gave such good service that after twenty years my father granted him manumission. Diocles stayed on in the household as a trusted and loved servant of the family. Now he raised his head. I saw his wrinkled face and faded eyes but his voice was firm as he assured my father that he would carry out his last wishes. This old man with only a few wisps of grey hair on his head, a body bent from hard physical work in his youth and with only a couple of teeth in his mouth, loved his master as if he were his own son.

'Well then, I think we are ready. Diocles, will you take my sandals, I shall have no further need of them.' But then my father hesitated. 'Lucius, I have been remiss. I have sent Publius to sit with your mother. Go now and send him to me so that I may take proper leave of him. Stay with your mother until he returns.' When I reached my mother's rooms Publius jumped up believing, I think, that I had come to tell him that his father was dead. After he had gone my mother patted the couch where she sat and asked me to sit beside her. I felt the dagger in my belt as I bent down. I wanted to hurl it away from my body.

'Where will you go?' she asked. 'Your father says that young Caesar, Gaius Matius and Carbo's son are also in danger. Apparently Sulla asked Caesar to divorce Cornelia and he refused. That was a brave thing to do.'

'I shall find Caesar tomorrow,' I replied. 'I propose to leave Rome with him and anybody else who will come with us. We can lie low in the hills around Praeneste until things

19

calm down. I know the area reasonably well from when we were besieged there last year.' My mother made no reply but put her arm around my shoulder and we sat silently in that sad room while I dreaded the return of Publius. Soon he came. Without a word he sank down on his knees and buried his face in the folds of my mother's dress. She turned to me, seeming to understand.

'Go now, you must do your duty to your father. Help him to die as a Roman should.'

When I reached the bath-house the steam made it hard to see at first. I found my father sitting by the water while Diocles knelt beside him. The slaves had gone and only the dim light from the oil lamps kept us company.

'Come down and sit next to me in the water,' my father spoke as if it were an invitation to a swim. He had not taken off his tunic and, like him, I sat on the side of the bath with my legs dangling in the water.

'I think, Lucius, you are cut out to be a soldier rather than a politician. Our family has many ancestors who have been consuls or praetors like me, but the system has become corrupt. Men seize office by force of arms or by bribery. There is no honour in it now. In any case I believe that Sulla has decreed that the sons and grandsons of the proscribed shall be disqualified from holding public office. So make your life with the legions and serve the State in that way. Perhaps one day public life in this city will regain its integrity. If that happens, then you may yet enter the Senate. Whatever the future holds, never forget the honour of our family. I know that you and Publius will uphold it.' He clasped me round the shoulders and I felt his lips pass across my cheek. He slipped off the side and sat on a step in the bath with only the upper half of his chest and head above the water. His tunic floated round him.

'Now pass me your dagger, please.' I drew it from its sheath and handed it to him. He pulled the blade firmly

20

across the inside of his wrist. Neither by the flicker of an eye nor by any movement of his lips did he betray any sensation of pain. The blood flowed out and spread on the water in a dark cloud. 'Quickly Lucius, cut the other arm for me. I do not wish to wait for the water to grow cold.'

I felt his eyes fasten upon mine. I took the dagger from his outstretched arm and cut hard into the flesh as he had done. Again blood spurted. I sensed him make me look up at him. He gave a little nod, saying, 'Good. I am glad you did not flinch.' I let his arm go and it dropped back into the water.

Diocles came forward and placed a cushion under my father's head as he sank back against the side of the bath. Still holding the dagger I watched the blood spread until the whole surface of the bath was stained like dark wood. It lapped around my legs but I did not move. My father spoke a few more words but I cannot remember them. Soon the colour went from his face and he began to slip under the water as he lost consciousness. Diocles supported him by the armpits. His breathing became noisy for a few moments, then gradually slowed until it ceased altogether. I do not know how long all this lasted. Sometime later Diocles and I lifted the body from the water. We summoned two slaves and together carried my father to the peristyle where we placed him on a table. Diocles called for bandages, a fresh tunic and oils. He bound the wounds, put on the new tunic and dressed my father's hair. Finally he placed round him his senator's toga with the broad purple stripe. 'I shall stay here with your father until it is light and we can begin the funeral procession,' he said. 'You should change your tunic too. It is better that your mother does not see you as you are.'

When I came back into the courtyard my mother and Publius were standing by the table. Both were calm. I believe that we felt a great release of tension. The crisis was past, father's pain was over. He was gone but he had escaped the fate that many would suffer, some brutal mugging in a corner of the Forum or even in their own house. My mother sent for wine and cakes. We sat there through the rest of the night with the old freedman, talking of the past. Nobody could sleep.

Shortly before dawn I must have dozed. I remember waking and feeling stiff from sitting in a chair. I looked up and saw kites circling in the sky. A smell of cooking came from the kitchens. My mother had gone but Diocles was there, supervising the placing of my father's body on a bier. I went into the tablinum and took down from the walls the waxen masks of our famous ancestors to be worn by hired actors in the funeral procession. I found the one of Caius Aurelius Cotta who became censor nearly two hundred years ago and after whom is named the Via Aurelia leading from Rome towards Pisa and beyond into Gaul. Handing them to a slave I made my way to the hall of the house where I knew my father's clients would be gathering as usual to offer greetings to him. The news of his death had already reached them. Many were crying out in anguish at the passing of their patron. I did my best to console them, telling those who came to comfort me that he had died nobly and to prepare for the funeral procession which would leave within the hour.

When all was ready Diocles harnessed two horses to the bier and led them on foot from the main door of our house. Immediately behind, Mother, Publius and I, dressed in grey as befitted mourners, walked together. Behind us came the actors wearing the family masks followed by a crowd of father's clients. It was still early in the morning. I had been anxious that we should be out of the city in good time so as not to attract more notice than was necessary. The sun was not fully up and there was still a chill in the air as we made our way down to the Porta Capena and out onto the Via

22

Appia. Here we were joined by other mourners of the Cotta family to whom I had sent messages. Another actor came and, in accordance with the tradition of noble families, he walked in front of the bier imitating the mannerisms of my father. The procession passed many other tombs and mausoleums which line the road. The bier jolted on the stones but Diocles kept the horses moving steadily. My mother looked neither to the right or left, keeping her eyes fixed on my father's body. Publius and I each held one hand. I noticed smoke rising from a pyre just off the road where another funeral was taking place. I guessed that this too would be a victim of the proscriptions, as normally such ceremonies would be held later in the day.

Just before the second milestone we reached the mausoleum of the Cotta family. I had given orders for the pyre to be prepared. Four of father's clients now came forward and unstrapped the body from the bier. Gently they placed it on the pile of wooden branches laid criss-cross to form a kind of platform. We surrounded the body with branches of myrtle until it was hidden from view. Mother stepped forward to offer a prayer to Jupiter Optimus Maximus. She touched the pyre which was the signal for Publius and me to put burning torches to the wood. As the flames rose, the onlookers burst into a lament. The myrtle gave off its scent, disguising the smell of burning flesh. Later Diocles would return, gather the ashes into a silver urn and place it on a shelf in the mausoleum. As the flames began to die down we set off back to the city. Publius claimed to see an eagle fly away towards the hills and said it was my father's soul gone to join the gods. Soon we were back within the Servian wall. Mother and Publius accompanied by Diocles and some clients returned to the house while I set out for the Forum where I hoped to meet Caesar, to whom I had sent word at first light.

I had almost reached the Via Sacra when I became aware

23

of the blaring of trumpets to my left. There on the road were about a dozen soldiers blowing their instruments to clear the way before them. I pulled the hood of my cloak over my head and drew inside a doorway. I had no wish to be recognised. Carts were bundled off the street and men hastily stepped aside. Street vendors who had tables displaying their wares pulled them back. Now I could see the reason for this commotion. Lictors were approaching, twenty-four of them in two columns of twelve, twice the number permitted to a consul. 'Mind what you shout and salute heartily,' I heard a man say to his neighbour, 'here comes the Dictator.' The lictors wore the toga and on their shoulders they each carried a bundle of rods, the symbol of their office. Since they were inside the walls of the city the axe-heads had been removed from the bundles. As they came past, they called upon the citizens to greet their dictator.

Dutifully men raised their right arm and shouted, 'Hail Lucius Cornelius Sulla, I salute you.' Behind the lictors followed a closed litter hung with pale blue silks. It was borne by four enormous black men, one at each end of the stout poles on which the litter rested. Perhaps they were slaves captured by Sulla during the war against Jugurtha. They wore only short tunics and large gold earrings. Their black skin glistened with sweat in the morning sun. In response to the shouts of the citizens an arm covered in blotchy skin emerged from the curtains of the litter and waved languidly in acknowledgement, but no face appeared. The little procession passed on its way towards the Forum and the Senate House. Behind, the street resumed normality. People crowded back onto it and the bustle of carts and tradesmen picked up from where it had left off a few moments before. Sulla had gone by, nobody was dead; everybody breathed more easily.

I reached the Forum. It was less busy than usual. A knot

24

of people had again gathered around the foot of the Rostra. Men walked quickly, exchanging a word of greeting with an acquaintance but not stopping to talk. There was an air of anxiety about the place. No persons of consequence were making their way to the law courts or to the Senate House escorted by their clients. The priests of the great temples were not in evidence. When you do not know who is your enemy and who is your friend you do not linger about your business. You could see the fear in men's eyes as they darted past. I reached the temple of Jupiter Stator where I had arranged to meet Caesar. Inside the gloom was lit by torches burning in brackets on the walls and incense rose from marble pedestals. For a moment I could see little, but as my eyes became accustomed to the shadowy light I spotted Caesar standing by a pillar not far from the main door. As I had hoped, he was alone.

'I am sorry to hear of your father's death,' he said gravely. 'He died honourably. The city is rife with rumours that Sulla will not stop with this first list. They say that there will be more proscriptions, that he is determined to wipe out those who sided with my Uncle Marius and with Cinna. We are both in the greatest danger.'

'My father told me as much,' I replied. 'He told me to leave the city immediately. Will you come with me? I think Carbo and Gaius Matius will come too.'

'Carbo has already left,' said Caesar. 'He is following his father to Africa. I spoke to Matius earlier today. He will fall in with any plan we have. I think we should go tonight.'

'I have to see my mother and Publius off to Baiae. Our house is forfeit and they are going to our villa there. I will come to yours at the beginning of the second watch. Can you organise horses – all ours are being used to transport as much as we can away from Rome.'

Caesar nodded. 'Leave the horses to me. Bring some money and food. Dress in coarse clothing. I will send to

Matius to do the same. Mind your back for the rest of the day.'

We left the temple separately and I hurried home through side streets. By the time I reached the house most of the carts were loaded. Father's old friend Gaius Sempronius arrived to take away some gold and silver for safe keeping. Mother and Publius were to travel in a covered carriage out of sight of curious eyes. With each cart Diocles had put two trustworthy slaves armed with daggers and staves to beat off any unwelcome attentions as they made their way to the south of the city. The carts left at intervals during the afternoon, each made to look like that of a tradesman or farmer making the journey back to his land outside the walls. The plan was to link up on the Via Appia at the fourth milepost and travel south in convoy. There would be brigands on the way but the slaves could offer some protection. It crossed my mind that they might conspire to kill my mother and Publius, but there was nothing I could do and I believed they would be loyal to a family who had treated them better than most.

Gradually the house emptied as slaves and freedmen departed. It was as if the life blood of our home was ebbing away. Nobody came or went with clothes from the fullers, with food brought from the market or with messages for my father or mother. There was no sound of activity from the kitchens, no boy going round to fill the oil lamps, no slave girl sweeping in the peristyle or tending to the flowers there, no stable boys carrying feed for the horses at the back. There was nothing but empty rooms where a few objects dropped or forgotten in the haste of departure lay on the floors. But I felt no sorrow – there was no time for that, only time to make sure that the others were safely on their way. Once again that day I went down to the Porta Capena, accompanying my mother and Publius in their carriage as far as there. At the gate we bade one another farewell, not knowing whether we should ever meet again. To see my father die and to part, perhaps forever, from my mother and brother in the space of a day made me both sorrowful and angry. I clasped them both, assuring them that it would not be long before we were together again, that they would be safe at the villa and that I would bring them back to the city one day.

I watched as the carriage bumped along in the wheel ruts between the rows of umbrella pines. The road ran straight as a javelin's shaft, away to the south, and not until the carriage was but a black speck in the distance did I turn back towards the house on the Caelian Hill for the last time.

I walked through the rooms I had lived in all my life. Only the sound of my sandals slapping against the floor broke the silence. I gathered together a few possessions such as I thought might be useful while we were hiding in the hills. The sun began to sink behind the roof of the peristyle where I sat in the shadows. I thought of my mother and Publius on their way towards Baiae. I prayed for their safety. I found a festival cake in the kitchens and placed it before the Lares on the hearth. It seemed fitting to make this symbolic sacrifice to the household gods as a way of saying goodbye to my home. It began to grow dusk. A gibbous moon rose in the pale violet sky and a few stars announced the end of that day and the end of our family life.

I slipped out of the house, making my way towards the Esquiline Hill. The streets were almost deserted. It seemed that the city lay cowed; there was a smell of fear in the air as men waited to see whom Sulla would choose next for his lists. Over to the west rose the Capitoline mount above the Forum and silhouetted on its summit I could see the great temple of Jupiter, Juno and Minerva, now lying in ruins since the mysterious fire of the previous year had destroyed it. The gods were angry with the people of Rome and with their rulers. I began to drop down into the Suburra and

27

made my way to Caesar's house. A slave conducted me to the atrium where I found him with his young wife Cornelia and his mother Aurelia, who enquired as to my mother's safety, for apart from being related, they were also close friends. As I was telling her about this, Gaius Matius was shown into the room. Like me he was dressed in coarse clothes and carried a bag over his shoulder. Aurelia smiled. 'The three of you look like ruffians and you Gaius Caesar nominated to be a priest of Jupiter! But it is as well. Make your escape while you can. I shall intercede for you while you are in hiding. I have the ear of Sulla's wife Caecilia who has promised to try to persuade him to let you return without punishment.' Caesar embraced his mother and led Cornelia to another room to take his farewell from her privately.

As we left Caesar told us that he had arranged for horses to be waiting for us at the first milepost beyond the Colline Gate on the Via Salaria. By now it was dark but the moon lit our way and soon we reached the city wall. The guards were dozing and took no notice of a trio of unkempt journeymen. Outside the gate the bleached skeletons of hundreds of men lay in the moonlight just as they had fallen the previous year in the great battle. For it was here that Pontius and his Samnites had made their last stand against Sulla, and Crassus had saved the day as Sulla's left wing was put to flight. Would that the gods had not preserved Sulla then. We should have been spared this grim parade and the crows and kites would not have grown so fat on the flesh of Roman citizens as well as Samnites. We walked on to the first milepost where we found one of Caesar's slaves who had tethered three horses for us. We were soon riding northwards and after a few miles we turned off the road into scrub land to rest for the night.

Chapter III

82 BC

When we awoke the following morning light rain was falling and the makeshift shelter of cloth stretched on the tree branches above our heads did not prevent the drips from the leaves dampening our clothes and spirits a little. We ate some bread and meat from our bags. Matius produced a flask of wine to which we added water for a drink.

'We must put more distance between ourselves and the city,' said Caesar. 'It is possible that search parties will be sent out. I know, Lucius, you suggested that we go towards Praeneste but I was told yesterday that Sulla is having the area surveyed. Apparently he is proposing to settle a lot of his veterans there. The place is thick with officials measuring out plots of land.'

'Why don't we ride northwards?' suggested Matius. 'I have a cousin with a sheep farm near Spoletium. He doesn't live there himself of course. He has a bailiff and slaves to run the place. I know the bailiff from visits there in the past. We could probably lie low in the area and get food from the farm.'

We agreed to head north and set off back to the Via Salaria, thinking to travel quickly before our disappearance was noticed in the city. The rain had stopped and I could just see through the trees the basalt paving stones of the road glistening and steaming in the rising sun. We were about to emerge from the wood when Caesar, who was in front, suddenly pulled in his horse and motioned to us to listen. At first I could hear nothing, then I made out the sound of horses' hooves somewhere in the distance but coming on steadily towards us from the direction of the city.

'That's not just a couple of horses, that's several,' said Matius. We turned about hastily and headed back up the slope out of sight. A few moments later I caught a glimpse through the trees of about thirty cavalry riding northwards towards Reate, a hill town some thirty miles away. Their helmets glinted in the sun as they trotted by and we wondered whether they had been sent to look for us. There was no question of our using the road and we began to travel through the hills and outcrops of the Sabine Mountains, keeping the Via Salaria well to our left. Most of the time we were able to ride, but occasionally where the going was too rough we had to dismount. It was slow progress and for quite long stretches there was no shade from the sun. Matius however, who was more used to the country than Caesar or I, had an innate feel for direction and the easiest route through the hills. He was a fine strong man of athletic build with a large crop of curly black hair and the long straight nose common to many members of his family. He could get a fire going from dried sticks in no time and knew how to hunt game and where to find it. Without him, Caesar and I would have gone very hungry in those first few days.

Eventually we came to the source of a stream quite high up in the mountains. It ran northwards and we decided to follow it as Matius thought that he remembered a lake in the area and hoped that the stream might lead us to it. Late in the evening the lake appeared in a shallow valley and we bivouacked by its shore. There we stayed for some days, catching fish which we cooked on a fire. There was grass near the water for the horses. We tried to catch some of the waterfowl as well but they either paddled off into the lake or took to the air before we could get near enough. Then one evening we saw some wild boar drinking on the shore and Matius thought we might be able to trap one. He fashioned a rough spade with his dagger and we found the track which the boar clearly used regularly on their way to drink. We dug a pit in the middle of the track and covered it with brushwood, trying to make it look as much as possible like the surrounding ground. Nothing happened for two or three days but one morning when we went over to check the trap we saw two wolves circling round it. They moved off at our approach. When we looked down into the hole we saw the reason for their interest. At the bottom a boar was grunting and butting with his tusks in a vain attempt to get out. Matius tied his dagger to the end of a stick and plunged it into the back of the beast's neck. It was not long before we had steaks of meat roasting over our fire. Gradually we made ourselves more comfortable by that lake. We built a shelter, washed our clothes and our bodies in the water and hunted for game to eat. We saw nobody and were not aware that anybody had seen us. In this we were mistaken.

One night I was wakened by the sound of a whinny from one of the horses which were tethered near to our shelter. Rolling over I propped myself on an elbow and looked outside. The lake gleamed like dull silver in the light of the moon and a flock of waterfowl rode on the water like a miniature fleet of warships. Looking round for the horses I made out two men moving towards them over the grass on the shore. In my sleepy state it took a moment to realise that they were intent on stealing our most valuable possessions. I shook the other two awake and we rushed out of the shelter pulling our daggers from their sheaths as we did so. In the darkness Matius tripped and fell cursing to the ground. One of the men had succeeded in cutting the tether of a horse. He scrambled onto its back and galloped off along the shore of the lake. Caesar gave chase but it was too late. Meanwhile I had reached the other man as he tried to cut free a second

31

horse. I grabbed the arm holding the knife and brought my own dagger down towards his chest. He was quick and just as I had caught his arm so he caught mine. He was strongly built and heavier than I. For a moment we wrestled, each seeking to stab the other. Then he brought his knee sharply up to my crutch, trying to force me to let him go but I had anticipated this and turned my body so that the blow struck my buttock instead. As I turned I twisted my leg round his and pushed as hard as I could. It caught him off balance and we both fell to the ground. Somehow he got himself on top of me and I felt the blade of his knife beginning to press against my ribs, for his arm was stronger than mine. Then suddenly his head jerked back and as his body slumped, I felt a spatter of warm blood on my face. I rolled away and, scrambling to my feet, saw Matius still holding with one hand the hair at the back of the man's head while with the other he withdrew his dagger from the thief's throat. His thrust had been so violent that the point of the weapon had come out at the nape of the man's neck.

It was too dangerous to remain by the lake. The thief who had got away might return with others to exact revenge for his partner's death. As soon as it was light we dragged the corpse to the pit which we had dug to catch the boar and flung in the body, covering it with earth. We dismantled our shelter and cleared away the evidence of our stay as best we could. Matius said that he knew of a man called Varro who owned stud farms at Reate for the breeding of horses and mules. It would be safer to get a replacement there than to try to buy a horse from one of the posting stations on the Via Salaria, where news travelled fast.

We headed due north following a path which ran alongside a river feeding the lake. Though we had only two horses now, it made little difference as we had to lead them through the rough country up towards the town. We kept a sharp eye on the crags above us but saw nothing other than a few rock partridge running about on the screes and the occasional eagle circling in the sky above. In the evening we camped by the river where Matius caught some trout with his hands, feeling for them under the banks. The night passed uneventfully except for the howling of some wolves somewhere close by and in the morning we came to a track leading up to a gate into the town. The Via Salaria lay a little way over to the west so we ventured through the gate to find a tavern where we sat down on a bench beside a wall facing the road. The innkeeper served us wine, bread and cheese, all of which he had made himself on his farm in the hills. Matius asked whether he knew of the man called Varro and where his estate was. The innkeeper not only knew but offered to take us there on his way to his smallholding – his son would look after the tavern and he needed to return home to tend his goats. He led us along a path which skirted the walls of the town and then dropped down into a grass valley, at the head of which stood a large villa surrounded by enclosures in which we could see horses and mules of all ages and sizes. The innkeeper bade us farewell and set off towards his farmstead farther down the valley. Round it lay a small field of barley with sheep and goats in the hill pasture above.

The entrance to Varro's estate had an imposing archway and drive of gravel up which we walked to the villa. As we came nearer the house a slave emerged from the courtyard carrying a basket of feed for some foals. Caesar ordered him to find his master as we had business to do with him. The slave hesitated for a moment, no doubt wondering about the young man who spoke with such authority but who was dressed so coarsely. The sun was nearly at its zenith and we sat down on a bench in the courtyard to wait. It was not long before there emerged from the villa a stout man of about forty. His ginger hair was thinning and his round face was freckled and pink. He had the expression of a man who enjoyed life to the full. Hearing of our need we were soon standing at the fence of a paddock while Varro had horses brought to us for inspection. We selected one and agreed a price of two hundred sesterces including a saddle. Varro ordered a slave to prepare the horse and to take our other two to the stables for fodder and water.

'Now, you three gentlemen must dine with me,' he announced in a tone which brooked no refusal. He led us into the villa to his triclinium. There couches were arranged round three sides of a low table. 'It is rare that I have guests from the city. I want you to tell me all the news. They say that Sulla is going to undo all the recent reforms and restore the power of the Senate. Tell me all about it.'

Cautiously at first, but with increasing confidence as we discovered where his sympathies lay, the three of us related the recent events at Rome, culminating in the proscriptions and our enforced departure from the city. As we talked, slaves brought a succession of dishes to the table. We started with Falernian wine from Campania and then a vintage Caecuban to be drunk with the meats. Fieldfares stuffed with walnut paste, a speciality we were told of the Sabine hill country, were followed by roast wild boar and baked peaches. Then a sucking pig garnished with a piquant sauce of garum, made from pickled fish, was wheeled in. We became increasingly merry as the wine flowed and Varro chuckled at our mishaps. Though Caesar was still a young man, the horse breeder was clearly a little in awe of him. He listened to the clipped accent of this patrician who claimed descent from the gods and was already nominated for the priesthood of Jupiter. He was amused by Caesar's slightly high pitched voice and expansive gestures as he emphasised a point. Matius and I too could not but be impressed as our friend explained so lucidly to his host the political situation in Rome. Varro wondered whether his young wife Cornelia, who was the daughter of Cinna, would be safe and Caesar assured him that it was only the men who would be in danger. The day drew on but we continued to feast on almonds, hazelnuts and pears followed by cake flavoured with honey. At length Varro summoned his young daughter Lepida to sit with us. She was a slim girl of perhaps seventeen whose mother had died in childbirth. With the help of a nurse her father had brought her up on the estate. Like him she had auburn hair which hung in long ringlets and gleamed in the light of the oil lamps. I could see that Matius was much taken with her and engaged her in conversation. She had a modest demeanour, smiling but never laughing at Caesar's witticisms about people in the city. She had not taken wine like the rest of us but sipped only water brought for her specially from a local spring.

'When it is safer, I shall take Lepida with me to Rome and find her a suitable husband,' said her father. 'Perhaps you gentlemen will help this country bumpkin to find one.' Lepida blushed and said she would rather stay with him in the country. 'You say that now, my dear, but there will come a time when you are bored of your old father writing his treatises on agriculture and horse breeding.'

That night we stayed at the villa. In the morning Varro saw us on our way. He had wanted us to stay longer but we pointed out that this would be dangerous for both him, if he were found to have given us shelter, and for ourselves as word of the presence of three strangers on the estate would be bound to get out.

Perhaps the great feast with which Varro had regaled us, though it was nothing unusual to have much more exotic and longer meals in the houses of the great families of Rome, had reminded us of how sparsely we had eaten until then, surviving on what we could catch in the woods and rivers. Whatever the reason, we decided to go back to Reate and buy some bread and meat in the market before going on. We rode up out of the valley and into the little town. In the centre was a tiny square; it could not be described as a forum. There we bought from the street vendors some salted sheep meat, bread, biscuit and nuts. The horses drank from a trough at the edge of the square and we turned to move off towards the town's northerly gate. As we did so, I became aware that there were two other horsemen approaching the water trough and behind them came a closed carriage followed by an open cart. The first horseman was clearly a man of substance. He wore a fine woollen tunic and a corselet of tooled leather. On his head was a broad brimmed hat decorated with egret feathers to protect against the sun. His companion rode a smaller horse and from his appearance might have been a bailiff or a freedman. As we passed one another I noticed a large gold ring on the first man's hand, a sign that he was a member of the equestrian order. He looked closely at each of us and I felt that he recognised Caesar and Matius, though his face meant nothing to me. As soon as we were through the gate Caesar said that he had met the man some months before at a dinner party in the house of Quintus Aurelius on the Esquiline hill.

'I cannot remember his name, but he is a close friend of Licinius Murena, Sulla's lieutenant. He will certainly report having seen us when he gets to Rome.' Caesar felt sure that he at least had been recognised as the man had bent down to the carriage and spoken to somebody inside while he pointed towards us. It was another warning that we had to be careful to avoid the main highways and towns.

Keeping to the mountains we made our way slowly northwards towards Spoletium. During the day we stayed on the high ground where there was little or no chance of meeting anybody except the occasional shepherd. In the evenings we would come down to a valley where there was shelter from the night's cold and pasture for the horses. Sometimes we saw tiny farmsteads and one of us would go for a little bread or cheese, whatever the smallholder could spare and was prepared to sell. On the upper slopes of the mountains there was less game to catch and we became increasingly reliant on what we could buy. It was a hard few days but eventually we came down to the Via Flaminia, the great road which runs from Rome all the way to Fanum on the Adriatic coast, south of Ravenna. The property of Matius' cousin lay to the west of the road which we crossed by night. In the morning we came to the estate belonging to Titus Matius, some miles south west of Spoletium. The villa overlooked a fertile valley in which vines and olives grew. The house itself was guarded by a wall about fifteen feet high with turrets at intervals, like the walls of a fortified town. Above and around the estate grazed thousands of sheep on their summer pasture. Matius led us through the main gate past ornamental gardens to a house laid out on three sides of a square. Apart from the family's villa, there were other great buildings housing oil presses and vats for storage, a barn for treading grapes with a stone floor in the centre of which lay a plughole allowing the juice to drain into containers below. Beyond was a complex of buildings for the keeping of pigs. We saw storage jars for wine and oil stamped with the initials T.L.M, Titus Livius Matius, stacked in the courtyard ready to be filled. In another barn about fifty slaves were eating a meal of mutton broth and bread under the eye of two gang masters. The men seemed well and fit. Matius told us that his cousin had long ago discovered that the better you treated a slave the better he worked. Round their necks they wore metal bands stamped with their owner's name.

The bailiff lodged in a small house close to the main villa. He was a freedman of about forty who had worked on the estate since birth. His parents were Thracians captured and sold into slavery after the conquest of Macedonia. Like many others, these slaves worked in gangs on the great estates of Italy. Aristo however, though born a slave because his parents were slaves, had pleased his master by increasing the productivity of the farm, particularly the olive oil and wine which were shipped all over Italy and as far as southern Gaul and north-eastern Spain. So he had received his manumission a few years earlier. He had a swarthy complexion roughened by years in the sun and under a crop of short grey hair protruded a long hooked nose. I counted five warts on his face. These combined with his great height and the absence of almost all his teeth gave him a fearsome appearance. In his belt he carried a whip with the thong coiled round his waist. The slaves did not linger in their execution of his orders.

'The villa, sirs, is of course at your disposal. I received a messenger on horseback some days ago from Rome ordering me to provide you with whatever you require, but on no account to reveal your presence here.' He confirmed that nobody had come in search of us but nevertheless we felt it unwise to stay too near to the estate. One of the horses, in fact the one we had purchased from Varro, had gone lame on the journey from Reate, so we changed this for another and restocked with food. Aristo provided us with saddle bags to enable us to carry more. Then Caesar wrote a note to his mother in Rome, asking whether she had made any progress in interceding for us with Sulla. The note was put into the hand of a young lad who, Aristo said, was his son by a woman who worked as a cook in the villa when the family of Titus Matius came to stay. He certainly had his father's nose and was nearly as tall. Caesar told him how to find his mother's house where he was to await further instructions from her. Within the hour the messenger was trotting out of the main gate towards the Via Flaminia and Rome. Aristo said he was a good horseman and knew how to look after himself. He would be back within five or six days.

Once again we set off northwards, planning to spend a few days more in the hills before returning to Spoletium to see whether there was any news from Rome. Leaving the Via Flaminia to our east we came eventually to a broad river

38

which Matius told us was called the Clitumnus and which he had visited as a small boy when he was staying with his uncle, old Livius Matius. We followed the river to its source where we found a hill covered with cypress trees. At its foot the river rose in a great spring feeding many different channels. These channels then unified into a wonderfully clear pool of ice cold water in which we swam, wondering at the brightness of the coloured pebbles on the bottom but which dimmed as soon as you lifted them out. The horses grazed on the lush grass and we lay in the sun drinking wine from our flasks. I thought again of my mother and Publius – had they reached Baiae safely? When would I see them again? I saw in my mind's eye the face of my father as I pressed the blade into his flesh, my flesh, his faint nod of approval and the pallor of his cheeks as the blood and his life flowed away. I wondered if I could be as brave as he and I resolved that I would try.

For five days we stayed by that beautiful river, lined with ash trees and poplars. We found a temple in which there stood an image of the god Clitumnus dressed in the robe of a magistrate. Round about were other shrines each containing a god, and having its own name and cult. There was a bridge too, made of stone which separated the sacred water from the ordinary stream. Close by we found a farmstead whose owner sold food and wine to people who came to take holy water from the pool and to worship in the temple. The farmer said there was a legend that Flaminius had stopped at the source of the Clitumnus on his way to oppose Hannibal and that an oracle in the temple had warned him to keep away from water, but that Flaminius in his impetuosity had forgotten and suffered the disaster at Lake Trasimene.

Almost regretfully we rode back towards Spoletium to see if our messenger had returned. Indeed he had and the news from Aurelia, Caesar's mother, was encouraging. Her contact had spoken to the Dictator who had indicated that we should return to the city where we were to attend upon him, but that our lives were not in danger. Aurelia did not think this was a trap and advised us to return without delay. We had been away almost three months.

The atmosphere in Rome was a little easier than when we had left. The reign of terror brought about by the proscriptions had ended. Many prominent citizens had died either by their own hand or had been clubbed down by Sulla's thugs. Now the Dictator was engaged upon his political reforms which were aimed at restoring the power of the Senate to initiate laws, packing the juries with senators and reducing the powers of the people's tribunes.

I stayed with Caesar at his mother's house while we waited for an appointment to see Sulla. One afternoon I walked over to our old family home on the Caelian Hill. It seemed little changed on the outside but I found it occupied by the family of one of Sulla's legates on the campaign against Mithridates, so I turned away and never went to that house again. I wrote a letter to my mother in Baiae asking her to send news and saying that I hoped to join her as soon as the business with Sulla was over. A few days later we received a note ordering us to attend upon the Dictator the following day in the Temple of Bellona after the business of the Senate was over for the morning.

Sulla sat on a great ivory chair surrounded by his lictors and a few servile-looking senators. Now in his late fifties his light coloured hair was turning grey but his eyes retained their piercing stare for which he was famous. His eyebrows were very thick and dark in contrast to his hair. The flesh on his face was blotchy and heavily pockmarked, while his neck had grown fat with excessive food and wine. In front of him stood the comedian Roscius, and Metrobius, a female impersonator. They were entertaining their audience with mime, portraying lewd acts and sexual perversions at which Sulla laughed uproariously. When he laughed the senators and lictors laughed too. We joined in, thinking it polite to do so. Sulla did not notice our arrival at first but once the actors had finished we caught his eye and he beckoned us before him. In those days Caesar was rather adventurous, not to say louche in his manner of dressing. That morning he was wearing a loose belt around his waist and on his tunic fringed sleeves reaching to his wrists. His hair had been prettily dressed.

'Oh!' said Sulla addressing Caesar, 'I thought I had just dismissed Metrobius for the day, but I see you are back already. Can you not resist me?' Everybody laughed loudly at this poor joke and my friend shifted uncomfortably as he stood beside me. Sulla raised his hand for silence. 'You see before you a perfumed youth whose life, against my better judgement, I have been persuaded to spare. But mark my words, there is in this boy more than one Marius and you will have to deal with him long after I have gone.' Turning then to Caesar he told him abruptly that his dowry from Cornelia was forfeit as were any legacies she might in future receive. Further, his nomination to the priesthood of Jupiter was cancelled. It was made clear that Caesar should leave Rome for some considerable time, otherwise Sulla might not remain so merciful.

As for me, I was informed that the death of my father and the confiscation of his property were sufficient punishment. In addition, like the sons of other proscribed men, I would be debarred from holding public office. Gaius Matius received a similar sentence though his father was already dead, having died at the siege of Praeneste where he had attempted to rally some young recruits to the Marian cause. With this we were dismissed, but not before Caesar had been made to dance a little jig with the Dictator who pretended to be in love with him, to the amusement of his companions. It was the second time that I had been in the presence of that man and been thankful that I was still alive.

Chapter IV

Not long after this I set off down the Via Appia southwards towards Campania and Baiae where I found my mother and Publius safe and well. I say that my mother was well, but she had clearly been under great strain to keep her composure following the death of my father. In the short time that we had been apart it seemed to me that she had aged. There was no spring in her step, her face had lost its freshness and her eyes betrayed the unhappiness inside her. She spent many hours in her rooms, often sending away uneaten meals with which her maids tried to entice her to regain her strength. Sometimes I would sit with her and we would reminisce about happier days in the city or their time in Sicily when my father was governor there. Gradually some vitality came back to her and one morning she announced that she had received a letter from the widow of Mucius Scaevola, the famous lawyer who had lost his life in the butchery which immediately preceded Sulla's return. The letter said that Publius would be welcome to return to the city and to stay with her while he continued his studies. So Publius went back to Rome and eventually on to the island of Rhodes to study rhetoric in the famous school of Apollonius, where Caesar also studied.

For a couple of years I stayed in and around Baiae, partly to keep my mother company and partly to help organise her affairs. She still had property in Rome and though my father's property in the city had been forfeit Sulla had chosen to ignore our estate in Campania, perhaps through the influence Caesar's mother or her contacts. Nevertheless my mother declined to return to Rome. It held too many memories for her and she said she preferred to spend her remaining days in the tranquillity of the villa's gardens which she took pains to improve. She loved to sit on the terrace in the evenings watching the sun go down over the sea to the west and the little fishing boats returning with their catch through water turned into shafts of splintered gold in the fading light.

But I was a young man. I needed more than estate management to fill my days. It was not long before I found my way to the colony of Capua, a little to the north of Baiae. Sulla had resigned from the dictatorship and gone to live in his villa at Cumae. Nevertheless his influence lived on in Rome where his reforms had restored to the Senate much of its lost powers and the position of the popular party had been correspondingly weakened. As the son of a proscribed man debarred even from standing for public office there was little opportunity for me to further my career in the city at that time. I reasoned that this state of affairs would not last forever, indeed Sulla died the following year, but meanwhile I must try to make what I could of the situation. Capua and Campania had always had Marian sympathies and been a stronghold of the popular party, so it was natural that I should gravitate in that direction where families who had known my father were willing to support me. I went therefore to live with the family of Tiberius Gutta, a member of one of the most distinguished families in Capua. Though he was a senator and was not therefore supposed to indulge in trade, Gutta had a thriving factory outside the town where he manufactured arms and equipment for the legions. Since the Marian reforms the state had increasingly relied upon private contractors to supply the army. Gutta had profited well from this. His labour consisted almost entirely of slaves, overseen by a few paid freedmen. The demand for arms and equipment was considerable and increasing as the influence of Rome spread. Every consul or proconsul seemed to want to raise legions to conquer more territory and create a new province, thereby qualifying himself for a triumph. Some provinces such as Spain and Macedonia maintained garrisons which had to be supplied. By the very nature of their purpose arms are always being damaged in battle and requiring replacement.

In the factory I watched the slaves as they glued together layers of wood and felt to make the oval shields. It was important that the shield should be as light as possible, for the legionary had much to carry, and yet offer the maximum protection. The men set up variations on the basic design, hurled javelins at them and shot arrows to see which combination and what thickness of wood worked best. Helmets were forged from bronze and their design too was examined and tested. The blades of the short stabbing sword, originally from Spain, were hammered out and sharpened on grindstones. Corselets of mail and tunics of leather reinforced with strips of iron were fashioned for every shape and size of chest. Javelins, of which each legionary carried two inside his shield, were made in their thousands, each with one iron and one wooden rivet after the innovation instigated by Marius, so that on impact the javelin bent or snapped and could not be thrown back by the enemy. Leather boots too were stacked everywhere, graded according to their size. There was the constant noise of metal being hammered into shape. In one part of the factory, which was spread over a large area, I found men twisting the sinews of oxen and women's hair to make the strings for catapults. The resulting plaits were then coated with animal fat to prevent them from drying out. Crossbows and other forms of artillery such as ballistas and scorpions of the lighter types were also made here. The engineers in the legions made the heavier ones from local timber when they needed them for a siege. All of the slaves working in the factory were either shackled to their workbenches or had heavy chains linking their feet. Foremen armed with swords and whips supervised each group and the whole place was surrounded by a high wall. At the end of each day the slaves, still chained, were taken out of the factory to another walled compound where they were given food and slept. Almost every day carts filled with weapons left the factory to be taken either directly to new legions being raised in Italy or to go down to Puteoli for shipment to the armies abroad.

I visited some of the gladiator schools of which there were several in the area of Capua. Ever since the incident with the horse thief I had been anxious to improve myself in close combat. The gladiators were trained specifically for this and I believe that what I learned from watching them stood me in good stead when I came to fight on campaign in Pontus and Gaul. They taught me to stand sideways to present a smaller target, one foot behind the other to prevent the enemy from knocking me off balance, how to use a shield and sword together to create the opportunity to strike where an opponent was most vulnerable, how to defend against a man who carried his weapon in his left hand and his shield in the right. I practised with a wooden sword and though at first I was knocked down and 'killed' several times by my opponents, I gradually improved as my feet began to move more quickly and I learned the technique of keeping out of range and then darting in to strike. In battle things are different. You are surrounded by others and a blow may come from any direction, but the experience in the gladiator schools probably enabled me to survive where others might have perished.

One evening I witnessed an incident which at the time seemed insignificant but which later assumed considerable importance, though I was far away in Pontus by then. I had been invited to dine at the house of a certain Lucius Magius, a member of another famous Capuan family with whom I came into contact during my time there. After we had supped and the light was beginning to fade, our host announced that he had arranged some entertainment. He led us to a circular courtyard surrounded by a portico under which chairs and couches were placed. We were invited to make ourselves comfortable while slaves brought wine and sweetmeats. Torches attached to iron brackets on the columns illuminated the courtyard which had been covered in sand to form a small arena. There, two gladiators stood a few yards apart. Each was chained by one leg to the ground. The chains were long enough to enable them to move around the arena and to reach each other, but not us. Both men were bare-chested and wore a kind of leather skirt with leather sleeves on their forearms. Each had a bronze helmet with a swaying plume on top. One man was black and we were told that he came from Africa. The other was a tanned Thracian and they matched each other for height and weight. They looked strong and fit, their muscles seemed to ripple as the light from the torches caught them. I heard the ladies sitting near me gasp with pleasure, particularly at the handsome Thracian. One giggled to her neighbour, 'I hope the white one wins. I shall run away with him afterwards.' I looked at her fat and drunken husband on the next couch, an empty goblet lying beside him on the ground, and felt some sympathy.

Lucius called for the master of the gladiator school, a certain Lentulus Batiatus, who said that the two men would fight to the death. To add spice to the occasion he told us that the pair were friends who had trained together. The African had a conventional short sword and a round metal shield upon which two serpents were embossed. He reminded me of a Greek hoplite. The Thracian was armed with a trident and a net which he carried in his left hand. The contest began. The guests fell silent, intent upon the deadly spectacle. In the arena the men circled each other warily, there was no sound except the clinking of the chains attached to each man's ankle. Of course, I had seen these contests before but never in a private house and at such close quarters. Neither man betrayed any sign of fear, but you could see the sweat break out in little beads on their biceps and the hair on the chest of the Thracian became damp and matted. They seemed evenly matched and neither could inflict any serious wound upon the other. The African would try to push away the trident with his shield and then thrust with his sword, but the Thracian was always too quick. His trident was longer than the other's sword; he could keep the African at bay while he threw his net and tried to entangle his opponent in it. Once he caught the African's shield and pulled him off balance but could not bring his trident to bear on the other's body because the African pressed down on it with his sword. The two rocked back and forth as each sought an advantage. The African managed to disentangle his shield and leapt back; as he did so the Thracian lunged with his trident and caught his opponent a glancing blow on the chest. Three streaks of red appeared and the ladies gasped, but the wounds were not deep and though the blood looked spectacular as it flowed down the man's skirt and then trickled down his legs, it did not hamper the African's ability to fight. Each man was breathing heavily now, oblivious of the spectators and intent only upon the grim task of killing or being killed. The Thracian was carrying his net at his side awaiting his chance to throw it. Perhaps he had momentarily forgotten the chain on his ankle, for he would not fight in a normal arena with such an encumbrance. For whatever reason the chain and net somehow became entangled and for a moment the Thracian stumbled as he sought to separate them. The African saw his chance, pushing the unbalanced Thracian over so that he fell on his back in the sand with the arm holding the trident pinned to the ground by the black man's foot and one leg entangled in the chain and his own net. He could not move; the African stood over him with his sword poised to plunge into his friend's throat.

There was a cry from one of the ladies. 'Do not kill him. He has fought bravely and the African has won by an accident.' The victor hesitated, looking to his master Batiatus for an order. The other women and some men too shouted that the Thracian should be spared. Little Clodia who wanted to run off with him, stood up and pleaded with Magius to let the handsome gladiator live. 'He is much too beautiful to die,' she sighed to her friend Vipsania, who was sitting next to me. Reluctantly our host ordered that the Thracian be spared. Both men were paraded before us. Their faces were expressionless; they looked only in front of them. The blood on the African's chest was like a daub of war paint. He still carried his sword and shield while the Thracian's weapons lay on the sand where he had fallen. When they came near to our seats, Clodia asked the Thracian his name, saying that she hoped she would soon see him fight again. 'My name is Spartacus,' he replied, without raising his head. So it was that this man survived to lead the gladiators and slaves in the rebellion which broke out a few years later. If he did not do so before, Spartacus learned that night to hate the Romans. He had been spared and thus humiliated.

Chapter V

75–66 BC

By the time I was twenty-five years of age I had grown bored of the provincial life in Capua. I wanted to be a soldier as my father had suggested. Nicomedes of Bithynia, a small kingdom on the Euxine Sea bordering our province of Asia, had died and bequeathed his realm to the people of Rome. A cousin of mine, Caius Aurelius Cotta, had become governor of Asia following his consulship. More importantly however, Caius' brother Marcus was appointed to a joint command with Lucullus to fight against Mithridates of Pontus who was again threatening to invade Asia, taking advantage of Rome's commitments against Sertorius in Spain. Despite the fact that it was his year of office when he would normally be required to stay in Rome, Lucullus received permission to leave immediately for Cilicia where the governor, one Octavius, had died suddenly.

Caesar had written letters to me from Bithynia where he had stayed at the court of Nicomedes following Sulla's order to leave Rome. Sometime afterwards he had fought at Mytilene on Lesbos and won a civic crown for saving the life of a fellow citizen in battle. Now I heard that he had joined a militia raised by our relative in common, Caius Cotta, to defend Asia against Mithridates. I was filled with envy at the exciting life he was leading and determined that I too would go to Asia to join the fight against the rogue King of Pontus. Lucullus had raised one consular legion in Italy and it was this legion which I joined as a junior officer in Cilicia at the age of twenty-six, having received a helping hand from my cousin Marcus Aurelius Cotta, the colleague of Lucullus in the consulship that year. The latter had been very thick with Sulla when he was alive, and but for my cousin's recommendation I do not think Lucullus would have accepted me. I had no military experience and would serve my time in the ranks until such time as I might qualify to be a tribune. There were ten cohorts in the legion and I took my place in the first cohort. My duties were to assist the tribune commanding my cohort, organising supplies, dealing with matters of discipline and the welfare of the legionaries and generally to act as a liaison officer between the tribune and his centurions. In battle I might act as a galloper between the general and the tribunes or legates commanding the various parts of the army. As the son of a senator and a scion of one of Rome's most distinguished families I would not normally march on foot with the legionaries but ride on horseback. Yet I wanted to prove myself, to show that I could march carrying the load of an ordinary legionary, covering twenty miles a day, pitching and striking camp each evening and morning. There would be time enough to ride a horse.

In addition to his own consular legion, Lucullus had assembled four others. Two of these, called the Fimbrians, had been out in Asia for over ten years and had acquired a reputation for erratic behaviour. It was not known how they would react to a member of the oligarchy such as Lucullus.

Within a few days of my arrival at the camp in Cilicia we received bad news from the north. Mithridates had invaded the newly acquired province of Bithynia and occupied the capital at Nicomedia without resistance. My cousin, Caius Cotta, had been forced to retreat with his hastily raised forces to the coastal town of Chalcedon on the Bosphorus, where he lay besieged by the Pontic army. On learning this Lucullus struck camp and his force, consisting of about

50

twenty-five thousand legionaries and a few Galatian cavalry, began its advance. Our way lay first over the Taurus mountains which were rugged enough going at any time, let alone for a new recruit such as I was. I soon learned what it was to be one of 'Marius' mules', as his soldiers had been called in the campaigns against the Cimbri and Teutones in southern Gaul some thirty years before. In addition to my shield and two javelins, I carried on my back my rations for three days, a saw, a pickaxe and a bucket. Strapped to my belt were my helmet and my short sword. I also carried a cloak into which I wrapped myself at night. We rose at first light and marched until the middle of the day when a brief stop was ordered. We ate a little cold porridge or biscuit and drank water or some wine if we were lucky. Then the bugles would sound and we were on the march again. In front of each legion the standard was carried, a silver eagle mounted on a pole in the charge of the chief centurion. The marching was not so much quick as relentless. We had to cover the requisite distance per day irrespective of the terrain. In the early evening we would halt, but there was no rest for the camp must be pitched. Riders would go in advance to select a site, preferably near a water supply and where forage was available for the horses. Then we set to work with our spades and pickaxes to dig the trench, piling the earth up on the inside to form a rampart into which staves from the baggage train were stuck making a palisade. Next, depending on what rations had been supplied, we would light fires to cook and perhaps talk a little before the bugle sounded again at dusk to mark the first watch of the night. We legionaries did not keep watch; this was the job of the skirmishers who screened the legions at the beginning of a battle. Soon after dark most men would be asleep and the sound of the bugle at the beginning of each of the other three watches did not wake us.

Once we were through the Taurus mountains and into

the central plateau of Phrygia the going became a little easier. It was a land of woods and hills with plenty of water and grass for the horses. There was wheat to make our cakes and porridge and even fruit if you were quick enough to beat the other man to it. Most of the men around me were Italians because the legion was newly formed. They came from Latium, Picenum and Campania. Some came from as far away as Apulia in the south and that part of Gaul around the Po in the north. For the most part I found them friendly but the speech of some of the men, particularly from Apulia, was hard to understand. Some of the legionaries, the poorest ones, were volunteers who sought to escape from the poverty which had afflicted Italy after the Social War and the turbulence caused by Sulla and others. Many had been dispossessed of their land or had sold out to big landowners like the cousin of Gaius Matius at Spoletium. Others had been enrolled by the levy and expected to serve at least six years and possibly for as long as sixteen. It was a hard life but the pay was regular, if not spectacular, and there was the prospect of booty and possibly the grant of a bonus and land on discharge.

As we continued our march through Phrygia, further bad news was brought by horsemen from Deiotarus, a chieftain from Galatia who had raised an army to defend his country. While my cousin Cotta had remained besieged in Chalcedon, his admiral, a man called Nudus, had fought a battle outside the city which had resulted in a victory for the Pontic forces. To make matters worse, the enemy fleet had succeeded in breaking through the bronze chain which guarded the entrance to the city's harbour and had towed away a large part of the Roman fleet. I felt ashamed at this humiliation of our forces and the dishonour which it brought upon my name. I longed to have an opportunity to restore some family pride. We were now approaching the border with Bithynia and intelligence from Deiotarus indicated that Mithridates was advancing towards us with part of his forces from Chalcedon. I had high hopes that we might do battle.

A few days later I had my first sight of the enemy. The army of Mithridates lay encamped on a plain at a place called Otryae. The camp was heavily fortified and the tribune in command of my cohort, Marcus Popilius, told me that they outnumbered our forces by more than three to one. They included a legion of exiles and renegades from Rome who had joined the Pontic army and were commanded by a man calling himself Marius, who claimed to be the son of the old general himself. Nevertheless Lucullus was eager to fight and for three days in succession he led us out of our camp to offer battle. Mithridates would not be drawn, though his cavalry must have been much more powerful than ours. We could see from our camp hundreds of scythed chariots lined up behind his defences. These were the King's new weapon which it was said he would use to break up the ranks of our legions.

One morning I was supervising some legionaries who were collecting kindling for their fires from the woods behind our camp out of sight of the enemy. I was on horseback to give me a better view. There were cavalry nearby who were watering their horses at a stream and at the same time acting as a guard for the men who were unarmed. Suddenly I heard bugles sounding the signal to prepare for battle and a galloper from Popilius arrived with orders to return to camp immediately. I rounded up the men and they ran with their bundles of wood back to the gates. As I rode I could see in the distance that infantry were emerging from the Pontic defences and forming up in line of battle on the plain which lay between us. I felt a sharp stab of excitement tinged with fear, but it passed almost immediately as I became caught up in the preparations for combat.

Inside our palisade everywhere was alive with movement. Men were putting on their iron corselets and helmets, others were strapping on their swords and fitting javelins inside their shields. As I passed down the main street of the camp a squadron of cavalry galloped towards the praetorian gate. Cohorts were forming up and marching out to be deployed with their legion. Tribunes barked orders to the centurions who in turn harried their men. I soon found Popilius and said that I wished to fight on foot as a legionary. He was too busy really to listen and with a wave of the hand indicated that I was free to do so.

Within half an hour of the first bugle note sounding the alarm I found myself in the front rank of the first cohort with about a hundred and fifty men beside me and another four hundred odd behind. Our legion lay in the middle with the two Macedonian contingents on either side. Behind us in reserve came the Fimbrians of whom Lucullus was still not confident. Our legion had deployed in a standard formation with the first cohort on the right and three more on our left. Behind us the other six cohorts were ranged in the gaps in two rows of three. This enabled us to move freely and quickly in any direction. The apparent gaps in the front line would be filled by the men in the second lines moving sideways and the rear cohorts filled in if the front line was broken. In front of us were some lightly armed skirmishers with slings and small catapults to harass the forward ranks of the enemy from a distance. They would run back through the legionaries as soon as the real fighting started.

Though I had never experienced battle before, I felt no sense of fear. I was young and fit. I believed that I knew how to fight another man and to kill him. I wanted to prove to myself that I could do this. The most striking thing as we awaited the order to advance was the quietness. Nobody spoke. Each man held one of his javelins in his throwing hand ready to let loose just before we closed with the front rank of the enemy. There was the occasional dull clang of metal on metal. Over to my left I could see the legion's standard held aloft in the middle of our line. We waited; one or two men coughed. I heard somebody behind make a joke and his companion laughed nervously. Though it was an overcast day some of us began to sweat. The enemy was probably at a distance of some five or six hundred paces from us. We heard the bugles sound the order for a slow advance and then there were shouts from the centurions. I began to walk forward and it was then that the fear gripped me. Like the man next to me and the man next to him, I could not show it; I would not show it. My nerves began to steady. I sensed the power of the legion around me. Well over twenty thousand men were walking with me; we walked steadily, we were disciplined, we were all armed in the same way and we knew that we were part of the most powerful military unit in the world, a Roman army.

The gap between us and the enemy had closed to about two hundred paces. Our skirmishers had loosed off their stones and arrows and were coming back towards us. Now we could see the faces of the enemy. There were infantry with round shields and long spears for stabbing rather than throwing. On the wings stood cavalry whose riders carried lances and had bows and arrows slung on their backs. Behind the front ranks we could see the scythed chariots poised to dash through and slice their way into us. We continued to move forward. Not a voice could be heard, only the rhythmic clunk of each man's sword chafing against his metal corselet as he walked. Moments later there was a great flash of light from above and an object engulfed in flame fell from the sky between the two armies. It seemed that the gods had thrown a boulder down onto the earth. The men on both sides took fright. It was an evil omen such as nobody had ever seen before. The soldiers in the foremost ranks of each army stopped. On either side of me I heard men exchanging anxious words. Nobody would advance in the direction of the flaming object that had crashed into the ground. A legionary shouted that Mars had decreed we should not fight that day. Others agreed. They would not move and no amount of coercion by the centurions, some of whom were equally alarmed, would make them. The Pontic forces too had turned about and were making their way back to their camp. Much later Lucullus told me that he was relieved in one way not to have to fight. Our forces were heavily outnumbered and he was uncertain how the Fimbrians might react against the legion of Roman exiles whom Mithridates had gathered.

So I did not get my first taste of battle that day. Instead we observed the Pontic army strike camp not long afterwards and march back into Bythinia. It soon became apparent that Mithridates was leading his troops to Cyzicus, another port on the Propontis lying far to the west of Chalcedon. If he could seize Cyzicus the King would be master of the Propontis and there would be no way through to the Euxine Sea for a Roman or any other fleet. Furthermore, his army would again be threatening the province of Asia and its cities where Mithridates had massacred eighty thousand Romans in the previous war. Lucullus had no alternative but to follow. It was a tough march, for the King pursued a scorched earth policy of laying waste to the country as he passed through it, so that there was nothing left for us. We requested supplies from Asia but these were slow in coming. Our rations were halved and often there was little water to drink as the enemy forces polluted the rivers and streams with animal dung.

Cyzicus was a port lying at the end of a peninsula jutting into the Propontis. On the landward side it had stout walls well sited to withstand a siege. The harbour had a very narrow entrance, easy to defend, so that the only practical means of attack was to storm the walls or undermine them while the Pontic fleet prevented supplies reaching the town by sea. A detachment of the enemy had marched to Cyzicus after the battle at Chalcedon. Now Mithridates came with the rest of his army to storm the city or to starve it into submission. At the base of the peninsula lay the mountains of Andrasteia which formed a barrier separating it from the mainland. On these mountains Mithridates at first took up his position, entrenching his army so that part of it faced into the peninsula where Cyzicus lay and the remainder faced outwards to the mainland. He then constructed trenches and earthworks to hem in the Cyzicenes and at the same time built moles to block the entrance to the harbour so that no supplies could reach the town by sea. His own supplies were secure as they could be delivered by his fleet onto the beaches controlled by his forces.

Faced with this situation Lucullus decided to bottle up the enemy and we constructed a long line of fortifications and ditches by means of which to prevent the Pontic army breaking out from the peninsula.

All that summer Mithridates battered the walls of Cyzicus without success. He erected a great siege tower called a sambuca which floated on two quinqueremes. This was brought up to the harbour wall and an assault column dashed forward from a drawbridge on the tower, but the attack was not pressed home and the Cyzicenes forced the quinqueremes to withdraw by pouring burning oil upon them. Meanwhile a landward attack had also been made on the town. The besiegers used battering rams and blazing barrels of tar thrown by catapults in their assault. Despite the desperate fighting the walls of the town held, except in one place where the intense heat caused the mortar to crumble and the wall collapsed in a heap of stones. Yet the stones were so hot that the Pontic infantry could not climb over them and by the time they had cooled the defenders had piled up another wall behind the collapsed one.

Meanwhile a strange thing had happened. For some reason which we could not understand Mithridates abandoned his impregnable defensive line on the mountains of Andrasteia and withdrew his forces further into the peninsula. At this Lucullus naturally ordered our troops to advance and we took over the old fortifications of the King's army. This meant that our lines were shorter and it was easier to keep the Pontic army hemmed in. Furthermore the citizens of Cyzicus could now see that an army lay beyond the besiegers and might assume that we had come to relieve them. But the enemy instead made capital of this. They shouted up to the citizens of Cyzicus that the forces encamped on the hills were Armenians sent by Tigranes to assist his father-in-law, and not a Roman army at all.

We knew from the capture of enemy soldiers that Mithridates had as many as three hundred thousand men in the peninsula, of whom only about a third were fighting troops. So long as the weather stayed fair he could keep these mouths fed by supply ships to the beaches, but Lucullus reasoned that once the winter set in it would be impossible to keep such a large number from starvation. The weather would prevent enough ships from landing sufficient stores on the open shore. If Cyzicus could hold on a little longer we could defeat the enemy without a battle. By now, however, the Cyzicenes were close to starvation themselves and there were rumours that they were about to surrender as they could see no way out from the siege. At this point a Greek mercenary named Archelaus, who had joined our army in Cilicia, came forward to propose that messengers be sent through the Pontic lines to tell the Cyzicenes the true identity of the army on the hills. This, said Archelaus, would encourage them to hold out long enough. So, for six successive days messengers were sent at night through the enemy lines, but none reached the town. We knew this because it was arranged that the messenger would have a red flag hoisted on the walls to show he had arrived.

For some weeks I had studied the defences of the King's army. They were indeed formidable and consisted of a series of ramparts and ditches with sentry towers posted at intervals of about a hundred paces. There were palisades where rocky outcrops made it impossible to dig ditches and guards patrolled throughout the day and night. Any man caught would be killed after being tortured to obtain information. From our position on the hills I had a reasonable view of the whole of the Pontic lines which stretched for about five miles round Cyzicus and ended with the sea at each end. I noticed that at the eastern extremity of the lines was a large rocky outcrop where it had not been possible to construct earthworks but which was protected mostly by palisades and sentries on the top of the rocks. I took my horse and rode to a place where I could have a closer look. At the base of the hill a ditch had been dug, presumably to prevent a sudden assault in numbers, but there was no other barrier, probably because the rock was so steep that there was no room for more than a few men to go up. The face of the rock appeared smooth from where I stood, but judging by other rocks on the mountains where we were camped I guessed that it might offer enough holds to climb it. About a hundred feet up there was a fissure, perhaps the width of two men, which led upwards at a slightly less steep angle towards the summit. The fissure appeared to run as far as the palisade and perhaps went under it. Guards patrolled the top of the rock and there was a watchtower about thirty paces from the fissure. I could not tell what was on the other side though I guessed that the land might fall away towards the sea.

That night I made my way to the part of the camp where the tribunes of our legion lodged. I found them seated

59

round a table playing dice and drinking wine from silver goblets. Slaves waited upon them with flagons to refill their cups and at the end of the wooden barracks by a fire were some women who I suspected had been smuggled in, for I doubt that Lucullus would have permitted them to enter the camp. On seeing me Popilius rose from the table. He looked a trifle cross at being disturbed and his eyes were bloodshot with drink. Nevertheless he treated me civilly enough for we had always got on well. I told him that I wanted to volunteer to try to reach Cyzicus.

'You're mad, my lad,' he laughed. 'Let's talk again in the morning. Now have a cup of wine and see if you can win some money back for me from these thieves.' He gestured to the table and nearly lost his balance as he did so. I thanked him but said I would see him on the morrow when he promised me that he would arrange an interview with Lucullus at his headquarters.

True to his word the following morning Popilius conducted me to the base at the rear of our lines where Lucullus had established himself and his staff. After giving the password for the day which I happen to remember was 'the she-wolf', we were admitted to a large wooden barrack with an anteroom occupied by guards and behind it a larger room where the general was seated at a table with three or four of his legates. On the table was a model made of clay showing the disposition of the Pontic defences and our lines. The walls of the room were draped with silks and on another table I saw sweetmeats laid out with silver plate and finely engraved goblets for wine. Slaves stood ready to serve food, with towels and water to wash the hands and feet of visitors. Lucius Licinius Lucullus at this time was about forty. He had a reputation for being a stern disciplinarian with the troops but face to face he could be kind and considerate. He was a patrician of the old school, believing in the traditional Roman virtues of simplicity and piety. In later years he became a gourmet and built his beautiful gardens on the Quirinal Hill in Rome where he grew some of the plants and shrubs brought back from the campaigns in the East. The Persian kings had parks in which animals could roam; they built pleasure domes surrounded by exotic shrubs, orchards and flower gardens with fountains. Lucullus saw all of this and it influenced the design of his gardens at Rome and at his villa near Baiae, where I got to know him better after he had retired. That morning I was conscious of the acute intelligence betrayed by his high forehead, the angular lines of his cheekbones and jaw. When he listened to you, his eyes seemed to penetrate into your brain so that you felt that he was reading your mind rather than paying attention to the spoken words.

Popilius led me forward and I stood awkwardly while the purpose of our visit was explained. Lucullus said nothing at first but looked steadily at me, appraising what he saw. 'So,' he said, 'you want to do something to redeem your family's honour, young man. I knew your father, a brave but mis-guided fellow, if I may say so. Your mother too I remember meeting at the house of Marcus Lepidus. You come of good stock. Now, have a look at this and tell me how you propose to succeed where six others have failed before you.' He raised an arm and beckoned me to the table. 'You recognise this, I trust?' I said that I did. 'Very well, perhaps you would elucidate your plan.' I sensed a lack of conviction in his voice and my finger was shaking as I pointed out on the model the rocky outcrop at the eastern end of the enemy defences. I explained how I intended to climb the face and crawl up the fissure which was too small to be shown on the model.

'The palisade may cross over the fissure as you suggest,' said the general, 'but you may be sure that the enemy will have blocked any gap underneath it. The guards patrol all the time and any noise that you make trying to unblock it

61

will certainly attract their attention. Even if you get through, what is on the other side?' I admitted that I did not know, that I would have to trust to luck and hope to evade detection in the dark. 'Supposing that you do evade the sentries, how will you reach Cyzicus itself? You can hardly approach the walls and ask to be let in.'

'I am a reasonably strong swimmer, sir,' I replied. 'If I can get down to the shore, I think it should be possible to swim to the harbour and climb onto the mole which Mithridates has constructed and perhaps make contact from there.'

Lucullus looked at the model for some moments. 'It all sounds rather vague to me, young man, and the sea will be very cold, even if you get that far. But I agree that the point in their defences which you have chosen offers the best chance of getting through.' He called for a secretary who appeared with a stylus and wax tablets, and dictated a short letter to the commander of the Cyzicene garrison, instructing him on the military situation and telling him on no account to surrender as the siege would soon be lifted in one way or another. This done he impressed his signet ring upon the wax which the secretary then enclosed in a thin wooden case. 'Strap that to your belt. They will kill you anyway, if you are caught, so it matters not if the letter is found on you.' Lucullus handed the despatch to me and with his other arm gave me a pat on the shoulder. 'Good luck, young Cotta, I hope that you will be more successful than your cousin at Chalcedon.' Then, it seemed as an afterthought, he added, 'And give my regards to your mother if you ever see her again.' He turned back to the table and I retreated with Popilius towards the anteroom and the guards. As we reached the door Lucullus called out, 'Lucius, I do hope you and I will meet again,' and he grinned as if there were some secret understanding between us.

'You seem to have made a hit with the old bugger,' said

Popilius with a hint of resentment in his voice as we made our way back to the legion. I was already thinking about what lay ahead of me.

It seemed to me that my best chance lay on a night which was cloudy and windy with some moon, but perhaps not a full one. The wind would muffle any noise that I might make and the moon would help me to plan my movements once it had gone behind clouds. We were approaching the equinox and it so happened that such a night came along three days after my interview with Lucullus. During the days before I had studied as carefully as I could the approaches to the rock. I should need help to cross the deep ditch which lay at its base. Two legionaries, Caius Appuleius and Septimius Varus volunteered for this. I decided to take with me a dagger, a knife to cut through any vegetation and some food in case I had to lie up for any length of time.

At the beginning of the second watch, having sent word to Popilius that I would make my attempt that night, the three of us made our way through our lines and emerged into a stretch of no man's land lying between the two sets of fortifications. There were a few trees and bushes which we tried to keep behind as we came nearer to the ditch dug by the Pontic forces. Where there were open spaces we moved very slowly on all fours to avoid being noticed by any guard who might be looking over the area from the hilltop above.

As I had hoped, the wind was blowing, clouds were scudding across the sky creating moving shadows in the faint moonlight and there was rain in the air making it even less easy to see any distance. At length we reached the edge of the ditch which had sheer sides and was about fifteen feet deep. The legionaries had brought with them a scaling ladder, dragging it along the ground behind them. Now they lowered this into the ditch and we climbed down easily enough and pitched it against the far side. Up I went and over the lip without difficulty. I had half expected to find some unseen obstacle on this side of the ditch but there was nothing. I signalled to Caius and Septimius that all was well by shaking the top of the ladder gently. It disappeared behind me and I could just see two shadowy figures as they made their way back across the ditch and out on the other side. Now I was alone in enemy territory and there was no way back, only forward.

I moved over to a shrub and tucked myself in behind it, waiting for the moon to appear to give me a look at the rock. It seemed a long time before the clouds moved away and I began to wonder how long I would shiver in the light rain which was falling. But the wind was still blowing and at last I got a better look at the rock as the moon emerged. I could not see the fissure; it was too dark and out of sight anyway. But I knew exactly where it was in relation to a jagged outcrop which in the daylight stood out like a broken tooth a few paces to the right and a little below where the fissure began. The broken tooth was silhouetted for a few moments in the moonlight. It seemed much further up than I had thought from my view of it behind our lines. I waited for the moon to disappear again and then moved out towards the rock which was only twenty or thirty paces in front of me. At this stage, even in daylight the guards on the top would not have been able to see me as the slope of the rock shielded their view of the base and others further away would not be able to see in the dark. I began to climb. The face was steep but not impossible. As I had expected there were occasional crevices upon which one could rest one's feet or grip with the hands. Once I dislodged a stone or a piece of rock and it clattered down to the bottom. The noise seemed deafening to me. I stopped to listen for a few minutes; all I could hear was the moan of the wind and a patter of light rain. I could see nothing of the barrier ahead or any guards, for the slope also blinded me from a sight of them. I set off again and eventually reached the jagged tooth where I sat down on a little ledge to rest.

Though I counted myself as fit and strong, I was not accustomed to the repeated exertion of pulling myself up by the hands alone and then seeking a foothold in the dark. However, I had made it and thought that the fissure would be easier as it had seemed to be less steep. Though I could not yet see it I knew exactly where it was and I crawled across the face of the rock towards it. The fissure proved to be less deep than I had thought from a distance. I could easily get my body into it, but I protruded above the rock on each side so that I felt visible to anybody who might look from above. I could only hope that the crack would become deeper as I got nearer the palisade. I started to climb again and after a few minutes I detected some way above me a darker shadow against the night sky. This I thought must be the palisade. I began to crawl more slowly, stopping every few feet to watch and listen. By now I was pretty wet with rain, but I welcomed it in the hope that it would discourage the sentries from emerging too frequently to patrol. Without warning, the moon slipped out from behind the clouds and for a moment I saw clearly the watchtower over to my right. The fissure led straight up to the palisade and as I had hoped it got deeper and wider as it climbed the hill. I saw no sign of life. The sentries would probably keep watch from the tower and occasionally patrol on the far side of the palisade. The rock on my side was completely bare and offered no cover.

The sky clouded over again and I crawled on my stomach towards the palisade. The watchtower was dimly visible but I was able to get right down into the fissure now and I doubted that anybody could see me. I became a little more confident and it was not long before I had reached the wooden barrier which was made of stout timbers with a battlement on top. I suspected, though I could not see it, that there would be a platform behind the battlement along which sentries could patrol, perhaps ten or twelve feet above me. In front of me the fissure was blocked with what felt like rocks and for some time I could find no gap of any kind. The moon came out again and I froze, wondering whether anybody in the tower could see me. I dared not turn my face to look in case the movement should attract attention. Then, as I examined the seemingly solid wall of rock I saw a chink of pale sky through a crack on one side of the fissure. Moments later it had disappeared as the moon went back behind the clouds. It began to rain harder and the wind blew. I felt round the rocks where I had seen the glimmer and discovered that some of them would move. It appeared that they had been tipped into the fissure simply to fill the gap between it and the base of the palisade. If I could move enough rocks at the top of the pile I would be able to crawl through to the other side. The problem was to move them without attracting the attention of the sentries, who could not be far away.

Gingerly I began to pull at a rock directly beneath the palisade near the side of the fissure, taking care not to disturb others. After about an hour I had removed six rocks and created a hole about the size of a man's fist through which I could see to the other side. Then I found that I could not move either of the rocks on each side of the hole and I had to start removing the ones beneath in order to enlarge it. This was risky as I might cause a collapse of the ones above and the resultant noise would rouse the sentries. But I had no alternative. I clawed away with my hands which by now were bleeding, feeling for the side of any rock and testing to see if I could move it. I sensed that time was passing, that it would not be too long before dawn began to break. I had to be through the barrier before then or face certain capture and death. I removed several smaller rocks

66

more quickly now, trying to expose a larger one which I could feel was loose but held by ones in front of it. At last I pulled the large one towards me and saw behind it a hole which I judged was big enough to crawl through.

I eased my way into the gap and within a few moments my head and shoulders were through to the far side of the palisade. The wind and the rain had slackened a little and I rested for a moment before making the final effort to pull my whole body through. I could feel my heart beating as I lay with my chest pressed against the rock beneath me. Turning my head I saw the watchtower as a dark mass over to my right. To my left the ground fell gently away and I sensed rather than saw the watchtower on that side, further down the slope. I put out my hands in front of me to get a purchase on the base of the palisade to force myself through. As I did so I heard the sound of footsteps and then voices speaking a language I did not understand. So far as I could tell they were coming towards me along the platform of the palisade. I heard the timbers above me creak as they passed over the spot where I lay and their voices gradually faded as they went on down the hill presumably to the next tower. It had probably been two sentries making a routine patrol, perhaps taking advantage of the slackening in the rain. Over to the east I made out a light grey expanse, the sea, and above it the sky was growing pale. It was now, I thought, that I should make a break; the sentries were unlikely to return immediately. In front of me the ground was bare offering no cover. Beyond, perhaps a hundred paces away and slightly to my right, there lay a jumble of rocks. If I could reach them I would be out of sight of the watchtower. I pulled myself completely through the hole and squatted for a moment looking to right and left. There was nothing to be seen or heard. Stooping forward to keep my body as low to the ground as possible I began to lope towards the outcrop of rocks. I had got about halfway when there was a shout. There must have been a sentry on the rampart where I could not see. I kept running and was soon among the rocks. From behind I heard more shouts and the alarm was raised.

The ground sloped downwards and I ran, crawled and slithered in a blind panic to get away. Once I had passed the rocks I came to a flatter area where bushes grew in the lee of the outcrop. They provided cover as I moved through them with the shouts of my pursuers audible above. Soon I was among trees. I slowed to a walk, pausing every now and then to listen. The darkness and the bushes had come to my rescue. The sentries had given up hope of finding me that night but no doubt they would be hard on my heels in the morning. The sky was beginning to grow lighter. I would not be able to reach the shore and try to make it to the harbour before dawn broke. In the darkness I had no idea where I was. I would have to lie up for the rest of the night and, the following day, try to plan my route in the daylight before setting out again once night had fallen. I made myself as comfortable as I could against the trunk of a fallen tree. My clothes were wet through from the rain, my hands were sore from the rocks, above all I was cold and frightened. I ate some of the biscuit and drank from the flask which I had brought with me. Slowly it began to grow light and I longed for the warmth of the sun's rays which would never reach me hidden under the trees.

Perhaps I dozed for a few moments. Suddenly I was aware of shouts somewhere close by. I could not tell whether they were sentries searching for me or perhaps just men gathering wood for fires. I looked round desperately seeking somewhere to conceal myself and found that the very tree trunk against which I had been leaning was virtually hollow. I eased my way inside feet first and pulled some foliage across to disguise the hole. I could hear more voices now; they were getting closer. From their shouts I sensed that they were sentries looking for me. I heard the sound of undergrowth being beaten down and breaking twigs as a man walked close to where I lay. My heart was thumping. A moment later I felt something cool and smooth begin to slither up my leg. I had disturbed a snake which had made its home in the rotten tree trunk. I could not move. The snake paused and then I felt it on my tunic as it came on up my body past my dagger. My arms were still up by my head holding in place the foliage. I could feel the weight of the snake on my left leg and the gentle sideways movements of its body as it slipped off my back and onto the crumbling wood beside me. Then a white and yellow head appeared within inches of my face. It rested on my wrist. Now that I could see it, the sensation of sick terror began to ease. I watched with fascination as the head turned this way and that looking to see if it was safe to emerge from the sanctuary of the trunk. I could still hear the sounds of the searchers but they seemed to be moving away. Eventually silence came back to the wood and with that the snake slithered over my hand and out into the undergrowth beyond. It must have been nearly the length of a javelin and when its tail at last flicked my arm, my skin felt warm from the friction.

I waited for some time until I was sure that my pursuers had given up the search. When at last I stood up I felt very stiff and cold. My dank tunic clung to my body. I tried to make a note of my surroundings in case I should need to hide again in the tree, then I started to walk in what I judged to be the direction of the sea. I needed to get my bearings and to find somewhere which gave me a view beyond the trees. By now it was fully light and a low sun was shining through the branches. Keeping a sharp lookout and stopping frequently to listen, I walked gently downhill until I came to a point where the trees became thinner and I could see the shore. Over to my right there were ships riding at anchor a little out to sea while others were pulled up on the beach. Smaller boats were plying between the larger ones and the beach, bringing provisions ashore where men were loading them onto carts. Over to my left about a mile away, perhaps more, I could see the walls of Cyzicus beyond which lay the town. Further away still rose what I guessed were the moles which Mithridates had constructed to prevent ships bringing supplies into the harbour.

Keeping out of sight in the trees I walked to my left until I could see round the hill. There below lay an enormous sea of tents, shelters, men and horses encamped before the walls of the town. A continuous stream of carts ran round the bottom of the hill from the improvised harbour to the besieging army. The sun was shining onto the walls of Cyzicus which in places were blackened by fire and tar. By the walls lay mounds of earth which were the spoil of operations to undermine the defences or possibly ramps to attack the battlements. I could make out battering rams and catapults but there was no sign of any fighting. Cyzicus looked almost serene in the sunlight and it was difficult to imagine the starvation and fear of those inside. From where I stood I had a good view of the approaches to the town. If I could get down to the beach I could walk along it until it ended in a large rock on top of which rose the rampart. To reach the harbour I would have to swim round the rock and then either climb over the mole constructed by Mithridates or, if there was a gap, swim past it. The beach lay on the far side of the busy roadway from the harbour to the Pontic camp. I could only reach it by night and I would certainly be challenged on the shore in daylight. I went back a little way into the trees and found some dense undergrowth into which I crawled. Though it was cool my clothes had almost dried. I made myself a sort of nest from twigs and leaves. I felt very tired and soon I was asleep.

When I awoke the sun had gone round the hill behind

me. It was late in the day and I crept forward again to survey the scene below. The roadway was still busy with carts but there were fewer now. Two of the large boats out to sea had disappeared and the shore was almost deserted. I tried to make a mental picture of the route I would take down the hill, across the roadway and out onto the shore where I judged I was least likely to meet anybody. The hill had little vegetation below where I stood and there seemed to be no gullies to provide cover for my descent. Between the road and the sea however were large bushes of gorse which would screen me once I had reached the beach. I ate a little more of my food and rested while I waited for dusk to fall. Soon the ground below lay in the shadow of the hill. The light began to fade and I heard birds in the trees behind me twittering as they found their roosts for the night. A bat flitted to and fro in front of me and the sea turned from dark green to dark grey. A light breeze sprang up and I was pleased to see a few clouds appear. I did not want moonlight as I left the shelter of the trees. One or two fires began to flicker where the boats were drawn up on the shore. I waited until it was completely dark but before the moon had risen, then I set out down the hill and it was not long before I had reached the roadway. Having crossed it without incident I walked through the gorse bushes onto the beach of shingle. I kept as close in as I could to the gorse so that I would not be silhouetted against the flat expanse of sea to my right. Way over to my left the night sky glowed faintly with the fires from the Pontic camps and I could hear the distant hum generated by the talk of thousands upon thousands of men.

Progress along the beach was easy and in a short time I saw the dark outline of the rock which marked the junction of the city walls with the sea. As I got nearer however, I heard the sound of voices. I edged into the gorse bushes and then crawled slowly forward until I was within about a hundred paces of the rock. So far as I could tell there were six or seven men seated in a group on the ground and further inland I saw a campfire burning. It seemed that I had run up against an outlying picket placed there either to prevent Cyzicenes getting out or possibly to prevent messengers like me getting in. I sat down to wait, hoping that an opportunity might present itself. For a long time the chatter continued. The moon rose and I could see six men sitting round in a circle on the rocks leading down to the sea. There was no hope of getting past them unobserved. Then, quite suddenly, they stood up and all but one of them set off inland. I sensed they were returning to the campfire. They carried shields and spears with them. One guard remained, his dark figure silhouetted in the moonlight against the background of the pale coloured rock behind him. For some while he stood motionless with his shield resting against his left leg and a spear upright in his right hand. On his head he wore a helmet whose plumes were occasionally disturbed by a gentle breeze off the sea. Using the bushes as cover I crept forward until I was not more than twenty paces from the man. By now he had sat down and I thought he might fall asleep if I waited long enough. But he showed no sign of this. At that time I had never killed a man. I wondered whether I could rush him and plunge home my dagger before he could raise the alarm – it seemed unlikely. There was open ground between us and he was a few feet up on the rock. He would have plenty of time to see me coming and be ready with his spear.

I went back the way I had come until I was out of sight of the guard and picked up some pebbles from the beach. Then I made my way back, keeping to the landward side of the gorse bushes until I reached a position some fifty or so paces from the guard but hidden from his view. I began to throw my pebbles one at a time at the rock – they clattered and fell back down to the ground. The noise sounded as though somebody might be trying to climb the rock and disturbing loose pieces as he did so. I watched the guard from the bushes. He had stood up and was peering about him trying to pinpoint the direction of the noise. I waited until he was looking up at the rock behind him and then threw two stones together at the part opposite me. Sure enough he turned, picked up his shield and began to walk towards the sound. Once he had gone past me I slipped out from the gorse across a few yards of open ground to a large boulder which concealed me from the landward side. Looking round it I saw the sentry still walking slowly and uncertainly inland, all the while looking up at the rock to see if somebody was trying to scale it. A few moments later I had reached the water's edge where the sea met the rocks on which the guard had been. I scrambled down out of sight and began to work my way round with water sometimes lapping over my feet. I had not gone far before the rock rose sheer in front of me. There was no way forward except by swimming round to the harbour. I could not see to do this in the dark so I sat on a ledge just above the waterline waiting for daylight. It was cold and there was little room to move. I tried to keep warm by swinging my arms and legs. I finished the last of my rations, hoping that my next meal would be inside the walls of Cyzicus if the starving citizens had anything left. The stars were out. I tried to identify the various constellations which my father had taught me. There was complete silence except for the gentle lapping of the Propontis against the rocks a few feet below me. Despite the cold I had to fight off the desire to sleep. Once I awoke with a start and only just saved myself from slipping into the water. To try to stay awake I fell to thinking about the past.

The sight of the great field of stars above me and the sound of the sea below reminded me of evenings spent with Domitia in the peristyle of her father's house in Rome where we had sat by the fountain and talked together through the warm nights, listening to the doves as they fluttered and cooed under the eaves. The image of her face became fixed in my mind in that dark and lonely silence. I heard her speaking to me, urging me to forget the past, to go on into a different period of my life with just her memory for company. I was tired and I began to weep. I told myself that it was merely a reaction to the fear I had experienced over the previous night and day. Then I saw her lying on the couch, dying slowly with her mother kneeling helplessly beside her. I became angry, the picture faded and my weeping stopped.

At last a pale streak appeared over the sea to the east. I heard some gulls overhead and the sun began to rise into a cloudless sky. I let its rays warm my stiff and cramped body before slipping down into the water to begin the last part of my mission. The sea was cold but within a few minutes I had adjusted to it. Keeping close into the rocks and sometimes clambering over them half in and half out of the water, I rounded the cliff and there beheld the harbour with the mole obstructing its entrance just beyond. The mole was occupied by what looked like Pontic forces, and ships which could only belong to the enemy were moored close by. Between me and the harbour the city wall ran along the top of the rocks which dropped steeply into the sea. I swam a little further and found a place where I could haul myself out. I rested briefly before beginning to climb up towards the wall, sometimes tracking sideways in search of clefts or gullies offering an alternative to the smooth rock on which there was no purchase. I reached a point a few feet below the base of the wall which rose another fifteen feet or so above that. I called out in Latin, trying to attract the attention of a sentry. The nearest Pontic vessel was moored about three hundred paces away. I could detect no movement on it. It was still not long after sunrise but I could not

74

afford to be seen, for it would have been the work of a few minutes to send a boat to capture me. I squatted down behind a rock and continued to call softly up to the wall. A face appeared over the parapet. I explained that I was a Roman soldier with a message from Lucullus for the chief of the city. The face stared down at me uncomprehendingly. I tried again in schoolboy Greek. The face disappeared without a word. Within a few minutes he had returned with three others. I repeated my message in Greek, having thought how to put it more clearly in the interval. Once again two of them disappeared, while the two who remained said nothing. I pointed to the leather pouch strapped to my belt saying that my message was inside. At length several men appeared and one who could speak Latin questioned me. He seemed suspicious and obviously feared that there was some trick. I explained again that I had a message from the Roman army encamped beyond the besiegers. I undid the pouch from my belt and threw it up to the guards. The man who could speak Latin read it and I heard an order being given. A scaling ladder was lowered, up which I climbed and so entered the city of Cyzicus a day and two nights after I had left our lines.

I shall not dwell long upon the events of the next few months. Suffice it is to say that the citizens of the town made me most welcome as the bearer of good news. Eventually Mithridates was forced through the gradual starvation of his army to abandon the siege. He made an escape by sea with his staff and his treasures. Many of his cavalry were cut down at the Rhyndacus, where they were caught by legionaries as they attempted to cross that river swollen by winter rains. The bulk of his army however, led by the renegade Marius, succeeded in evading our forces by a night manoeuvre and marched away to the west in the direction of Lampsacus. At another river, the Granicus, Lucullus caught them and killed a vast number of soldiers and camp followers. Then he made a formal entry into Cyzicus where I had waited as a guest of the citizens.

Shortly after his entry into the city I was summoned to the general's headquarters, a large Greek villa which he had requisitioned. Lucullus was seated on a dais surrounded by his legates with a secretary or two at a table to one side. He was not dressed in military uniform. Instead he wore the toga with a garland of plaited jasmine on his head.

'I was confident we should meet again, young man,' he said, beckoning me to stand before him. 'Tell me how you got through. Did you have to kill?' He listened without interruption as I told my story. When I had finished he turned to his legates and said, 'I think you will agree, gentlemen, that Lucius Valerius Cotta has distinguished himself. I propose to award to him the corona vallaris.' And so saying he stepped down from the dais and placed upon my head the crown which is awarded to a Roman soldier who is the first to cross the entrenchment of a fortified camp. I was so surprised that I could only splutter thanks. In a daze of pride I walked back to the lines surrounded by men who came forward to congratulate me when they saw the wreath upon my head. I was proud to be a Roman soldier in a consular legion.

Chapter VI

75–66 BC

The following spring saw our legions concentrated in Galatia. We had made progress in the war against Mithridates in the sense that the provinces of Asia and Bithynia were now secure. The King had been driven back into his own territory and Lucullus decided that we should invade. Our fleet was coasting along the northern seaboard threatening the cities of Heraclea, Amisus and Sinope on the Euxine. Inland, large parts of Galatia had been ravaged in fighting between their chieftain Deiotarus and a Pontic mercenary called Eumachus. The army could not march through this wasted country without provisions. Lucullus, however, devised the idea of employing porters who would carry the necessary rations. Some thirty thousand men were rounded up by Deiotarus and loaded with sacks of flour to keep us fed as we marched through Phrygia and Galatia into Pontus. Once we had crossed the border, the supply situation became very different. This was a land of plenty which had enjoyed peace and sound government for many years. There we found corn and herds of cattle to keep us fed.

As we advanced further into Pontus we came to a river called Thermodon which runs through a valley said once to have been inhabited by Amazons. It was a land of woods, valleys and hills sometimes shrouded in mist. These Amazons had come over the mountains of the Caucasus far away to the east and settled in the fertile countryside by the river.

77

There they had built a great fortress which they named Themiscyra after one of their queens. It was this fortress which was our next objective. For two days we marched beside the river until there appeared before us a great rock, the summit of which was swathed in cloud and mist. We made camp for the night, wondering what we would see when the skies cleared. In the morning we were confronted by a castle gleaming in the sunlight on the top of the hill which rose steeply on all sides but one, where it was guarded by a sheer cliff. The engineers were set to work to build heavy-duty catapults with which to bombard the walls and to lob rocks and beams onto the garrison behind. Other men began bringing up soil to pile against the walls. On the ramps of soil we would mount siege towers to gain the advantage of height over the defenders. All this was routine work in the assault upon a town or city which dared to hold out against a Roman army. Lucullus was confident that we would soon break down the defences.

Yet all did not proceed well. The slopes leading up to the walls of Themiscyra were so steep that it was difficult to stabilise the ramps. The rain and wind washed the earth back down the hill almost as quickly as the legionaries could pile it up. Then we found that the catapults had little effect because the trajectory was so high that the missiles had lost all impact by the time they reached their target. Battering rams were similarly at a disadvantage as the men had no level ground upon which to work at the base of the walls. The garrison too were adept at throwing down projectiles of flaming oil and naptha on the shelters under which the men operated.

It was decided that we should sap the walls. We began to dig tunnels. To deceive the enemy we started digging in several places but did not continue with all of them. The legionaries went to work with picks and shovels. Others carried the spoil back to the tunnel entrance while engineers erected the heavy wooden props to support the sides and ceiling. Sometimes a rock would force the tunnellers to change direction to bypass the obstacle, but the underground passages advanced gradually towards the base of the walls. The principle is simple. Once under the wall of the besieged fort you enlarge the area of the tunnel by widening it on each side, holding the ceiling up with dry timbers. Then straw is piled into the cavity and set alight. The timbers burn and collapse, bringing down with them the soil and wall above, or at least causing a substantial subsidence which attackers above ground can make into a breach.

The Pontic defenders watched all this activity from their walls. They countersapped, building tunnels to meet ours. Now began frightening underground warfare. Each side dug to find the tunnels of the enemy and destroy them. In the eerie gloom the legionaries hacked at the earth, sweating in the claustrophobic heat and coughing at the fumes from the brands providing a dim smoky light. Men pushed and shoved against each other in the cramped space, some carrying buckets of earth while others carried beams to hammer into position. There was a cacophony of swearing, banging and the clang of picks on stone and rock. Every few minutes the centurion in charge would order silence. Men stopped what they were doing, there was heavy breathing and the occasional cough, but they were listening, listening hard for the tell-tale sound of the enemy working towards them. Usually there was nothing, occasionally we could hear men scraping and digging close by. It was often difficult to be sure from where the sound came. The legionaries would gesticulate and point in silence as they tried to fix the direction of the noise. Then it would stop and you knew that the enemy were listening too. On several occasions there was fierce hand to hand combat where sappers, unaware of what lay in front of them or perhaps above or below, broke into a defenders' tunnel to find the enemy lying in wait in the darkness. Then man fought man in a confused brawl, not knowing whether he had stabbed his enemy or his friend. Behind in the tunnel but unable to help, others listened to the screams and groans of the wounded. Then, as suddenly as it had begun, there would be silence. Legionaries would crawl forward, having to clear away fallen earth and rock, groping in the darkness to find their wounded comrades or guided by their moans. Many died in these brutal encounters or were asphyxiated when the enemy succeeded in breaking into a tunnel, cutting off the workers at the face by collapsing it behind them and setting fire to the timbers. We killed the enemy too as this bloody struggle continued in the darkness. Once I was standing at the entrance to a tunnel and heard shouting as one side or the other came under attack. Moments later three men ran out, their heads crawling with bees which the enemy had released into the shaft.

The garrison of Themiscyra had prepared well for our attack. Some legionaries believed that the defenders had dug countersaps before we began our siege, constructing listening chambers from which they could detect our approaches to the walls. We strengthened the protection for the sappers, sending in escorts of armed men who lined the passages.

One day I was supervising in a tunnel which we believed had remained undetected. It was not far from the base of the wall according to our measurements. The men had begun to widen the chamber. The work was slow for they had often to pause and listen. There were four men working at the face in front of me, clearing earth and rubble. At intervals others came forward to fit the beams while the men with shovels and picks retreated to make way for them. I watched a man as he placed a timber against the side of the chamber, ramming it into position with a padded sledge hammer. Without warning the earth beside the timber poured onto the floor of the gallery as if it were being pushed from behind. A hole appeared and the soldier jumped back, fearing a collapse of the outer wall. Then through the gap sprang two great cats, leopards with cruel yellow eyes gleaming in the half light of the torches. One crouched down, growling and swishing its tail angrily, but the other leapt at the throat of a man carrying a beam. He fell back onto the ground with the cat's jaws clamped around his neck. Before I could draw my sword another legionary rushed forward and buried his pick in the leopard's flank. There was a great roar as the animal released its grip. For a moment it rose to its feet before collapsing with its paws flailing the air. I finished him with my sword. This was enough for the other animal who turned tail and fled back through the hole from which it had come. I gave orders that the injured man be carried back to the casualty station, though there was a gaping wound at his throat and I feared he was already dead. We piled straw hurriedly into the half-completed chamber and set it alight. Once outside we watched hopefully but there was no effect upon the wall above. We had been forced to abandon the sap too soon.

The grim struggle continued for another month. Autumn was approaching. Lucullus decided to leave us at the siege and march away to the coast to threaten the cities there. Shortly after his departure we noticed that one part of the wall was at last showing signs of subsidence. Our engineers thought that it might be a combination of our own tunnels and the countersaps of the defenders which had caused this, for we had not lit fires close by. The legionaries dragged heavy timbers up the sides of the hill under dense fire from arrows loosed off by the defenders. With the timber, platforms were constructed to provide a level base for two catapults at a distance of about fifty paces from the walls. Round these we stretched screens of oxhide to protect the operators. The defenders fired flaming arrows at the screens and lobbed cylinders of burning oil while our legionaries doused the hides with water from the river to keep them from burning. Our archers and slingers kept up a continuous barrage at the men above the wall. Under this cover the legionaries carried heavy boulders up the hill to the platforms from which the ballistas hurled them at the masonry where cracks had appeared. For two days and two nights this assault continued. We could not stop the attack, for if we did so, the defenders would seize the opportunity to repair the breach. At night rivers of fire glowed like lava flowing from a volcano as the besieged rolled barrels of burning tar and naptha down from the walls towards the platforms and the archers below. The legionaries replied with flaming arrows which flashed like shooting stars against the dark sky. Many men suffered terrible burns and lay screaming or groaning on tables where the surgeons waited for them to die; there was nothing they could do.

At length the wall began to crumble. First, parts of the battlement came loose, then larger rocks and stones began to fall away and roll down the slope. Some were used by the catapults to fire back into the breach which gradually increased in size until we could see through it. One afternoon, as the light began to fade, the second cohort of the first legion moved up to the base of the hill. When dusk fell the archers redoubled their showers of arrows to keep the heads of the defenders down while the legionaries advanced with their shields above their heads. They came on steadily up the slope in two columns each of about two hundred and fifty men. They had almost reached the platforms on which the ballistas stood when a great wave of flame tumbled down from the wall above. The defenders had wrapped sheaves of straw round wooden beams and soaked them in oil before lighting them and pushing them over the ramparts. Men were engulfed in flames as the sheaves rolled through the ranks; others managed to dodge the beams and charged toward the breach. Some died under a hail of arrows before they had reached the base of the wall, while the rest, maddened by their wounds or those of their comrades, scrambled over the fallen masonry in the breach and into the fortress. As this assault took place, men of the first cohort ran forward with scaling ladders and set them against another part of the wall. The sentries above, preoccupied with defending the breach, were taken by surprise and several men of the first wave up the ladders succeeded in scaling the battlement. There we formed a bridgehead from which we gradually moved round, using our swords to kill defenders armed only with bows which were no protection at close quarters. Below us legionaries swarmed through the breach and up the alleyways inside, hacking and stabbing their way past all resistance. The carnage lasted until dawn, by which time there was no man left alive among the defenders, apart from a few hundred mercenaries who surrendered without a fight and were chained up ready for sale into slavery. The legionaries, freed from the stern discipline of Lucullus, had raped the women and then gorged themselves on wine. Many lay in the streets and alleys in full armour, besotted with drink. From their mouths dribbled the red liquor while on their arms the blood of their victims had congealed. So ended the siege of Themiscyra.

Chapter VII

75–66 BC

For the next two years the campaign in Pontus continued. One by one the strongholds of the interior were reduced and the seaports on the Euxine were taken, until at last Mithridates was forced to flee to Armenia and take refuge in the kingdom of his son-in-law, Tigranes. Lucullus had no particular wish to carry the war into Armenia and his mandate from the Senate gave him no authority to do so. But precedent at least required that he should send an embassy to Tigranes demanding the surrender of Mithridates. There was also the fear that so long as the old King of Pontus remained alive and free, he would raise yet another army to threaten the safety of the Roman provinces in Asia. Besides, no Roman general ever willingly accepts that his campaign is over and that he must lay down his command.

At headquarters in Cilicia serving as a military tribune was one Appius Claudius Pulcher, the brother of Lucullus' wife. Claudius was a member of one of the most distinguished patrician families in Rome, and it was his ancestor who had constructed the Via Appia. Though intelligent and charming, Claudius was extremely arrogant. He boasted the handsome features for which his family was well known and regarded non-Romans as nothing more than barbarians. Despite his youth and inexperience, Lucullus, himself no great manager of his fellow men, chose Claudius to lead the embassy to Tigranes to demand that Mithridates be handed over to us. On arrival at the King's court in Antioch, Claudius harangued his host for some time, making no attempt to disguise his contempt for all things Armenian. In full view of the royal court he demanded the immediate handing over of Mithridates as a prisoner or Lucullus would invade. Tigranes did his best to negotiate by sending lavish presents to the Roman embassy but these were refused and Claudius returned empty handed.

In the face of this blatant refusal to surrender the Pontic King, Lucullus was obliged as a matter of honour to attack. By this time our army was reduced to only two legions, consisting of about ten thousand men, and some mercenary cavalry. The other three legions had been left behind as garrisons for Pontus, Pergamum and Bithynia. As we marched through Cilicia and Commagene towards the border with Armenia and the great river Euphrates, legionaries could be heard muttering that this was a campaign too far. We had been fighting for four years, the army was too small, the odds were too great, we were entering territory where no Roman army had marched before. Whisperings reached us that leaders of the popular party in Rome were speaking out against Lucullus, saying that he was simply a bloodthirsty warlord invading Armenia for the sake of it and without the authority of the Senate.

Without favourable omens I believe that the army might have refused to cross the Euphrates and the opportunity to win the most brilliant victory in which I ever took part would have been lost. When we finally reached the banks of the river, we found it impossible to ford the waters which were swollen by winter rains. Lucullus gave orders to pitch camp and for boats to be built which were to be roped together to make a bridge. On the following day, however, as we looked out across the river, we could see islands revealed by a sudden fall in the level of the waters overnight. The tribunes and other officers, no doubt encouraged by Lucullus, were quick to point out that this was a clear sign from the gods that we should cross into Armenia. Soon a ford was found to the first island and led by the standard bearers the legionaries began to wade through the shallow water. The cavalry splashed on to the far bank via two more shoals and within half a day the entire army was across. On the other side we found cattle wandering in the pastures. The local inhabitants worshipped them as sacred and one cow was found standing at an altar as if waiting to be offered to the gods. Lucullus, who admired the Greeks and knew his mythology, seized the opportunity to sacrifice the animal in front of us to the goddess Artemis, who soon after she was born had helped her mother Leto across the narrow straits between Ortygia and Delos. Now the legionaries knew that the gods were with them and thus encouraged we pressed on towards Tigranocerta, the great artificial capital which the Armenian King had constructed roughly in the middle of his realm and peopled with settlers dragged there from Persia and Cappadocia. On the way we were attacked by a small force of cavalry which Tigranes had sent against us, thinking it would be sufficient to dispose of an impudent invader. They came charging at us over the plain where our outriders had spotted them some miles before they reached our columns. Orders were given to form squares and we watched as the squadrons thundered towards us with pennants flying and lances held horizontally to skewer our bodies. At forty paces we unleashed our javelins with devastating effect. Horses reared and collapsed on their riders, other men tumbled from their mounts which turned and ploughed back into those coming behind them. The second flight of javelins poured into the confused mass of screaming flesh and kicking hooves. The bugles sounded the charge and we went to work with our swords on the dying while our cavalry gave chase to the remnants that had survived. On hearing of this defeat Tigranes fled northwards pursued by a detachment led by Murena whom Lucullus had ordered to give chase. Murena caught the baggage train before Tigranes escaped to the mountains of Taurus.

Our army of two legions continued to Tigranocerta where we sat down to lay siege to the city which was defended by high walls with a small garrison of whom some were only Greek mercenaries. Meanwhile Tigranes was at last taking the threat to his kingdom seriously and assembling a colossal army in the mountains to the north. The summer drew on. We dug trenches round the city and began to sap the walls. However, our forces were so stretched by the length of the siege lines and the shortage of men that it was not difficult for the Armenians to break in and out. Then in the hills to the north we began to see a huge army gathering. Our scouts reported that thousands upon thousands of soldiers were mustering from all parts of Armenia under the flag of the Great King Tigranes. Their tents covered whole hills and the rivers were running dry as men and horses consumed the water.

Lucullus held a council of war. In addition to his legates, the tribunes in command of the cohorts were also summoned to attend. I had been promoted by Lucullus to be the tribune in command of the fourth cohort of the first legion, to replace Rubirius Piso who had died of a wound while fighting on the river Lycus the year before. There were perhaps twenty of us who gathered outside our general's tent. He sat as usual on a dais and we disposed ourselves in a row before him. First, he told us that the scouts had estimated the enemy's strength at around two hundred and fifty thousand foot with as many as fifty-five thousand horse. Some of the horse were heavily armoured cavalry called cataphractarii and many of the soldiers were mercenaries who might be unreliable in a pitched battle. There was no question, he said, of retreat. The enemy's cavalry would harry us as we marched back towards Cilicia.

They would deny us food and forage for our horses while the Tigris and the Euphrates would provide excellent opportunities to attack the legions as they tried to cross the rivers. Instead we would strike the enemy where they stood. By discipline and courage we could rout the barbarian horde just as the Greeks had triumphed at Marathon over the Persians four hundred years before. 'Each of you,' he continued, 'must march on foot with your cohort into battle. I shall lead you from the front where the legionaries can see. By my side will walk the standard bearers carrying the silver eagles of each legion. Your men know the shame that will be heaped upon them by their fellow citizens if either of those standards is captured. Now go to your maniples and cohorts, speak to your centurions and tell them that tomorrow they can show the Great King what a real soldier is.'

We gave a cheer and raised our fists in salute. Murena, who was to remain behind with a detachment to see over the siege lines, ran forward to stand beside his general. Then, turning to us, he raised his voice: 'Soldiers and citizens of Rome, let us lead our men as Lucullus leads us. Mars will guide our swords so that at the end we shall prevail and salute our general as imperator!'

I summoned the men of the fourth cohort and told them that we would fight on the morrow. Some muttered that the following day, the sixth of October, was an unlucky day for Rome as it was the anniversary of a great defeat, but even as I was speaking a shout went up from another part of the camp. Looking up, we saw two eagles circling in the sky above us. The legionaries watched as they flew slowly off towards the hills where the Armenians lay. The eagles were our two legions and the signal they gave was to attack. Nothing could have been a better omen and the men set to with a will to check their equipment and ready themselves for battle.

That night I could not sleep. At the end of the second watch I rose and walked up through the lines towards the northern rampart of the camp. Almost everywhere I could hear the sound of men talking in low voices. There were many like me who were too tense to rest properly. On the rampart sentries patrolled, looking out towards the sea of lights produced by the campfires of the enemy. It seemed to me that they outnumbered the stars above us. I spoke to a sentry whose name was Spurius Festus. He had originally owned a small farm near Praeneste. It had been seized by Sulla's veterans at the time of the proscriptions and he had drifted into Rome to join the city mob. There he had found work as a butcher cutting up sheep meat before realising that the urban life was not for him. When the rickety block of apartments in the Suburra where he had a room burnt down he had been homeless for a few months. The chance came to join a legion and he had no regrets. He had signed up for six years and hoped eventually to obtain his discharge with enough money to buy a smallholding and perhaps get himself a wife. He had lost two friends from burns at Themiscyra. His own death he did not fear because nobody depended on him. He had no relatives and only his fellows in the maniple would miss him, for a few days. He smiled grimly and said as we parted, 'I intend to take a few Armenians with me if this is to be my last day as a Roman soldier. That's what I'm here for.' I wished him good fortune. He was a soldier who would fight to the last drop of blood; he knew nothing else was enough and that it was his only hope of getting back to the land where he really belonged as a peasant farmer.

Dawn broke and the soldiers made a meal of wheat porridge over the campfires. Then we armed ourselves for battle and the two legions marched on to the plain in perfect formation as instructed by Lucullus. He intended to demonstrate to the enemy the discipline and training of his army, to show that his commands were instantly and precisely obeyed. A river ran across our front and to approach the enemy it was necessary to ford it. This we now did and reformed again in rectangles of individual cohorts. Between the two legions was a gap of perhaps a hundred paces. In front of each cohort stood the commanding military tribune. My cohort was deployed in the van with three cohorts to my right. Behind us three cohorts filled the gaps between those in the front line and then came three more making up the third line. The second legion to my left was drawn up in the same fashion. Way over to the right, shielded by a low hill and woodland our cavalry was secluded, having made its way there under cover of darkness. Before us, we could see the dense mass of the enemy's troops, so tightly packed together that it would be difficult to manoeuvre. We stood motionless with the rising sun glinting on our armour. A solitary bugle sounded and there was Lucullus arrayed in full armour with his red military cloak flowing out behind him as he strode up between his two legions. On his head he wore a helmet with a great white plume to ensure that his men could see him. In his hand he carried his ivory-hilted sword. On each side of the general walked the standard bearers carrying the two silver eagles escorted by the chief centurion of each legion. A great cheer broke out in the ranks as the five men walked steadily forward until they were a little in advance of the front line. There, Lucullus stopped and raised his hand. The cheering instantly ceased and at the signal of another bugle my cohort and the first cohort of the second legion deployed to fill the gap between us and came in behind the standards. It was a theatrical display of military drill calculated to overawe the enemy by its precision. They watched uncertainly from the rising ground in front of us, incredulous that such a small force should dare to attack in the face of overwhelming odds.

Again Lucullus raised his arm, but this time with his sword

aloft. He brought it slowly down to point towards the enemy. The bugles sounded the advance and Lucullus, who was by now about forty-five years old, led us into battle. The Armenians were not ready. It had not occurred to them that we would attack first. They had assumed that they would make their dispositions in their own time to annihilate our puny force. The heavy armoured cavalry, the cataphractarii, had not deployed. They were still cramped together with their long lances pointing forwards between the ranks in front of them. So intent had they been in watching our manoeuvres and Lucullus in his white plume that they had not noticed our cavalry sweep in to take them in the flank. The cataphractarii were helpless. They could not bring their lances to bear upon their attackers and were thrown into confusion. Meanwhile we advanced against the enemy foot and began to cut and hack our way through troops so closely packed that they could not wield their arms. It was bloody work but Lucullus ordered us to keep strict discipline throughout the line, each man keeping abreast of those on each side and thereby protecting one another. The enemy did not relish close combat for which our shortswords were ideal to stab and slash where there was little room to move. We slaughtered almost at will, burying our blades up to the hilts into the guts of Cappadocian and Persian mercenaries. At one moment I pinned a man to the ground with my sword but could not withdraw it from his body. The blade had become trapped in some piece of the armour or a buckle. For a few seconds I stood defenceless with only my shield to ward off an aggressor. One of my centurions, seeing my plight, thrust his sword into my hand, saying that it would only be the work of a moment to replace it. With that he crashed his shield into an infantryman, pushed him to the ground and bent back his sword arm till the man had stabbed himself in the throat.

We broke through and rallied round Lucullus on a hillock

behind the enemy. Then we charged down upon the rear of the Armenian cavalry which had already been severely mauled by the earlier attack from our own horse. This was too much for them. Their riders panicked and turned to flee before us. They rode straight into the ranks of their own infantry who in turn rushed headlong into the reserves behind. The butchery was terrible and we estimated the losses of the Armenian army that day at about a hundred thousand while we lost only a handful. The slaughter would have been greater but for the desire of the men to get their hands on some booty from the enemy camp. Tigranes himself escaped on horseback. Later that evening a cavalry-man rode in with his crown which had been found lying in a ditch where the terrified King had tossed it to avoid detection as he fled the field. We presented the diadem to Lucullus who disdained to put it on, saying it was not worthy of a Roman. Never had one of our armies defied such great odds and secured such a decisive victory as on that day in Armenia.

Yet after the glory of Tigranocerta our campaign gradually lost momentum. The war meandered on for another two years. We marched northwards as far as the Armenian capital of Artaxata and laid siege to it until the bitter weather forced us to retreat, leaving the city untaken. We were obliged to march back southwards past Lake Van into Meso-potamia where we attacked and captured the city of Nisibis. It was there, at the point where Lucullus should have been free to pursue the war in almost any direction he chose, that disaster struck. The troops refused to march. They had had enough. We had been campaigning for five years. We had marched the length and breadth of Asia, further east than any Roman army had previously penetrated, almost to the Caucasus, fought many battles against great odds and endured hunger and cold for long periods. Though person-ally Lucullus was a kind and civilised man with whom I became friends in later years, he had no real feeling for the men he commanded. Of his bravery there could be no question, but he was the sternest disciplinarian who required his troops to live in rough wooden huts during the winter season when they were not campaigning, instead of enjoying the pleasures of the town or city where they could indulge themselves in women and drink until spring came round again. He permitted them to plunder when they stormed a town or fortress yet took care to see that the communities of Asia were not pillaged and robbed as had happened under Sulla. Indeed he received many gifts from the cities of the province who were grateful to him for relieving their financial distress. Quite legitimately Lucullus became a wealthy man as a result. His legionaries came to resent the luxury in which he lived and compared unfavourably the silk hangings, the fine wines and the soft couches of his quarters to the draughty huts and the cold porridge which were their lot. To make matters worse, the soldiers knew that back at Rome there were moves afoot to replace their unbending general. A message came to us from the Senate that Acilius Glabrio had been appointed to the command in Asia and would arrive in the spring. Until such time as the new governor reached us Lucullus was forbidden to take action of any kind. Meanwhile Tigranes and Mithridates had raised another army and the old king was once again back in Pontus opposing an army led by Triarius, the commander of our garrison in Asia. Powerless to march in support of our own forces we heard that Rome had suffered a defeat at Zela in central Pontus. The wheel had turned full circle. Mithridates had recovered control of his kingdom while we, having left Syria, drifted in confusion back to Cappodocia. By now the men were virtually in open mutiny. The pleas of Lucullus and the officers loyal to him, of whom I was one, went unheeded. The legionaries, particularly the Fimbrians, who had rejoined us, complained of hard treatment, lack of plunder and fatigue. There was nothing to be done but wait for the new commander. Acilius Glabrio, however, never arrived.

For many years the seas of the Mediterranean had been plagued by pirates. From the pillars of Hercules in the west to the coast of Syria in the east their ships had attacked and robbed merchantmen. Recently they had become so confident as to land on the shores of Italy and steal the goods of traders on their way to Rome. Even Gaius Caesar had been captured by a band of pirates while on campaign in the Aegean, though he had bought them off with a ransom and then taken care to return and crucify his erstwhile captors. The situation had become so bad that the corn supply to Rome itself was threatened with being cut off. The people began to agitate and at length a tribune named Gabinius came forward with a proposal that Pompeius Magnus should be invested with supreme power at sea and provided with a fleet to sweep the Mediterranean from west to east. Further, Pompeius was to have power to act in the coastal provinces where the pirates had their lairs, in order to exterminate them. News of this great command came through to us in camp in Cilicia where we lingered, paralysed by the orders of the Senate and the mutiny of the legions. Though the pirates had bases in many countries, some of their biggest nests were in the bays and inlets of the Cilician coast south of where our army lay. Hither Pompeius made his way, having swept the seas in a matter of months in a campaign which, it was thought, would take years. He then started to settle the pirates in Cilicia with grants of land, creating colonies to enable them to live by honest means. Naturally the Senate and the people of Rome were delighted with the quick and effective cure which Pompeius had provided for the pirate menace. Hard on the heels of the Lex Gabinia we now heard of the Lex Manilia. Apparently another tribune of the people, Manilius, had proposed a law giving Pompeius the supreme command in Asia, to deal finally with Mithridates and to settle matters generally in that area.

So Pompeius never left Cilicia but marched north to confront Mithridates. Meanwhile a group of us accompanied Lucullus on his journey south to the coast where we were to take ship for Italy. On the way the two commanders met. Pompeius, flushed with his triumph against the pirates, treated Lucullus with arrogance, mocking him for the apparent lack of progress in the war. He was a few years younger than Lucullus with short curly hair and a very small mouth. His eyes had a complacent look born of the easy successes which seemed always to attend his undertakings, though I never had any great admiration for him as a general. He had a knack of arriving to finish a job when others had done the hard work before him. Crassus had discovered this at the time of the slave revolt led by Spartacus.

'Well Lucullus,' Pompeius said half jeeringly, 'you and Sulla seem to have been outwitted by that old man in Pontus. I never heard of a general who won so many battles but could not win a war.'

Lucullus flushed deeply at this taunt and I saw the knuckles on his fist grow white as they tightened on the hilt of his sword. 'I am relieved,' he replied, 'that the Republic can supply carrion crows like you to finish off the carcass.' With that he turned on his heel, mounted his horse and we rode down to the ships waiting for us on the coast. It was true, Mithridates might still be alive and have a small army, but he was so weakened that Pompeius' task of bringing the campaign to a conclusion was a negligible one. We had done the real fighting.

A surprise awaited me when we reached the sea. My brother Publius was there to greet me as we boarded the galley which was to transport us to Italy. He had been appointed to command one of the ships assigned to Pompeius in the campaign against the pirates. He was grown tall with a beard since last I had seen him a good ten years before. As he came forward to embrace me I gave a start for he so resembled our father that I could not see for tears at first.

The galley was a powerful warship with a square rigged sail and two rows of slaves to man the oars. On the prow was set the head of a giant bird whose beak provided a battering ram with which to pierce the hull of the enemy. A great yellow and black eye was painted on either side of the bow and as we stood above on the deck we heard the chanting of the galley slaves in rhythm with the banks of oars. Along the coasts of Cilicia, Pamphylia and Lycia we sailed until we came to Rhodes where we hove to, so Publius could show me where he had studied at the school of Apollonius. Then on we sped past the Cyclades and the three peninsulas of Achaia, across the Ionian Sea and up through the straits of Messina, hugging the Italian coast until at last the familiar shape of Vesuvius dented the horizon. We docked at the naval base at Misenum where it was only a short ride on horseback to the villa at Baiae. My mother came out to greet me, but old Diocles had died the year before and the faces of some of the household slaves were not familiar. Mother had grown frail and her grey hair was thin and wispy. She could no longer see to stitch or weave. Instead she sat for many hours on the terrace receiving visitors from other villas nearby. Occasionally people came to stay from the city. She never left the villa to go anywhere but walked in the gardens, instructing the slaves in the care of the plants and the construction of the marble pavilion which had been begun before I left and was now complete. She listened attentively as I related the stories of the war in Pontus, sometimes asking me to repeat what she had not heard properly. I noticed that she had usually forgotten the next day what I had told her on the previous one. She was full of gossip about the new people who had established themselves in

96

villas close to Baiae. Many of them had made money in trade and she thought them and their tastes most vulgar. Though she lived in considerable luxury, my mother's values were of the traditional Roman matron who had loved and obeyed her husband without question, living quietly and simply. When I reached Rome again I realised that there were very few such ladies left.

Chapter VIII

65–63 B C

Having settled my affairs in Baiae where I stayed for a few
months, I returned to Rome to live in a house belonging to
my mother on the Quirinal hill. It was a fine building
constructed of limestone, tufa and brick with the walls
decorated in pleasing patterns of the different materials.
One entered through a front door giving directly onto the
street. On either side were two rooms, one of which I used
as a dining room and the other as a study. The passage
between led to the tablinum, the main room of the house
where I received visitors. Beyond this lay a spacious atrium
surrounded on all sides by a colonnade supporting inward
sloping roofs. Round the pool of the atrium I had a garden
of shrubs and roses with benches of marble upon which to
sit in the shade of an umbrella pine. The house was of two
storeys and I could accommodate several slaves without
difficulty. Here I lived happily for four years until I left for
Spain as Caesar's legate during the consulship of Messala.

I had been back in the city for a couple of years when
Lucullus approached me, encouraging me to stand for the
aedileship. The aediles are minor magistrates who are
charged with many duties relating to the life of the city. For
example, they look after the street markets, the corn supply,
hygiene, water supplies and funerals. It is also their responsibility to keep the roads in repair and free from obstruction,
to maintain the temples and to hold games for the people.

Another important task is to supervise the firewatchers, for in a city full of tall wooden buildings packed closely together, fire is a constant hazard.

I pointed out to Lucullus, whose great villa and gardens were close to my house on the Quirinal, that I was the son of a proscribed man and therefore debarred from holding public office. He promised that there would be no difficulty about this. His influence in the city was considerable and many of his veterans had come to Rome where they were waiting to take part in his triumph following the campaigns against Mithridates. So it was that in the consulship of Lucius Julius Caesar, a kinsman of my friend Gaius, and Gaius Marcius Figulus, I was elected one of the curule aediles for the following year. My colleague as curule aedile was to be Publius Cornelius Lentulus Spinther.

I entered upon my period of office with some trepidation. Early in the year a tribune of the plebs, supported by Caesar, had sought unsuccessfully to introduce a law in the assembly to remove the political disabilities of the sons of proscribed men. I felt sure that my position would be challenged but the weeks passed and no move was made. Evidently Lucullus had done his work well. I knew that he was anxious to promote his lieutenants and I was the first beneficiary.

At that time Rome was a troubled city, as it had been for the previous twenty odd years and was to remain until well after Caesar's murder. There were many who were disaffected in one way or another; debtors in the vice-like grip of creditors charging usurious rates of interest, veterans of Sulla's armies who had dissipated their gratuities or failed as farmers and drifted back to the city, men from the provinces and townships of Italy overburdened with taxes or denied full citizenship, and thousands who lived in extreme poverty, relying upon cheap or free distributions of food to keep them alive. In this atmosphere, where people crowded together in the narrow lanes and alleyways, jostling in the

99

markets, plying their trade from shops, taverns and work-shops opening directly onto the street, violence was never far from the surface. With my colleagues it was part of my job as aedile to try to keep the peace and to bring prosecutions against malefactors of every kind. It was not long before I became aware that gangs of slaves were operating in the street markets, particularly at the crossroads, where farmers bringing produce in from the country and other tradesmen were wont to display their goods. I began to receive reports of stalls being overturned and the wares being destroyed or stolen, of shopkeepers being threatened with daggers by mere slaves operating in groups of three or four, of the removal of large quantities of food and wine without payment. In the vegetable market by the Tiber between the Fabrician and Aemilian bridges I saw members of the Esquilina and Suburana tribes attacked. It was intolerable that Roman citizens, of however inferior a tribe, should be treated in this way by slaves acting under the orders of some other citizen. I assumed this to be the case, for no slave would dare to behave so outrageously unless his master had instructed him.

I spoke from the Rostra in the Forum, encouraging the people to come forward, to tell me what they knew, to report incidents and to identify culprits. But I received little or no intelligence by this means. It was clear that the shopkeepers and stallholders were being intimidated. Provided that they paid what little money they had or handed over goods in place of money, they were allowed to continue to trade, and this they preferred to the risk of extreme violence and the destruction of their assets. I therefore gathered together some of the firewatchers and instructed them to track the gangs who were now disrupting the streets almost every day and find out who was behind this thuggery. It was not long before I had my answer and it caused me great anxiety. The gangs were seen to be coming in each morning from a large villa just outside the city belonging to none other than Metellus Scipio, probably the greatest aristocrat in Rome at the time. The Metelli, of whom there were several branches, traced their ancestry back many centuries and boasted consuls, praetors, censors and great generals throughout our history. The name Scipio, of course, needs no elaboration from me. But despite his great name and family, Metellus Scipio was known to be an extremely arrogant and corrupt man. On one occasion, so I had heard, he had attended a dinner party where the host had decked out the house as a brothel and noble ladies had performed with the guests. He was also profligate and though exceedingly rich with estates throughout Italy and abroad, he was permanently short of money. It appeared that he was maintaining his income by operating a protection racket via slaves who had so cowed the street traders that nobody dared to identify him, even if they knew, which seemed unlikely.

I raised the matter with my friend Gaius Caesar who had been curule aedile two years previously during the consulship of my cousin Lucius Cotta and Torquatus. We discussed the possibility of a prosecution against Scipio but the chances of securing a conviction were slim. The jury would inevitably be bribed, witnesses would be slow to come forward for fear of reprisals and the jury would be packed with senators who would be unwilling to convict one of their own. At Caesar's suggestion I went to see the consul, Marcus Tullius Cicero, who promised that he would call upon me in the Curia to address the senators concerning the matter. This I did a few days later. My audience listened in silence as I set out the problem and hinted that the slaves of a man belonging to one of the most distinguished families in Rome were responsible for the outrages. There were murmurings in the marble seats on either side of me as I spoke from the centre of the chamber. Out of the corner of my eye I could see Scipio occupying his customary position. He pretended not to be listening and to be preoccupied with the purple edging of his toga while he engaged in occasional asides to his neighbours. When I sat down I heard one or two voices of support while others made light of the matter, saying that the street markets had always been tinged with violence of this sort. As the presiding magistrate, Cicero raised his hand for silence and then, to my surprise, invited Caesar to speak. Caesar had not warned me of his intention to say anything in my favour. Now he came forward with brave words.

'Fathers of the State,' he began, 'I have heard with great concern the words of my friend Lucius Cotta. I too was a curule aedile in the consulship of our kinsman and I am well acquainted with the problem which he describes. From my own observations I can say that the situation has grown worse in the first few months of this year to the extent that it now poses a serious threat to the well-being of the city. The slaves of this man run riot in our markets, blackmailing the street traders with threats of murder or destruction. They steal goods at will and do violence to citizens. Lucius Cotta refrained from mentioning by name the member of this house who is responsible for these outrages, hoping no doubt that he will be shamed into restraining his slaves. But I fear that the arrogance and cupidity of the man in question are such that he will not be deterred by this tactful approach. Indeed, as Cotta spoke, I observed the demeanour of Metellus Scipio, who did not even deign to attend to the words of the curule aedile.'

At the mention of Scipio's name, there were shouts of 'Shame!' and 'Sit down, you're a liar!' particularly from the group of optimates sitting near to Scipio, such as Catulus and Hortensius.

Cicero called for order and Caesar resumed. 'Yes, I dare to name Metellus Scipio as the man responsible for these crimes and I call upon this house to witness that he should now come forward and deny the matter if he is as innocent as his friends suggest.' Scipio flushed a deep red all over his large flabby face but he did not stir from his seat. Instead Quintus Lutatius Catulus stepped forward to address the chamber. It was not difficult to anticipate his attitude. Only two months previously Caesar had unexpectedly defeated Catulus in the election for the post of Pontifex Maximus, the chief priesthood of the city. A young upstart several years the junior of his highly aristocratic rival had beaten a distinguished ex-consul and moved into the official residence on the Via Sacra. Catulus did not like Caesar before the election and hated him afterwards, especially as he was well aware that it was the sesterces of Crassus that had bribed the electors and secured victory for a man who had no interest whatever in the gods.

'Caesar,' Catulus spat out the word, 'our duly elected Chief Priest should know better than to utter a vicious slander against my distinguished friend.' He turned to smile at Scipio who twisted uncomfortably in his seat and leered back. 'What evidence does he have for this outrageous allegation? He cites no witnesses, he names no names identified with the accused and he recounts no incidents where slaves of Scipio have been involved. If this matter was a problem when he was aedile, why did he not raise it then? On behalf of the great family of the Metelli Scipiones I demand an apology.' There were roars from the optimates that Caesar should withdraw his allegations and apologise; others remained silent eyeing Scipio and asking themselves why he did not assert his innocence.

Caesar rose in his seat and when the hubbub had subsided said simply, 'If Metellus Scipio is innocent let him sue me in the court. I shall be ready for him.' Then Cicero drew the discussion to a close asking the Senate to support any steps which the aediles might see fit to take to alleviate the problem. This motion commanded the assent of the whole house as neither the optimates nor the popular party could oppose it. The incident was particularly interesting to me in that it was the first time I had experienced the deep antagonism of the optimates towards anything which threatened their positions of privilege and influence in the State. This deeply held obstructive attitude of the optimate party manifested itself again and again in the next few years. It resulted in our crossing of the Rubicon to start the civil war.

For some time after the confrontation with Scipio in the Senate the situation in the street markets improved. I suspected that the slaves had been called off to allay suspicion, although of course it had the opposite effect in that the change of atmosphere merely served to convince me that we were right about the man behind the thuggery. But as the weeks went by there was a gradual deterioration. Groups of slaves reappeared with their demands and menaces. I decided to take practical action and risk prosecution after I had left office for having exceeded my powers and damaged another citizen's property, that is, his slaves. I hired about two hundred of the Lucullan veterans and armed them with stout cudgels which they were instructed to keep hidden from view. These men I stationed at the most important markets, particularly in the Forum Boarium and the Forum Holitorium, and at certain crossroads frequented by traders. The veterans mingled in the streets in groups of three or four, watching for signs of intimidation. It was not long before they made their mark. Some of the slaves armed themselves with daggers. There were fights between the ex-legionaries and Scipio's men who were no match for the veterans. Several slaves were killed and others beaten almost to death. Within a few weeks the problems of the street traders were cured. Scipio made no complaint and never acknowledged that it was his slaves who had been killed and injured. One of my responsibilities as aedile was the maintenance of the roads and those of the slaves who had not been killed by the veterans I set to work on repairing the

Via Flaminia. I received a vote of thanks in the people's assembly for my efforts but Cicero tactfully made no mention of the matter in the Senate.

Later that summer Lucullus gave a great party at his villa on the Quirinal. This was to promote the candidature of Lucius Murena, his legate in Asia, who was standing for the consulship in the following year. Although the gardens were not yet finished they provided a wonderful setting for the occasion which took place during the early evening and night. I remember looking out over the city from a vantage point. The sun had begun to set. In the long shadows I could make out the shapes of the barges from Ostia moored against the banks of the Tiber. The buildings on the Capitoline rose silhouetted against the southern sky, shielding from view the temples and law courts in the Forum. On the air floated strange scents from flowers and shrubs which Lucullus had brought back from the East. I smelt jasmine and myrrh from Parthia while brightly plumaged pheasants from Colchis strutted on the paths or sought a perch for the night among the trees. Slaves, dressed as Pontic and Armenian soldiers to recall our great victory at Tigranocerta, served food and wine. By the pools and fountains musicians played the lute and the zither to which young Numidian slave girls danced in the light of lanterns hung from stakes or the branches of trees. In the centre of the gardens stood a lifesize statue in gold of Mithridates and we dined off the golden and silver plate taken from his court. Scattered about the grounds were dimly lit arbours and pavilions into which men who had held high office in the State and well bred ladies were seen to retire, sometimes with their husbands or wives and sometimes not. I spent a few minutes chatting with Caesar. As usual Servilia, the wife of Decimus Junius Silanus, was on his arm. She had been his mistress for years but Silanus, who was also a candidate for the consulship, never seemed to care or was persuaded that it was in his best

105

interests not to do so. The sun disappeared behind the Janiculum hill in the west and it was not long before solid figures began to dissolve into shadows. It became difficult to discern who was who and the continuous flow of wine had its inevitable effect. I was vaguely aware that Caesar and Servilia had left me for the pleasure of their own company in a dark corner of the arbour behind me. Not wishing to disturb them I walked for a while by myself, simply enjoying the sweet evening air and the wine which I sipped from a silver goblet. I sat down by one of the fountains and watched the fantastic shapes of the dancers and their shadows as they cavorted in the light of the torches. I looked up and saw the crescent moon which had risen above the temple of Juno Moneta. It hung in the indigo sky like a golden sickle in a field of stars. I remembered sitting on evenings such as this in the atrium of my father's house and with Domitia when she was dying. Perhaps I fell into a reverie induced by the intoxicating effect of the wine and the mulling over of memories of life before my father's sudden death.

I cannot say how long I had been sitting there but I awoke suddenly to find that it was quite dark and that a lady was beside me with her arm around my waist.

'Hello,' she said brightly, 'I thought you looked a bit lonely so I came to sit next to you.' I rather liked the feel of this warm female body nestling against mine, so I made friendly noises and said she could sit next to me as long as she liked. We began to chat. She told me her name was Fulvia and that she was of noble birth, which I already knew from the way she spoke. We talked of nothing in particular but I did gather that she had been or perhaps still was the mistress of one Quintus Curius who, I happened to know, led a raffish life mixing with others of dubious morality. I remembered he had been expelled from the Senate some years previously for a scandal involving young boys. It had happened while I was away in Pontus and the characters involved meant little to me. I found that my goblet was empty and we went in search of more wine and something to eat. In the light of the torches I noticed that my new friend was not unattractive, with golden ringlets of hair hanging down on each side of a pale oval face set off by a rosebud mouth. I had some more to drink and listened earnestly as she prattled on about the gossip and love affairs which were the eternal topics of her class. We began to stroll, perhaps a little unsteadily, back towards the bench where we had been sitting, but when we reached it I propelled the lady Fulvia past it and into the shadows of a pavilion. Judging by the giggles and whispers which emanated from the darkest corners it was already well occupied. I tripped over somebody who cursed me roundly and then let out a loud belch. Even in the gloom Fulvia recognised him as Publius Autronius Paetus, a man well known for his debauchery and sexual excesses. 'Publius,' she hissed, 'you have a vocabulary like the great sewer of Rome and you smell like it.' We passed on as Publius gave vent to a further stream of abuse. My eyes had now grown a little more used to the dark and I found an unoccupied niche with some cushions where we made ourselves comfortable.

'I can't stand that Publius,' Fulvia whispered a few minutes later.

'Oh,' I said, 'why?' My attention had been occupied by the gentle curves of her body which were a great deal more interesting to me than some drunken oaf on the floor a few yards away.

'He's a friend of Sergius Catilina, you know, the man who stood for the consulship last year.'

'Indeed I do know him,' I replied. 'He is standing again this year. Is there anything wrong about that?'

For a while Fulvia did not reply and I resumed my amorous activities, made braver but more clumsy by the wine I had consumed. Just as I thought that I had the lady's

107

undivided attention she sat up and straightened her cloth-ing. She lent over and kissed me, passed her hand through my hair and said, 'Lucius, I must go now. Quintus will be furious if he finds out where I have been. I hope we meet again soon, but do not try to contact me.' She paused and seemed reluctant to continue. I started to speak but she laid her hand over my mouth. 'Listen,' she whispered, 'there may be trouble with Catilina and some of his friends.' I asked what she meant. She shook her head and bit her lip, as if regretting what she had already said. 'I can't say any more now and it may not come to anything. You're a magistrate. May I come to you if I need help?'

'Of course,' I replied. I told her that I lived close by on the Quirinal and she could rely on my discretion. She kissed me again and stood up. I made to follow her but she pushed me gently back.

'Wait till I have gone,' she mouthed and disappeared into the night. I lay there for some minutes in the dark, feeling a little frustrated and a little foolish at the same time. The wine had made me behave indiscreetly. It was hardly suitable for a curule aedile to be indulging in such activities with a woman whom he had never previously met. I grinned to myself and reflected that in the pavilion about me were many others for whom such a dalliance was a regular occurrence. Such was Roman society at that time. Then I fell to wondering about what Fulvia had said of Sergius Catilina. There had been rumours in the city of clandestine meetings, even of conspiracy against the State. Catilina was a firebrand who stirred up the feelings of the most dissolute elements in the aristocracy and the common people. He himself had been prosecuted but acquitted the previous year at a court presided over by Caesar enquiring into murders alleged to have been committed under Sulla. He had gath-ered round him a group of men who were conspicuous for their gambling, debauchery and general notoriety. To the people he had made speeches, during his candidature for the consulship both the previous year and for this year, which were calculated to appeal to the worst elements. He had advocated the cancellation of debts and other measures designed to weaken the structure of the state, including the power and influence of the Senate. What did Fulvia mean by her vague assertion that there might be trouble from him? Was it anything to take seriously or was it just the talk of a woman whose tongue had been loosened by wine? Was it merely the gossip that occupied the aristocratic ladies of the city or was there something more sinister behind it?

I got up and made my way out of the pavilion. There were still plenty of people about. I passed a group of elegantly dressed men and their ladies standing by the statue of Mithridates. One of them called out to me, 'Hey, Lucius, I see the lovely Fulvia has taken you on. I saw her cuddling up to you on that marble seat. You really must stop going about alone. She'll have all your money, you know. That's why she's fallen out with Quintus Curius, she's spent all his.' It was a friend of mine, Marcus Vatinius, who had recently returned from a posting on the staff of the governor of Further Spain. We joked about old times. We had been pupils together at the school of a teacher called Caepio who used to beat our knuckles with his stick when we had not learnt our Greek sentences properly. I asked him about Fulvia. He told me that she was the daughter of Gaius Fulvius, an impoverished aristocrat who lived in a villa in the Alban Hills. Apparently she had had a longstanding affair with Curius though had recently been seeing less of him, partly because of money problems. She was not a bad girl but her connection with Curius had brought her into contact with Catilina and other undesirables. I walked home and was soon sleeping off the rich food and wine.

It must have been about ten days after the great party for Murena that I was preparing to retire to bed. I had been entertaining a few friends to supper. We had been discussing the forthcoming elections for the consulship which had been delayed beyond their usual date in midsummer but were to take place shortly. One of my body slaves was washing and oiling me while another gently massaged my neck and shoulders. They had almost finished when a knock on the door brought in a young Greek with a message from his mistress. It was from Fulvia asking if she might call upon me within the hour. She apologised for disturbing me but the matter was urgent. I of course agreed and put on a robe ready to greet her in the tablinum. It was not long before a litter draped with curtains to conceal the occupant arrived at my door and Fulvia was shown in. The slaves bearing the litter were ordered to the back of the house where they could not be seen.

Fulvia took a little time to compose herself. She was frightened and most anxious that her visit to me should not be observed. I soon gathered that there had been a row with Curius. It was partly her fault. Apparently Curius had promised her money to spend on clothes and jewels. In reliance upon this she had got further into debt. Now Curius, who had become rash with his promises to try to retain her affections, announced that he could not pay. Others, he said, had let him down, although Fulvia suspected that he had wagered large sums on chariot races in the Circus Maximus and lost. He was a fervent supporter of the greens who were having a bad run at the time. He had called for wine and drunk a considerable amount before collapsing onto a couch where he had lain muttering about the injustices which had afflicted him and his friends. Later, no doubt affected by the drink, he had brightened up and assumed a confidential air. 'All will be well soon,' he announced, 'when Catilina is in power. Then I shall be able to resume my political career, obtain the governorship of a lucrative province and get all my money back and more.'

'What happens if Catilina does not win the consulship?' Fulvia had asked.

'Don't worry, my dear, he will. And even if he doesn't, we have plans. Forces are being raised in the country, particularly in Etruria where we have agents at work. Here in the city too, men are ready at the given signal to raise the rebellion and seize power. We have been denied once. We shall not be denied a second time.'

Hearing this Fulvia had pleaded with Curius not to be involved. In response he had grown violent and threatened to kill her if she revealed anything of what he had said. Eventually he had left the house but not without holding the point of a dagger to her throat and making her swear by the household gods to keep his secret. I asked if she knew the names of others involved in the conspiracy. It appeared that apart from Catilina, Curius and Publius Autronius Paetus, there were other men from distinguished families. In addition, from something that Curius had said, she thought that a senior magistrate for the current year might be implicated. She knew nothing more and dared not ask.

It was clear that something serious was afoot, but there was little evidence as yet and we had to be discreet. I sent Fulvia back to her home ensuring that she left by a door which was not overlooked. By this time it was well past the midnight hour and I sent torch bearers to guide the litter. She promised to keep in touch by messenger and to tell me of any developments.

For some time that night I lay awake turning over in my mind what I should do. By morning I had decided that the matter must be reported to the consuls, in particular Cicero. His colleague Antonius was a poor fish and unlikely to take decisive action; besides I felt it was even possible that he might have links with the conspirators. Soon after dawn a number of clients had assembled to greet me and escort me to the Forum where I had business in the assembly. However, I informed them that my normal judicial duties for the day would have to wait and sent a message to Cicero at the house he was renting from my mother while he was building his own on the Palatine. Having heard from the consul that he was at home and ready to see me, I walked down to the Forum escorted by only a few retainers, as I wished my visit to Cicero to remain unremarked.

Cicero received me with great courtesy. Despite the fact that he was a new man and I from one of the great noble families of Rome we had always had good relations. I recognised the qualities of intelligence and determination which had brought this provincial from Arpinum such great success at the bar and then successive magistracies culminating in the supreme office. I was not long in telling him what I had learnt the previous evening, except that for the moment I withheld Fulvia's name. I knew that Cicero would soon discover her identity when he made enquiries about Curius. The consul was not as surprised as I had expected him to be. It was clear that he already had suspicions about Catilina. He told me of the contents of a private address which Catilina had made a few days previously, about which I had not heard as I had been down at Baiae on family business. Apparently he had spoken of the many miserable people in the State, people oppressed by debt, others who had been dispossessed of their land or had lost their money in failed enterprises, men without legal rights and lacking all worldly goods. His words had been highly inflammatory and calculated to stir up a rebellion of which Catilina implied he would be the leader. Cicero had been so concerned that he had persuaded the Senate to postpone the elections while the matter was investigated. My information served to confirm that Catilina and his associates were not merely talking about rebellion but were actually concerting plans. Nevertheless, there was little firm evidence of conspiracy and the identity of others in the plot was not known. Cicero there

112

fore asked me to maintain observation on Curius and try to discover more from my informant; meanwhile he would hold the elections in the normal way while keeping a close eye on Catilina.

No doubt Cicero informed his friends and clients of his suspicions and vague rumours began to circulate in the city. Despite these, on the appointed day the consular elections were held in the Campus Martius. As presiding magistrate Cicero appeared, wearing underneath his toga a breastplate which he took no pains to conceal. He also surrounded himself with a powerful bodyguard of volunteers, as the Senate had not seen fit to provide one. He told me that he feared an attempt would be made on his life if Catilina were not elected. In the event Decimus Junius Silanus and Murena won the consulships, the latter being helped by his lavish bribes to the city tribes and the presence of Lucullus' veterans. Before the ballot Cicero made a brave speech criticising Catilina for his wild promises to the people. His oratory, I believe, helped to sway the result and for the second time the rebel was forced to accept defeat. What would Catilina do now? I watched him slink away from the Campus Martius surrounded by some of the city mob. He kept strange company for a man of such a patrician family.

I made my way on foot to the office which I occupied in the Vicus Jugarius at the foot of the Capitoline where a number of grain merchants presented a petition with regard to a proposed amendment to the laws relating to the corn supply. I had just dismissed them with a promise to look into their grievances and was about to have a meeting with my colleague Spinther concerning arrangements for the Roman Games when a message arrived from Fulvia. Curius had told her that he was meeting Catilina and others that night to discuss plans following the defeat at the election. I immediately despatched a slave asking if she knew where the meeting would be held and received a reply that she did not, but that Curius was at her house playing at dice with a few cronies and could presumably be followed from there.

I sought out Cicero who was in the Forum, still surrounded by his bodyguard and taking the auspices before conducting further business. He handed over to his colleague Antonius and we were able to talk in a quiet corner of the Temple of Castor. Cicero had great intellectual talents but he was not physically brave and I could see in his face the fear of a man who felt that the assassin's dagger was never far away. Nevertheless he recognised too the grave danger to the State and remained calm and decisive in dealing with the situation.

'Get hold of this man Curius by any means you can,' he instructed me, 'but be discreet. If we can extract names and plans from him, we can take countermeasures and denounce the plotters in public. Perhaps a little pressure would bring Curius over to our side. You are an experienced soldier. I'm sure you know how to make a man talk.'

Understandably the consul wished to remain in the background at this stage. Meanwhile I knew that I had his support to do whatever was necessary. I therefore sent for six of Lucullus' veterans who had served in my cohort in Pontus and Armenia. I instructed two of them to take up position immediately outside Fulvia's house not far from my old family home on the Caelian Hill and to follow Curius wherever he went. A third veteran was to act as messenger between me and the trackers while the remaining three would be available if force were needed. The afternoon and early evening remained uneventful. I returned to my house on the Quirinal having declined an invitation from Caesar to dine at his official residence on the Via Sacra where he was celebrating his election to the praetorship for the following year.

Soon my messenger Helvidius arrived to report that Curius had left Fulvia's home and gone to a house belonging to one Gaius Cornelius Cethegus a little way from the Forum on the Vicus Cuprius. I knew Cethegus to be a rash and impetuous man who was always urging the Senate to take action before giving proper thought to the consequences. He seemed a likely associate in the reckless enterprise of Sergius Catilina. Curius had indicated to Fulvia that he would return to her house after the meeting and so I now wrote a note requesting her hospitality for the evening. She replied that she would be pleased to receive me and I set out in a hooded cloak escorted by my three veterans. The Vicus Cuprius lay on our way. There I found my two trackers waiting in the shadows a little way from the house of Cethegus but with a sight of the entrance. They had established there was no other exit and I instructed them to follow Curius when he left, telling them that I expected him to make his way to Fulvia's property on the Caelian hill. They had seen about six other men arrive for the meeting. It had been impossible to identify them in the poor light at a distance.

I have to confess that the prospect of an evening in the company of Fulvia did not displease me. It was unfortunate that it was likely to culminate in an unpleasant interview with Curius. Awaiting his return, however, would not be tedious, far from it. The memory of her lightly perfumed body and the kisses in the shadowy pavilion at Lucullus' party still lingered. I realised that I had been hoping to see her again ever since her nocturnal visit to my house a few weeks previously. Then, the fear on that pale face framed by the golden tresses had made her even more appealing and desirable. I hurried on with my three veterans for company up the slope of the Caelian hill. On arrival the old soldiers were sent to a dining room where Fulvia gave orders that they should be provided with food and wine. I was led into a reception room which looked out onto the peristyle. Sweetmeats and a chased silver flagon of wine stood on a

115

low table next to a couch. Fulvia motioned to me to sit while a young female slave gathered up the combs and mirrors with which she had been tending to her mistress's hair and then silently withdrew.

The room was decorated with beautiful wall paintings which the oil lamps bathed in a gentle light. Behind me I saw Hercules standing in his lion skin on Mount Cyllene. He rattled the bronze castanets given to him by Athene and then loosed off his arrows as the startled birds rose in clouds from the Stymphalian Marsh below. Birds flew or tumbled in a riotous confusion of colour and shapes against a yellow background. Fulvia had lain down on the couch opposite me and above her Aphrodite rose from her scallop shell to step ashore on the island of Cythera where grass and flowers sprang in anticipation of her landing. The body of the goddess was carelessly draped in a thin veil and it seemed to me that her face bore a close resemblance to my hostess. I asked and Fulvia smiled. It was indeed a portrait done by a Greek named Pollio who was fashionable at the time for his decoration of houses. On the third wall Helius rode over the Acropolis in his golden chariot drawn by four winged horses and Zeus extended his hand towards the city of Athens in confirmation of his gift.

Fulvia pressed me to eat and drink a little for which I was grateful as I had not dined. She touched me lightly on the arm when she poured wine for both of us and I felt a tremor of excitement at this trivial physical contact. She moved back to her couch unconscious of the effect that she had had. I realised that her mind was on the events earlier in the evening.

'What will you do when Curius returns?' she asked. I explained that I had spoken to Cicero who wanted me to extract information from him by any means necessary. 'And if he refuses to say anything?'

'I believe he will cooperate when he realises how much we already know.'

'And if he doesn't?' I detected a slight tremble in her voice.

'Well then, we may have to use other means to obtain what we need.'

'You mean torture, don't you?'

I didn't reply but took another sip of my wine. She looked away and then I saw a moment later that she had begun to weep. I went to sit beside her and she made no resistance when I put my arm round her waist. We sat in silence for a few minutes and she stopped crying. 'You see,' she said, 'I still love him a bit. It's a legacy from all the good times we had before he got mixed up in the gambling and this business with Catilina. He was kind to me when Trebonius was killed. I didn't have any money or anybody to look after me. Curius filled the gap, I suppose.'

'Who was Trebonius?' I asked.

'Oh, didn't you know? He was my husband. We married just before he left to go to Greece with Sulla. I was only fifteen years old. My father was anxious for me to marry into a good family. Anyway, straight afterwards he went off as a military tribune to the campaign in Greece against Mithridates. He was killed by a stray arrow at the siege of Piraeus. It hit him in the leg – nothing really, but they think the arrow tip was poisoned. He died three days later.' She bit her lip and the tears came again. I mumbled something inadequate about how sorry I was. She shook her head. 'It's a long time ago. We didn't even know each other for more than a year.'

'So how did you come to know Curius?' I asked.

'Oh, it all started soon after I knew that Trebonius wasn't coming back. Curius was one of the young men about town. He was good fun and he seemed to have lots of money. I

117

was very young and naïve, I suppose. But it wasn't just him, I had lots of friends. There was Aemilius Lepidus, Metellus Celer, Lucius Torquatus and quite a few others. We knocked around together. We had wild parties at a villa near Praeneste – sometimes they went on for days. Somehow I always ended up with Curius. He became a quaestor and seemed to be doing quite well.' She stopped and a little smile came over her face. It seemed as if she were reliving the happy times they had enjoyed together. I said nothing but kept my arm around her waist. For a woman of nearly forty years of age she was extraordinarily attractive and I found it hard to believe she could be as old as that.

'Then after his year as a magistrate,' she continued, 'it all began to go wrong. He started to gamble heavily on the chariot races in the circus. He won quite a bit to begin with. That was the trouble. He thought he couldn't lose. He started to put on very large bets and lost a lot of money. Then he borrowed to try to win back what he had lost and lost even more. I think he owes Marcus Crassus about two hundred thousand sesterces. He started to drink heavily and to play at dice. That was when he fell in with Catilina and his crowd. I've tried to stop him, but he's just addicted to gambling. He has the income from an estate in Etruria – that's what keeps him going; of course it isn't enough. He was expelled from the Senate a few years ago, you know. The censors told him his way of life was so scandalous that they had to strike him off the list. You wouldn't remember – it was while you were away in Pontus.' She smiled ruefully. 'You've got to be pretty bad to be expelled from the Senate these days. Just think of the rogues there at the moment.' Another pause and then, 'Now all we do is argue. He comes here out of habit really and because I give him food and a little money. I inherited a bit from my mother when she died last year and my father gives me a small allowance though he doesn't have much. I haven't told Curius about

118

the legacy – he'd only try to get more out of me. Anyway I need it to pay off my debts. I can do it slowly if I'm careful.'

'But you love him still, despite all this?' She turned her face towards me and gave a little shrug.

'I don't know. I don't know. I used to, but he's changed. The gambling has poisoned him. His character has changed – he's never nice to me any more. He even threatens me with a knife sometimes. He flies into rages at the smallest thing. I don't think he loves me now – he just relies on me to help him out. You can't go on like that for ever, sooner or later the flame goes out, doesn't it?'

'I suppose so,' said I, not without feeling a little spark of encouragement at this admission. At that moment there came a gentle knock on the door and the slave girl appeared to say that Helvidius was outside and wished to speak to me. Curius had left the house in the Vicus Cuprius in the company of a man whom Helvidius described as very fat. Instead of coming this way they were heading slowly towards the Forum on foot and without escort of any kind. I returned to Fulvia to say goodnight. When I mentioned a fat man she immediately said that it might be Lucius Cassius Longinus with whom Curius was very friendly. Longinus was a noble who had stood for the consulship the previous year and like Catilina had failed. He had a house at the foot of the Capitoline and it seemed likely that the pair were going there. I bade farewell to Fulvia, kissing her several times on the mouth and eyes. My hands strayed down to her hips playing gently up and down them.

She clasped me round the waist for a moment and then pushed me away with a little laugh. 'I mustn't keep an aedile from his business, I'm in enough trouble already.'

I hurried down the hill with Helvidius and the three veterans. The Forum was in darkness apart from a few torches maintained in brackets on the walls of buildings so that the firewatchers could see about their business. We soon found the two trackers who reported that Curius and Longinus had gone into the house on the Capitoline as I suspected they would. Fulvia felt sure that Curius would eventually go back to her but now the opportunity presented itself to question him elsewhere, so that he did not necessarily connect his unmasking with her. I ordered the men to wait for Curius to leave, then seize him and take him to my office on the Vicus Jugarius, provided that this could be done under the cover of darkness. I set off for home taking Helvidius with me. We had covered only a short distance when one of the veterans caught up with us to say that Curius had left the house and had been taken by force to my office where he was now being held.

I found Curius tied to a pillar while the veterans gazed at him impassively as he raged and swore, demanding to be released. I told him that he could go once he had answered certain questions which I had to put to him concerning rumours which were circulating in the city and elsewhere.

'I have no idea what you are talking about and I certainly shan't be answering any questions from a mere aedile,' he sneered. I decided to let him know that we already had a lot of information in the hope that this might dupe him into parting with more.

'You were at a meeting this evening with Cethegus. Catilina, Longinus and Paetus were also there in company with others. You are all members of a plot to overthrow the State and to foment rebellion in the provinces where you have agents already working for you. If you want to tell me more about it, it is possible that your life will be spared. Otherwise it is inevitable that you will be arraigned for treason and condemned to death or perpetual exile.' Curius looked at me and said nothing. Then he suddenly spat in my face. One of the veterans drew a dagger from beneath his cloak and pressed the point against Curius' stomach. But I did not want a dead witness, what I wanted was one that would talk.

I pushed down the dagger and told the veteran to bring one of the oil lamps from the table.

'Now,' I said to Curius, 'this oil lamp produces only a small flame but it is hot enough to cook your testicles if we are patient.' I turned to the veteran and told him to pull up Curius' tunic which revealed a loincloth. 'Rip it off,' I ordered, 'and start cooking.'

It is difficult to be brave in the hours just before dawn, when you have had more than enough wine and you are tired. Curius was not a brave man and it was not long before he had given me some information in exchange for the preservation of his manhood. As the sun began to come up we let the miserable wretch go with the promise that his life would be spared for so long as he supplied information. Fulvia's name had not been mentioned and I had let it be known that our knowledge of the conspiracy came from a letter by Catilina which had been intercepted. This of course was a fiction. I was anxious that Curius should not suspect his mistress.

Without returning home I waited upon Cicero at his house to give him the information which I had gleaned. First, I had the names of the other significant conspirators which included Marcus Porcius Laeca, Quintus Annius and most importantly Publius Cornelius Lentulus Sura, who was a serving praetor and presumably the magistrate to whom Fulvia had referred. I also reported that one Gaius Manlius, Catilina's agent at the elections, was to be sent to Faesulae in northern Etruria to organise the recruitment of rebel forces. There were plenty of impoverished peasants in the area together with brigands and Sullan ne'er-do-wells who would be easy to seduce into joining the cause. We knew too that there were plans to send agents into other parts of Italy and that gladiators within the city were to help bands of Catilina's supporters to seize control and remove the consuls. While we were talking, none other than Marcus Crassus

121

arrived with his entourage. He handed to Cicero a bundle of letters including one to himself which, he said, had been delivered to his house. Each letter warned the recipient of an impending massacre and advised him to leave the city. The letters were all in the same hand, probably that of a slave, and were unsigned. It was never discovered where they had come from.

Armed with this information Cicero went to the Senate where members vacillated and demurred in their customary pusillanimous way, but did at least encourage the consuls to raise levies. Then an ex-praetor named Quintus Arrius reported that Manlius was actually recruiting troops in Etruria as we had anticipated. At last the Senate was galvanised into action and Cicero persuaded them to pass the Ultimate Decree authorising him to take whatever measures were necessary to save the State. There was growing alarm among the citizens. The companies of gladiators in Rome who could not be trusted were sent away from the city, mostly to Capua where the biggest schools were situated. I was authorised to raise a troop of vigilantes to police the streets and to assist the firewatchers. The greatest fear of the citizens was arson. It was known that agents of Catilina had orders to torch certain buildings at a given signal. I instructed my vigilantes to patrol each of the old four regions of the city day and night. They were armed with swords and daggers. Outside the city we heard reports of gatherings of malcontents in several regions. Quintus Marcius Rex and Quintus Metellus Creticus, both former consuls, took control of special levies in Faesulae and Apulia. Others were given leave to raise troops where danger threatened. Catilina meanwhile brazened it out and acted as though nothing at all were amiss. He even attended meetings of the Senate. This put Cicero in a difficult position. As he pointed out, all that he had was hearsay evidence that Catilina was plotting against him, there was nothing concrete. The old aristocratic members of the Senate inevitably sided against 'the new man' who aroused all their prejudices. Sergius Catilina was a member of an ancient noble family – one of their own whom they were reluctant to condemn. After all, Cicero made disquieting speeches and hurled allegations at this man, but where was the hard evidence? Did a guilty man behave as Catilina did, attending the Senate and public games at every opportunity? A young nobleman called Aemilius Paullus had prosecuted him for instigating public violence. What had Catilina done? He had offered to place himself in the custody of Cicero himself. Dates upon which Cicero had announced that there would be uprisings came and went – nothing happened. Some senators began to mock Cicero, saying that he was just a scaremonger. I heard Aulus Gabinius shout at him in the Forum that he ought to get himself back to Arpinum if he was too frightened to run Rome.

Eventually, however, my bargain with Curius paid off. He did not communicate with me directly but told Fulvia there was to be a final meeting of the conspirators at Laeca's house in the Sicklemakers' street. It was too dangerous to keep a special watch on the house as Cicero was anxious that the conspirators should not discover we were being kept informed of their movements. However we needed to learn quickly of any decisions which the conspirators took and I therefore sent a message to Fulvia that I would come by covered litter to her house and wait for Curius who was to return there as usual after the meeting.

Fulvia welcomed me again in the painted room which was now heavily curtained against the chill of autumn. She told me that Curius was close to breaking point, terrified at the thought of being discovered in his betrayal of the conspiracy which he knew would result in slow torture and death. At the same time he was trying to appear normal and to play an active role in the preparations. She begged me to keep him in my house after that night until matters were resolved one way or another. He had evidently worked upon her affections since our last meeting and I felt myself flush with irritation. I pointed out that such an act would immediately expose him, that we might still need information and that he would have to carry on a little longer in his double game. The rest of the evening passed pleasantly, though we were both tense, waiting for Curius' return which was just before midnight. His news was dramatic. Catilina had at last decided to leave Rome and go to Etruria to take command of the army raised by Manlius. Other commanders had been appointed for the various regions of Italy while Lentulus, the praetor, would remain in Rome to direct the rebels in the city. Then came the vital part: it was planned to assassinate Cicero that morning. An equestrian called Gaius Cornelius and a senator, Lucius Vargunteius, had volunteered to make a formal call upon the consul at an early hour and cut him down on his own threshold. There was no time to lose and I went immediately to Cicero's house where his servants woke him.

'At last,' he said. 'Lucius, this is what we have been waiting for. Tomorrow, we shall have firm evidence for the Senate. Catilina is going to break cover and we may even be able to arrest the would-be assassins.' He seemed almost gleeful as we made arrangements to surround his house with armed guards and gave orders that nobody was to be allowed to enter without giving the password.

Alas, it was not to be so simple. In the morning I had a number of scouts posted to watch for the approach of Vargunteius and Cornelius and indeed they were spotted together in the Forum. I think however that they must have sent somebody to reconnoitre, who would have seen that Cicero's door was heavily guarded and realised that they were expected. Nevertheless Cicero summoned a meeting of the Senate in the temple of Jupiter Stator on the Palatine

124

for the following day, instructing me to post guards around it. The temple was easier to protect than the Senate House. Once again Catilina wrongfooted us. He attended the meeting, assuming his usual air of injured innocence. There was no doubt that Cicero was stunned and upset by this. He had expected to address the house in the knowledge that Catilina had left the city and thereby demonstrated his guilt. Yet there he sat, although I noticed that nobody cared to sit near him. Even the most conservative and blinkered senators were beginning to have doubts about their fellow patrician. Cicero launched into his attack, pointing a withering finger at the isolated figure hunched in his seat, continually adjusting his toga. At this distance I cannot remember the exact words of Cicero's speech and although he published it later, it had been much edited. His words were something along the following lines:

'Gentlemen, we meet here surrounded by an armed guard but the enemy is within this temple as well as without. It is personified by that man over there, Lucius Sergius Catilina. Never in the history of this city has it been so brazenly betrayed as by this monster and his evil associates. I have addressed you on this subject previously and there have been some of you who either could not see or did not wish to see what was laid plainly before them. Perhaps you believe it impossible that a man who springs from a noble family with a long tradition of service to the State could act so treacherously against it. But I view him in a different light, the cold light of knowledge. The wretch who sits here with you is prepared to stop at nothing to seize power and to overthrow the rule of law for his own ends. For some weeks now he has been laying plans with his fellow conspirators to raise troops in the provinces who will then march upon Rome. Simultaneously, agents in the city will rise up and kill the magistrates, set fire to buildings and massacre those who oppose them.'

At this Catilina rose in his seat saying with a sneer, 'The consul makes a pretty speech but where is his evidence?' As he sat down there was a murmur round the chamber and I sensed a degree of sympathy for him, as usual from the most conservative elements.

'Catilina asks for evidence. We have already plenty of that. You know that an attempt was made a week ago to seize Praeneste under cover of darkness. Fortunately, the troops which I had put in place were ready and the attack was easily repulsed. Now let me tell you something that you do not know. Last night, at the house of Marcus Porcius Laeca in the Sicklemakers' street a meeting of the conspirators was held. Catilina as leader was present. Two of their number, Lucius Vargunteius and Gaius Cornelius, were detailed off to murder me at my house this morning. I am only before you now because we are privy to their final plans and can take the appropriate precautions.'

'I deny it!' shouted Catilina. 'If the consul thinks I am guilty of these crimes, let him put it to the vote.' But he was clearly disconcerted by the detailed knowledge which Cicero displayed and some of the senators began to cry out, 'Enemy' and 'Traitor'. Seeing this Cicero gave way and Catilina then spoke, playing to perfection his role of a man wrongly accused.

'Fellow senators, I am innocent of everything which Cicero says against me. Like the barrister he is, he lays before you wild allegations which he does not substantiate. He tells you that last night I plotted to murder him. Where are the witnesses for this accusation? He says that I am plotting insurrection in the countryside, to set fire to buildings in the city. What evidence does he have to connect me to these activities? Does this provincial from a small country town seriously suggest that I, whose family history is scattered with men who have performed great services for the State, would act to bring it down? What could possibly be achieved by

126

this? I am one man, I have no army, no means to bring about a revolution and no wish to do so. It is impossible to disprove these allegations but I ask you to accept the word of a noble Roman who seeks only to serve his country, rather than the wild assertions of an ambitious lawyer seeking to expand his reputation.' Catilina spoke quietly and modestly throughout. He was the supreme actor who by his sheer effrontery left many of his audience in doubt, despite all that they had heard over the previous months. He walked slowly to the door where he turned and said, 'As a guarantee of my good conduct, I am ready at any time to place myself in the custody of any person nominated by this house. I believe that my actions are better evidence than the words used so freely and erroneously by the consul.' With that he left and Cicero rose to give further details of the conspira- tors and their plans. Many senators were now convinced of Catilina's guilt but others still wavered and Cicero declined to put the matter to a vote.

After the meeting Cicero was downcast by the attitude of the Senate but events now moved swiftly to prove him right. The following night we learnt that Catilina had slipped quietly out of Rome and was thought to be heading for Etruria. Nevertheless he still maintained a veil of innocence, writing to Catulus that he had been shunned in his efforts to serve the poor and the dispossessed, that he had been ill- treated by his fellows from whom he was entitled to expect the rewards due to a man of his rank and dignity. He told Catulus in the letter, which was read out in the Senate, that he would go into exile at Massilia to escape the forces massed against him and entrusted his wife Orestilla to the care of his friend. I don't know whether Catulus believed all this. Cicero certainly thought that the letter was a ruse to allay suspicion and to gain time to raise more troops in the north of the country. It was not long afterwards that news reached us of Catilina's arrival at Manlius' camp. Matters

127

were now out in the open. The Senate passed a resolution outlawing both Catilina and Manlius. The other consul, Antonius, was empowered to levy troops and lead an army against the rebels, while Cicero remained in Rome to organise the defence of the city.

The feast of the Saturnalia was approaching, a time of great merrymaking and disorder. Cicero was worried that the rebels might strike, taking advantage of the general licence. Though Curius could tell us nothing, there were rumours of a plot to kill both consuls and to set fire to the city in several places at once. I redoubled the patrols of vigilantes and took with me an armed escort of twenty men whenever I had business which led me through the streets. I sensed that there were many who were hostile to the authorities and sympathetic to Catilina, whom they saw as somebody who would relieve their hardships without effort on their part.

As it had been during the proscriptions of Sulla, the air was thick with rumour and you felt that the assassin's knife might strike at any time from any quarter. Accusations were made by Catulus and others that Crassus and Caesar were in the plot, despite the fact that it was impossible to see how either could gain anything from being involved. For my part, I realised that I could be a target. I was helping Cicero with the defence of the city and it was possible that my link with Curius had become known to the conspirators.

On the last night of the great festival the streets around the Forum were lit up with processions. People were dancing and drinking, many wore masks and waved bunches of rushes made in the shape of human beings. With these they then simulated acts of copulation in honour of the god Saturn who watches over the fertility of our soil. Masters and slaves exchanged places for the evening. I saw members of the equestrian order serving food to their own household slaves as they sat in a tavern. Amidst these celebrations we

128

kept careful watch for any move by the rebels, but the night passed peacefully.

On the following day there was a meeting of the people in the Forum at which a tribune called Calpurnius Bestia addressed the mob from the Rostra. I knew him to be an enemy of Cicero and sympathetic to the cause of Catilina, so I decided to keep an eye on events. Bestia did not name Catilina but made no secret of his desire to see reform for the benefit of the lowest classes. He spoke of increased supplies of free bread, of the cancellation of all debts above a certain figure, and of grants of land to every citizen of Rome. His words were calculated to stir up general indignation and hatred towards the governing classes. He even suggested that a time might soon come when the people would have an opportunity to seize power for themselves and that they should be ready for the signal. I heard the names of many leading men in the city, including my own, declared to be oppressors of the people. The crowd hooted at the mention of each name and Bestia whipped them up into a fine frenzy. I had listened long enough and ordered my vigilantes to break up the meeting. I told Bestia that if he spoke again in the same manner I would bring a prosecution against him for public violence. He stalked off with his cronies, uttering threats against my life.

It was shortly after this speech by Bestia that I had a narrow escape myself. I had retired as usual to my bedroom soon after midnight. It was cold and overcast so that there was no light to speak of. A little oil lamp which stood on a table where I had been reading some documents had expired for lack of fuel. Before dozing off I remember hearing the shutters at the window rattle in the wind. Some time later I awoke with a start, conscious that something had happened to rouse me. The wind had dropped and there was complete silence. I could see nothing for it was pitch black inside my room. I lay there for a few moments wondering what had disturbed me. Then I saw a narrow vertical shaft of light. In my drowsy state it took me a second or two to realise that the door had opened a little and the light which I could see came from a lamp in the passage where my slave boy slept. Now I could detect a hand holding the edge of the door. Something told me that it was not the hand of my young slave but of somebody else, an intruder who meant no good. The door opened a little more – I saw the figure of a man and silhouetted against the light, a knife in his right hand. I sensed that he was peering into the room trying to make out where I was. For a moment I had the advantage; I could see him whereas he could not see me. My couch lay to one side of the door from which the man appeared to be looking straight ahead. I rose to my feet as quietly as possible but my assailant heard the movement and turned toward me. I rushed him, aiming a blow at his head with my fist and grabbing the hand which held the dagger at the same time. He fell backwards, striking his head against the door, his feet gave way and he slid down to the floor with me on top of him. Either the punch to his head or the blow against the door had virtually knocked the man senseless. I pulled the knife from his hand and plunged it into his throat. As I rose to my feet I saw the body of my slave slumped in the passage. He had been stabbed, probably while he was asleep. This caused me great distress for he was the son of two slaves who had worked for my father and then followed my mother to Baiae. Though a slave is merely a piece of property it does not stop one from becoming fond of those who serve faithfully for a whole lifetime.

I had no idea who had broken into the house. He looked like one of the city mob and had no great physique. He had probably been offered a sum of money to kill me. I would never be able to discover by whom. I doubt that he ever knew the identity of his paymaster in any event. I took steps

130

to make the house more secure at the back, where it seemed most likely that the intruder had scaled a wall, and instructed the slaves to maintain a patrol throughout each night.

In the city itself the common people continued to be restive. We heard that there had been risings of Catilinarians in north Italy, in Picenum, in Bruttium and as far south as Apulia. These had been suppressed, as had a rebellion in Cisalpine Gaul where Gaius Murena was in charge of our forces. However in Etruria Catilina had succeeded in raising an army equivalent to about two legions. They were not properly armed or equipped but the consul Antonius had proved himself ineffective in engaging his opponent. Catilina seemed to be evading battle while he waited for his co-conspirators in Rome to strike. The situation had reached an impasse.

It happened that at this time a delegation from the tribe of the Allobroges who hail from southern Gaul were in Rome. They had come to seek redress following the depredations of certain Roman financiers. They had met a committee of senators who not surprisingly had refused their request for relief from the harassment of their colleagues administering the province. Lentulus Sura, the serving praetor and conspirator who was in charge of operations for the rebels in Rome, thought he saw an opportunity of securing some outside help. The Gauls have always been strong in cavalry. He therefore proposed to the leaders of the Allobroges that, in return for financial assistance, they should provide a force which would create a diversion in Cisalpine and Transalpine Gaul and cause troops that might otherwise be used to attack Catilina in Etruria to turn north to defend the provinces. Lentulus himself, of course, was careful not to be involved personally with the negotiations but instructed another conspirator, Publius Gabinius Capito to deal with the Gauls. Gabinius was a man of extraordinary stupidity and rashness, for not only did he reveal the details of the conspiracy to the Allobrogians, he even supplied the names of the principal men involved.

The Gauls, we were told later, debated among themselves for some time what they should do. They were still in Rome and I suspect that when they made discreet enquiries they discovered that Lentulus was not in a position to deliver on his promises and that if he did not, revenge would be swift and merciless. The patron of their tribe was a certain Quintus Fabius Sanga whose family had long represented their interests. In the end they decided that they should tell him of the approach by Gabinius. Sanga very properly went immediately to Cicero and reported the matter. It so happened I was with the consul at the time, as we were discussing further measures to protect the city against arson which was a constant source of concern. We were sitting in a room off the main chamber of the Senate House. It was late afternoon and already getting dark. We had been talking for some time. I noticed that the consul was beginning to show the signs of his age. He had been born six years before me and I calculated that he must be about forty-three. His year of office now drawing towards its close had been a strenuous one. The hair was receding from his very high forehead where two wrinkles ran in parallel lines above his eyebrows. Round his ears the hair had turned white and if his eyes retained their brightness, there were shadows beneath them. He spoke of the problems of resolving the affair of Catilina. Antonius it seemed was incompetent and he feared that at any moment there might be a wholesale attack on prominent people and buildings within the city.

It was at this rather depressing time that Fabius Sanga brought in his news of the approach to the Allobrogians. Cicero leant back in his great curule chair and closed his eyes as he listened to the details. At the end a slow smile came over his face which became suffused with an energy missing only a few moments before.

'Fabius,' he said, 'I think the conspirators may have at last played into our hands, but the greatest discretion is required. Do you think you can persuade your clients to cooperate with us and lead the rebels into a trap? I believe that they have confidence in your family, isn't that so?'

'Within reason,' replied Fabius. 'I think that they will do anything I propose provided I can reassure them about their physical safety.'

'Very well. I would like you to go back to them and instruct their leaders to simulate collaboration with Gabinius. Tell them to ask him for a letter from Lentulus and the other conspirators in Rome setting out exactly what is being asked of the Allobrogians in return for which they would receive financial assistance. Your clients should say that they must be sure of the authenticity of the letters as they will need to convince the leaders of their tribe when they return to Gaul. On no account must they leave Rome until they have the letters in their possession. I suspect that they will be nervous at undertaking such negotiations. It will be for you, Fabius, to convince them that they can trust you.'

Fabius was even more successful than we could dare to hope. A few days later he returned to Cicero with the news that the Allobrogians had obtained letters signed and sealed by Lentulus, Cethegus, Gabinius and a man called Statilius of whom we had not previously heard. Cicero thereupon told Fabius that his clients might now leave Rome, taking care to carry with them the incriminating documents. There were, as I recall, about twenty of the Allobrogians and they were staying as guests of a number of members of the equestrian order near the Via Lata in the Campus Martius. Cicero was anxious that nothing should go wrong. I was instructed that as the Gauls made their way up to the Milvian

Bridge and the Via Flaminia I should post vigilantes at intervals to ensure that there was no interference from conspirators who might have got wind of a trap.

On the appointed evening, when darkness had already fallen, I watched the Gauls assemble. They were heavily cloaked. Some rode horses while others were carried in carts covered with skins against the wind and rain which they would meet as they travelled northwards. They had their own small escort commanded by a man called Titus Volturcius. My men remained in the shadows ready in case of trouble. The little procession set off and I rode some distance behind. Soon the Tiber came into view with the bridge spanning it lit up at each end by torches and dark shadows in between, for there was no moon. I could just discern the shapes of the houses which lined the road on both sides of the river. There, soldiers commanded by one of the praetors waited. As the Gauls reached the centre of the bridge the trap was sprung. Soldiers closed off each end, arrested the Gauls and took possession of the letters. It was the work of a few moments. Volturcius and his men were overpowered without bloodshed. Having satisfied ourselves that the letters were all there I delivered them to Cicero shortly before dawn. He took care not to break the seals. Instead soldiers were despatched to detain the conspirators and an urgent summons was sent to all senators for a meeting that morning. As we waited, a message came in from the praetor in charge of the Allobrogians that one of the Gauls had told him that Cethegus was storing a large quantity of arms in his house on the Vicus Cuprius. Cicero gave instructions for the property to be searched and this produced a number of swords and daggers greatly in excess of what Cethegus could need for his personal use. Cicero could not contain his excitement. He strode up and down the room muttering to himself, 'I have done it. I have saved the State. At last, at last. Now surely the Senate will recognise my services.' I had great respect for the consul and I too was elated at his success, even if the last act was still to come. It was only later that I, and many like me, became tired of Cicero's conceit and his constant harping on about his consulship and his handling of the great conspiracy. The trouble was that he always wanted to be thanked and to be reassured. Perhaps it was his provincial background. Despite his great intellectual gifts he was cordially disliked by many, though Caesar got on tolerably well with him until the civil war broke out.

Later that morning the Senate met in the Temple of Concord. The conspirators who had been detained were brought in followed by the Allobrogians, looking about them. They were fearful that the letters were about to be used against them to show that they themselves had been plotting against Rome. Sanga, however, moved amongst them, reassuring them that there was nothing to fear. Thus encouraged and prompted by questioning from Cicero they willingly recounted the story of the approach by Gabinius and the proposed use of their cavalry. There was a mildly amusing if pathetic incident concerning the praetor Lentulus who stood with the other prisoners in the centre of the chamber watched over by guards. You will recall that his full name was Publius Cornelius Lentulus Sura; in other words he was a member of the great patrician family, the Cornelii. Of imposing appearance and good looks with a fine speaking voice, the wretched Lentulus was not blessed with great intelligence. He had got hold of a Sybilline oracle from Delphi which foretold that Rome would be ruled by three members of the Cornelian tribe. In his mind Cornelius Cinna was the first, followed by Cornelius Sulla and he would be the third. When one of the Allobrogians revealed this tale there were gasps of astonishment among the senators followed by laughter. Lentulus gazed around him wondering why his colleagues should find his pretensions so ridiculous. The man was no more fitted to be a ruler of Rome than a litter bearer. Admittedly he had once been consul eight years previously when the votes had been bought by lavish bribery of the people. He had been expelled from the Senate a year later, at the same time as Curius.

One by one the conspirators were brought forward. As they stood before him, Cicero opened the letter which each had written, having first obtained the acknowledgement of the prisoner's seal on the document. Cethegus and Statilius soon confessed under the weight of the evidence. At first Lentulus denied everything, accusing the Gauls of treachery and seeking to cast blame on Volturcius. Then Cicero produced the letter which Lentulus himself had written to Catilina encouraging the latter to take up arms, enlist recruits wherever he could find them and generally to promote the rebellion. In the face of this Lentulus bowed his head, nodding as Cicero asked him to agree that he was guilty with the rest. Next it was the turn of Gabinius who also tried to deny his involvement, at which the Gauls repeatedly asserted that he had conducted the negotiations with them, and that it was he who had handed over the letters to them while at the same time swearing them to secrecy. In the end Gabinius confessed to everything; the weight of the evidence left him with no alternative.

Cicero was triumphant. The conspirators stood silently on the floor of the chamber, their arms chained behind their backs and guards with drawn swords surrounding them. Lentulus was shaking with fear and seemed almost unable to stand. As a serving praetor he held imperium and was therefore immune from prosecution until he left office. Cicero addressed him and suggested that if he wished to preserve any semblance of dignity, he should resign forthwith. Again, without speaking, Lentulus nodded his assent and was placed under arrest with the others. At that time

136

the city lacked a prison large enough to accommodate these men and several others whose arrest the Senate now authorised. Accordingly each one was placed in the charge of an individual senator. Gaius Caesar took Lucius Statilius into custody and Crassus assumed responsibility for Gabinius. Before the house rose a solemn thanksgiving to the gods was decreed for the services of Cicero in saving the State. As he kept telling everybody afterwards, it was the first time in the history of the city that such an honour had been voted to a magistrate while not exercising a military command. It was also the first and only time during his year of office that I observed the Senate unitedly behind Cicero. It was no more than he deserved.

Now came the consul's great dilemma. What was to be done with the conspirators? So long as they remained under arrest, they would be a focus for malcontents within the city. There was a risk that attempts would be made to rescue them by violent means. Indeed it was rumoured that gangs had been hired to free Lentulus and Cethegus within hours of their being led away from the Senate House. Cicero was terrified that all his work could be undone if the conspirators were to escape. He pondered the question of putting them on trial which might have seemed the logical step. But, as he pointed out, the outcome of such proceedings would probably be banishment to some foreign country or even a town in Italy beyond the jurisdiction of Rome, where the convicted men might live out the remainder of their lives in relative comfort or even recommence their rebellious activities. This hardly seemed an adequate punishment for their crimes. It was most unlikely that any court would sentence the conspirators to death as such a penalty was to all intents and purposes non-existent for citizens. That evening Cicero debated the question over dinner with some of his friends and the praetors who were in Rome at the time. I was not invited but learnt afterwards from him, when we

137

met later that night to discuss security arrangements, that almost everybody present had advised him to refer the matter to the Senate. This accorded with his view and the meeting was set for two days later. Meanwhile we were all very shocked to hear that a certain Lucius Tarquinius had appeared in the Senate claiming that he had been entrusted with messages for Catilina in Etruria from Marcus Crassus. Personally, I didn't like the look of Tarquinius. He had a shifty appearance and I felt that he might have been bribed to implicate Crassus who could use his political weight to save the conspirators. Many senators were in the financier's debt, including myself, of which I shall say more later, and Crassus was certainly in a position to sway votes, but he had nothing to gain from such manoeuvres. I thought Tarquinius was lying, as did many others. He was kept in chains until his release the following year, yet he never admitted that he had lied. Nobody dared to question him too closely. If Crassus was in fact implicated it would have embarrassed too many people.

The great debate on the fate of the conspirators opened in the Curia which was ringed by guards as the Temple of Jupiter Stator had been. Cicero called first upon the senior consul designate, Junius Silanus, for his opinion. Silanus took the view that the only adequate sentence was death and this was echoed by many of the most experienced members of the house. Then came Caesar who spoke persuasively and at length. He pointed out that under the strict terms of the law the death penalty could not be imposed. The Senate was not a court of law, the debate was not a trial and the accused had no opportunity to speak nor were there witnesses available to check the evidence. Instead Caesar proposed banishment to various towns in Italy where the conspirators would remain incarcerated for the rest of their lives. It struck me at the time as a slightly illogical solution, given that Caesar had viewed the question from a legal standpoint and now proposed a punishment, namely life imprisonment, which was unknown to our legal system. Nevertheless many members of the house who had supported the execution of the prisoners were impressed by the speech and I could see Cicero stir uncomfortably in his seat – it was not what he wanted to hear. After Caesar had sat down, Tiberius Claudius Nero, a rather pompous old aristocrat, one of whose ancestors had defeated Hasdrubal on the River Metaurus, rose to suggest that the whole question be postponed until after Catilina had been defeated and the remainder of the conspirators were captured. Then further and better information would be available and a more reasoned decision could be taken. This seemed to throw many senators into confusion. The earlier determination to execute the accused faded in a babble of disordered discussion. At this point Silanus announced that he had changed his mind and would support Nero's position. For Cicero, this was almost worse than Caesar's proposal. The prisoners would be detained in Rome indefinitely until the rebellion was put down with all the attendant risks in the interim. Fortunately for him, help was at hand in the figure of the tribune designate, Marcus Porcius Cato. He could be relied upon to disagree with anything which Caesar suggested, for Cato hated him more than any other man in Rome. Cato poured scorn on his enemy's speech. He pointed out that treason was unlike other offences in that once it had been successfully committed, it could not be punished for the traitors were then in charge. Accordingly, the remedy was to prevent it happening at all and this could only be achieved by the execution of those who attempted such a crime.

'These men,' he went on, 'many of whom belong to the noblest families in our city, have plotted to set fire to our buildings, to summon Gauls to aid them in their attack upon our institutions and support Catilina who stands at the head of an army in Etruria which even as we speak is poised to march against us. Surely, there could be no graver crime than this. Supposing they had succeeded in their plans, how many of us would be alive now? You may be sure that we should have been struck down to a man. The sentence must be death, the safety of the city demands it.' These remarks were received with general acclamation and turned decisively the opinion of those who heard them. Cicero restrained himself, as befitted his position of president of the Senate, from appearing too partisan in his closing speech in which he summed up the arguments. Nevertheless one could tell that he favoured the death penalty. The motion for it was carried by a large majority.

Cicero now had what he wanted. Yet, as Caesar had pointed out in the debate, the motion of the Senate could not override the laws of the State which decreed that every citizen had a right to be tried before being sentenced. As a lawyer Cicero was well aware that if he put to death any citizen without trial he ran the risk of being prosecuted himself for a capital offence. Once again he paced up and down the room in the Curia reserved for the consuls. 'I have the authority of the Senate, the safety of the City demands it,' he repeated to himself. He sat down in his chair and gazed in front of him for some minutes, ignoring a cup of wine offered to him and seeming not to hear those who spoke to him. At last he stood up, looked round at us and said, 'It must be done, now before nightfall. Assemble the prisoners and the guards, Lucius. The praetors and I will accompany the conspirators to the Tullianum for execution. Send a messenger to the triumvirs to make everything ready.'

The walk from the Senate House to the Tullianum is a short one across the Forum. There were five prisoners: Lentulus, Cethegus, Statilius, Gabinius and a man called Caeparius who had also incriminated himself with a letter to the Allobrogians. Lentulus walked beside Cicero while the other conspirators were each accompanied by a praetor. I supervised the guards who walked in pairs, two in front and two behind each prisoner, with their swords drawn. The little procession walked in silence except for the clink of the chains round the wrists of the prisoners. A few passers-by stopped to look but did not shout or jeer. The news of the debate in the Curia had not then spread to the streets, although small knots of people were beginning to gather asking for news.

When we reached the Tullianum a member of the triumvirs led us down some steps into a dungeon several feet underground. It was a dark airless chamber lit only by a couple of shafts covered by metal grills. In the middle of the floor was a hatch from which a ladder led down into another chamber below. A large dark-skinned man wearing a leather apron stepped forward.

'Which is the first, sir?' he asked Cicero.

The consul replied, 'This is Publius Cornelius Lentulus Sura. The senate has decreed that he should die.' The man advanced upon Lentulus, placed an arm around his neck and with his other arm pushed the wretched praetor violently down the hatch. We heard a thud as his body hit the ground several feet below.

The same procedure was repeated with the other four men after which the executioner turned to Cicero and said, 'They will now be garrotted in accordance with your orders, sir. Do you require a witness to attend and formally report the deaths? It is usual.'

Cicero, who looked shaken by what had happened already, turned to me and muttered, 'Lucius, would you mind? I have no stomach for this.' The executioner indicated that I should follow him down the ladder. The dungeon below was even darker than the one above. In one corner smouldered a fire of logs from which a little smoke curled up through a great chimney into daylight about twenty feet above. I noticed several irons glowing in the embers. The room was almost unbearably hot and there was a sickly smell of blood. From the stone roof hung a row of nooses into each of which was twisted a shaft of wood. From the floor beneath each noose rose a wooden beam with ropes attached to it. There were two other men besides the first executioner and each wore the same leather apron.

'We shan't keep you long, sir,' said one to me. With that two of them picked up Lentulus where he still lay on the floor bleeding from a blow on the head as he fell down the ladder, and pulled him upright. They tied him to one of the wooden beams and placed his head in the noose above. From behind the third man began to twist the stick round and round to tighten the rope. Lentulus' head jerked back, his body seemed to stiffen and then his face turned deep red. His eyes bulged and I saw his feet twitch in the final agony of death. The executioner stopped twisting but held the stick firmly. The body sagged and went limp. 'Just hold on to this, mate,' he said to one of the others who stepped round and took the stick while the first man helped the third to hoist Cethegus into position and tie him to the next beam. As they made him secure Cethegus was sick over the foot of the man nearest him and received a punch in the stomach. He doubled up but within seconds his head was in the noose and the stick was twisting.

'All right, that first one should be finished now,' said the head executioner. His assistant released the stick at the back of Lentulus' neck so that it spun back until it hung limply behind him. Within a few minutes all five conspirators were slumped forward, held upright only by the nooses round their necks and the ropes round their bodies. The chief executioner then took a knife, lifted each head in turn from its noose, pushed it back against the beam and slashed each throat. He wiped the blade on his apron, turned to me and said, 'Always do that, sir. Can't be too careful.' He passed a

142

weaty arm across his forehead, leaving a red smear. The
mell and the heat were sickening. I climbed back up the
adder. It had reminded me of the fighting in the tunnels at
he siege of Themiscyra.

In the chamber above I found only a couple of guards
vho escorted me to Cicero waiting with the others above
ground. I confirmed that the conspirators were dead. While
had been in the Tullianum a sizeable crowd had gathered,
naving heard the news of the Senate's decree and the
ubsequent decision to execute the prisoners. Cicero
tepped forward and raised his hand for silence. 'They have
ived,' he said simply. The throng broke into a cheer and
escorted the consul back to his house, praising his conduct
of the whole grim business. Caesar caught hold of my tunic
and took me off to his official residence. The sun had by
now set and he summoned slaves to wash and massage me. I
vas glad to rid myself of the stench of the execution
chamber and then to take wine with my old friend.

Shortly afterwards Catilina was killed and his vagabond
army defeated in Etruria, thus putting an end to the rebel-
ion. Poor Quintus Curius was found battered to death near
he fifteenth milestone on the Via Flaminia. I went to break
he news to Fulvia. I was surprised by the calmness with
vhich she received it. 'It doesn't really come as a shock,' she
aid, 'I have been half expecting it. Towards the end he
became very tense and drank even more than before. When
ne got drunk, he used to talk too much. I think he let on to
a few people that he was spying on the conspirators for
Cicero, trying to make himself seem important. Sooner or
ater somebody was bound to hear about it and punish him
or betraying their cause.'

'You may be right, but it's possible that he fell victim to
common criminals. There are plenty of brigands who prey
upon travellers without an escort.' She shook her head and
miled sadly. I think we both knew that she was probably

right. Curius had never said anything about leaving Rome unless of course he had decided to head for his estate in Etruria and lie low there. Somehow it seemed unlikely. He was a man who needed company in the gambling and drinking dens of the city and could never have stood the isolation of an estate in the country.

I began to visit Fulvia frequently. We became lovers when she took me to see her old father in his villa overlooking the lake at Albanum. It was rather a difficult interview because Fulvius had gone very deaf and most of the conversation was taken up by my trying to explain that I came from a different branch of the Cotta family from the one he had known in his youth. Eventually he fell asleep on his couch and Fulvia and I retired to another room, both of us rather relieved to escape. Fulvius still maintained a good stock of wine despite his straitened circumstances. He had some Opimian, named after the consul Opimius, which was very fine indeed. Fulvia poured more for each of us as we sat together on cushions which she spread out on the floor. She wore a rose coloured dress tied loosely at the waist. Her breasts were pale with a shadow where they parted and were concealed by her bodice. In the flickering light of the fire I saw the line of her thighs and hips as she lay back and laughed at some joke I made about the conversation with her father. The ringlets from her hair spilt over the cushion and her eyes sparkled. I put down my goblet, lent over to kiss her on the lips and then drew back fearing I had been too presumptuous. But she caught me by the shoulders and pulled my face towards hers, saying, 'I thought Roman soldiers were a bit more determined than that.' I began to kiss her on the eyes and forehead, letting my hands run through her pale hair which felt like the silk they bring from the orient. My hands strayed to her breasts which I stroked as we kissed. I found my body pressed against hers and she wrapped her legs around mine. I could feel the smooth skin of her thighs as she rubbed

144

herself against me. She trembled as I entered her body. She was very beautiful; I gasped at the pleasure which she gave me. It had happened so suddenly without either of us expecting it, although I had longed for her on many occasions previously.

After that night at Albanum we made love on many occasions, mostly in the little painted room at her house on the Caelian Hill. The desire grew as we learned how to please each other. I had never known a mature woman in this way. Domitia and I had been very young; we were still at the stage of exploring each other when she fell ill. With Fulvia there were no inhibitions. She made love with all the vigour of somebody much younger. I had had little contact with women in the years of campaigning in Pontus. Since returning to Italy I had found myself too busy to form any serious attachment. Now Fulvia had come into my life and I became infatuated with her. The touch of her hand, the smoothness of her skin, the gentle contours of her thighs, the shiver of excitement as I penetrated her body occupied my mind in a way that nothing had ever done before. When I told her this, she would smile and stroke my chest almost reprovingly for taking her so seriously. For all that she abandoned herself to me in the act of love, there was always something which she held back, in her mind rather than her body. I asked her once if she would marry me but she shook her head. She said that one husband had been enough. I think she had suffered greatly when Trebonius went away never to return from Greece. It had left an enduring wound in her as a very young girl, though she professed that it had long been forgotten. One day she suddenly asked when I would be off on campaign again.

'Oh, I'm not sure about that,' I replied, for at the time I had no plans to resume my military career.

'You are a soldier, Lucius, not a politician. Sooner or later you will be off somewhere with an army. I can't see you

145

staying in the city indefinitely, bribing your way to becoming praetor and then perhaps consul.'

'But,' I protested, 'becoming a praetor or even consul is the only way to get a command. Look at my friend Gaius Caesar, when his year as praetor ends he will get a province and probably two legions. Why should I not do the same?'

She smiled, put her arms round my waist and shook her head. 'When we are with your friends, you talk only of military tactics, of the campaigns against Mithridates, of how the might of Rome can be expanded by more conquests. I never hear you talk of politics. Even during the great conspiracy of Catilina it was not the political situation which interested you, but the question of how to protect the city from attack.'

'Well, that was my job at the time,' I pointed out. But I knew that Fulvia was right. Once my year of office as aedile drew to a close I would be looking round for something to do and the political chicanery of the city held little appeal for me. The experience of my father under Sulla had left its mark. Fulvia knew this. She accepted me for what I was. She understood that one day I would be off and she could not face the prospect of widowhood for a second time. Meanwhile, on this tacit understanding, we enjoyed each other's company and made love. It was the best kind of relationship because each of us was giving, not taking. I like to think that she was as happy then as I was.

Chapter IX

During all the business of Catilina's conspiracy I had also to carry on with my ordinary duties as curule aedile. In the early autumn it was my task with my colleague Lentulus Spinther to organise the Roman Games, which we sometimes call the Great Games. We managed to borrow some money from a few friends but, as usual, the greater part of the expense of financing the games fell on our shoulders. I was determined that we should provide a good spectacle and Cicero too was anxious to distract the people from the rumours of rebellion outside the city. In the end I was forced to obtain a large advance from Marcus Crassus, about half a million sesterces so far as I can remember. He seemed anxious to lend the money knowing that I would from then on be under an obligation to afford him political support. There were many men, not least Gaius Caesar, who owed money to Crassus, with the result that his influence in the city during the decade leading up to his death at Carrhae was as great as anybody's. People whispered that he was involved with Catilina. Nobody dared to accuse him. I could only hope that in some future military campaign I would have the chance to pay my debts from the spoils, as most did when they returned from a province. That chance came a little sooner than I expected.

On the day appointed for the opening of the games a magnificent feast was held on the Capitol attended by the

147

magistrates and the most distinguished people of the State. A sacrifice of white bulls was made before we all processed from the Capitol to the Circus Maximus. Cicero, as presiding consul, led the way, representing Jupiter himself and dressed in a purple toga with a garland of oak leaves on his head. Behind followed the serving praetors, quaestors, aediles and tribunes in their civic robes and the senators swathed in their purple-edged togas. Next came the tribes of citizens drawn up in their centuries, with the charioteers competing in the races that day behind them. Round the competitors frolicked clowns, mime artists, flute players and satyrs in a carnival atmosphere of music and dancing. The young men posing as satyrs wore goats' ears, tails, legs and horns. Some had large phalluses dangling between their legs which they poked into the unsuspecting bottoms of those in front of them. As the procession wound its way past the Palatine Hill down to the Circus, the porters bearing the treasures of the city on litters came into view. For these games the golden and silver plate in the temples is brought out together with jars filled with rare spices and ointments and sometimes trophies of war. On this occasion the golden statue of Mithridates was borne on a wooden carriage. Last and most important came the gods: the Capitoline triad of Jupiter, Juno and Minerva, then Mars, Venus, Vesta, Bellona, Saturn and others. Each image was carried to the Circus on the shoulders of a burly citizen. There they were placed on the sacred couches enjoying the best view of the spectacle. Not until each god had been installed could the games begin.

That first day we saw eight fine chariot races, some with teams of four horses, some of two. The drivers came mostly from Rome. Others had journeyed from Capua, Corfinium and even as far as Ravenna to try their luck. At that time Serpennius was all the rage and usually started as favourite. He had been brought up on the estates of Pompeius in Picenum where his father had been a bailiff. I once saw him

148

thrown from his chariot in the early stages of a race, wait for his team to come round again, leap back into the chariot and go on to win the race. Afterwards a fight broke out because many of the bookies refused to honour bets placed on him as he had not been in the chariot for every lap. That day he was matched against a man called Rusillus who was the champion from Capua. The crowd booed as Rusillus took his place in the starting booth next to the team of four horses belonging to Serpennius. The latter raised his fist in salute as the crowd chanted 'Serpennius, Serpennius'. I dropped the white cloth to start the race, the barriers fell and the two chariots shot down the side of the Circus to the other end where in a flurry of dust and sand they rounded the spina before racing back towards us. As they completed the first lap one of the seven giant eggs hanging from the spina was removed to signify that six more laps remained. To begin with it was neck and neck. Both horses and men seemed evenly matched; first one obtained an advantage and then the other caught up. Rusillus' horses were slightly faster in the straight, but at each turn Serpennius made up the lost ground. They came to the final turn, each seeking the advantage of the inside. Relentlessly Serpennius pushed Rusillus towards the turning post but the latter held his line; he knew that to touch the post would almost certainly cause his chariot to overturn. As they came into the corner their wheels touched, there was a sharp crack of splintering wood and the inside wheel of Serpennius' chariot flew off, careering into the crowd where it struck a man on the head, killing him instantly. Meanwhile his chariot had slewed round the turn and slid with a violent crash into the side barrier. The horses rolled over, kicking their hooves in the air and screaming with pain. For a moment Serpennius lay still, then staggered to his feet, cut himself free from the leather reins fastened to his belt and walked round to look at his horses. Seeing one of them with a badly broken leg, he cut its throat. The crowd groaned. Meanwhile Rusillus had fared little better. His chariot had broken up in the impact of the collision and he had been dragged down the last straight entangled in his reins. Luckily for him, one of his stable men had succeeded in stopping the horses but by this time Rusillus was unconscious and his body was a mass of bruises and cuts. The people cheered both men for their display of courage and the race was declared void. None of the other contests quite lived up to the first one, but by the end the people had seen enough blood and injury to satisfy them for one day. As they left they were given wine and sweet-meats which Spinther and I had paid for.

On the second day we turned the floor of the Circus into a landscape of hillocks, trees, bushes and a couple of streams which we fed with water diverted from the Tiber. When the people saw it excitement mounted as we announced a display of lions being hunted with elephants. They craned their necks trying to spot the lions while the elephants, all unsuspecting, grazed on the shoots of young trees which had been planted for the occasion. I had procured four lions from Africa. They were released into the arena in pairs, one pair at each end so that the people would have no difficulty in spotting them among the greenery. Soon the Circus was echoing to their roars. The archers on the backs of the elephants let fly with arrows, most of which missed. Occasionally one struck home and quivered in the flank of its target. Suddenly there was a gigantic roar of rage from one of the animals. Its paw had been pinned to the ground by an arrowhead. In a moment it had freed itself but the shaft remained embedded in the beast's foot. It could only hobble painfully on three legs towards a clump of trees. The archers closed in and more arrows rained into the flanks of the wounded animal. As it collapsed the pursuing elephant, goaded by its driver, drove its tusks into the underbelly of the great cat. Another lion, however, was more cunning. It had observed the tusks of the elephant and began to stalk it from behind. When the elephant was turned to provide its riders with a view of their target, the lion hid behind bushes or hillocks out of sight, only to emerge a moment or two later, once again behind the hunters. The people shouted and gesticulated trying to tell the archers where the lion was. The elephant lumbered past some undergrowth and the lion, sensing its chance, sprang from behind sinking his great claws into its rear quarters. There was a shrill squeal from the elephant who reared up on his back legs tipping two of the archers out of their seat. Then he set off at a canter trumpeting and flailing his trunk as he tried to dislodge the big cat which began to clamber up on to the elephant's back. The remaining archer screamed with terror. Nothing could save him. The infuriated lion clamped his jaws on the man's head and shook him from side to side before dropping his lifeless body to the ground. But now the lion looked a little uncertain. He crouched on the back of the elephant which continued to run one way and then the other; loud roars and trumpeting competed. The crowd was in a frenzy of excitement. Another elephant with its archers approached. They began to fire arrows at the heaving sides of the lion, failing to score a hit. He roared back defiance at them, his tail swishing and thrashing against the elephant's ears. The elephant lay down on the ground and began to roll over on its back which caused the lion to leap off and retreat snarling into the undergrowth. More archers came up and volley after volley of arrows flew into the bushes until at length the great tawny body was pulled out and held up to the crowd who applauded its bravery.

For the third day one of the displays involved the use of twenty criminals who had already been condemned to death. We had a pit constructed in which were placed twenty jackals who had been kept hungry and had acquired a taste for human flesh. Across the pit was erected a gangway having a

151

length of some seventy paces, a width of only five or six paces and no parapets. Each of the prisoners drew by lot a tablet numbered one to twenty and received a sword and a light shield but no armour. The man who had drawn number one took his place on the gangway where he had to fight the man who had drawn the tablet numbered two. The object was to kill your opponent or to push him over the side into the pit where he would be attacked by the jackals waiting below. The winner remained and had to fight the holder of the next number until only one man survived who would be spared his life. Since the contestants were mere criminals, many had no training in armed combat and they had not been matched for weight or size. The crowd roared with laughter at some of the feeble yet desperate skirmishing which usually ended with one of the contestants losing his balance and being pushed over the side with or without a wound. Below, the jackals closed in upon each new victim and tore at his flesh for a few minutes before turning to the next one. One man refused to fight; instead he ran onto the bridge and tried to fall on his sword which skewed out of his side leaving him screaming in agony until his opponent despatched him with a further blow and kicked him over the edge. Two men became so locked together that neither could get a blow upon the other. As they wrestled they came closer to the edge until one thought he had the advantage and gave a great heave so that his opponent went over the side, but the latter managed to cling on to the rim of the gangway with only one hand and then both, while his legs dangled above the pit. The man still on the bridge brought his sword down on the other's fingers to end the contest. The criminal who had drawn tablet number sixteen might have survived if he had not sustained a gash in his thigh against his third opponent, so that he was barely able to stand when the nineteenth man came on. He proved to be a Samnite slave condemned for stealing a swarm of bees. He was by far the largest and heaviest of the convicts and had no difficulty in finishing off the wounded man who was dead before the jackals got him. Number twenty ran around seeking to escape from his more powerful but slower pursuer and then jumped into the pit where he tried to scramble up out of the side. A jackal sank his jaws into the man's leg and dragged him down. By the end the muzzles of the animals were matted and red with blood.

For the final day of the Great Games we had a temporary amphitheatre constructed in the Campus Martius and hired professional gladiators from a contractor. The show was to be a re-enactment of the legend of the Wooden Horse of Troy. The night before, in the customary manner, a sumptuous meal was served to the gladiators taking part in the spectacle. For many of them it would be their last dinner. Sightseers came to watch the men as they ate, marvelling at their carefree demeanour as they swapped toasts and joked with their neighbour whom they might be trying to kill the following evening. These men were supremely fit, well trained athletes who might attain their freedom if they could survive three years in the arena. Then they would carry the wooden staff, the symbol of the retired gladiator. That night, no longer mindful of the special diet imposed by their master, they ate and drank copiously, though I noticed that some were careful to add plenty of water to their wine, knowing that speed of reaction might be the difference between life and death on the morrow.

The show was timed to begin after dusk to obtain the best dramatic effect. The wooden horse which stood about forty feet high was pulled into the arena by slaves dressed as Trojan soldiers. Such was the weight that it took nearly a hundred men to manoeuvre it into position. The colossal animal blotted out the night sky to the 'Trojan' nobles and their ladies who dined and drank in the arena below, waited upon by slaves and entertained by flute players and dancing

153

girls. The whole scene was lit by torches round the edge of the arena while the audience sat above in the darkness watching the feasting. King Priam made a speech in which he celebrated the departure of the Greeks and the victory for Troy, toasts were drunk until at length the ladies withdrew from the arena and the men, who were of course gladiators, lay down to sleep. Silence descended for a few moments, before an expectant murmur rippled through the audience. Suddenly the great horse came to life. Trap doors sprang open, ropes and ladders fell out followed by men dressed as Greek warriors, but with the arms of the different types of gladiators. The Trojans were roused from their pretended slumber and each set of gladiators took up a position round the outside of the arena, forming a circle in the centre of which stood the horse. Torches in brackets attached to the legs and belly of the wooden animal were lit to form a great illuminated arch under which the contests took place between a 'Trojan' and a 'Greek'. Each fighter displayed great skill and courage; two were spared death because they had been exceptionally brave in defeat. One continued to defend himself successfully for many minutes even though his right arm had been virtually severed at the elbow and he had only a short sword with which to ward off his opponent. He was carried from the arena still breathing but died in the surgeon's room afterwards. The flickering torches, the black hulk of the horse towering over the stage, and the gladiators and their shadows jumping and darting at each other in and out of the light combined to make a fine show with which to end the games for my year as curule aedile. I was now heavily in debt without any immediate prospect of being able to repay Crassus or some of my friends. My only comfort was that in those days in Rome I had plenty of company in a similar position.

154

Chapter X

62 BC

It was in the early summer of the following year that I received a letter from Baiae to say that my mother had died. I had been on the point of going south in any event to visit her and was greatly saddened that I had not been with her at the last. Fulvia came with me to the villa where we stayed for some months to settle my mother's estate. There were also houses in Rome of which I later sold two to pay off pressing creditors. My brother Publius had by this time settled in Brundisium where he was running a most prosperous business, importing goods from the Orient and corn from Egypt. After Pompeius had swept the Mediterranean of pirates many of the ships which he had requisitioned for the purpose had been available for purchase at cheap prices. Publius, as one of Pompeius' captains in the campaign against the pirates, had seen his chance. He had borrowed some money and bought up a dozen or so of the boats, converting them into a merchant fleet which he operated with great success in a sea now free of the predators who had plagued so many traders until then. Pompeius had supported him, using the ships as part of the fleet required to ferry troops and supplies for his campaigns against Mithridates and the East generally. Publius had done very well and I rejoiced in his success. It seemed that perhaps both of us had done something to restore the family's dignity since my cousin's disasters in Bithynia.

He brought to Baiae his wife Sempronia and their two sons, young Publius and his brother Valerius, both well built and strong. I envied him these sons to whom he was obviously devoted. I wondered whether I would ever have children of my own. Fulvia sensed this. She watched as I played with them or we went hunting in the woods or bathing in the sea. Sometimes Publius and I would disappear into the rough country near the Lucrine lake and leave a trail for the boys to try and track us. We would circle round behind and jump on them as they followed us. We went out in pursuit of wild boar, teaching them how to throw a spear properly and to fire an arrow. Here at least I had a little more experience than my brother. Fulvia liked the boys as well. She was a little reserved at first with Sempronia, believing the other regarded her as rather vulgar. When she realised that Sempronia thought nothing of the sort they struck up a firm friendship. Once the shadow of my mother's death had faded, it was a happy family. We spent a wonderful summer at the villa, enjoying the simple pleasures of life in the country, away from the political intrigue and the violence of the city. I was never so content, before or since.

One evening when we were sitting alone, Fulvia took my hand and said, 'You know, Lucius, that I am much too old to have children. But you, you should be a father. I have watched you with these boys. They love you almost as much as their own father. It is such a shame that you have no sons of your own.' She let her hand slip from mine and looked at me as if she were afraid of my reaction. When I said nothing, but perhaps by my look betrayed my subconscious longing for a family, she added, 'You don't have to stay with me for ever, you know. You could almost take your pick of the most beautiful and well born women in Rome and soon have a family.'

I laughed and pulled her to me. 'I am not quite as

156

desirable as you think. I am the son of a proscribed man. My family still has enemies and as you know, I still have debts. Who wants to marry a soldier who may go off at any moment to fight a campaign and get himself killed? Anyway, I have you and I thank the gods for that.'

'But you should have children,' she insisted, 'the family name must be carried on. Besides, who will run the estate here when you have gone?' I could feel the effort that she was making to say these things. On the one hand she wanted to stay with me, to continue to make me happy; on the other, she had seen the effect of my nephews upon me and knew that to be truly fulfilled I needed something which she could not give. I tried to reassure her, to make her feel that this was something which would never come between us. That night we made love with a greater passion than usual. It was as if each of us was trying to prove to the other that nothing and nobody else meant anything. And yet, for a long time afterwards I could not help remembering what she had said that evening, when we were watching the dying sun sink into the sea and turning the villa imperceptibly from a pale to deep pink while the faintest breeze stirred the umbrella pine above our heads and the cicadas began to sing. She had touched a little spot in my psyche from which we had both shied back, fearing the emotional consequences. Perhaps Fulvia regretted sowing the idea in my mind. Perhaps I loved her too much to risk losing her for the sake of finding another woman who might or might not give me children.

The months of summer drifted by. We became almost drugged by the long lazy days of heat. Publius and his family returned to Brundisium where he had to attend to his business. The villa fell quiet; no longer were the boys running about in the courtyards, playing with the dogs or splashing in the sea below. Everything seemed to doze in the baking sun; the lizards basked on walls too hot for

157

human hands to bear, the dogs lay sleepy and silent in any shady corner they could find, the slaves moved slowly about their tasks. Nothing moved out in the bay except the occasional boat coming into or out of Puteoli, propelled by galley slaves for there was no wind to fill a sail. Sometimes in the dark we could hear nightingales in the woods below, but during the day no birds sang. It was as if they found it too much effort. Even the little plume of smoke from Vesuvius in the distance seemed to hang languidly like a wreath around the summit, unable to move away so still was the air. Fulvia and I used to bathe in the sea in the morning and then lie on the rocks until they became too hot. Sometimes we might take a stroll in the woods or go down to the stream at the bottom of the hill and watch for the kingfishers. The afternoons were spent lying in the shade of the umbrella trees in the peristyle. Often we dined there before going to the terrace to watch the sun set in the west over a sea which was so calm that it gleamed like polished marble. Later a slave would come round to light the oil lamps and once again the long silence of the day would be broken by a chorus of unseen cicadas.

Of course all this had to end. Fulvia received a letter from her father asking her to come back to the city. He intimated that his life was drawing to a close and he wanted to see her before it was too late. I too had to get back to Rome and set about finding myself something to do. Crassus would not wait indefinitely for his money. One morning, when there was just a hint of autumnal chill in the air as the sun came up, we set off, with Fulvia riding in a closed carriage while I trotted alongside on my horse. I was sorry to leave the calm of the villa, the beautiful garden which my mother had cared for so well and the view across the bay. At the same time I felt ready for something more stimulating, just as I had done years earlier when I got my chance to go on campaign with Lucullus. I was delighted therefore when I reached my house on the Quirinal to find a letter from Gaius Caesar waiting for me. 'Welcome back to the action,' it read, 'I have just heard that I have been allotted Further Spain as my propraetorian province for next year. Would you come with me as one of my legates? I need your military experience.' I could not have asked for anything better. This was exactly what I wanted, a chance to go on campaign again and also a chance to make some money to pay off my debts. I wrote a note immediately to Caesar to say I would be glad to go with him. I could hardly contain my excitement and went round to see Fulvia who smiled sweetly and then laid her head on my chest saying, 'Why do I always fall for soldiers who go off to fight? I knew this would happen.' She shook her head a little sadly while I reassured her that I would not be gone for more than a year and that I would return once Caesar had completed his time in the province.

Chapter XI

On my return to the city I had found the place alive with scandal. Publius Clodius, whose brother had been such a nuisance on campaign with Lucullus, was thought to be in love with Caesar's new wife Pompeia. It was said too that she was not over-zealous in rejecting his advances. It was rumoured that Caesar for his part had been conducting a clandestine affair with Mucia, the wife of Pompeius, while the latter was away in the East. There may have been something in this because I heard afterwards that Pompeius divorced Mucia immediately after his return to the city. Clodius, however, had overstepped the mark during the festival of the Good Goddess which that year had been held in the house of the Pontifex Maximus and from which all men are always excluded. Defying the ancient custom Clodius had infiltrated his way into the house, presumably with the object of making contact with Pompeia. This attempt to trespass upon the secret rites of the Good Goddess by a man was the most outrageous piece of behaviour, even for Clodius who was notorious for his arrogance and capacity to cause trouble. Fortunately a maid of Aurelia, Caesar's mother, who was helping with the ceremonies, had challenged Clodius on meeting him in a passage. Despite his make-up and woman's attire, the maid had realised from the voice that she was speaking to a man and immediately reported the matter to her mistress.

160

Clodius was prosecuted for sacrilege and pleaded not guilty even though Aurelia affirmed that she had found him hiding in a cupboard in the house. When the trial came on Clodius claimed that he had not been in the city at the time of the alleged offence, but Cicero broke this alibi by declaring that he had observed Clodius in the Forum on the relevant day. Despite the evidence, Clodius was acquitted, although we all knew that the jury had received large bribes to bring in this verdict. Afterwards in the Senate there was an amusing exchange when Clodius, cock-a-hoop at his acquittal, sneered at Cicero, pointing out that the jury had not believed him. 'Of those jurors who handed in legible verdicts,' replied Cicero, 'I think you will find that twenty-five of them trusted my word since they voted against you. The other thirty-one certainly did not trust yours, since they did not vote for you until they had received your money.' The senators roared with laughter and Cicero, if he had not already done so, made a dangerous enemy for which he was to pay later.

Shortly after my return I called on Caesar at his official residence on the Via Sacra to discuss arrangements for the journey to Further Spain. As I was shown into the atrium I noticed Mucia accompanied by two maids stepping into her litter. She gave me a slightly self-conscious smile knowing that I must have seen and recognised her. Her face was a little flushed and her normally perfectly arranged blonde hair hung loosely instead of in a circlet round the top of her head secured by a ribbon which she now held in her hand. Perhaps there was substance in the rumour after all and I wondered idly whether Caesar had discarded Servilia, his mistress of some years' standing. The man himself however appeared completely unruffled as we walked in his private garden. It was planned that we should leave within a few weeks and make the journey on horseback to Spain, travelling as lightly and as fast as possible. First, however, Caesar

161

had to resolve the matter of his creditors, who were pressing hard. His year as praetor had cost money and the office of Pontifex Maximus also carried with it financial burdens. The creditors were not prepared to let him leave the city without at least something on account. He would have to borrow even more cash to stave them off and the only solution was to apply once more to Crassus. Evidently the financier recognised in Caesar a sound political investment for he readily advanced or guaranteed no less than eight hundred and thirty talents to keep the hounds at bay until Caesar could enrich himself in his province.

Once the money problems had been settled, Caesar, accompanied by a small staff of about ten including myself and a cavalry escort, set out from Rome early in the new year. We maintained good speed travelling along the Via Aurelia up the west coast of Italy, through Cosa, Pisa and Luni, then on into Transalpine Gaul where the road clings to the side of the mountains which plunge directly into the sea and seemed sometimes to hang over our very heads as we rode. Occasionally we halted at wayside inns for the night, but very often we bivouacked by the road to save time. We were up at first light and stopped only to water the horses and for whatever was available to eat at midday before riding on till it was too dark to see. This was my first experience of Caesar's capacity to travel great distances very swiftly. Frequently he would confound his enemies on campaign by appearing in places which it was thought impossible to reach in the time available. He developed an ability to ride for hours, even a whole day, without stopping for food or water. He would then think nothing of dictating orders or notes to a secretary until late in the evening before calling for something to eat. His food was invariably simple for he took no interest in it, regarding eating as merely a necessary task to be accomplished with the minimum delay.

During the journey we encountered weather of every

kind. As we left Rome and travelled north it was sleet which whipped our faces every day. I wrapped my cloak tightly round my body but my hands and feet were numb for much of the time. One or two who had no military experience found the going too tough and dropped back to join the secretarial and administrative staff who were following at a slower speed in covered wagons and carts. Gradually the weather improved and I remember clear mornings with frost glistening in the trees on the mountains above us as we clipped along the road leading to Narbo far away in the west. On the left the sea gleamed like burnished bronze when we were high above it. Then the road would dip down towards the shore and we would take the horses out to splash in the spray and cool their legs for a while.

In about ten days we reached Massilia where we stayed for a night at a villa which our old friend Gaius Matius was renting. He was establishing contacts in the area for the export of wine and oil from estates in Italy and importing lavender to the city where there was a growing market for the scent. He had also found gold and silver cheap to buy and was selling this on at a profit to merchants in Rome. We spent the evening reminiscing about our time on the run from Sulla. Then Matius asked for news of events in Rome and the personalities of the day, for he had been absent from the city for nearly two years. Caesar began to talk about Pompeius first.

'He's a wonderful administrator but I'm not convinced that he is a great general,' he said, taking a sip of his wine which I noticed he now drank sparingly. 'If you consider his victories, it seems to me that they have all been won against enemies who were half-beaten already, like Mithridates and the slaves who rebelled. Take the pirates as well. That was really a piece of good organisation rather than a military campaign. As soon as he came up against an able general like Sertorius in Spain he failed, even with forty thousand troops at his disposal and the help of Metellus. In fact if Metellus had not come to the rescue on the Sucro, Pompeius would probably have been captured and killed. I think Lucullus was right when he said that Pompeius was no more than a carrion crow feeding off prey which others had already killed.'

'Do you think he is the most powerful man in the city?' asked Matius.

'It's hard to say whether he or Crassus is the most powerful at the moment,' replied Caesar. 'Crassus has enormous influence because of his wealth. He can buy votes for his friends to obtain political office and he can bribe juries if he needs to. But like most creditors, he is not loved. He is jealous of Pompeius, particularly as he got most of the credit for suppressing the slave rebellion even though Crassus did the donkey work. If the two of them could sink their differences, then they could control Rome completely. But so long as they remain hostile to each other, there's a chance for the rest of us.' He pushed aside a plate of asparagus offered to him by a slave and began to chew on some grapes.

'What about Cicero?' asked Matius. 'I hear he did well in the Catilina affair.'

Caesar smiled. 'Dear old Marcus Tullius. He's like a young puppy anxious to please his master, in this case the old fogeys in the Senate. Of course he is up from the country, Arpinum I think he comes from. Nothing wrong with that but he can't forget that he's a provincial. Subconsciously he wants to be accepted by the ancient noble families of Rome. He wants to join the club. His other big problem is his capacity to annoy people, particularly by making jokes at their expense in court or in the Forum. People do not like being made to look a fool in public. Then he is always writing letters or making speeches about how he saved Rome in its moment of greatest peril. All right, Catilina did present

164

a considerable threat and I think Cicero handled the situation pretty well, but we are all getting bored of his constantly harping on about it. Having said that, he's the greatest living writer of Latin, both prose and poetry, and there is no man I would rather have to defend me in the courts.'

'How about your friend Cato?' asked Matius, with a mischievous grin. Caesar spat out a couple of grape pips with more force than usual.

'To me he represents all that is worst in the Roman State. He's completely stuck in the past. The stupid man just cannot understand that Rome is the most powerful city in the world and that it can no longer be ruled as if it were still a small country town. We are building an empire. We need to adapt our political system to enable it to govern that empire. It cannot be done by a few privileged men from noble families who rotate the various magistracies and governorships between them. That way lies corruption and bribery which is what we have now. Cato himself is not corrupt, indeed he is a man whose whole life is devoted to the old Roman traditions. I admire him for that but the trouble is that others do not have his virtues. If only he were less obstinate and could see that change is not necessarily bad and that institutions like the Senate must adapt and change with the times.'

We talked on into the night. I began to see in Caesar a man who was very different from the young fop whom I had known not so many years previously. This was not the playboy who dressed in rather raffish clothes and was as happy to go to bed with a young boy as with a girl, the youth who was rumoured to have been the plaything of King Nicomedes of Bithynia for many months. Here was a man who was ambitious and who had begun to analyse the political scene at Rome. I sensed in him an urge to take control. He saw the chaos of the previous thirty odd years as the Republic teetered from one crisis to the next, from Marius to Cinna and Sulla as they blackmailed the city in turn at the head of their legions and massacred its citizens. If the Republic did not work then the Republic would have to be replaced by something which did. I asked him if he meant that we should go back to the kings of earlier times. He replied that the city was not yet ready to accept kings again; the very word king was anathema to a Roman. Some permanent institution to rule the empire would have to be devised which was not subject to bribery and violence and which would have to be supported by an administrative class such as did not exist then. He lapsed into silence and then said quite suddenly, 'When I think of what Alexander achieved in his life of thirty-three years and what I have achieved at the age of thirty-nine, I am ashamed at how little I have done.'

I began to realise I was in the presence of a man who believed that his destiny was to rule Rome and thence to rule the world. From then on I could see that his every thought and action were directed towards this end and that he had complete confidence in his ability to achieve it. His family claimed to be descended from the founders of Rome, from the Trojan prince Aeneas and from the goddess Venus. It was the gods who had ordained his destiny.

After Massilia we followed the coast to Narbo and then into the mountains separating the Province from Nearer Spain. As before, we made swift progress. 'The sooner we reach Further Spain the sooner we can start to raise troops for a campaign. I want to use this year as a launching pad for the consulship,' Caesar told me one night as we camped round a fire somewhere on the banks of the Ebro. He knew that Spain represented an opportunity to gain military experience and possibly to be awarded a triumph. There would be booty as well to repair his financial position. The following year he would be eligible to stand for the consul-

166

ship at the age of forty-one, two years earlier than usual because of his patrician birth. The night was cold and it was not long before we went to our tents. As we did so I saw three bears shuffle off into the trees close by. Perhaps they had been attracted by the light of the fire or the possibility of some food. I pointed them out to Caesar who said that a soothsayer had told him the year before that the number three would play a significant part in his life, but he could not tell in what way. Later as I lay in my tent I wondered whether the three might not represent Pompeius, Crassus and Caesar. If the latter was to assume supreme power in Rome he might have to use the other two in an alliance and then as stepping stones. How much more bloodshed was there still to come?

As soon as we reached headquarters at Corduba we began to recruit troops to supplement the twenty cohorts already stationed there. Within a few weeks we had an additional ten cohorts which I set to work with, to train them up to legionary standards. These men were excitable and of unpredictable humour, but I found them to be brave and able to march great distances in the mountainous country which surrounded us. They had lithe wiry bodies so that climbing a hill or a mountainside was to them no more difficult than marching on the flat; it came naturally to them. At first the centurions whom we transferred to command the new recruits had problems in making themselves understood, but the slap of a sword on a man's back or a sharp prod with a javelin soon improved their wits.

Caesar was not displeased to find that in the mountains to the north of the province there lived large numbers of bandits. These bandits were forever raiding the more law-abiding tribes who occupied the plains. He resolved to drive them out of the hills and either to force them into sub-mission or, if necessary, to exterminate them. We advanced with a large force into the area between the Tagus and the

167

Durius, gradually driving the Callaici and the Lusitani northwards. This had a threefold purpose in Caesar's mind. First, we were able to launch a military campaign which, if successful, would entitle him to a triumph on his return to Rome. Secondly, he was able to exact from the towns and cities of Lusitania tribute and gifts, some of which could be remitted to the city and the remainder of which the governor might keep for his purposes, including booty for the troops. The third benefit was the extension of the boundaries of the province as more territory was conquered and its people brought under control.

Nevertheless these mountain tribes were capable fighters. They had the advantage of knowing the country. They avoided at all costs direct confrontation with the legions. They employed hit-and-run tactics similar to those with which Sertorius had plagued Pompeius and Metellus. Caesar knew he could not match them in the mountains. Instead we advanced steadily from one town or city to the next, accepting the surrender of the citizens and taking hostages to ensure their good behaviour. To the bandits we denied food by cutting off their access to the plains where they could steal crops or obtain forage for their horses. We crossed the Durius and advanced into the north-western corner of the peninsula.

On one occasion there was an incident which nearly cost Caesar his life. We were reconnoitring country some way south of Brigantium. The legions were resting in camp after a long series of forced marches as we drove northwards into the country of the Cantabrians. Caesar was anxious to see what lay in front of us and to make a final push which would drive the brigands to the shore of the ocean which marked the edge of the world. We set out one morning with a squadron of cavalry numbering about two hundred men. A patchy mist lifted sometimes to allow a clear view of the hills around us, then at others was so low that you could see only

168

for two or three hundred paces. In front of us, I remember, lay a line of jagged crags intersected by valleys the floors of which were wooded before gradually giving way to scrub and bare rock at the top. Beyond this natural wall, the scouts had told us, lay an area of lower land where the remaining rebels were thought to have congregated in large numbers. I could see Caesar's red cloak as he rode some way in front of me near the head of the column. He made for one of the valleys which seemed to offer a passage right through the crags to the far side. However the gap was relatively narrow and the only way through was along the course of a dried up river bed separating the trees growing on either side. There was room perhaps for two men to ride abreast and I saw the leaders begin to file into the mouth of the valley where thin mist was still hanging just above the treetops. Suddenly a great hue and cry arose. I could not tell whether some brigands had sprung an ambush or, more likely, had been disturbed as they gathered fuel or forage for their horses. In any event about a hundred of our men including Caesar were inside the valley and apparently under attack from both sides. Caesar had the presence of mind to order his men off their horses immediately. They could only be an impediment on the rocky bed of the river. I saw the men form a tight column with each of them facing one side of the valley or the other from where the attacks were coming. The enemy was invisible among the trees. We heard the crash of breaking timber as rocks and boulders were sent tumbling down the crags onto our men below. Horses screamed as they were hit while others tried to run back towards the valley entrance careering into each other and their riders as they panicked. In no time the river bed was blocked by a sea of flailing hooves as horses struggled to escape from the jagged rocks beneath their feet and the rain of boulders from above. Caesar could not retreat through this carnage and I saw his men begin to advance slowly along the valley floor, presumably hoping to fight their way through to the far end. I turned to the two men beside me and ordered them to ride at full speed back to the camp to summon reinforcements. At this moment a slight breeze arose and the mist lifted to reveal the tops of the crags on each side of the valley. On the one to the right I observed a ridge about a hundred feet below the summit and some way above the tree line. Caesar had seen it too, for I saw his men turn and strike up through the trees. I sensed that his purpose was to try to occupy the ridge in the hope that I could protect him from above by seizing the top of the crag. I urged my horse forward and with about a hundred men we galloped to the base of the hill. The slope was too steep for the horses and we were forced to leave them tethered to trees. This was dangerous. If the horses were taken by brigands we should be highly vulnerable, but there was no alternative. We scrambled up the face of the crag. Men cursed as they slipped and cut themselves, one man fell so that both he and the man beneath crashed down to the bottom and had to begin again. Once we had gained the summit I drew up the men in two ranks. Some way ahead of us we could see about three or four hundred of the enemy, waiting above the ridge to block Caesar's escape. My cavalrymen had only light armour and the short Spanish stabbing sword. I ordered them to draw these and to advance at a fast walk, keeping formation as well as the rough ground would allow.

I have found that advancing in orderly ranks has a much more intimidating effect on the enemy than a disorderly charge. The brigands turned to face us. Many of them had no weapons at all while others had only daggers or implements for cutting forage. As we came within range we were met by a volley of rocks and stones. The small cavalry shields were not much defence against this and one or two men went down. I gave the order to charge and we went in hard

170

with our swords striking down on the unprotected arms of the bandits. In no time they were fleeing in every direction and we were masters of the crag above the ridge. Below I saw Caesar with about thirty survivors struggling up towards it. Between them and us were more of the enemy rolling anything that came to hand down onto Caesar's men. I saw one soldier no more than five paces from Caesar struck by a boulder. His body seemed to leave the ground for a moment before crashing back into a tree where it lay inert against the trunk. Leaving half of my force on the summit, the rest of us began to clamber down a steep slope of tufty grass and loose rock towards the ridge where most of the enemy were lodged. Seeing us coming from above and what remained of Caesar's men beneath, the bandits sought to make their escape along the side of the hill. Some slipped down a scree and disappeared into the trees below, one or two were caught by my men and killed, the rest got away. Caesar and I met on the ridge. He and most of the survivors with him were covered in cuts where they had been hit by rocks. One man had lost an eye, another had been dragged up the slope by two comrades; his leg was broken and I could see where the bone had come through the skin. When the reinforcements arrived we made a stretcher for him and took him back to the camp where the surgeon cut away the leg. He died later from an infection.

We had now driven the men of the mountains to the very shores of the great ocean. There the brigands had embarked on ships and sailed for an island off the coast. Caesar however was not to be deterred. He had a fleet of his own boats brought up from Gades. With these we forced a landing on the island and there a few cohorts exterminated the last of the rebels. In a campaign lasting only a few months Caesar had greatly extended the boundaries of the province of Further Spain. He had eliminated the mountain bandits and had been able to send to Rome large sums of money by way of tribute from the towns and cities which had opened their gates to us. The legionaries had also benefited greatly. Caesar always made sure that his men were well paid. He understood only too well that the extent of a man's loyalty was in direct proportion to the rewards he received. Not surprisingly the army acclaimed him imperator when we landed back on the mainland after the successful expedition on the great ocean. On our arrival in Corduba his quaestor Vetus handed him a despatch from the Senate announcing that he had been voted a triumph.

Caesar took all this success in his stride. Like a man running a long race, he noted each marker as he passed it and set off for the next one. The aims with which he had arrived in the province had been achieved, but they were only the first of a long flight of steps which he intended to ascend to make himself the most powerful man in the world. He rose at dawn to hear disputes between citizens and receive deputations. He passed legislation to relieve debtors from having to pay the whole of their income to their creditors and reduced it to two-thirds. He established good relations between the various cities within the province and achieved many improvements in the general administration. Nearly ten years previously he had served in the same province as quaestor. Now, at the end of his propraetorship he could set off for Rome to claim his triumph and stand for the consulship. The gods might have decreed his destiny but there was no doubting the determination of the man to fulfil it. He had proved to himself that he could lead troops and be a successful general. 'Now,' he said to me, 'I believe I am ready and equipped to be the equal of Pompeius and Crassus. Give me another few years and I will be their master.' The words were said without a trace of arrogance, almost in a casual manner by a man who was certain of himself and confident in his ability. He would stop at nothing to achieve his ambition and many men would pay the penalty for attempting to prevent him. Sulla had been the first to discern that in the playboy there burned a unique flame which would one day be the catalyst for the destruction of the Republic. Now others would begin to feel the heat of that flame. As we began the journey back to the city my emotions fluctuated between admiration for the man and fear for the future of the State.

Chapter XII

60–59 BC

In early summer we started the journey back to Italy. Caesar was anxious to be in Rome in good time for the consular elections to be held in July. This meant being in the city about a month beforehand to present his name as a candidate. We had reached Luni when a letter arrived from the serving consuls, Lucius Afranius and Metellus Celer, reminding Caesar of the law which forbade a general seeking to celebrate a triumph from entering the city before the triumph was held. This of course presented Caesar with a problem in that he had to enter the city to put his name forward for the consulship. He therefore wrote to the Senate seeking permission to be allowed to stand in absentia and was hopeful that this would be granted as it had been on a previous occasion to Pompeius.

Travelling with us was a certain Lucius Cornelius Balbus, whom Caesar had got to know during his two spells in Spain as a quaestor and then as a praetor. Balbus was a most handsome young man who had also been befriended by Pompeius during his campaign in Spain against Sertorius. Not only was Balbus endowed with great good looks, which certainly endeared him to Caesar, who lost nothing of his sexual appetite during his governorship, but he was also highly intelligent and a skilled negotiator. Caesar recognised in him a potential link between himself and Pompeius.

A day or two later a courier arrived to say that the request

o stand for the consulship outside the city limits had been
alked out by Cato. On the only day available for the Senate
o debate the matter Cato had risen to his feet and spoken
or several hours until the sun had set in the sky after which
o vote in the house was valid. 'Very well,' said Caesar
ersely, 'that man can fight me with his words and speeches.
 have other more powerful weapons which I shall not
esitate to use if I have to.' His face had assumed an
xpression of controlled anger and those of us with him at
he time did not care to ask what those weapons might be. I
hought again of the words of Sulla who had recognised
nany Mariuses in the young Caesar. What forces would he
nleash on the Republic if obstinate men like Cato got in
is way?

   For the time being Cato had won and Caesar resolved to
orego his triumph for the more important prize of the
onsulship. We entered Rome where Caesar began at once
o make speeches to the people, pointing out the revenue
/hich his campaign in Further Spain had brought to the
ity and promising a bill to distribute some of the public
and to the poor and dispossessed. At the same time bribes
/ere discreetly distributed to leaders of the city tribes and
thers who could influence the vote. There was nothing out
f the ordinary about this. It had become commonplace to
ffer bribes when standing for office. Indeed the other main
andidates, Bibulus and Lucceius were engaged in the same
usiness. I too made a couple of speeches from the Rostra
n the Forum praising Caesar's past deeds both in the city
nd in Spain and pointing out the benefits which his policies
romised to bring. My main task however was to speak to
he leaders of the city tribes to try to make sure that they
oted for Caesar on the day and to see that bribes were
hannelled to the right people. Once again Caesar needed
noney to finance the election but did not feel able to
pproach Crassus on this occasion. In fact he borrowed

money from his rival candidate Lucceius who seemed strangely willing to lend it. I did not ask Caesar why this was so and he volunteered no explanation.

Meanwhile the reactionaries in the Senate, led by Cato now that Catulus had died, had not been idle. They anticipated that Caesar would win the election for one of the consulships. However, before the elections took place it was the custom for the Senate to nominate the provinces which the two victors would govern following their year of office. An ancient aristocrat, one of the Metelli clan so I was told came up with the idea that the provinces should be the forests and cattle tracks of southern Italy. The Senate at once seized on this idea and passed a resolution to this effect. Afterwards there was much smugness and self-satisfaction in the optimate party. They had succeeded in delivering a severe slap in the face to Caesar's military ambitions by depriving him of a province where he could wage war and acquire wealth and power. He would need no legions to look after forests and cattle tracks. Once again Cato and his cronies had made clever use of the constitution to block Caesar even before he had become consul. The man himself however was unconcerned. 'What the Senate has resolved can be unresolved. The governance of this State cannot be left in the hands of a few senile and obstinate reactionaries.'

We were in the dining room of Caesar's residence on the Via Sacra. The slaves had been dismissed and the three of us, Caesar, Balbus and I, were eating figs and drinking wine at the end of the day. It was a hot summer evening. The doors giving onto the peristyle were open wide to catch what cooling breeze there was. Even the marble floor felt warm to the touch and we reclined on our couches dressed only in the lightest tunics. Dusk was falling as a slave moved outside among the lamps lighting each one with a taper as he went. The consular elections were to take place later that week in the Campus Martius and Caesar, leaning back on

176

the end of his couch with his goblet resting on his chest, began to talk of the political situation.

'Let's take the Senate first. Suppose that I succeed in the election and become one of the consuls. Cato, Bibulus, Domitius and the rest will do everything they can to oppose my programme. Their only interest is to preserve their ancient privileges, to block any kind of reform and to rotate the magistracies among a few noble families to keep their influence and power. Given their attitude I cannot see how I can expect to achieve anything through the Senate.' He paused and took a couple of figs from the low table beside him. 'So I must look elsewhere; to Pompeius. He is anxious to have his eastern settlement ratified. It is an affront to his dignity that this has still not happened. That's why he has promised discreet support for my candidature. But there's another point to consider. His relations with the optimates have worsened since he divorced Mucia.' Balbus and I exchanged amused glances which Caesar pretended not to notice. 'Her half-brothers, Metellus Celer and Metellus Nepos are annoyed about this. They see it as an insult to the dignity of their clan which after all is one of the most powerful in Rome. Pompeius is a little beleaguered at present. He is short of political friends.' Again Caesar paused, gazing at the ceiling. Balbus and I knew him well enough not to interrupt. He was thinking and when he was ready he continued, 'Pompeius has veterans in and about the city. With my position as consul, if that happens, and his soldiery I reckon that we can get legislation through the assembly irrespective of what the Senate may say. Then we'll see how powerful Cato is with his mischievous speeches and machinations. By the way, you know that Pompeius proposed himself in marriage to Cato's niece but was rejected out of hand. That's another reason for him to be feeling a little miffed with the optimates. I think, Balbus, it's time for you to pay a visit to your old patron to see if he and I can't come

177

to some working arrangement. He's staying in his villa in the Alban Hills for a few days. I know he likes and trusts you. Let's see if we can bring him onto our side.'

'What about Crassus?' I ventured.

'That, Lucius, is the other factor we have to consider. He has his problems as well at the moment with the Asian tax collectors' contract. They have bid far too much for the right to collect the revenue and now they're squirming and saying they want to renegotiate the terms. Of course "money bags" is supporting them but with their usual obstinacy the Senate won't budge. Cato says the contractors must stick by the bargain they struck – typical. I have no doubt that Crassus has a massive financial interest in seeing the contract altered – I can't imagine he's siding with the tax collectors for nothing; so, if he thought that I could achieve that for him, I should be surprised if he didn't offer us his support.'

'But,' broke in Balbus, 'how do you get Pompeius and Crassus to work together? They've never liked each other since the end of the Slave War. Crassus is intensely jealous of Pompeius and believes that he stole his thunder when it was Crassus who did all the hard work to see off Spartacus.'

'I agree that it may be difficult,' said Caesar, 'but Crassus is a practical man. If he knows that Pompeius and I have reached an understanding, to put it no higher, then I think Crassus will realise that he needs to be in with us. If he refuses to join us he will be weaker for it and he will be no further forward with the alteration of the tax contract.'

The evening broke up. Now all depended on the election which took place a few days later. As everybody expected, Caesar was triumphant and led the poll. In second place however was the arch conservative Calpurnius Bibulus who had served as a colleague with Caesar both as an aedile and praetor. Cato and the optimates had secured the election of their candidate by a massive bribery operation. Caesar could hardly complain given the money that had also been spent on his campaign.

Fortified by the result, Balbus went to see Pompeius and I went to see Crassus. Both were reluctant at first to become involved with Caesar. They recognised however that Caesar had the political ability to deliver what each separately desired for himself and that to stand aloof would inevitably weaken their respective positions. About two months after the election a secret meeting took place in Pompeius' villa outside Rome where the three principals conferred with their aides in attendance. Nothing was written down but an understanding was reached to seek the political objectives which Caesar had outlined. Caesar also mentioned the question of the allocation of provinces following his year of office. It was agreed that this would have to be considered at a later date. For the time being the alliance between the three men was to remain secret although its existence would become apparent once Caesar embarked on his consulship at the end of the year. It was fascinating to watch as Caesar, by far the least influential of the three at the time, manipulated the political naivety of Pompeius and the greed of Crassus to establish a relationship which could only lead in the end to his own supremacy. Here I watched him put into place the two stepping stones to power which I foresaw that night as we camped on the banks of the Ebro.

With Pompeius and Crassus safely in the net, Caesar turned his attention to Cicero whose support he desired for the sake of appearances. For all his faults of vanity and exaggerated ideas of his own significance in the political life of the city, the orator still commanded the respect of the people and of many of the nobility. His suppression of the Catilinarian conspiracy had not been forgotten and his eloquence both in the Senate and the law courts was admired. His support would lend respectability to Caesar's

179

actions. And so it was that one afternoon in the early autumn Balbus and I climbed the slope of the Palatine Hill to Cicero's newly-built house. The year was beginning to turn and the occasional leaf swirled around the columns of the great buildings in the Forum behind us. One of my slaves had brought with us a large dish of oysters which were part of a consignment sent to me regularly from the beds near the Lucrine lake at Baiae. We found our host sitting at his table where he had been writing a letter to his friend Atticus. He thanked me briefly for the oysters and sent them to the kitchen to be prepared. I introduced him to Balbus whom Cicero had not previously met and then we talked for a few minutes about the past, particularly of course about our times together when I was getting information from Fulvia.

'But I understand, Lucius, that you have not called on me simply to share a dish of oysters. I fear some less pleasurable purpose is in the mind of you and your friend. You have a message perhaps for me from the man who once danced at the behest of Sulla and now seeks to take his place.'

'Not a message, merely a proposal,' I replied, ignoring the more sinister reference to Sulla. Balbus and I explained the reason for our visit which was to invite Cicero to join Caesar and the other two in the private understandings which had been reached. Cicero listened carefully, looking intently at each of us as we spoke. At length when we had finished he rose from his chair and began to pace up and down the room. Then he spoke, almost as if he were addressing a jury in the law courts.

'What Caesar is proposing seems to me to be an attack on our great Republic. You are suggesting that I should join a group of three powerful men who could effectively arrogate to themselves all the functions of the elected magistrates, the Senate and the people's assembly. I cannot support what amounts to the abolition of our constitution and its replacement by a few men who would really be dictators. What we

180

should be doing now is to restore the strength of our existing institutions, getting rid of the bribery and corruption which plagues our elections and improving relations between the Senate, the equestrian order and the common people. Only in this way can we preserve our liberties and prevent the tyranny of generals at the head of legions. I seek a balance between the social classes of our state, the rule of law, the preservation of the rights of property and the free working of the constitution as it has developed over the years since we expelled the kings. You are asking for all this to be thrown away in favour of dictatorship.'

'I believe that Caesar would agree with much of what you have said,' intervened Balbus. 'But he sees the lifeblood of the Republic being squeezed out by the reactionary elements in the Senate. There is no longer leadership from the noble families. They act only from motives of self-interest and bribe the people to keep them in the magistracies. The system is irretrievably corrupt and needs reform. The old methods of governing the State are breaking down. Unless we make changes to the system the Republic will tear itself apart with faction fighting against faction.'

Cicero shook his head. 'I accept that the Republic has its faults. We need to cure them and get back to the stability which prevailed before the days of the Gracchi brothers. I believe that this can be done by men of goodwill. We need to persuade citizens of all classes that it is in their interests to cooperate to this end.'

'But surely if you were to join with Caesar and the others, this would give you the influence and platform on which to put forward your policies,' I said. 'Caesar has repeatedly told me that he desires your advice on how to proceed when he becomes consul. I know that he has the highest regard for you, both in questions of politics and literature, where he says you have no equal.'

Cicero turned and looked thoughtfully towards us. 'I

181

know that Caesar has a high regard for me. He has often been kind enough to say so to my face. But in the end there is an unbridgeable divide between us. I shall always be for the Republic, however weak and corrupt it may be. I prefer liberty however poorly administered to tyranny however efficient it may be. I do not believe that Gaius Caesar sees any future for the Republic. He is intent upon a different future for our State and I cannot join him there.'

'Are you not painting too black a picture of the intentions of Caesar?' asked Balbus. 'After all he has not done or said anything to indicate that he wishes to abolish the Republic. Certainly he is bitterly opposed by Cato and his faction in the Senate who see him as a threat to their interests, but that is very different from sweeping away the constitution which you suggest is Caesar's ambition. And take Pompeius with whom Caesar wants to work. When he returned to Italy from the East he did not threaten Rome with his legions, he dismissed them. Since then he has sought by constitutional means to have his actions in the East ratified and his veterans settled. He has never threatened violence to achieve these ends. Do you imagine that he would countenance violence by Caesar? You may say that Crassus is greedy and uses his money to influence events, perhaps to bribe juries and generally to further his own political objectives. But again, there is no evidence that he seeks to change the political system and to develop some kind of dictatorship.'

Cicero resumed the seat at his desk. He was now a man of forty-six years of age. His appearance remained imposing despite the strains endured during his consulship and the succeeding couple of years, as he sought to promote his ideas of concord between the classes. The lines on his forehead and cheeks seemed deeper. He drummed his fingers lightly on the table and then nodded his head very slightly as if he had finally composed his thoughts.

'Even if what you say is true and Caesar's intentions are

182

not as I think they are, I could not work with the other two. They have caused great affront to me in the past and I do not believe that either appreciates what I have done for the State. When I wrote to Pompeius outlining my achievements in suppressing the conspiracy of Catilina and comparing these with his great settlement in the East, he did not even condescend to reply to my letter. He clearly does not appreciate me. As for Crassus, I suspect that he was responsible for bribing the jury in the acquittal of Clodius and I am not convinced that he had nothing to do with the conspiracy. Do you remember, Lucius, what Tarquinius said when he appeared before the Senate on the day before we had the debate on what to do with the conspirators? He told us that he had been sent by Crassus to tell Catilina not to be dispirited by the arrests, but to make haste to reach Rome and rescue his friends. Do you expect me to trust and work with a man who then accuses me of having put Tarquinius up to the whole thing?' As ever Cicero was harking back to his year as consul. His vanity was such that he bore a grudge against Pompeius simply because the other neglected to answer his thinly veiled request for praise. Perhaps his dislike of Crassus was more soundly based. The incident with Tarquinius in the Senate had certainly been curious.

Cicero was speaking again. 'Caesar seeks to flatter me by asking me to join his group. I do not believe his desire is to make use of my advice as you suggest, but to manipulate me as he will manipulate Pompeius and Crassus. The other two delude themselves if they imagine that they are joining a partnership with Gaius Caesar. They may achieve short-term gains from their association with the consul-elect, but in the long run it will be he who benefits most and who will emerge as the most powerful. For my part, I shall continue to try to restore the authority of the Senate and to bring about a harmonious relationship with the equestrian order despite the efforts of others to exacerbate the differences between us. Perhaps I shall fail in this. Even so, it is a more worthy aim in life than to join with men who do not seek the preservation of the Republic, only their own political advantage.'

Cicero rose somewhat wearily from his seat. 'There, gentlemen, I have given you my answer. No doubt you will report what I have said to your master. I hope that my predictions are wrong and that Caesar will prove it to us. If I am not wrong, then the days of this great Republic are numbered. It will be crushed like a nut between the reactionary pressures of Cato's party and Caesar's overweening ambition.'

Cicero's attitude disappointed and angered Caesar. There was an exchange of letters between them towards the end of the year. Caesar felt that he could talk Cicero round and was surprised by the latter's curt rebuff. I think Caesar secretly admired the orator's great gift for the Latin language. Years later when we were in Gaul they kept up a correspondence about questions of style and grammar, commenting on each other's work and asking for advice. On this level they remained friends, but the political gulf grew wider as the years went by and they drifted apart.

In recounting to you the events immediately following our return from Spain, I have omitted to mention a personal matter. Naturally I was looking forward to renewing my relationship with Fulvia. The rigours of a campaign and camp life with the legions allow little scope for a man to enjoy the company of women, let alone sleep with one. So it was with considerable enthusiasm that one afternoon shortly after our return I made my way again to Fulvia's house on the Caelian hill. Her maid led me through the familiar passage to her little painted salon where she stood waiting for me in the doorway. As I bent to kiss her and clasp her round the waist she drew back a little, gave a nervous laugh, then took my hand and led me into the room.

184

'Lucius, how nice of you to call,' she seemed to be addressing me as if I were some favourite nephew, not the passionate lover with whom she had groaned in ecstasy on the couch behind her. I now saw the reason for this less than enthusiastic welcome. On the other couch, where I had been accustomed to recline, I saw a young man who was quite clearly familiar with his surroundings; he had the air of a frequent visitor. I noticed that his sandals were on the floor and he swung his legs off the couch as I entered the room.

'Livius,' said Fulvia, turning to the man who did not rise to his feet, 'this is my dear old friend Lucius. He has been away with Gaius Caesar in Spain. You remember, I have often talked about him.' This last remark contained a hint of pleading in it, as though she was anxious to show that I was not forgotten. She chattered on to avoid any break in conversation and motioned me to sit on her couch, then sent for more wine. She sat down herself on the floor beside the couch on which Livius lay. His arm slipped down to drape itself around her naked shoulder. It was clearer than any verbal statement could have been. My place in that salon had been taken by Livius Gallus, a rather insipid young fellow, I thought. His hair was so pale that his eyebrows were invisible. His face was long and solemn except for a rosebud mouth which gave him a slightly effeminate appearance. I thought I detected a hint of perfume about his body. He told me that he was studying to write poetry under Catullus. Fulvia looked fondly up at him and said that he had written two beautiful sonnets to her. Livius inclined his head, deprecating his efforts with a tiny gesture of the hand which then rested on Fulvia's cheek for a moment. I finished my wine and made some excuse to leave, hardly knowing what I was saying.

I felt confused and foolish as I walked back down to the Forum in search of company. It had never occurred to me that Fulvia would find someone else while I was away. How naïve I was. And yet I had felt there was a bond between us, especially after that summer in Baiae. Who was it who had laughed at me at Lucullus' party when he saw me with her? Evidently he knew something which I had never known. We saw each other once or twice after that, but only at the houses of others. I heard that Livius had moved in with her and that she was supporting the struggling poet who read his works to aristocratic ladies in their salons or to men who cared to listen at the baths. He was certainly not the soldier type that Fulvia had fallen for before, but then she had always said that she could not bear another separation and there was no question of that man going off to war. My pride was wounded. The dream of lying with her again, which I had often thought about in camp, seemed rather silly. Caesar roared with laughter when I told him the story.

'My dear chap,' he cried, 'you can't possibly take women that seriously. If you do, they create terrible problems. Just enjoy them while you can; they say there's an awfully long time afterwards when you can't.'

The year turned and Caesar entered upon his consulship with Bibulus. One day as he entered the Senate I saw Domitius approach Caesar. There was an exchange between them which ended with Domitius saying that Bibulus would keep his colleague chained up like a dog during their year of office. 'We shall see who is the dog and who is the master,' replied Caesar and one of his lictors gave Domitius a little push with his bundle of rods as the consul passed into the chamber. It was a sign of things to come.

Soon enough Caesar introduced his first agrarian bill, the purpose of which was to provide land for the city's poor and also for Pompeius' veterans as he had promised. The proposals were perfectly reasonable. They involved the appointment of a commission of twenty men to oversee the acquisition of the necessary land from property owned by the state for which proper prices would be paid. Caesar observed constitutional propriety by presenting the bill to the Senate for their consideration before taking it to the people's assembly. Cato and his party immediately set about blocking the bill which they held to be revolutionary. Cato played his old trick of trying to talk it out so that no resolution would be passed by sunset. I watched as he talked and talked, mostly upon subjects irrelevant to the proposals before the house. He ranged from bribery at the elections to the fleecing of provincials by the governors of Asia, Sicily and Spain, to the question of the tax collectors' contract and any other subject which kept him on his feet. Whenever he was invited to revert to the matter in hand or to sit down, the claque of senators behind him shouted out that they wanted to hear everything he said and that he must be afforded the opportunity to speak for as long as he wished. Caesar remained calm until at length Cato went too far by beginning to talk about public morals, in particular those of magistrates who had engaged in sodomy with the kings of client states. How could such persons be fit for office, he asked, gazing pointedly at Caesar, while behind and around him came cries of, 'Hear! Hear!' and senators whose morals were certainly no better than the consul's smirked. Amid the hubbub Caesar rose to his feet and summoned his lictors to drag Cato out of the house and take him off to prison. 'We shall see for how long he can talk without an audience,' he muttered to me. When the lictors arrived Cato shook them off and told them that he was perfectly capable of walking to the cells without their assistance. He emerged from the Senate House and began to walk through the Forum where a crowd had gathered. When they saw Cato and heard what had happened many of them shouted their support for him and booed the guards. They began to follow, chanting Cato's name and hissing at Caesar as the little procession with Cato at its centre walked to the prison.

Now it was the consul's turn to be a little ruffled. 'I must admit that the blasted man has turned the situation to his advantage,' he said, surveying the scene from the steps of the Senate House. 'I had fully expected him to summon a tribune of the people to intercede and prevent his incarceration. I cannot let him actually go to prison – it will not go down well with the voters.' So saying, he gave orders that as soon as he reached the prison house Cato was to be released and escorted to his home. I heard that he was followed there by a large crowd who cheered and clapped him. It had not been an auspicious start to Caesar's programme, but he had proved his point that it would be impossible to work with the Senate. It seemed to me, however, that the reactionaries had behaved remarkably stupidly. The bill which Caesar proposed was a sensible solution to the problem of the urban plebs and the veterans. The Senate had chosen bad ground on which to oppose Gaius and he was astute enough to recognise this.

A few days later Caesar took himself to the assembly of the people and addressed the representatives of the tribes. He set out carefully in his speech the advantages which his bill would bring to the people and anybody who looked could see that plenty of Pompeius' veterans were among his audience. They shouted out in support of his proposals. Then, to the general consternation, both Pompeius and Crassus came forward to speak in favour of the bill. Up to this time nobody had been aware of the association between the three men. I saw a lot of worried faces looking up as they stood together on the platform. I heard an old senator called Considius turn to a friend and say, 'Look, our Republic has given birth to a three-headed monster. We shall have to mind out that it does not eat us.' Then Bibulus came forward to try to block the proposals on the basis that they had not been approved by the Senate or by himself. He was supported by two or three tribunes who interposed their veto. At this point it looked as if Caesar might have to accept defeat when suddenly a number of soldiers burst into the assembly and set about roughing up the opponents of the bill. The tribunes were forcibly restrained and from somewhere a bucket of excrement appeared which was emptied over Bibulus. In the general fracas his insignia of office were smashed and several people emerged with bruises and cuts, though nobody was killed.

It was said afterwards that the soldiers belonged to Pompeius and that he had lent them to Caesar in case they should be needed, yet nobody would admit to having given them orders to interfere. The upshot was that Caesar's proposals were enacted by the assembly, which had been thoroughly cowed by the violence. Many jurists and other leading citizens were firmly of the view that the law was a nullity. Caesar therefore, in an attempt to bolster it up, made all the senators and candidates for the various magistracies swear an oath not to oppose it. Even Cato submitted. He told his friends that it was better to do this and continue to oppose Caesar than to be killed, which he feared would happen to those who refused to speak a few meaningless words. The atmosphere in the city was changing. I noticed that the reactionaries had become much less vociferous in the meetings of the Senate. Indeed many of them stopped attending, saying that it was a waste of time so long as Caesar remained consul. Meanwhile the latter got on with implementing his new law and appointing his commission of twenty men. One of those chosen was our old friend Varro who had entertained us so well on his estate when we were on the run from Sulla all those years ago. He was a man of extraordinary energy, already in his late fifties then, writing books on agriculture and animal husbandry as he continues to do even today.

With all the fighting and upheavals which have taken place in the last fifty years it is hard to recall that the people still retain great respect for the institutions of the State. The procedures of the Senate and the assembly are regulated by customs and laws which have developed over centuries. In addition it is important to observe the correct religious practices before embarking on public business. For example, a praetor or a consul must first take the auspices, assisted by the augurs, to ensure that the omens are favourable. If the augur decides that, say, the entrails of the sacrificed animal or the flight of some birds in the air is not propitious the magistrate will not proceed with the business in hand. Of course, many of the better educated and governing class have little time for such rituals which in private they dismiss as mere superstition. But in public it is an unwise magistrate who does not observe the correct religious procedures which the college of augurs are anxious to maintain for the sake of their own livelihood and importance. The people too believe strongly in the significance of omens. If the augur pronounces that entrails betray some sign of disease no magistrate dares to proceed with public business for he would be defying the gods.

Caesar's colleague Bibulus now took advantage of this concern for omens and the taking of auspices. After the shambles in the people's assembly he decided that his best method of opposing his fellow consul was to shut himself up in his house, which he proceeded to do for the rest of the year. From there he announced that his consent to all future meetings of the Senate would not be forthcoming. Since neither consul could summon the Senate without the agreement of his colleague, this meant that all such meetings called by Caesar alone and any resolutions passed would be invalid. Then Bibulus went even further by invoking the provisions of the Lex Aelia Fufia which had been passed about a century earlier. By this law any senior magistrate could announce that he was 'studying the sky', in which case all public business had to be suspended until the will of the gods had been ascertained. Bibulus had several notices stuck up round the Forum and on the walls of public buildings saying that he would be studying the sky for omens until the end of the year. Furious arguments broke out between Caesar's supporters who maintained that Bibulus was behaving in a ridiculous manner and his opponents who said that Bibulus was perfectly entitled to invoke the laws of the State to prevent Caesar from acting illegally. From the Rostra men made speeches denouncing one consul or the other, while round the Forum and at dinner parties jurists debated with one another. Meanwhile Bibulus, who was not without a sense of humour, kept up a stream of scurrilous propaganda. He had messages and witticisms posted up for the people to read at street corners and in the markets. Sometimes the notices caused traffic jams as people abandoned their carts or market stalls and crowded round to read the latest joke or poem to emerge from Bibulus' house on the Capitoline hill. I remember reading one which caused particular amusement, though not to Gaius Caesar. It read something like this, so far as I can remember:

> To the Senate and people of Rome
> And that dirty old queen of Bithynia
> (when he's not having sex with Servilia)
> You may wonder why I stay at home.
> Well, of consuls we used to have two
> But Caesar says, 'Just one'll do.'
> So I'm watching the skies for the birds
> While he throws his brickbats and turds
> With Pompeius and Crassus for crew.

The common people took great delight in reciting this to each other for some weeks afterwards. Indeed it was not impossible to overhear it repeated with some gusto in the houses of the nobility. Bibulus also sought to take advantage of the fact that Caesar, of all people, as pontifex maximus, ought to be guided by the religious practices of the state. He ought to have been the last person to ignore the provisions of the Lex Aelia Fufia. Caesar, however, was fully aware of his duties in that respect and took care to distinguish between his roles as chief priest and consul.

One morning he was walking in procession to the Capitol where he was to sacrifice a white bull at the Temple of Jupiter on the anniversary of his ancestor Marius' great victory against the Teutones at the battle of Aquae Sextiae. Before him walked his twelve lictors and behind came the college of priests in their ceremonial robes. They were about to ascend the Clivus Capitolinus on the last part of the Via Sacra when one of the tribunes of the people, a certain Lentulus Nero, stepped forward from the crowd of bystanders and sought to address Caesar. Two of the lictors pushed Nero aside and told him to make way for the consul, but Caesar reprimanded them, saying, 'Surely you are aware that the person of the tribune is inviolate. Let him speak if he wishes.'

Somebody in the crowd shouted out, 'Nice to see one of the tribunes is inviolate. They didn't get much protection in the assembly the other day.' Caesar ignored this and asked Lentulus what he had to say. The tribune, who had evidently been put up to it by the reactionaries, told Caesar that he was breaking the law by carrying on public business in the face of the veto imposed by Bibulus and that he would bring down the wrath of the gods on the city for ignoring his duties as chief priest.

'Young man,' said Caesar as the procession halted and people gathered round to listen, 'the governance of the Republic is not a game to be played out by a few reactionaries for their own amusement and profit. Rome rules the world from the Great Ocean bordering the shores of Further Spain to the forests and mountains of Armenia. Do you seriously suppose that the world will wait while one man shuts himself up in his house to look at the sky? It is outrageous to seek to immobilise public business in this way. There are laws to be passed, taxes to be collected, elections and trials to be held, citizens to be fed, governors of provinces to be appointed. Are all these and more to stop at the whim of one man who disagrees with his colleague? Have I not as much right to carry on the business of a consul, the purpose for which I was elected, as Bibulus has to do nothing? And,' he continued, turning at this point to the people, 'I certainly carry out my duties as chief priest. Indeed I am on my way now to sacrifice to Capitoline Jupiter. Before the start of business every day I assist the augurs to take the omens in the time-honoured way, as the people would wish it to be. Is that not so?' There were many in the crowd who now shouted their support for Caesar, agreeing that he had never failed in his priestly duties. Listening to this I had to smile to myself. Times without number Caesar had told me that the taking of the auspices was just a ritual of no significance whatever, though it had a useful purpose in that it enabled a magistrate to put off business if it were convenient to do so. Lentulus retired in some disorder and was jostled by a few of the crowd for his trouble.

Caesar remained quite unperturbed by the attempts of Bibulus to frustrate his programme. As far as he was concerned it was just one opposing voice fewer in the Senate during debates. Every now and then he sent round slaves during the night to erase the messages put up by his housebound colleague. Bibulus however was quick to have replacements in position and on one or two occasions I witnessed brawls between opposing bands of men scrawling notices on walls which others then scraped off. Inevitably Caesar won the battle.

It was at about this time that I noticed Pompeius had

become an increasingly frequent visitor to Caesar's house. I assumed that they were discussing the ratification of Pompeius' eastern settlement which Caesar was now pushing through as part of their bargain. Then one evening when I was at the baths I fell into conversation with Servilia's son, young Brutus, who told me that Pompeius had fallen in love with Julia, Caesar's daughter by Cornelia. Brutus told me that his mother was most concerned at the attention which Pompeius was paying to Julia, who was thirty years his junior. Apparently Servilia had hoped that Julia was going to marry one of her nephews. The thought of her marrying Pompeius instead was a considerable blow to a woman who spent most of her time intriguing among the nobility to advance her relations to positions of power. I often thought that her long relationship with Caesar had more to do with politics and power than any sexual urge. To make matters worse I knew that Pompeius had murdered her first husband, Marcus Brutus. Cato, who happened to be Servilia's stepbrother and disapproved strongly of her adulterous relationship with Caesar in any event, now urged her in the strongest terms to tell him that if Pompeius married Julia that would be the end of their affair. Brutus said that his mother was furious with Caesar and had refused to sleep with him until he promised that Julia would go to her nephew as arranged. Caesar, however, said to me with a little gleam in his eye, when I asked him about the matter, that he intended to let nature takes its course.

'Servilia is a great ride, never known a better one. But I should not think much of myself if I could not do without her. Besides, I really believe that Julia and Pompeius are made for each other. Julia is flattered by the attentions of such a famous man and he wants to show that he can still do it even at the age of forty-seven.'

I had to admit that when I saw them together a few days later it was obvious what pleasure they took in each other's company. Pompeius laughed and joked like a young man. He was telling Julia about one of his villas by the sea, somewhere near Terracina, I think, where he had a pleasure boat. It seemed that Julia had very rarely been to the seaside. Pompeius invited her to stay with him for a few days. Caesar readily gave his consent for he was delighted by this turn of events. A marriage alliance with Pompeius would immeasurably strengthen his hand and the happiness of his daughter added to his satisfaction.

Not long afterwards it was announced that Pompeius would marry Julia and a great celebration was arranged. Among the reactionaries the prospect of a blood relationship between Caesar and Pompeius caused great alarm. There were whispers of a dynasty being born, of the Republic being cast aside in favour of a family who would effectively become dictators. To make matters worse, Caesar, who had divorced Pompeia after the Clodius affair, now announced that he proposed to marry Calpurnia, the daughter of Lucius Piso. This was a particularly cynical act as Caesar had no affection for this rather plain lady, but her father was consul-elect for the following year. Given that most of his actions as consul were viewed by many jurists as illegal, it suited Caesar well to have as his successor a man who would be obliged to support him. Piso was a rather boring man with his head stuck in books most of the time. He could be relied upon to do as he was told. He also balanced Pompeius' nominee for the consulship, his old ally Gabinius.

The next thing I heard from Brutus was that his mother had received a long letter from Caesar in which was enclosed a very large brooch made from a beautiful pearl set in gold. In the letter he explained that Julia was deeply in love with Pompeius and he asked for Servilia's understanding in giving his daughter to the man who would make her happy. Brutus, who had no illusions about his mother, had been amused as he watched her fondle the brooch while a maid held up a mirror for her to try the jewel in various positions on her dress.

'It will not be long,' he told me, 'before she is back with Caesar. She is captivated by his charm and he makes her laugh with his jibes about Cato and the rest. Mother will always side with a winner. She has a nose for it. I shall never understand why she married my stepfather Silanus.' He gave a little laugh and for a moment he looked uncannily like Caesar, so much so that I have often wondered since who his real father was. Certainly Caesar always displayed immense affection for him.

In the face of all these developments it was not surprising that rumours began to circulate in the city of plots to kill both Caesar and Pompeius. A man called Vettius claimed that a group of conservative elements in the Senate were conspiring against them and Caesar was most upset to find that Brutus was included in the list of those alleged to be involved. When confronted, Brutus flatly denied it to both him and Servilia. A few weeks later Vettius died mysteriously in prison where he had been held after being interrogated. Nobody asked how he had come to die. Caesar remained unruffled by the rumours and refused to change any part of his routine to make him safer from attack. Nevertheless, those of us close to him became vigilant and tried to ensure that even when escorted by his lictors there were others present who could protect him where he was exposed to the public.

The celebration of Pompeius' marriage to Julia took place over three days and culminated in a great party held at Caesar's official residence on the Via Sacra. At some stage I found myself in conversation with Balbus and a rather vulgar young man called Publius Vatinius. Vatinius had not long previously been identified by Caesar as a potential ally among the common people. He possessed a ready wit, told rude jokes and was a favourite in the Forum, where the crowds always gathered to listen to him. He was not a man whom I would have readily invited to my house as a guest for dinner. Apart from anything else, his upper body and face were covered in blotches and pustules caused by some disease of the skin, so that his appearance at close quarters was unattractive. However, I have to admit that he was good company. He was busy telling us how he had planned to catapult dead chickens over Bibulus' house on the Capitoline.

'Well,' he explained, 'if he's going to watch the sky, we might as well give him something to look at.'

Caesar was horrified and immediately forbade it. If word had got out that he had permitted such an act the people would have been scandalised. The hot-headed Vatinius had also proposed to drag Bibulus from his house and cart him off to prison. I had to persuade him that it made no difference to Caesar whether his colleague was at home or in prison, so that idea was firmly sat on as well. Nevertheless, Caesar knew that Vatinius had a strong following among the common people, not for any particular policy which he advocated, but simply because he was an amusing character who relieved the tedium of their day by his wit. Behind the wit, however, Caesar detected a certain hardness and an ambitious streak. Soon Vatinius became a tribune of the people, in which position he rendered good service to his patron later in the year.

Talking of Vatinius has caused me to digress from the wedding festivities for Pompeius and Julia. We had been reclining for some hours in the gardens under the umbrella trees where benches and couches had been placed for the convenience of the guests. The dancing girls had finished and now only a few slaves moved among us with silver flagons of wine, while a very young man dressed as Pan with goat's horns attached to his head pranced about playing his reed pipe and occasionally blowing it into the ear of some somnolent guest. Caesar was deep in conversation with Pompeius, both quite unaffected by the drink of which as usual they partook sparingly. I happened to be close by with Balbus and Vatinius when I noticed a slave approach with a large platter. It was some time since everybody had finished eating and I thought it strange that this dish should suddenly be brought in. I therefore beckoned the slave over. On the platter were displayed one of Caesar's favourite dishes, roasted thrushes with asparagus and the garum sauce to which he had become addicted in Spain. I asked the slave why these had been produced now and he explained that a servant from outside had brought them to the door, saying that they had been sent by a 'well-wisher'. 'Did the well-wisher have a name?' I asked, but the slave said no name had been left. I ordered him to feed the contents of the dish straight to the house dogs. I was not particularly surprised to be told the following day that two had died and one other was very sick.

The festivities accompanying his daughter's marriage to Pompeius and his own to Calpurnia did not distract Caesar from his legislative programme. He pushed through a new deal for the tax contractors in Asia, reducing their obligation to account by a third, thus redeeming his promise to Crassus and receiving a large commission in the process. His first agrarian law, however, had not been particularly successful because the commissioners found that the owners of the land to be redistributed were demanding excessively high prices. He therefore brought in a second bill to requisition the remaining public land in Campania and this time the terms of purchase were fixed at much lower levels. He then had the land parcelled out to more of Pompeius' veterans and to his own clients from the city. Cato spoke vigorously from the Rostra against the new law and there was an ugly scene when he was beaten up by some thugs who dragged him from the platform. I could not help admiring the man's courage. He never flinched from what he saw as his duty and never fled when the attackers came at him with sticks or their fists. Seeing him attacked, many citizens ran to his aid, making a circle round him and escorting him to his house.

Though Cicero did make a speech early in the year, during his defence of his old colleague Gaius Antonius, in which he made disparaging remarks about the state of public affairs, he later retired to his estate in the country from where we heard very little for some time. Caesar was somewhat relieved by his absence. He had expected Cicero to be at least as outspoken as Cato. 'But you can be sure,' he told me, 'that as soon as the cat leaves Rome the mouse will return, so I shall have to set a trap for him.'

In a further attempt to embarrass Cato, Caesar produced a bill by which all the acts of the assembly and decrees of the Senate were to be published. In this way the people would be made aware of the obstructive attitude of the reactionaries. The optimates could hardly object to this measure or to a further law providing for the governors of provinces to be made answerable for extorting excessive sums from their subjects. These however were minor matters compared with the major problem which exercised the consul's mind, that of his province when his year of office expired. He had no intention of becoming a cowherd in Apulia, to which the resolution of the Senate had effectively condemned him. For some time he had talked about the country north of Transalpine Gaul. 'This is territory ripe for conquest. It is the logical next step in the expansion of the empire. If we leave that area as it is, the Germans and all the tribes east of the Rhine will eventually flood into it. Then we shall be threatened by them just as the Cimbri and the Teutones threatened us fifty years ago.'

Yet it was not easy to see how Caesar could secure a command which would enable him to mount a campaign in 'long-haired' Gaul as it was known. The consuls of the previous year, Afranius and Metellus Celer, had been nominated to the governorships of Cisalpine Gaul and Narbonese Gaul respectively. Afranius, however, was not a particularly strong character and Pompeius persuaded him, at Caesar's instigation, to stand aside from the appointment to Cisalpine Gaul in return for a large bribe. At this time both Pompeius and Caesar were particularly flush with cash as they had just induced King Ptolemy of Egypt to part with a colossal sum of money in return for the Senate recognising him as that country's lawful monarch. Having bought Afranius, Caesar now induced Publius Vatinius to put a measure through the assembly whereby Caesar, instead of being consigned to the forests and cattle tracks, received as his post-consular province Cisalpine Gaul with Illyricum. The appointment was to last not for the usual one or two years, but for five. The Senate, who had not even been consulted, were furious. Bibulus, who was still sitting in his house, declared the law invalid and there was uproar when the matter was debated. Insults flew back and forth. One old senator shouted out that the consul was mounting them like a man, at which another induced gales of laughter by pointing out that this was a position which it was not possible for a woman to assume. For a moment Caesar looked discomforted but then smiled grimly, remarking that the Amazons and Queen Semiramis of Syria had been more than a match for young and healthy men, let alone old and senile ones. With that he stalked out of the building and left behind him a lot of Roman nobles who suddenly realised how powerless they had become.

The appointment to Cisalpine Gaul also brought with it three legions which were stationed at Aquileia. In addition this area of northern Italy provided good recruiting ground for the other two legions which Caesar eventually mobilised. Most of the communities north of the Po had only semi-

Latin status in that officials became Roman citizens while the ordinary people had no such rights. Caesar ignored this and treated the whole community as having Roman citizenship. In this way he gained a large body of clients who could be relied upon to support him. Some of these could, as occasion required, be sent down to Rome to vote in elections where Caesar had a candidate. By treating the inhabitants as Roman citizens he was also able to circumvent the law which stated that only citizens could be recruited into the legions. Once a man had enrolled as a legionary his loyalty would inevitably attach to the man who would reward him with booty and perhaps a grant of land at the end of his service. As for Illyricum, this might present the opportunity for conquest which Caesar passionately sought. To the north and east lay the kingdom of Dacia under Burebistas. A vast region bordered by the Danube and the Black Sea lay waiting. 'If I cannot conquer Gaul, then Dacia and beyond will do very well.' Somebody pointed out that a Roman general was not supposed to make war beyond the boundaries of his province unless he could show that the security of the province was threatened. 'Who is going to stop us? In any event, the city will be happy enough if we are able to send back booty and revenue from the conquered areas. Even the Senate won't complain about that.' Caesar had already asked me to go with him as one of his legates and before the end of the year I travelled to Aquileia to review the state of the legions there. 'They will become fit and hardened again once we get them on the march, but make sure that their equipment is in order and that we have proper supplies of replacements. Men who have been in garrison for some time become sloppy. I want to develop the best fighting machine the world has ever known.'

Before I could leave Rome there occurred an event which in retrospect seems like an act of the gods. Perhaps history will mark it as one of the turning points in the story of our city. Certainly if it had not happened my life and more significantly that of Caesar would have been very different. One evening I was dining at the house of Gaius Memmius. He had also invited two poets, Titus Lucretius and the young Valerius Catullus, who had fallen in love with Clodius' sister Clodia and was always writing verses in her honour. After we had eaten, Memmius asked Catullus to read some of his work. I have to confess that under the influence of the wine I dozed on my couch and heard little of the poetry, in which I was not greatly interested. In due course I called for my litter and bade good night to my host and his two friends who were deep in discussion of each other's work. As my bearers carried me up towards my house on the Quirinal we passed by the home of the consul of the previous year, Metellus Celer, governor designate of Narbonese Gaul. I had been aware that for some time he had been suffering from a fever but it was not thought to be serious and his doctors were confident he would recover. Indeed I knew that Metellus was anxious to take up his appointment and extend the province with a view to obtaining a triumph for himself. Now as I passed the house I heard the sound of wailing and upon enquiry of a slave at the door I was informed that his master had died about an hour earlier. The significance of this was not lost on me. If Metellus was dead, then the governorship of Narbonese Gaul was vacant. Caesar had to be informed at once. I sent for fresh torches and my bearers retraced their steps to the house on the Via Sacra. When I arrived I found Caesar dressed in a night robe dictating to a secretary who was promptly dismissed. On hearing my news he sat down on the folding chair which the secretary had been occupying. The light from an oil lamp played over his face as the very faintest breeze came through an open window. There was no sound from the house or the city beyond. The hair on his forehead was receding, so he kept it brushed forward to cover as much of

202

his scalp as possible. His eyes were sunk in shadow but I detected an expression of conviction in the firm line of his mouth and jaw, just a little thrust out. 'So Lucius, the gods have decided to offer fate a little helping hand. Now we must give it a good slap up the backside. Then perhaps we can launch our campaign in Gaul after all.'

Within a few days Pompeius was proposing in the Senate that Caesar's province be enlarged by the addition of Narbonese Gaul. It was not an unprecedented arrangement in any event for the two Gauls to be under one command. Pompeius argued that the appointment should be on an annually renewable basis, rather than for the five years granted in the case of Cisalpine Gaul and Illyricum. Nevertheless the significance of the additional province was readily apparent to all those who knew of Caesar's military ambitions. A base beyond the Alps afforded the opportunity to conquer the vast areas of Gaul lying to the north, which indeed the dead Metellus had been hoping to exploit himself. Cato and several of his claque arrived at the meeting dressed in mourning, saying that they had come to attend the funeral of the Republic. As usual Cato himself made a long speech in which he reviewed all the illegal acts of Caesar as consul. Occasionally there were murmurs of support. Other senators sat in glum silence, either too frightened to register their feelings or resigned to what would happen.

'If you pass this motion, fellow senators, you will have placed the tyrant in his citadel and the last vestige of freedom will be gone. My noble ancestor, Marcus Porcius Cato, used to finish every speech to the Senate with the words, 'Carthage must be destroyed'. From now on, so long as I am allowed to speak, and it may not be for much longer, I shall finish every speech to this house with the words, 'Caesar must be destroyed." He sat down to a long silence. Every senator there, bar a few, knew that Cato had spoken

203

the truth. But perhaps the moment of resistance had passed in any event. For if Pompeius' proposal had been thrown out it would have been a simple matter to take it to the people and have it passed by the assembly. As it was, the Senate accepted the inevitable and Caesar's appointment to replace Metellus was confirmed.

Ironically, Cato's persistent rejection of all Caesar's proposals had in the end been fatal to the preservation of the Senate's influence. If he had only shown some willingness to compromise I believe Caesar would have at least tried to work with him. Indeed, with the introduction of his first agrarian law, Caesar had very properly consulted the Senate for its views, but their unreasoning rejection of the bill had convinced him of their implacability. Although we did not realise it at the time, I think the Republic died that day and was already dead when Cato pronounced his funeral oration. After that I never heard the Senate pass a resolution or the people's assembly make a law which was not instigated or suggested by powerful men at the head of legions.

With his year of office drawing to a close Caesar could look back on it with considerable satisfaction. He had cemented his alliance with Pompeius and Crassus and secured his own political objectives. He and Pompeius had greatly enriched themselves over the affair of King Ptolemy. Despite the machinations of the Senate, Caesar had obtained a military command lasting not just one year but five. He began to think about his governorship and the lieutenants he would need for the campaign which he had in mind. In addition there was the problem of Rome. Caesar knew perfectly well that his actions as consul would be attacked as soon as he left office. He needed to preserve influence and a power base in the city while he was away. Having seen his selection of Balbus and Publius Vatinius I was not at all surprised when he told me that he had decided on Clodius as the man to look after his interests.

'The odious Clodius has just the right blend of arrogance, lack of respect for the constitution and capacity for outrageous behaviour to keep the Senate occupied while I am away. He also knows how to organise a bunch of thugs.'

'But,' I pointed out, 'he has no political clout, he has never held any magistracy and spends most of his time either pimping for his sisters or, even worse, going to bed with one or other of them. He is a man whose lack of moral principle stands out even in this society.'

'Precisely,' replied Caesar with a grin. 'Just the sort of man I want. And if I can get him made a tribune of the people, then I think he will lead the reactionaries a merry dance if they start to attack me or my legislation while I'm away.'

'How can Clodius possibly become a tribune of the people when he is a patrician? He is debarred by his birth from standing to be a tribune,' I said.

'I've had a word with him about that. We're going to get him adopted into a plebeian family, so that he becomes a plebeian himself. He thinks it's a splendid idea, you know how he likes to outrage everybody. The person he's chosen to adopt him is several years younger than he is!'

And so it happened. Caesar asked me to attend as one of the witnesses while he presided over the proceedings in his capacity as chief priest. Clodius was led into court by a man who was said to be his father, but quite obviously was no such person. In accordance with the ancient law the alleged father sold Clodius to the buyer, a plebeian of no importance whose name I forget, who then promptly released Clodius from his power as a father. The alleged father then repeated the sale and the buyer again released Clodius from his power. On the third sale however, the alleged father brought an action seeking a decision of the court as to who was the rightful parent of the smirking Clodius. Caesar, who maintained a straight face throughout, then referred to

Pompeius who was acting as augur. Pompeius announced solemnly that he had searched the sky and found no omen to prevent the action from being concluded, whereupon Caesar pronounced judgement in favour of the plebeian father. Clodius marched out of the court followed by his new father, who was about half his age. I have not mentioned this before because I have got so used to referring to him as Clodius, but he only began to spell his name with an 'o' after he became a plebeian. His real name was Claudius. He changed the spelling to distinguish it from the aristocratic Claudian clan to which he belonged.

Caesar's scheme with Clodius soon began to pay dividends. With the aid of a good deal of bribery and Clodius' own skill in addressing the common people he was duly elected a tribune for the following year. By now Cicero had returned from his estate and Caesar was fearful of his influence. It was certainly not advisable to leave him in the city to stir up trouble with the power of his oratory. But how to get rid of him? The mouse, as Caesar had said, must be trapped. Clodius lost no time over this. He made a speech in the assembly reminding everybody that no citizen could be put to death without trial. He then referred to the great debate which had taken place in the Senate four years previously at the end of which Cicero had caused the Catilinarian conspirators to be summarily executed without trial. He demanded that Cicero should go into exile as punishment for this alleged crime and whipped up the people into a frenzy of support, aided and abetted by a bunch of thugs whom he appeared to have recruited from the Guild of Carpenters. I thought for a little while that I might get caught up in the affair, having been aedile and attended at the execution of the conspirators, but evidently Caesar had told Clodius to keep my name out of it. Cicero withstood the pressure for a few weeks, claiming with some justification that he had had the authority of the Senate for his actions. He even called round to see Pompeius to elicit his support. Unfortunately the latter had slipped out of his back door while Cicero was knocking at the front. In the end he felt obliged to leave the city and went off to live in the East somewhere for about a year and a half. Then Clodius managed to persuade Cato that he was required to supervise the annexation of Cyprus from Ptolemy of Egypt's brother. I think Cato probably went out of a sense of duty, but the prospect of a battering from Clodius' hooligans may have encouraged him.

The new praetors were Lucius Domitius Ahenobarbus and Gaius Memmius, with whom I had dined on the night that we heard that Metellus Celer had died. Within a matter of days of Caesar leaving office they called a meeting of the Senate at which the motion was put that all Caesar's acts during his consulship be declared null and void. Naturally Calpurnius Piso and Gabinius, the new consuls, opposed this. Caesar, however, sensed that it would be dangerous to delay his departure from Rome. He therefore went to stay just beyond the city limits where he was immune from prosecution on the grounds that he was absent on official business, for he was entitled to assume his office as proconsul even though he had not yet reached his province. It would be nine years before he returned.

Chapter XIII

58–54 BC

I shall not recount in detail the various campaigns to achieve the conquest of Gaul. These occupied eight years and the *Commentaries* which Caesar wrote up at the end of each season are a brilliant account of events. He was helped in this by his secretaries Pompeius Trogus and later Aulus Hirtius who actually wrote the last instalment. Caesar himself dictated notes while in the saddle or travelling in his closed carriage, for he was a man who could not bear to waste time.

Besides the staff which he maintained at headquarters in Ravenna and on campaign in Gaul, Caesar kept an office in Rome while he was away. This office was organised by Balbus, assisted by an equestrian called Oppius. From it there flowed a constant stream of letters and communications by which Caesar kept his finger on the political pulse in the city. Even when we were in the far north of Gaul in the territory of the Nervii or the Eburones, Caesar would know within a few days of any significant event at Rome. A team of riders and good Spanish horses were always at hand to deliver his own letters to Clodius, Vatinius and others whom he had chosen to watch over his interests. Another to whom he wrote frequently was Servilia, who kept him informed about the social scene, who was bedding whom and who might be susceptible to a bribe in return for political support. Nobody of significance moved or spoke in

Rome without Caesar knowing of it almost as quickly as if he were still in residence on the Via Sacra.

As I have said, it is not for me to write the history of the conquest of Gaul. I shall deal only in brief outline with that, to enable me to set in context the part which I played as Caesar's constant companion and aide-de-camp. For I was not one of the generals in command of a legion, such as Titus Labienus, Gaius Trebonius or young Publius Crassus, who proved to be a highly effective cavalry officer and whose death at Carrhae we all mourned after he left us to join his father's expedition to Parthia. No, my task was to be a sounding board for Caesar's ideas, to offer advice and to liaise with the generals, Mamurra, the chief of staff, and Publius Ventidius, who was in charge of supplies.

In the first year of his governorship of the province, during the consulship of Piso and Gabinius, Caesar found that the Helvetii who inhabited an area of the Alpine region just to the north of the River Rhone were planning to migrate across Gaul with a view to settling in the far west. It appeared that pressure from Germanic tribes east of the River Rhine was causing this. At first Caesar tried to prevent the migration by destroying a bridge at Geneva, but with only one legion in Gaul at the time he had insufficient troops. He therefore enrolled two new legions in Cisalpine Gaul and I brought the three legions stationed at Aquileia to join him. The two new legions were numbered XI and XII to add to legions VII, VIII, IX and X which had been assigned to the province. Caesar, with these reinforcements, pursued the Helvetii, brought them to battle and in due course obliged the survivors to return to their own territory and rebuild their homes which they had destroyed before leaving. He thus restored the buffer which they had previously formed against invasions from the east. The Sequani who inhabited territory just to the north of the Helvetii between the River Saône and the Rhine then requested

Caesar's help against the German chief Ariovistus who had occupied their land. Initially Ariovistus had come to assist the Sequani in their dispute with their neighbours the Aeduii, but now he refused to leave. Caesar immediately perceived that the Germans constituted a threat to the security of the province and demanded that Ariovistus and his men withdraw across the Rhine. When the German King refused we fought a battle some fifteen miles from the river, routing the enemy, many of whom drowned as they tried to make their escape. Thus, by the end of that first year, as the legions went into winter quarters, Caesar could justifiably say that he had removed a serious threat to the security of the province of Transalpine Gaul, and established Rome's military authority in the area of southern Gaul.

In the following year, when Lentulus Spinther and Metellus Nepos were consuls, two more legions, numbers XIII and XIV were enrolled. During the winter in northern Italy, Caesar had made the decision to attempt the conquest of the whole of Gaul from the seaboard of the Great Ocean in the west to the Rhine in the east. To this end we had advanced into the country of the Belgae in the north-eastern part of Gaul. Having received their surrender we marched towards the territory of the Nervii who were supposed to be the best and bravest fighters of all the Gauls. We were met however by a curious obstacle in the form of great hedges planted with briers and thorns, so thick that it was impossible for cavalry to manoeuvre and through which nothing was visible. The Belgic prisoners told us that the Nervii planted these hedges to impede the progress of raiding parties into their territory and because they had few cavalry of their own. We were not far from the river Sambre where, according to our intelligence, the Nervii had concentrated with their neighbours the Atrebates and the Viromandui. Their womenfolk and old men had hidden in the marshes where they awaited the outcome of the battle.

Being hindered by the hedges in assessing the territory through which we were advancing and also uncertain as to the whereabouts of the enemy, Caesar decided to send forward a party of cavalry to find a suitable site for a camp near the river. Then, instead of the six legions advancing each with its own baggage train immediately behind it, he brought them all forward together and posted the baggage train in the rear where it was guarded by the newly enrolled legions XIII and XIV. The site chosen for the camp was a hill which sloped gently down towards the river. As I came up on my horse I could see on the far side of the river, which seemed at this point to be quite shallow and readily fordable, a piece of flat ground on which were stationed a few pickets of enemy cavalry. It was a fine afternoon and the horses, which presumably were those of the allies of the Nervii, grazed peacefully in the sunshine. Waterfowl could be heard quacking and flapping about in the reeds which skirted each bank. Some way beyond the open ground on the far bank of the river there rose a hill not dissimilar to the one which had been selected for our camp, except that it was covered with a thick wood.

The legionaries began to fortify our camp, digging the trenches and preparing the rampart. As usual they stuck their javelins in the ground and some removed their helmets from the strap on their chest where it was normally carried on the march. Others were sent out to forage. Seeing the enemy cavalry on the far side of the river, Caesar despatched some of our units to engage them together with a party of slingers and archers. The enemy showed no particular inclination to fight and I watched as they gradually pulled back towards the wooded hill behind them, drawing our cavalry on. In the distance to my right I could see the baggage train escorted by the two new legions filing through gaps in the hedges which we had previously cut. Without warning there was a great blowing of trumpets behind the enemy pickets and a horde of Gauls ran out from the wood where they had lain concealed, waiting for the order to attack. As our cavalry units fled, the Gauls rushed down the slope rank upon rank and began to wade across the river, shouting and waving their swords and spears to encourage one another. Many of them wore trousers woven into patterns; some had stained their faces with blue or red dye. The chieftains wore golden torques round their necks and thick bracelets on their arms in place of armour, which they professed to despise. Even their sword handles were encrusted with jewels which glistened in the sun. In no time the leaders were beginning to come up the slope towards our unfinished entrenchments.

We had been caught badly off guard and every man had to look to himself in great haste. Fortunately the legionaries were already experienced men who did not panic. Some had to go into battle still strapping on their helmet or with their shield cover still on, joining not their own cohort or maniple but filling a gap in the line wherever it appeared. The trumpet signal for battle had been sounded immediately and the flag ordering every man to run to his arms had been hoisted on the poles at each of the camp gates. I happened to be close to the tenth legion where Caesar, without a helmet but wearing his distinctive red cloak, soon appeared. The troops raised a cheer on seeing him; he urged them to live up to their reputation and, instructing them to obey my orders, told me to try to attack the Nervii as they emerged from the river some two hundred paces to our front. Meanwhile he galloped off to rally the ninth away to our left. I shouted to a trumpeter to signal the advance and sent for the standard bearer who came with his pole mounted with the silver eagle. I dismounted from my horse. Experience with Lucullus in Pontus had taught me that men will follow an officer who advances with them on foot much more readily than one who stays mounted on his horse.

Some had no javelins, others no helmet or shield but all had their shortswords which never left their belts.

Even though they had not been ready for the attack, discipline quickly asserted itself. With pride I saw that they formed into orderly ranks as we advanced. The enemy were already scrambling up the banks of the river and up the slope. At a distance of perhaps fifty paces I gave the order to discharge such javelins as we had; the bugle sounded and I heard the grunts of the legionaries around me as they launched their weapons. A first grade centurion marching beside me thrust into my hand a shield and clapped a helmet upon my head, apologising for his familiarity as he did so. I thanked him and drew my sword, for we were now coming to close quarters. The next moment I felt a terrific thump on my left shoulder and fell sprawling on my back. A spear had pierced my shield, splintering the wooden frame, and had struck the leather strap of my breastplate. A legionary helped me to my feet and I pulled the spear right through the shield, which was still serviceable apart from the hole to one side. My shoulder ached but there was no wound.

Soon we were engaged in fierce fighting with the Atrebates who were at a disadvantage as they tried to scramble up the banks of the river, still breathless from their charge down the slope and wading through the water. We drove them back, dispatching many as they tried to retreat across the river which became crowded with bodies tangled up in the reeds or floating slowly downstream with trails of blood in their wake. I ordered our men to stay up on the bank where they had the advantage and not to pursue the enemy down to the water itself. A runner arrived from the ninth to our left where Labienus was in command. He proposed a joint assault upon the enemy camp now that they were in full retreat. I sent back a message that the men of the tenth were ready. We began to wade across the river and to advance up the slope towards the wood. The enemy in their wild enthusiasm had not thought to have an effective guard so that we had soon taken possession of their camp. As we reached the higher ground, however, a disturbing sight met our eyes. Legions VIII and XI were engaged in fierce fighting with the Viromandui further down the river, while legions VII and XII were formed up in a square on the slope leading to our camp. They were surrounded by a large force of the Nervii some of whom had broken off and were assaulting the camp from which servants and baggage drivers could be seen fleeing. The legions looking after the baggage train were approaching but had not yet reached the hilltop to give assistance.

Thus we had hardly reached the enemy fortifications before I ordered the men of the tenth to turn about, race back down the hill, re-cross the river and relieve the pressure on our own camp. Many of the legionaries were tired, some were wounded and without proper equipment, yet they did not hesitate as they perceived the danger to the whole army. I saw several men stumble in the river, either from exhaustion or wounds; others immediately carried or pulled them to the bank. One legionary had a friend on his back while with his free arm he supported another who had the shaft of an arrow impaled in his thigh. With what strength we had left we began to climb the slope towards our half-completed entrenchments.

My left shoulder was giving me some pain and I could hardly support my shield; my eyes stung with sweat while the muscles in my legs felt as though a dagger had been plunged into them. Even the sword in my hand began to feel heavy. I had killed two men on the bank of the river and from one I had seized his round shield to replace my broken one. It was made of wicker with an iron rim and a bronze boss in the middle.

As we mounted the slope our appearance gave encouragement to others. The cavalry, who had been routed in the first charge of the Nervii, re-concentrated and launched an attack on those who had breached the camp's defences. Even some of the non-combatants inside began to offer resistance. Others who had stopped fighting, either through exhaustion or wounds, on seeing the example set by the tenth, picked up their arms. The legionaries were anxious to show to Caesar that his confidence in them had not been misplaced. I gave the order to charge into the Nervii despite the slope of the hill which gave the advantage to the enemy. At the same time the leading units of legions XIII and XIV appeared on the hilltop above us. A desperate fight ensued as the Gauls, now assailed both from the front and the rear, fought ferociously. As one man went down another stepped into his place, until their bodies were piled one on top of the other like a human rampart. Others ran forward to pull back the wounded and grab their weapons. I saw a man pull the spear from the gut of another who lay screaming with pain and plunge it again into the man's chest to put an end to his agony. Then he turned to fling it down at us. But the bravery of these Gauls was not enough. The other legions came up in support after overcoming their opponents, to help us cut the remainder to pieces. The men of the Nervii were almost removed from the face of the earth by the end of that sunny afternoon on the banks of the Sambre. Meanwhile, far over in the west on the shores of the Great Ocean, Publius Crassus had obtained the submission of the Veneti to complete our campaign for that year.

As winter approached the legions went into quarters and Caesar returned to northern Italy where he held assizes. At the turn of the year the new consuls, Lentulus Marcellinus and Lucius Marcius Philippus, entered office. We started to receive reports of the deteriorating political situation in Rome where rioting and violence were becoming commonplace. These had their roots in two issues which in those days periodically sparked trouble; the supply of corn to the city and the problem of Egypt, which had been reopened following the unseating of Auletes, whom Caesar had put on the throne during his consulship.

I must go back a little further to explain. During the previous year Pompeius had watched with increasing anxiety the advances which Caesar was making in Gaul. The latter's victories at that time paled into insignificance when set against the military triumphs which Pompeius had enjoyed against the pirates, Mithridates and in his campaigns in the East. Nevertheless his bright blue eyes were sharp enough to discern the star of a rising man whose capacity to manipulate events and military genius were already being discussed admiringly in the salons of Rome. Servilia in a letter told Caesar that she had been amused one evening to watch Pompeius sulk in a corner at a dinner party where all the conversation had centred upon Caesar's victory against Ariovistus. Pompeius had begun to feel the need of a spokesman to remind the people of his past achievements and perhaps even to secure him some great new command. His thoughts turned to Cicero, then in self-imposed exile thanks to Clodius. With the help of the consul Lentulus Spinther who brought forward the necessary legislation, Pompeius secured the recall of Cicero who made a triumphant return in the autumn.

Cicero was not slow to repay the obligation under which Pompeius had placed him. Within a week of his return he was promoting in the Senate a motion that Pompeius be put in charge of a special commission to deal with the problem of the corn supply. The position however was complicated by a further proposal put forward by a tribune called Gaius Messius, who wanted to give Pompeius even greater power than Cicero had proposed, involving a fleet of ships, an army and authority over all the provincial governors, not to

216

mention as much money as he liked. This placed Cicero in a difficult position. His own more modest proposal was unpopular with many senators who did not wish to see Pompeius presented with the prize of the corn commission in any event, and the sweeping powers advocated by Messius were anathema to them. Pompeius, as usual in these situations, equivocated, though from our position at Ravenna it was clear that he was quietly backing Messius with a view to acquiring as much power as possible.

The dispute between Clodius and Cicero had also flared up again. Cicero, before his departure, had built himself a fine house on the Palatine close to the one which he had rented from my mother. Clodius however had arranged for the property to be demolished and replaced with a shrine dedicated to the goddess Liberty, an ironic touch considering what a political lout he was. On his return Cicero was anxious to have the consecration of the shrine annulled by the College of Pontiffs so that his house could be rebuilt on the site. The College of Pontiffs included many leading senators whom Cicero could not afford to offend by pushing too hard for the appointment of Pompeius to the command of the corn supply, in whatever form. He therefore avoided the subject for the time being and received his reward when the College voted to let him rebuild his house. Clodius tried to frustrate the work of reconstruction by getting the priest who interpreted the omens to pronounce that certain subterranean disturbances experienced during the rebuilding were caused by the wrath of the gods at the defilement of consecrated ground. Cicero managed to persuade the Senate that this was nonsense and the work on his house continued, but not without further attacks on it by Clodius and his gang, who also set fire to a neighbouring property belonging to Cicero's brother, Quintus.

Meanwhile the question of the corn supply had been settled on the basis of a bill brought forward by Spinther and Metellus Nepos which granted to Pompeius the more limited powers which had first been advocated by Cicero. Pompeius, we heard, had said that this was all he wanted in the first place. In any event the opposition to the proposals of the tribune Messius was so widespread that he would never have got his legislation through.

Every day a despatch rider from Caesar's office in Rome arrived at Ravenna bringing with him a report from Balbus or Oppius. By this means Caesar maintained discreet contact with Clodius, though he never wrote to him directly as far as I was aware. Balbus would pass on, by word of mouth only, suggestions which emanated from 'an old friend in northern Italy'. Clodius usually needed no second invitation to act and was rewarded with gifts of money from time to time. He spoke up vigorously in opposition to Messius, partly because he felt there was interference with his own corn law, and partly also because Caesar was anxious that Pompeius should not be invested with so much power that he would no longer feel the need for cooperation with himself and Crassus. As for Clodius' antics against Cicero, Caesar would smile wrily, for the orator had not endeared himself to the general since his return to the city. Early in the new year Cicero had undertaken the defence of a man called Publius Sestius who was charged with provoking a riot and other disturbances designed to prevent Clodius being elected as an aedile. One of the witnesses for the prosecution was Publius Vatinius who as a tribune had forced through the assembly of the people the law allotting to Caesar the province of Cisalpine Gaul for five years. During his cross-examination of Vatinius and in the presence of Pompeius, who was in court to give evidence, Cicero had seen fit to make widespread criticisms of what had gone on during Caesar's consulship, in particular the disregard of religious proprieties, the violence and the illegality of some of the legislation. Caesar remarked that he could hardly be expected to restrain Clodius if

Cicero was going to sound off in this way. Balbus, in one of his letters, said he felt that Cicero must be receiving some tacit support from Pompeius to give him the courage to speak so freely. Then a few weeks later Cicero obtained the Senate's agreement to reopen the question of the Campanian land which had been the subject of Caesar's agrarian legislation. This was another indication that he was intent on trying to break up the coalition between Caesar and Pompeius. He could hardly be doing this without encouragement from his rescuer from exile. Cicero was becoming a nuisance.

Relations between Pompeius and Crassus were never good at the best of times. Worse was to come. There was a tough young man called Titus Annius Milo who as a tribune had supported the recall of Cicero from exile. He had about the same regard for the rule of law as Clodius and had recruited a gang of ruffians, including a squad of trained gladiators. Now the two of them fought tooth and claw for control of the city. After the attacks on Cicero's and his brother's houses on the Palatine, Clodius and his gang had attempted to set fire to Milo's house as well, from which they were driven off with heavy losses. There followed moves in the Senate to curtail Clodius' activities. These were obstructed by his powerful relatives, his cousin Metellus Nepos who was consul and his elder brother, the praetor Appius Claudius. Milo then threatened to prosecute Clodius who, however, was standing for the aedileship which would give him immunity. Milo thereupon sought to occupy the Campus Martius to thwart the election at which Clodius was successful. In his turn he brought a prosecution against Milo.

Pompeius hated Clodius who, he believed, was plotting to kill him. He also knew or sensed that Clodius had at least the tacit backing of Caesar and Crassus in some of his activities. Milo he saw as a counterweight to Clodius. In addition he brought into the city some of his clients from

Picenum where he had large estates. Matters came to a head at a preliminary hearing of the case which Clodius had taken against Milo. Pompeius appeared in court to speak on Milo's behalf, during which the followers of Clodius hurled abuse and generally shouted him down. Clodius, in his turn, received similar treatment from the supporters of Milo, whereupon he engaged his own adherents by asking questions such as, 'Who is starving us all to death?' to which the reply came, 'Pompeius!'

Then, 'Who wants the job in Egypt?'

'Pompeius!' shouted his claque again.

'Whom do we want to go to Egypt?'

'Crassus!' they yelled back to him. Tempers rose as Clodius whipped his followers into a frenzy until at length Milo's gang charged and knocked him off the platform.

From headquarters in Ravenna Caesar watched all these events in Rome with care. His own relationship with both Pompeius and Crassus was unimpaired, particularly now that his daughter Julia was married to Pompeius. It was clear, however, that Pompeius and Crassus had never been on worse terms. Indeed Pompeius had told friends that he believed Crassus to be behind the plot of Clodius to kill him. Pompeius had always been terrified of assassination, so Caesar took this with a pinch of salt. Nevertheless it did not alter the fact that if the understanding between the three of them was to be patched up, he, Caesar would have to take the initiative. The conversation then turned to Clodius.

'He was useful in getting rid of Cato and Cicero after my consulship, but I think he is now doing more harm than good,' said Caesar as we discussed the situation one evening. 'His attacks on Cicero are all very well, but his attitude to Pompeius is driving a wedge between him and Crassus and sooner or later Pompeius will blame me for not keeping him under control. As for Cicero, I am beginning to think he is the most dangerous of all. He is not a crude political bully like Clodius. He is more subtle.'

'Do you think Cicero is trying to break up the coalition between the three of you?' I asked.

'That is exactly what I believe,' replied Caesar. 'I don't know whether his recent remarks in the Senate about the possible repeal of the Lex Campania are inspired by Pompeius. Whether they are or not, I suspect that Cicero's objective is to try to wean Pompeius away from me and back towards the optimates.'

'Surely,' I said, 'the Campanian land law has benefited Pompeius as well as you. So why should Cicero use that to try to win back Pompeius?'

'It's true that the first agrarian law that I brought in as consul did settle many of Pompeius' veterans. It's not that law which Cicero is seeking to reopen. It's the Lex Campania itself which mostly benefited the urban proletariat. If that were repealed it would hardly affect Pompeius' veterans and it would be popular with the Senate because it would restore a large slice of income to the public treasury. Cicero is calculating that if Pompeius were to give his support to such a proposal, it would go a long way to restoring his popularity with the optimates and perhaps persuade him that he no longer needed the coalition.'

'And of course,' I pointed out, 'if Pompeius does a good job in restoring the corn supply, the people are going to like him for that.'

'There's another problem on the horizon,' added Caesar. 'A letter from Balbus this morning tells me that the optimates are planning to put forward Ahenobarbus for a consulship next year and that he is openly saying he wants to take over the command from me in the province when my tenure of office expires the following spring. I doubt whether I can complete the conquest of Gaul by then. I suspect we still have lot of fighting to do before we can quell all the tribes of such a vast area. I need more time to finish the job and strengthen my political position.'

'Some of your enemies are still talking of prosecuting you once your command expires. They have not forgotten what happened during your consulship. Cato, Bibulus and probably Cicero will all be thirsting for blood.'

'Yes, I am only too aware of that,' replied Caesar. 'But suppose I could contrive to prolong my command until I was eligible to stand again for the consulship; then I would remain immune from prosecution.' He let the thought hang in the air. Ten clear years needed to elapse between consulships; that was seven years away. A lot could happen in seven years, as indeed it did.

'I think I need to see Crassus, bolster him up and then try to see Pompeius separately,' said Caesar, suddenly recovering from the reverie into which he had fallen after his last remark about prolonging his command.

A few days later Crassus arrived at Ravenna, accompanied by Appius Claudius and a considerable entourage of hangers-on. I noticed that the great financier had to be helped down from his carriage on his arrival at the villa which had been set aside for his accommodation. He was now in his late fifties and years of good eating and drinking were beginning to take their toll. His face had become heavy and the girdle of his tunic supported a paunch which the folds of his toga could not disguise. Really, he cut a sorry figure beside Caesar who was at least ten years his junior in any event and retained a lean athletic figure by dint of sparse eating and continuous exercise. Nevertheless Crassus still spoke crisply after the manner of his training as a successful advocate.

The old jealousy of Pompeius soon emerged in his talks with Caesar, who had clearly taken the right decision to speak to them separately. Caesar was tactful enough to let

Crassus have a free rein in his complaints. Pompeius had made all sorts of unwarranted allegations against him; Pompeius had brought back Cicero against his wishes; Pompeius had been given the corn commission; Crassus had got nothing; now Milo, backed by Pompeius and some of his clients from Picenum, was causing trouble.

Caesar understood Crassus very well. Above all, what Crassus wanted was a military command. He wanted to show that he was the equal of Pompeius as a general. His victory over Spartacus in the Slave War had never been properly recognised. Worse, Pompeius had claimed much of the credit for it. Looking on, it didn't seem to me that Crassus was young enough or fit enough to assume command in anything but a nominal capacity. Crassus himself perhaps sensed this. Caesar began to talk of his son, young Publius Crassus, who was doing so well in Gaul where he had shown himself to be a fine leader of cavalry. 'Suppose,' suggested Caesar, 'you were to have the command against Parthia. Your son Publius could go with you. I should miss him, of course, but I would be happy to see him at your side in such a great expedition. The combination of your experience and his youthful dash would be invincible.'

The lure of a great military campaign to re-establish his reputation as a soldier and Caesar's flattery were irresistible. Crassus liked the idea. But Caesar had not finished. 'Of course,' he pointed out, 'we have to be in a position to secure such an appointment for you. I propose that you and Pompeius should stand for the consulship next year. I think I can assure you of a victory in the election by arranging for enough of my legionaries to have some leave and come to Rome to vote. Publius could bring them down to the city.' Crassus took a slug of wine from the goblet at his side. He could hardly restrain himself from smiling at the prospect. Gone was the slightly sulky expression with which he had entered the room.

Then he looked up and said, 'Of course, Pompeius will want something as well.'

'Naturally,' replied Caesar evenly. 'He must not feel left out.' Caesar was giving Crassus the impression that they were arranging things between themselves, that he was taking the older man into his confidence.

'Well,' went on Crassus, 'he already has the corn supply to look after. What else do you think he would need?'

Caesar did not reply immediately and seemed to be turning things over in his mind, though I suspected that he had considered this long before Crassus even arrived in Ravenna. Eventually he said, as if the thought had just occurred to him, 'Well I suppose if you were to have Syria to launch your campaign against Parthia, it would do no harm for Pompeius to have the two Spains.'

Crassus nodded. 'I don't see why he shouldn't agree to that. I am sure I can work with him for a year as consuls before we go off to our respective commands. And how about you? I imagine you haven't asked me here just to propose commands for Pompeius and me.'

'You're quite right,' replied Caesar. 'But I am not seeking any fresh command. What I need is a prolongation of the present one to enable me to finish the job in Gaul.'

'That seems reasonable. How long do you think you will need?' By now Crassus was beginning to assume a much more confident air, as of a man who had suddenly seen a bright new future open up before him, with the opportunity for military glory and the acquisition of large sums of money, the latter of which he certainly didn't need.

'I thought perhaps we would make all three commands of five years' duration,' said Caesar. 'That would be fair to all of us; would you agree to that?' Once again he was drawing Crassus into his confidence so that the latter began to feel that the whole scheme was his rather than Caesar's.

The following day Crassus climbed back into his carriage

224

to return to Rome. There was a trace of swagger in his step. The two men had promised to keep secret their plans for the future. Caesar hoped to see Pompeius within the next few days to outline what had been agreed between them. Crassus was well pleased with the outcome of his journey to Ravenna. He had made some ground on Pompeius. He and Caesar had arranged things very satisfactorily. Caesar had seen a lot of sense.

Hardly had the dust from Crassus' carriage settled in the courtyard of Caesar's headquarters than an urgent message was being despatched to Pompeius. As luck would have it, we knew that Pompeius was about to set off for Sardinia on the business of his corn commission and to see one of his legates there, Quintus Cicero, the orator's brother. Caesar invited him to stop at Lucca on his way to sailing for the island. On receiving an acceptance of the invitation Caesar and I, with Appius Claudius, took horse and made our way across country to the small border town still just inside Cisalpine Gaul.

I think Caesar was a little concerned about what reaction he might receive from Pompeius when he outlined his proposals. In the event the meeting went much more smoothly than we had expected. In the first instance, as with Crassus, Caesar let Pompeius give full voice to his complaints, particularly against Clodius, of whom he seemed genuinely frightened. Appius Claudius thereupon undertook to call upon his brother to moderate his attacks, particularly against Pompeius. Caesar too promised to exercise such influence as he could in this direction. In return, he asked Pompeius to grant a similar favour in relation to Cicero whose eloquence and standing with the people Caesar in his turn feared. Pompeius for his part undertook to speak to Quintus Cicero about this and make sure that the great orator was made to behave. I had thought that Pompeius might be less cooperative about renewing the coalition, particularly with Crassus, whom he loathed. In the end he chose to stay with Caesar on the basis that it was better for him to alienate the optimates who continually failed to give him what he wanted than to alienate his father-in-law. In his mind the suppression of Clodius was uppermost and he believed that Caesar could deliver that. His only stipulation was that he should be entitled to stay in the region of Rome, effectively in command there, rather than travel to his provinces. This put him in a very powerful position to influence events in the city. I detected that Caesar felt this a small price to pay for the prolongation of his own command.

In the space of a few days Caesar had achieved a great deal. He had patched up the rift between Pompeius and Crassus and arranged for Cicero's dangerous speeches to be silenced. More importantly, he had obtained the extension of his command in Gaul which effectively removed the threat of prosecution for a further five years and gave him the opportunity to extend his influence and wealth. As we rode back to Ravenna I asked what pleased him most about the outcome of the talks. 'I have gained the time to train my legions into the most formidable fighting force the world has ever seen. Pompeius may have legions in Spain but they will go soft in the sun. They will have forgotten how to fight. As for Crassus, his will disappear into the shimmering deserts of Parthia – mark my words.' Poor Crassus, it was a far cry from the days of his youth when somebody had described him as being 'like a bull with hay on his horns', which the farmers say to show that an animal is dangerous.

Following our return from Lucca I was engaged for a few weeks on administrative matters in preparation for the campaigns of the coming summer. After two years in the field the legions were in need of further supplies of equipment, particularly boots, but also swords, shields and other pieces of armour. It was necessary to collate the requirements of each legion, stationed in their winter quarters. The legionaries themselves, many of whom were skilled in working with timber or metal, spent much of the winter in repairing or manufacturing arms, especially the spears and javelins. From my position in Ravenna I liaised with the state arms factories, of which I had acquired some experience during my time in Capua. I corresponded also with Mamurra and Ventidius in Gaul to make sure that the equipment, properly escorted through sometimes hostile territory, reached the legions safely. There was the question too of payment for these supplies and for the new legions which Caesar had enrolled since his appointment as proconsul in Gaul. The state treasury had agreed to undertake this for which there was much documentation to complete and I was kept busy for some time in dealing with this.

I shall not dwell for any length upon the campaigns of that year. Publius Crassus in the west had victories over the Aquitani and the Cantabri. Meanwhile we marched against the Morini and the Menapi far up in the north-eastern part of Gaul, where there are many rivers and the country is often difficult to penetrate as it is covered with marshes and forests. We fought some indecisive engagements in which the enemy refused to be drawn into pitched battle. Instead they contented themselves with harrying our foragers and then melting away into the marshes or retreating across rivers so that we could not pursue them. We could only ravage the countryside, burning villages and looting anything of value.

In Rome there was great unrest. The triumvirate, as the coalition of Caesar, Pompeius and Crassus was now known, had kept secret the arrangements reached at Ravenna and Lucca. Despite this, many senators and others were deeply suspicious. Pompeius and Crassus were repeatedly asked if it was their intention to stand for the consulship and answered evasively. The consular elections normally held in July were continually being postponed due to the disturbances in the city. Clodius was active again, but now as people observed, he seemed to agitate in the interests of Pompeius. What had happened to change matters? The truth was that Appius Claudius coveted a consulship and had promised the support of his brother if in turn the triumvirate would support his candidature for the following year. So that was why Appius Claudius had accompanied Crassus to Ravenna and then journeyed on to Lucca. It was all becoming clear; the people smelt a rat, especially when towards the end of the year the city began to fill with Caesar's veterans 'on leave' from Gaul.

The announcement that Pompeius and Crassus would stand for election as consuls together produced an upsurge of violence and howls of protest from Cato, Domitius and many others. Domitius, who did not lack courage even if he was a fool, refused to stand down and went while it was still dark to the Campus Martius on the night before the elections were due to take place. Balbus reported to us that Cato had accompanied him with a number of supporters in the hope of preventing the soldiers on leave from bullying the other voters. As they milled about in the early hours, waiting for the voting pens to open, they were suddenly set upon by a gang of masked men carrying wooden cudgels. One of Domitius' torchbearers was killed in the ensuing scuffle and Cato himself received a blow on the head. Nobody seemed to know who the attackers were but Clodius must have been behind them. His elder brother was evidently fulfilling his part of the arrangements reached nearly a year before. Not surprisingly Pompeius and Crassus were duly voted in, while many outraged senators continued to go about in mourning.

A few days later Caesar received a letter saying that his daughter Julia had miscarried. Apparently Pompeius had been caught up in further violence following the voting in the Campus Martius and his toga had been splashed with blood. A slave duly carried it back to his house where Julia had fainted at the sight, believing that her husband had been killed, and then lost the baby.

The campaigning for the new season opened with an unexpected invasion of north-eastern Gaul by German tribes from across the Rhine. There were two tribes in particular, the Usipetes and the Tenctheri, who had invaded the territory of the Eburones who live in an area not far west of the Rhine and straddling the River Meuse. Realising that the Germans posed a threat to the area and wishing to demonstrate to the Gallic tribes that he would not tolerate their presence, Caesar demanded that the Usipetes and their allies retrace their steps and go back across the Rhine into Germany. The Usipetes protested that they could not return to their homelands, from which they had been driven by the fiercest of the German tribes called the Suebi. Caesar dismissed their envoys saying that he had arranged for them to be admitted into the country of the Ubii, another tribe who lived on the far side of the Rhine. Negotiations continued during which there was an attack on our cavalry by the Germans who followed their usual practice of jumping down from their own horses and stabbing ours in the belly. We lost a large number of good men, whereupon Caesar resolved to drive the invaders back into Germany without further ado. Their leaders, who had come to apologise for the treacherous attack upon our cavalry, were detained and we advanced quickly to seize the enemy camp. It turned out to be full of women and children who had accompanied their menfolk across the river in search of a new home. Without their generals the Germans had fled in all directions. We hunted them down with our cavalry, killing many thousands as they tried to cross the Rhine near where the Moselle flows into it. It was estimated that the enemy was up to four hundred and thirty thousand strong including non-combatants, yet we lost not a single man during this engagement. I think that as many of the enemy were drowned as were killed by the legionaries. When I reached the bank of the river you could almost have used the bloated bodies floating in it as a causeway to reach the other side.

We pitched camp on the banks of the Rhine. That night as we dined in the large tent which Caesar used when he wanted to call a meeting of his staff officers, we discussed whether it would be advisable to cross the river and campaign on the other side. All agreed that the natural boundary of Gaul was the river itself and that it would be foolish to invade an unknown territory which was thickly forested and populated by tribes who had a reputation for producing the fiercest warriors. The army would be difficult to supply and in any event there was no prospect of establishing a colony, let alone a province, on that side of the river. Nevertheless, Caesar was anxious that both Gauls and Germans should know that the river of itself presented no barrier to the advance of Roman arms whenever we deemed it expedient. A large body of the cavalry of the Usipetes and Tenctheri had escaped back into Germany where they had joined forces with the Sugambri, to whom Caesar had sent envoys demanding their surrender. The Sugambri had replied haughtily, saying that the Rhine was the limit of Roman sovereignty and that they would not recognise any authority east of the river. Caesar also reported that the Ubii were being oppressed by the Suebi and were earnestly requesting us to cross over into Germany in a show of strength, saying that if we would only do this it would be sufficient to deter the Suebi from molesting a declared ally of Rome.

One of the first-grade centurions, whom Caesar always invited to such councils of war, for he valued greatly the opinion of the legionaries themselves, suggested that we should send an expeditionary force across by boat. Others argued that this would be easy to oppose if forces were assembled on the far bank to attack our men as they came ashore. It would in any case require the construction of a large fleet to get a force across in sufficient numbers. Then Publius Rutilius, the first centurion of the ninth legion, suggested that a bridge might be built. This immediately commended itself to everybody, especially Caesar, who foresaw the wonder and admiration that such an enterprise would arouse in Rome. The following day the engineers set to work to design the bridge and men were despatched to chop down trees for the timbers, while others forged the metal braces and prepared the ropes to hold the structure together.

Even now I wonder at the speed and skill with which the bridge was put in place. Pairs of piles were sunk into the bed of the river at a distance of forty feet apart, the upstream pair inclined slightly in the direction of the current with the downstream pair inclined slightly against it. Between each pair of piles was laid a great timber crosspiece to form an arch held in place by iron brackets. The arches continued across the river joined by lengths of timber running in the direction of the bridge. On top of the decking we laid smaller poles and bundles of sticks to provide a firm footing for both men and horses. The downstream piles were further strengthened by more timbers laid obliquely against them, driven into the river bed and wedged to the original supports. Upstream we placed vertical piles at intervals to act as buffers and prevent the Germans from attempting to demolish the bridge by floating tree trunks downstream onto it. The whole work of construction was completed within ten days.

With the bridge in place Caesar led the bulk of the army across, leaving me in command of the guard which consisted of six cohorts. During the building of the bridge I had given orders for a number of large rafts to be prepared. These had been moored against the bank upstream of the bridge.

231

I envisaged that they might be useful if we were to be attacked by boats coming downstream. The rafts would provide a floating platform which would rest against the buffer poles and from which the legionaries could defend the wooden supports of the bridge itself. As soon as we could get sufficient men across to the far bank, I constructed a ditch and rampart fortification in a semicircle round the German end of the bridge. Less elaborate defences were also in place at the Gallic end. Despite the fact it was summer I had noticed that in the evenings a mist often settled over the river so that when it was dark it became very difficult to see anything at all. At every arch of the bridge therefore I attached to the rail, which ran the length of each side of the deck, burning brands which the sentries from time to time renewed. In the mist these gave off an eerie orange light which helped the sentries to maintain contact with one another and to see a little further. In the middle of the bridge I placed a temporary shelter which housed a hundred men and acted as a command post. Three of the cohorts I placed within the fortification on the German side of the river and the remainder of my force were either on the bridge itself or inside the fortification at the Gallic end. I had a squadron of cavalry which I ordered to patrol both upstream and downstream to watch for any signs of activity.

One evening, I think it was the sixth day after Caesar had crossed with the army, I stood on the bank of the Gallic side of the river. Behind me the sky was a little lighter where an invisible sun was going down concealed by thick cloud. In front a shallow blanket of mist hung over the river so that I could see only the upper part of the bridge and the parapet, which seemed to hang suspended in the air, held up by unseen hands. At intervals above the parapet I saw the figures of sentries, their helmets and the upper parts of their shields silhouetted against the grey sky. Every now and then one set off on his beat, looking out over the river which he could not see for the white shroud which swirled beneath him. I sensed but could not make out the far end of the bridge and the tall pine trees which came down almost to the bank. We had felled many of them to use in the construction of the bridge and the fortifications. Immediately beneath my feet the river hardly stirred. Only the drift of some bits of vegetation and sticks betrayed the direction of the current beneath the surface. Two herons came flapping ponderously upriver, just cleared the bridge and then alighted on some rocks in shallow water close by. The men were either sleeping, in readiness for the night watches or eating a meal of biscuit and corn mash. There was no wind, no movement and no sound to speak of. Everything was still as we waited for nightfall. There would be no moon.

My thoughts were disturbed by the arrival of Aemilius Cimbro, the captain of the cavalry squadron, with his evening report. His men had ridden for some miles both upstream and downstream on our side of the bank and had found nothing sinister. On the far side it was difficult for cavalry to patrol. The forest reached almost to the riverside and there was little or no open country to survey for enemy activity. It was impossible to know what might be concealed by the trees.

'This would be a good night to attack, wouldn't it, sir,' said Aemilius, who had divined my thoughts. 'If they come down the river, we won't be able to see them until they're virtually upon us.' I agreed and told him that as soon as it was dark he should post pickets at intervals along our side of the bank in the hope that they might be able to pick up any sign of movement on the river and give advance warning of an attack. Then I arranged for one of the maniples to carry on to the bridge a collection of stones, each about the size of a man's fist, and deposit small piles of them at intervals where they could be used to throw down upon anybody trying to damage the bridge supports. Next I sent a message to the military tribune in charge of the cohorts on the far side of the bridge, a certain Titus Verrianus, who had acquired a good reputation in the battle against the Nervii, to double the guards on the rampart. Having issued the password for the night, 'Janus', I retired to my tent to try to catch a little sleep. It was my intention to spend the middle watches on the bridge at the command post.

A couple of hours later, as the bugle sounded for the beginning of the second watch, I was wakened by my body slave. I strapped on my breastplate and my sword belt and made my way up onto the bridge. The torches had been lit and the double row of smoky flames cast a pale light on the mist which still shrouded the river. Above, the sky had cleared a little and the stars hung like glow-worms on a backcloth of jet. No moon had risen. As I passed the sentries each man demanded from me the password and received it. All reported that they had seen and heard nothing. There was a chill in the air, and I pulled my red cloak round my waist and fastened it. At the command post I found the centurions had a brazier lit.

About halfway through that second watch we heard a great clamour break out at the far end of the bridge on the German side. Accompanied by half a dozen legionaries I hastened over to see Verrianus, who reported an attack on his fortifications. We had cleared a large patch of ground beyond the ditch and rampart when constructing the bridge. Here we saw great numbers of Germans gathered, apparently intending to fill in the ditch with earth and sticks and then storm the rampart itself. Arrows and other missiles to which burning cloths had been tied were being fired into our camp. Under cover of this barrage men were moving bundles of sticks forward towards the ditch. Verrianus had mounted catapults surrounded by leather shields and these were firing arrows and heavy bolts into the massed enemy with considerable effect. In the dark it was difficult to tell their numbers but there was a great deal of shouting and clashing of arms. There seemed, however, to be no real vigour in the attack and as I watched I sensed that this was a diversion designed to draw our attention away from an assault on the bridge itself. Verrianus had the situation well under control. His legionaries would soon put paid to any foolhardy Germans who came within range of their spears.

I hurried back onto the bridge and was not surprised to find our men hurling javelins and stones at boats which had floated downstream keeping to the German side of the river where they could not be detected by our pickets. The enemy had anticipated that they would be attacked from above and had constructed floating huts with pitched roofs of leather braced with iron. From these they were attacking the supports of the bridge with axes when they could get close enough. Hearing the sounds of an attack but not being able to see much in the mist, our legionaries had immediately launched their rafts and were now among the boats of the enemy. Using hooks provided for the purpose they pulled the attackers' boats away from the bridge supports and then jumped aboard, killing and capturing almost at will, for the Germans put up little resistance when they found themselves assailed both from above and behind. The weight of their roofs caused some of the boats to capsize so that many men either drowned because they could not swim or were picked off in the water as they struggled to get ashore. Others clung to the piles which minutes before they had been trying to hack through, only to be cut down by the legionaries on the rafts. It was soon over. We lost ten men either killed or drowned. Of the enemy there must have been several hundred washed up on the bank in the morning or floating up against the supports of the bridge.

By daylight we found two of their boats which had become trapped between the vertical piles acting as buffers and the timbers of the bridge itself. Inside one of these floating huts lay the body of the biggest man I have ever seen. When we stretched the corpse out on the bank it measured nearly seven feet. On his head he wore a round helmet surmounted by the skull of a wolf. His hair was very blond and reached halfway down his back. He wore no armour, instead his upper body was covered with the skin of a black bear and on his legs he had patterned trousers. We found no trace of a wound on him and wondered if he had taken poison when he saw that the assault on the bridge had failed. I ordered his body to be strung up by the legs from the deck of the bridge along with those of one hundred others who were hanged similarly on each side. There the corpses swung and twisted in the wind for another ten days or so until Caesar returned. I intended to let both Gauls and Germans know what fate awaited any other would-be attackers. By the time the legionaries marched back from their expedition the bodies were beginning to turn black and the carrion crows had fed well on the eyes and any flesh they could get at.

Upon his return Caesar immediately destroyed the bridge. His foray across the Rhine had achieved nothing in military terms, but the fact of his having crossed the river with such ease had taught a sharp lesson to the tribes on both sides. The effect in Rome was even more dramatic. Caesar was demonstrating what an army led by him could achieve, both by the skill of its engineers and in battle. Let the citizens of Rome take notice.

Later that year and again in the following year, by which time the consulships had passed to Caesar's old enemy Lucius Domitius Ahenobarbus and to Appius Claudius, we mounted two invasions of Britannia, an island lying across a short stretch of sea to the north of Gaul. These invasions were little more than reconnaissance expeditions and to show the Roman people that even the sea was no barrier to the army of Gaul. The Britons make much use of chariots, which were long ago abandoned by us as a weapon of war.

236

We found that the best tactic against them was simply to separate as they charged and to throw our spears from each side as they passed between our columns. In this way they became isolated from the main body of their own infantry. We seized a quantity of booty and took hostages before leaving.

In the summer of the consulship of Domitius and Claudius, Caesar received terrible news from Rome. His daughter Julia, who had already miscarried once and was of a delicate disposition in any event, was expecting a child by Pompeius. Balbus and others wrote saying that she was having a difficult pregnancy, not helped by the hottest summer the city had experienced for many years. The Tiber was very low and the city's great drain stank as there was insufficient water to carry away the effluent and human excrement. In the Subirra there was disease which had killed many while it was said that others had died from heatstroke. Because of the drought, fires readily broke out and spread through the closely-packed houses and wooden apartment blocks. Cato and others of his party tried to make out that the gods were punishing the people for the atrocities which he claimed Caesar was committing in Gaul. Balbus and his staff in Rome worked hard to counter this propaganda, pointing out the great benefits that Caesar's victories in Gaul were bringing in the form of tribute to the state's treasury. At the height of all these difficulties, Julia died in the process of giving birth. The child survived only a few days. The news reached us far away in the north of Gaul, as we prepared for the second invasion of Britannia. It was early in the morning when a rider came into the camp with a letter from Lucius Rufus who acted as adjutant to Pompeius. On reading it Caesar turned to me and said simply, 'Today I shall think only of Julia and of my life with her until now. Tomorrow I will again be Caesar.' With that he entered his tent ordering his guards to let no one disturb him until he emerged again.

He remained alone for the whole of that day and night, taking no food, though I believe he had water and wine with him. The following morning he sent for me. I found him dressed and ready to resume command. On his table I saw letters addressed to Pompeius and to Servilia. I never heard him mention Julia's name again. I believe the memory of her was too painful to him. Despite his long relationship with Servilia, it was Julia and her mother Cornelia who were the women that he really loved. His mother Aurelia was too ambitious and scheming while Pompeia and Calpurnia were not much more than political pawns. For a few days he was quieter than usual. Once he said to me, 'Now Pompeius will think himself free of me, but he cannot escape me.'

In Rome the people poured out their grief, sensing perhaps that peace might be maintained between the two great generals while Julia was alive. They wondered now what the future could hold. Originally Pompeius had planned that Julia would be buried at his villa in the Alban Hills, but the people, much to the irritation of Ahenobarbus, made a funeral pyre on the Campus Martius and there her body was burned amid great lamentations. It marked the end of an unhappy and uncomfortable summer for the people of the city.

The troubles of that year were not at an end. A Gaul called Ambiorix deceived the fourteenth legion under the command of Sabinus, together with five cohorts in the charge of my distant relative, Aurunculeius Cotta, into leaving their winter camp. They were ambushed in a defile by a force of Eburones, who cut them down almost to a man. Those who escaped back to the camp fell on their swords during the following night, so ashamed were they of what had happened. Six thousand of our men had died. Caesar did not shave or have his hair trimmed until we avenged the defeat some weeks later.

Chapter XIV

54–52 BC

In Rome Crassus was preparing to set out to take up his appointment as proconsul in Syria, where everybody knew that his main objective would be to mount an expedition against Parthia and win military glory. Many people objected to this plan, saying that Crassus had no business to be making war on a country which had a treaty of friendship with Rome and presented no immediate threat. One of the tribunes of the people, a man called Ateius, went so far as to have Crassus arrested by his attendants as he was making his way out of the city. The appearance of Pompeius, whom Crassus had asked to see him off, encouraged the people, and other tribunes then forced Ateius to release Crassus. When the procession reached the gates of the city they found that Ateius, undeterred, had set up a brazier upon which he threw incense and libations. He then proceeded to invoke the names of strange and terrible deities and to call down upon Crassus mysterious and ancient curses. From then on many were convinced that his expedition to Parthia was doomed because once a man had been cursed in this way he could not escape failure and death. When news of the defeat at Carrhae reached the city a year later Ateius was vilified in the streets for having been responsible for Rome's worst military disaster since Hannibal's victory at Cannae.

Caesar had agreed at Ravenna that young Publius would join his father once he was installed in Syria. Thus the day came when he rode away from us, taking with him one thousand prime Gallic cavalry who were to accompany him all the way to his father's province. I had grown fond of this dashing officer who was married to Scipio's daughter Cornelia. She was a most beautiful young woman who had learnt geometry and philosophy but retained a gaiety and zest for life unusual in one of such intellectual leanings. never knew a daughter more different from her father whose disgusting habits I mentioned earlier. Publius too was different from his greedy, calculating and obscenely rich father. His passion was riding and the cavalry. Tall and good looking, he led his men with indomitable courage, never hesitating to throw himself into the thickest fighting. His men loved him for he treated them all as his equals.

'If you ride into battle beside a man who may perhaps have to save your life, even though he may lose his own in the act, how can you regard him as anything but your equal if not your superior?' he would say. He cared nothing for money, perhaps because his father had so much, and often gave away to his men booty which had been presented to him. I was sad to see him go. The night before his departure we drank long into the night. I gave him a cloak made of leopard skins which I had brought back from the campaign with Lucullus. In the morning he was wearing it as he rode round the camp where the legionaries all raised a great cheer and wished him well. Perhaps because of what Caesar had said and because of the curses that had been called down upon his father, I had a premonition that I should never see him again. I stood watching as the figure of that noble young Roman, laughing and joking with his escort, slowly receded, riding into the morning sun until they all merged into a single spot on the horizon. I remembered watching in the same way all those years ago after the death of my father, as the carriage carrying my mother and brother bumped away down the Via Appia to the south.

When the news came of his death we were told that he
ad fought desperately to save his father's army. They had
een trapped in the desert sands by the Parthians, sur-
ounded by archers who had rained myriads of arrows down
on them. Two Greeks who lived in the village of Carrhae
ear to the scene of the disaster had offered to guide
ablius to a city called Ichnae where he could take refuge.
e told them that no death could be more terrible than to
andon his men who were even then dying for his sake.
hereupon he seized his sword in his left hand because his
ght arm had been badly wounded by an arrow, rode his
orse into the thickest of the battle and was struck down
on afterwards. The Parthians cut off his head and paraded
on the end of a spear up and down the columns of
gionaries. Publius paid the highest price for the stupidity
d greed of his father who had only invaded Parthia to get
is hands on even more riches and in a futile attempt to
mulate the military achievements of Pompeius and Caesar.

For our part in Gaul we had seen many widespread revolts
different parts of the country. Caesar had been obliged
recruit a new legion to replace the lost fourteenth and
ompeius had agreed to lend him one, so the strength of
e army reached ten legions with large numbers of cavalry.
deed at the beginning of the following year we were
cruiting more men in Cisalpine Gaul when news reached
s that Clodius had been killed in a clash with Milo's gang
ear a village called Bovillae, south of Rome on the Appian
Vay. Apparently Clodius had been wounded in the first
ncounter and carried into a wayside tavern where one of
filo's ruffians had finished him off. When his body was
rought up to the city the people carried it into the Senate
fouse, made a funeral pyre of anything they could lay their
ands on and set it alight, with the result that the building
ad burnt to the ground. The disorder in the city was worse
han ever. No consuls had been elected for the year and

eventually Pompeius was appointed sole consul on the motion of Bibulus, supported by Cato. Caesar received the news of Clodius' death with equanimity. The rabble-rouser had outlived his usefulness. In any event there were other matters to engage his attention, in particular a Gallic prince called Vercingetorix, a leader of the tribe called the Arverni who occupied territory to the north of the province.

Vercingetorix was a young man of almost boyish appearance. He had ginger hair which curled at the nape of his neck. His nose was very long and straight and his eyes seemed to protrude slightly from their sockets. Unusually he had no beard but beneath a rather small mouth there was a large and determined jaw. He was the son of a man called Celtillus who had once ruled over the whole of Gaul Perhaps it was this fact which above all inflamed Vercingetorix with his fanatical hatred of Rome. Deep down he believed that the invaders were depriving him of his rightful inheritance. This Arvernian prince, however, was different from other Gallic leaders we had encountered. He saw that the only way to liberate his country was to unite all the tribes in a great alliance, but not necessarily to fight us in pitched battles. Instead, Vercingetorix decided to adopt a scorched earth policy and to try to deny Caesar the supplies needed to sustain his legions. It was not long before he was elected commander-in-chief and had gathered round him a very considerable force from many different tribes. He gained their respect by the strength of his will and ruthlessness. He thought nothing of cutting off a man's ears or gouging out his eyes, even for the most minor misdemeanour. For a short while he served in our cavalry, a couple of years before the start of his great rebellion. I once saw him whip a slave close to death for having fed his horse too much grain so that it could not gallop. There was a fire burning in him that I have never seen in any man before or since. He took advantage of his service with us to learn something of

242

rategy and tactics and to observe a legion at close quarters, ow it fought and how it was supplied.

It so happened that at the very beginning of that year hich had begun in Rome with no consuls elected, there ere a number of circumstances which encouraged the ,auls to think that this might be the moment to throw off he Roman yoke. They had heard of the defeat of Crassus at :arrhae. The Parthians had shown that Rome was not ivincible. Rome itself was gripped by political violence, pitomised by the death of Clodius. It was rumoured that :aesar would not leave northern Italy while the turmoil at .ome lasted. The Gauls themselves were deeply angered by he execution of one of their chieftains called Acco. The evolt in central Gaul began to gather pace. We received eports of a massacre of Roman citizens at Cenabum in the erritory of the Carnutes. There were threats against the rovince and Vercingetorix was concentrating a large force orth of the Cevennes mountains.

We left Cisalpine Gaul, travelling on horseback with only small escort, making for the city of Narbo. Before leaving, :aesar ordered the drafts which had been recruited during he autumn to follow by forced marches and to concentrate outh of the Cevennes which separate the province from the ountry of the Arverni. Meanwhile he posted detachments f troops from the province's garrison along the northern order and encouraged them to resist the raids led by a ;aul called Lucterius. Then we marched with the remainder f the garrison to meet the troops coming from Italy and ffected a junction with them just to the south of the nountains. There Caesar called a council of war and xplained his predicament to the military tribunes and the enior centurions. The legions in their winter quarters in iorthern Gaul were separated from him and the province)y the force which Vercingetorix had assembled and by the nountains which were said to be impassable in winter. In order to rejoin them Caesar must either travel north through very hostile territory with a small escort and run a high risk of being captured, for there were spies everywhere reporting his movements, or he must order the legions to march southwards and run the risk of their being attacked without their general to guide them. They would be denied supplies on the journey and Caesar feared that without his presence to steady them, Vercingetorix might inflict heavy losses which would encourage the remainder of the country to join his rebellion.

There was however an alternative which he wished to put to the meeting for its opinion. He had obtained the services of two guides who said that they could lead the army through the mountains. It would be very hazardous; thick snow lay on the ground and the legionaries would have to dig their way through it. It had never been attempted before and Vercingetorix was banking on the fact that it could not be done now. But if he, Caesar, could appear with a substantial force having crossed the mountains in the depths of winter, this would demoralise the enemy and discourage others from joining the rebellion. He asked the centurions whether they thought the men could do it. The centurions were unanimous that the attempt must be made. If Hannibal could cross the Alps, which were now a well worn thoroughfare, then a Roman legion could cross the Cevennes. Caesar praised the centurions for their enthusiasm, repeating that the task would not be easy. We would have to travel with the minimum of supplies as it would be impossible to get the wagons which carried the heavier equipment and provisions through the snow.

The next day was spent in preparing for the journey and marching to the foot of the mountain range. There we camped for the night and at first light the following morning the column set out with Caesar riding ahead, his red cloak soon becoming flecked with snow which was falling again

244

he men had wrapped strips of cloth round their arms and
gs for greater warmth. They carried double rations of
iscuit and corn. Since it was very unlikely that we would be
ttacked during the passage of the mountains Caesar had
rdered the javelins and spears to be carried by packhorses,
ut the legionaries still had the rest of their equipment,
including their spades which would be vital if we were to dig
ur way through.

At first the going was reasonable and we made steady
progress. The ground rose very gradually, the snow was not
eep and the cohorts at the head of the column flattened
nd impacted the snow on the tracks, making it easier for
hose who came behind. When a cohort had been in the
an for an hour it stood aside to let the column come past
nd then rejoined at the rear so that the work was evenly
hared. Sometimes it stopped snowing and from the seat of
ny horse I could see the whole length of the column
vinding its way upwards, accompanied by a long trail of
loud above the soldiers' heads as their breath vaporised in
he cold air. Instead of the mixture of sounds which an army
n the march normally makes, the clatter of horses' hooves,
he clang of metal on metal, the bawdy songs which the
egionaries sing to amuse themselves, there was only the
teady and continuous clump of thousands of boots as they
runched the snow beneath them.

Soon the helmets and shoulders of each man bore a white
overing. Every now and then one would stop to shake
imself free of it and brush down his shield with a hand
vhere only the ends of his fingers protruded from the cloth
vrapped round his arms. The packhorses and mules seemed
o have fires in their bellies as their nostrils exhaled billows
of steam. Then the snow would begin to fall again, obscuring
verything, and we would all be cocooned in our little
groups consisting of the few men around us whom we could
till see.

245

As we went forward the slope of the track became steeper. Occasionally the whole column came to a halt because the path was blocked by a snowdrift. Now the leading cohort were having to shovel almost all the time, using their entrenching tools to dig the snow away. Some used their shields to push it aside. The work of the men in the van became harder and the changes of shift more frequent as fresh hands moved up to take the place of those exhausted by the sheer weight of the snow to be cleared. In the fading light the painful advance continued. Caesar knew that we had to get through the pass quickly or the men would die of cold in any event. The work kept them warm. Braziers were lit at the head of the column and as the legionaries shuffled past they received a drink of warm wine mixed with water. Some tried to linger by the fires but were pushed on by those coming up behind. Torches were lit and fixed on the end of stakes stuck into the snow. Fortunately the guides were good. Even in the dark and with the features of the country obscured by the blanket of white, they did not lose their way. At about the beginning of the first watch a slight breeze got up. The sky cleared and a pale moon rose over the mountain above us. This helped us to see our way but the wind came straight through our clothes so that many men could not hold their spades properly for the numbness in their fingers. One soldier accidentally struck another on the leg with his spade, causing a large gash in his calf and staining the snow red. The wounded man said he could feel nothing. The gash was bound and to keep warm he resumed work rather than be relieved. I had long since dismounted from my horse as had all the other officers. We walked up and down the column encouraging the legionaries to keep moving when they were waiting for the way to be cleared in front.

At about midnight we reached the top of the pass. It was blocked with drifts up to six feet deep. The wind had risen a little and moaned around the heights above our heads. The cold was intense. Caesar, who had not dismounted, rode up and down the column encouraging the men. He even managed a few jokes with those he knew from the garrison. Despite the appalling conditions the legionaries had faith in their general and their discipline did not fail. They grouped together with their shields turned towards the wind and each man shuffled round the outside of his century or maniple until it was his turn gradually to move into the centre where protection was greatest. In this way they kept on the move and gave each other temporary respite from the worst of the cold. Meanwhile at the front of the column the leading maniples worked furiously to clear the way.

Eventually we began to advance again. The legionaries gave a muffled cheer. They had seen the silver eagle on the standard, lit up by torches carried alongside it, top the pass and then begin the long descent. Many men were close to exhaustion. Their cloaks were heavy and damp from melted snow. The cold and above all the wind were unrelenting. There was an old legionary called Sergius Rufus who had fought bravely with the seventh in the battle against the Nervii five years previously. He had lost an eye and been wounded in the leg. When Caesar returned to Ravenna for that winter we took Sergius with us. Caesar employed him on general duties at headquarters, thinking he could serve out his time there. The leg had recovered and Sergius had requested that he be allowed to come with the new recruits to rejoin his legion. He was nearing the end of his enlistment for sixteen years and he wanted the chance of a good gratuity before he retired. Now I saw him half shambling and half supported by two men. He was barely conscious. There was nothing to be done; if he stopped moving he would die quickly in the cold. I passed on down the line cajoling and encouraging as I went. Half an hour later I caught up again with the two men who had been helping Sergius. They said he had suddenly let go of them and collapsed to the ground. When they bent to help him to his feet they found that he was dead. They had laid him at the side of the track and then covered him with snow. Going up the column a little further I found a mule on its back in a dip into which it had slipped, breaking its leg. Its shrill braying filled the crackling air as it thrashed about with the three uninjured limbs while the broken foreleg hung uselessly. The muleteer despatched it with his knife and began to unstrap the load of javelins from its back, throwing them up on to the track where they bounced and clanged on the rock hard snow. As they passed slowly by, each legionary stooped to pick up a javelin and sling it on his shield. In a matter of minutes the incident was over. No words had been spoken; all energy was concentrated now upon the task of survival, of getting through that wall of snow. Sergius Rufus was dead but nobody had the strength to care. Four other men died of cold that night. We buried them with a few shovels of snow beside the track and moved on.

Once we started our descent from the head of the pass conditions improved a little. The wind dropped and the snow stopped as the sky cleared again. The track wound downhill through great white banks which towered above us like the shoulders of some giant. The men sensed that the worst was over, their pace quickened a little and before long we glimpsed the faintest hint of a lighter sky over to our right where the sun would rise. The silent shuffle of the column was now broken by occasional snatches of conversation, a sure sign that morale was rising. We pressed on. Caesar was determined to be through the mountains by daybreak, out of the wind and onto lower ground where the winter sun might help the legionaries to rest and recover. It was still very cold and the troops must be kept moving at all costs. He dismounted from his horse and walked at the head f the column with the standard bearer by his side. The military tribunes took their places at the head of each cohort, exhorting the men to make the last effort. Gradually the elation at reaching the top of the pass dissipated as the men realised that there was still a long way to go before they could rest. The conversations faltered and the column fell silent. The only sound was the clump of the soldiers' boots as they trudged on, heads down, not looking where they were going, simply intent upon following the steps of the man in front. Occasionally somebody stumbled and fell. Others then barged into the back of one another, not seeing what had happened. There were muttered curses. After a few moments of disorder the file in which the man had fallen righted itself and the steady trudge began again.

At last the sky lightened to let the stars fade to invisibility. The first rays of the sun began to touch the tops of the hills, turning the snow from white to pale pink while below we remained in black shadow. The sun itself was hidden by a great ridge rising steeply from the valley down which the track led. In the distance we could see that the ground levelled out and as we watched the plain in front of us was suddenly suffused with light. The dawn welcomed us to another day that many of us had not thought to see.

We stopped on a small hill which gave a good view of the surrounding country. With lookouts posted there could be no question of a surprise attack. Caesar ordered that we should rest until midday when we would again advance for a couple of hours before pitching camp for the night. Most of the men were too exhausted to do anything but lie down where they had halted and sleep. Some simply wrapped themselves in their cloaks and lay out in the winter sun. Others erected tents which had been brought on the pack-horses. In the distance I saw a group of perhaps twenty horsemen who observed us from the corner of a wood. At length they turned away and set off northwards. It would not be long before Vercingetorix knew that Caesar had crossed the mountains.

That evening while we were waiting for the camp servants to prepare the evening meal I found Caesar in impatient mood. Now that we had got this far he was anxious to join the legions and re-establish the credibility of Roman arms before the rebellion spread even further.

'This man Vercingetorix,' he said as he paced up and down the tent, 'is a far abler general than we have faced before. Until now we have been up against tribal chiefs who considered only their own position and the territory which they governed. Vercingetorix is looking at the broader picture. He understands that the only way to beat Rome is to unite the whole country and then to starve us of supplies. He knows that the legions need feeding and so do our horses. Now, when there is little or nothing in the fields, is the time when we are most vulnerable.'

'So what do you propose?' I asked.

'I propose, Lucius, that we leave tonight and ride with a small escort to the winter camp in the Lingones' territory where we have two legions. Once there we will summon the other legions and conduct a swift campaign. I want to avenge Cenabum first. We cannot let atrocities like that go unpunished. Then we will move against Vercingetorix himself, though I suspect he will be too canny to risk a pitched battle.'

'Will you leave young Brutus in charge of the troops here?'

'Yes, he can do the job, I think. I shall have a word with him in a moment. If he sends out the cavalry to do as much damage as possible in this area it may cause the Arverni to summon assistance from Vercingetorix. I should like him to be marching south while I assemble the legions round Agedincum.'

'We are going to struggle to keep the army fed,' I said.

'That's the gamble, Lucius. Somehow we have to keep the supplies coming, even in this weather. The Aedui have been reasonably reliable allies and we should be close to their territory. But the snow and the rain will make it difficult to move wagons and Vercingetorix will do everything he can to stop us using the rivers.'

As we ate Caesar issued a stream of orders to a secretary and spoke to Brutus. It was to be put about the camp that Caesar had returned to the province for a few days to attend to some business but would be back shortly. Some German horsemen, part of a troop of four hundred we had brought up from Narbo, were instructed to make their way to the Aedui with orders that certain of their chiefs were to report to Agedincum where they would be informed of our needs.

Taking with us a guide named Lato, we rode out of the camp late that night. We had with us an escort of only ten men from a cavalry squadron provided by the Remi, our most loyal allies. Fortunately the sky was cloudless and the moon was nearly full. The snow was only a few inches deep and presented no difficulties to the horses who maintained a steady trot as we rode northwards. The trees of the woods and forests were black and forbidding. We skirted past them, never too far away in case we needed to disappear quickly. At length we came to a river running due north which we followed for several hours, occasionally having to ford streams flowing into it. We rode past settlements which appeared deserted and bore traces of having been burnt.

'I think we shall see a lot of this,' said Caesar indicating what looked like a hay barn which was still smouldering. 'If necessary, Vercingetorix will starve his own people if it means that he can also starve us.' At daybreak we pulled away from the river and bivouacked in a wood. I made a bed of twigs to keep me off the ground. When I awoke it was late afternoon and the light was beginning to fail. The men had reconnoitred and finding the area deserted, had lit a fire.

My hands and feet were numb. I was glad of the warmth and the hot corn mash.

Before dusk we were on the move again. The countryside seemed abandoned. There was no trace of movement of either man or animal. I was struck by the silence and the stillness. The only sound to break it was the rhythmic beat of the horses' hooves. The sky was overcast and uniformly grey. The scene reminded me of the black and white mosaic floor round the baths of our old home in Rome. Soon it grew too dark and we were forced to stop. We found a deserted settlement where we made ourselves as comfortable as possible in a crude house built of rough stone and a timber roof lined with straw. We noticed that two barns, which had probably contained hay, had been burnt to the ground. In another building there was cattle dung which looked fairly recent. During the night I heard wolves calling and in the morning we found traces of their footmarks in the snow. It was the first sign of life that we had seen for two days.

Caesar, determined that we should lose no more time, decided to risk travelling by day. We continued northwards, still following the banks of the river flowing southwards. There was less snow now but it began to drizzle. I longed for the sun and tried to imagine myself back at Baiae sitting on the terrace overlooking the sea with the scent of the roses on the air. The drip of icy rain down my neck and the splash of slush on my legs as the horses waded through sodden fields brought me back to reality. We were hungry as well, for the provisions had been rationed carefully from the start in anticipation of not being able to find food on the way.

On the fourth day we came to a junction of rivers where Caesar had arranged for us to be met by a force of cavalry which had been in the area for some time. We changed horses and struck off to the north-west, heading for the country of the Lingones in which the ninth and tenth legions were quartered. With fresh cavalry to escort us we increased speed, reaching their winter camp late the following day. The legionaries gave a great cheer when they recognised Caesar as he rode through the gates. Many ran out from their barracks or dropped what they were doing to throng round his horse. They had known within two days of our crossing of the Cevennes. The Gauls communicate by shouting their news from village to village. Our allies in the Gallic cavalry had picked up the message while out foraging. Nobody would believe that Caesar had got a force across the mountains until the shouted messages confirmed that the Arverni were pleading for help. Now Caesar had rejoined his men I could see the relief on their faces. They had implicit faith in his leadership, believing that so long as he was in command they would always be victorious. Nevertheless, they had heard about Vercingetorix and had felt threatened and isolated in the middle of a very large hostile country where great forces were being assembled against them.

Caesar for his part was delighted by the welcome he received. He told the legionaries that they had become the finest fighting units in the world. Looking down on those rough weather-beaten faces, I could see what he meant. The men were hard and lean. Their dark bodies ingrained with dirt were toughened by the rigours of long marches under arms, with trenches and ramparts to fashion at the end of the day. They had fought and won many battles over the previous six years. They were experts in the use of swords, spears, catapults and other artillery. They could build bridges, construct terraces and siege towers under fire from the enemy or sap the walls of a besieged town. Above all, they were experienced and confident. They kept their discipline under pressure when each man knew his place and what was required of him. Caesar now had ten such legions at his command, double what he was supposed to have if he had obeyed the instructions of the Senate. Truly he was the most powerful man in the world. Yet this power would evaporate if we could not defeat Vercingetorix and finally subdue Gaul. The last round was about to begin.

Chapter XV

52 BC

Caesar moved swiftly to concentrate the other legions around Agedincum. Then, leaving the two least experienced to form a garrison there and to secure our supplies from the north, we began to march towards the Bituriges where Vercingetorix, distracted southwards as we hoped, was besieging a town called Gorgobina. On our way we attacked a stronghold of the Senones called Vellaunodunum and then swung westwards to the River Loire and the town of Cenabum where the slaughter of Roman citizens had taken place earlier in the year. The legionaries put the citizens of Cenabum to the sword before burning it to the ground. We re-crossed the river and hurried southwards while Vercinge-torix, hearing of our approach, raised his siege of Gorgobina and manoeuvred towards us, harrying our foragers with his cavalry.

Supplies were a perpetual problem for us. The Gauls, under instruction from their commander-in-chief, had burnt all their stored crops and driven off the cattle. We were able to get some food from the north via Agedincum and boats came down the Loire bringing grain. In addition the Aedui had been instructed to furnish provisions, but they were slow and irregular in coming. We suspected that they were under pressure from other tribes to withdraw their support for Rome and in any event did not wish to commit them-selves too much to one side or the other while the outcome of the struggle remained in the balance. Every day we saw smoke on the horizon all around us. The Gauls were burning everything we might find to eat. At night the sky glowed as the clouds reflected back the fires of the burning towns and villages below. Smoke hung in the air and smuts settled on our cloaks and tunics. It was too early in the year for anything to grow in the fields. The cavalry were forced to travel further and further in search of forage. Sometimes they were ambushed by the enemy's horse and we suffered losses.

Amidst all of this we received intelligence that the Gauls had resolved, contrary to the advice of Vercingetorix, to spare one town from this policy of destruction because it was thought to be impregnable. It was a place called Avaricum, a large town of the Bituriges which was almost completely surrounded by a river and marshes. Caesar decided to attack. If we could capture such a stronghold it offered the chance of booty and supplies, to say nothing of the effect on the morale of the enemy. We hoped also that Vercingetorix might be induced to offer battle in order to draw off our legions from the siege.

On reconnoitring the land around the town we found that there was a narrow gap in the marshes where we were able to pitch camp. The walls of the fort had been built in the usual manner of the Gauls who are very skilful at this. They construct great box frames of timber which are fastened together and then faced with heavy dressed stone presenting a smooth and impenetrable barrier. The timber frames are filled with tightly packed rubble which it is impossible to knock down with a battering ram. The only solution was to build a terrace so that our men could scale the walls. Caesar gave orders accordingly.

For the next few weeks the legionaries worked in terrible conditions to construct the platform. On most days it rained. The ground became sodden, forcing us to build timber rafts on which we pitched our tents. The tracks from our camp to the walls of the town turned into a morass of mud. We built causeways of stone and logs to provide a road along which the legionaries brought tree trunks in wagons from the forest. These were then laid on the ground a little distance from the base of the wall and parallel to it. The next layer of trunks was laid at right angles on top of the first layer and so on, until an enormous terrace had been raised to a height of eighty feet and a length of some three hundred and thirty feet. To protect the men constructing the platform there were wooden sheds covered in hides. These long covered passages ran up to the base of the platform and were also placed on top to shelter the legionaries who were building the next layer. On the far side from the town walls, the platform rose in a series of steps so that when the time came to attack a large number of men would be able to reach the top together. On the ground we mounted catapults which maintained a continuous fire of bolts and arrows at the top of the wall. Nevertheless the Gauls were still able to shoot arrows and hurl spears at our men. They threw down rocks which tore the hides of the covered ways and poured boiling pitch into the tunnels which we had dug towards the walls in an attempt to undermine them.

To make matters more difficult the Gauls had erected towers at regular intervals along the walls. These were furnished with platforms protected by hides. From these more projectiles were fired down on our men who sometimes could only approach the terrace by locking their shields together above their heads. Although we suffered few fatalities many legionaries received burns or were wounded by arrows in the arms or legs. At night the work continued. The carts led by torch bearers lurched along the causeway bringing the next loads of timber. The horses neighed and reared under the lash of whips as their drivers urged them forward. The camp was filled with the sounds of hammering and sawing as men fashioned timber for the covered passages or made props for the subterranean galleries. Others winched more logs into position on the terrace. Arrows hissed from the catapults towards the enemy's towers. Burning brands and braziers smoked in the damp atmosphere. Men coughed and swore. Occasionally a shout or scream came out of the dark. Men would run forward with a stretcher in case the wounded man could not walk. On top of the terrace heavily armed legionaries waited in the sheds to repel any attack which might be launched from the wall on the men laying the timbers. Below, the mud clogged everything. Horses and wagons became stuck in it. Men shouted for assistance. Every night through all of this Caesar supervised, cajoled, encouraged and advised. He walked about in his red cloak splashed with mud. Wearing no helmet, a shield-bearer protected him when he was within range of the defenders' missiles. He took trouble to talk to the legionaries as they worked, praising their resolution and making sure that each man felt himself valued. Many of the centurions he knew by name. Sometimes he would carry a vinestick, the badge of a centurion, which he found useful when making a point or to indicate something. If a man had acted with great bravery in a battle or at a siege, Caesar liked to decorate him there and then in front of his fellows. The award might take the form of a torc suspended from a shoulder strap, a medallion worn on the chest, a bracelet or even the oak-leaved corona civica. These Caesar would present with a short speech praising the man's achievements.

One night a chief centurion called Junius Strabo, in charge of the guard on top of the terrace, was brought down with an arrow in his neck. The men who carried him said that he had been hit while dragging to safety a legionary who was lying unconscious after a rock thrown from one of the defenders' towers had struck him on the head. Despite

258

a hail of arrows Strabo had rushed forward and had been wounded as he pulled the man back to the shelter of the covered passage. The surgeon pulled the arrow from his neck. For a few minutes he regained consciousness as he lay on the table in the dim glow of the oil lamps which lit the tent. On hearing the news, Caesar hurried over and was able to speak to Strabo before he lapsed again into unconsciousness. He died with Caesar clasping his hand. When Caesar rejoined me a few minutes later at the command post I saw that he had been weeping. He muttered something about finding the death of brave men hard to bear and then hurried off to inspect progress on two towers which were being built to mount on the terrace.

Caesar himself was physically brave and he admired this quality in others above all else. He knew that the battlefield produced two kinds of courage. There was the man who without thought or out of instinctive aggression performed some act of valour, risking his own life in the process. But there was another kind of bravery; that of the man who pauses, realises the mortal danger to himself, and then overcoming his fear goes through with an act to rescue his comrade. Junius Strabo was such a man. When the seventh legion was surrounded by cavalry and chariots while fetching corn during the first invasion of Britannia, it was Strabo who had rallied the men by refusing to retreat and calling on them to stand firm until Caesar arrived with reinforcements.

The following morning, which for once was fine, the seventh were drawn up in their ranks outside the camp. The circular war trumpets sounded the order for silence. Then six men from the first century of the first cohort carried Strabo on a litter up and down the files so that each man might see him and pay his last respects. In front of the camp gates a pyre had been built beside which Caesar waited with the legates and military tribunes. He wore full uniform with his scarlet cloak and the oak-leaved wreath of the corona civica on his head. The men bearing the litter came forward and placed Strabo on the pyre. Not a word had been spoken and nobody moved until Caesar stepped forward.

I had thought that he would make a short speech praising Strabo's life and achievements. Indeed I think that this was what Caesar intended but he could not bring himself to speak. Instead, he suddenly removed the wreath from his own head, stepped up to the pyre and placed it on the head of the dead man. Then he bent forward and kissed Strabo on the forehead before stepping back and raising his right hand in salute. Behind him the whole legion raised their hands as Caesar had done and chanted, 'Strabo! Strabo! Strabo!' A torch bearer lit the pyre and the flames leapt up into the morning sun.

This was a hard time for the legionaries. The incessant rain meant that they were often damp and cold. Many had fallen ill. There was a serious shortage of food. Vercingetorix had made no attempt to attack us during the siege but had pitched camp a few miles away. From here he maintained a close watch, particularly on the foraging parties. We tried to vary the routes, times and places of the outings. We strengthened the escorts and on many occasions beat off attacks from the enemy's horse. Nevertheless Vercingetorix had his spies everywhere and many parties were ambushed. The situation improved a little when a herd of cattle was discovered. We were able to drive them in and slaughter them before the Gauls realised that we had found them. At one point Caesar even contemplated raising the siege but the troops clamoured to be allowed to finish what they had started. Their dignity required it.

Not long after the death of Strabo when the terrace was almost complete, we were watching as the men worked through the night to prepare for the assault on the walls. The Gauls had sensed that the attack was imminent. They saw the two towers in position on the terrace, placed there so that our men could rush out from gangways which would be dropped down onto the top of the wall. Suddenly we saw smoke rising from the terrace. The defenders, who were skilled miners of the iron ore found in their territory, had dug tunnels under the terrace and were now setting light to the beams and straw which would fall in, undermining the ground upon which the terrace stood. At the same time Gauls rushed out from the gates in the wall on either side of our towers, flinging burning torches and pitch onto the terrace itself which was engulfed in flames and smoke. Soon the covered sheds which protected the soldiers were alight. Men choked and spluttered in the oily fumes, groping forward to rescue others who had been caught in the first onslaught. Caesar, however, had foreseen that such an attack might take place. Two legions were held perpetually in readiness just back from the siege operation. Men from these now came forward quickly to operate a system of pulleys and buckets with which water was carried to the surface of the terrace. Others began to douse the fires at the base, using water from two lagoons which we had constructed nearby in the marshy ground.

I led a cohort from the eighth legion up the steps at the rear of the terrace. At first it was impossible to see anything or to know what orders to give. I sent men forward under the cover of their interlocked shields to pull back our towers and prevent them being captured and destroyed. Others worked to douse the fires which had sprung up everywhere. I tore a strip of cloth from my legging and soaked it in a bucket before tying it round my mouth to avoid inhaling too much smoke. Many did the same. Wounded men were carried back down the steps while others scrambled up to replace them. Meanwhile the defenders continued to fire arrows down from their towers and to hurl burning pitch,

261

causing many injuries. We witnessed great acts of bravery by the Gauls who knew that they must destroy the terrace or lose their town and probably their lives.

In the archway of one of the gates from which they had rushed out we saw a man silhouetted against the fires and smoke billowing around him. A line of men behind was passing up lumps of burning tallow and pitch which he then tossed onto the flaming terrace a few yards away. I instructed a legionary to train his catapult on the man and in a few moments he was struck by a bolt and fell dead. Immediately another took his place, making no attempt to protect himself by a shield or otherwise. The legionary took careful aim and felled him with his first shot. A third man stepped forward, pulled away the two prostrate bodies and began to throw the tallow and pitch as the others had done. He too was killed by a bolt which struck him in the chest with such force that he was knocked backwards several yards. This ritual dance of death on the little stage framed by the gateway continued for some time as man after man sacrificed himself.

Gradually we brought the fires under control and resumed possession of the terrace. It had been a fierce struggle which lasted until nearly first light. The Gauls had poured hundreds of men onto the walls in a vain attempt to throw us back and re-ignite the fires.

After this the defenders seemed to lose heart and one morning we noted that their guards were not well posted. It was raining heavily which made it difficult for their lookouts to see what was happening. The legionaries assembled at the foot of the terrace out of sight. At the given signal they rushed up to the top where one of the towers was rolled forward and men scrambled across onto the wall almost before the Gauls could raise the alarm. The sentries were soon dislodged and our men ran round to occupy the entire circuit of the wall. The siege had lasted several weeks. The

262

egionaries had suffered great privations with many deaths
and injuries. When they came down into the town itself they
spared neither man, woman nor child. A few escaped to tell
the tale to Vercingetorix in his camp a few miles away. The
rest were put to the sword. The stench of blood mingled
with the rain. The streets were filled with corpses where the
water ran red as the shortswords of the legionaries did their
deadly work amidst the screams. The fury of the troops was
frightening and seemed to feed upon itself. Some men, half
starved over the previous weeks, crammed bread and other
food into their mouths as they worked. Then they slaked
their thirst on wine. By the end of that day many lay in a
drunken stupor amongst the corpses of their victims. Thus
the siege of Avaricum ended and with it the lives of nearly
forty thousand people.

The rebellion, however, continued to spread. The destruction of Avaricum had convinced the tribal chiefs that a
scorched earth policy gave them the best hope of defeating
us. Vercingetorix summoned contingents of cavalry and
infantry from all Gaul. A great council was held at Bibracte,
where he was appointed commander-in-chief. As we
marched towards the territory of the Sequani, he dared to
attack us. We immediately formed a hollow square with the
baggage train inside. Then our German cavalry, reinforced
by lightly-armed men trained to run alongside the mounted
troops, counter-attacked, chasing the enemy horse down to
a river and massacring them in great numbers. This bloody
repulse caused Vercingetorix to make a fatal mistake. He
retreated to the stronghold of Alesia and shut himself up
there with his army.

It was late afternoon when we pitched camp on a hill
which looked across to the town of Alesia, perched on a hill
of similar height on the other side of a narrow valley. Caesar
decided to reconnoitre immediately. Labienus, Trebonius,
Marcus Antonius and I went with him. We saw that it would

be impossible to storm the town itself. On the south side of the hill there rose some sheer cliffs and the remaining sides were steep with strong fortifications. We observed, however, that to the north and south of the hill there flowed two streams which looked adequate to flood ditches. To the west, still flanked by the streams lay a large area of fairly flat, low-lying land. The eastern slope of the hill was occupied by a camp crowded with Gallic troops. As we re-climbed the hill to our own camp Caesar gave orders for a council of war to be held that evening.

After the fortifications had been completed and the sentries posted, the senior officers gathered. There must have been about forty of us including seven or eight legates, some military tribunes and the senior centurions from each legion. As usual Caesar was calm and analytical but I could tell that he was also exhilarated at the prospect of bringing Vercingetorix to bay. The faces of the centurions were in shadow as they watched and listened to their general. Most of them had been with Caesar since the beginning and had belonged or still served with the seventh, eighth, ninth or tenth legions. Some had transferred to the more recently recruited legions to provide experienced leadership. Most knew each other as old friends while preserving a healthy spirit of rivalry, for each legion sought to outdo the others in valour and hardiness. Make no mistake; these men were the bravest of the brave and the toughest of the tough. Almost all were tall and well built; others had worked their way to the position of first spearman by the sheer force of their personality or their courage in the heat of battle. These were men who knew their business. They came quietly and squatted on the ground or sat on benches in front of the dais which had been set up for Caesar. He joshed with a few of them before he began to speak.

'On the hill over there to the north of us lies Vercingetorix with his army of about eighty thousand men. He has

264

taken over the town of the Mandubii called Alesia. It seems that he and his chieftains have been thoroughly frightened by the recent victories of our cavalry over his. Now I believe is our chance to bring his rebellion to an end. If we can defeat Vercingetorix here it is certain that the rest of Gaul will recognise the supremacy of our arms and the conquest of the country will be virtually complete. But we must not repeat the mistake of Gergovia where our men in their enthusiasm for glory tried to achieve the impossible. Instead we shall besiege the town and starve Vercingetorix and his henchmen into submission. This will require fortifications round the whole of the hill upon which the town stands, a distance of about ten miles. We shall dig a trench of a width of twenty feet first. Set back about four hundred paces from that inner trench and depending on the lie of the land we shall dig two more trenches of a depth of about fifteen feet. You may have seen that two streams flow to the north and south of the hill. We shall divert these to flood as much as possible of the inner trench. Behind these trenches will be the palisade and rampart with large forked branches of trees projecting from it to hinder the enemy in any assault. At the moment our camps lie to the south of the town. Tomorrow each legion will receive orders to set up camp on one of the main hills surrounding Alesia itself. These camps will be placed immediately behind our lines of fortification which will have redoubts and towers at regular intervals along the line of the rampart.'

An experienced centurion of the tenth stood to ask Caesar whether he anticipated that the Gauls would send a relieving force. Surely such a wily campaigner as Vercingetorix would not have led his army into this position without considering the consequences.

'At the moment,' replied Caesar, 'we have no information about this but I agree that it is very possible that he will ask his allies to march to his assistance. If that happens we shall have to construct a line of fortifications facing outwards, using the terrain to make sure that any relieving force has to attack from below. That is why our camps will be pitched on the high ground surrounding the town.'

'We can do this,' remarked Marcus Antonius, 'except in two places. On the plain to the west where the ground you can see is level. There is also a large hill lying to the north of Alesia. From here it is not visible but we rode over it when we surveyed the area before sundown. I think this hill is too big to include within the circuit of any outer fortification which means that our men would be forced to defend any assault from attackers on higher ground.'

The appearance of Marcus contrasted sharply with the centurions. His craggy face was framed by a mane of long gingery hair combed back loosely over the nape of his neck. He had a louche look about him and it was said that he could seduce high-born women faster than any other aristocrat in Rome. Nevertheless he was brave and Caesar often sent for him to inspire the troops where the fighting was at its thickest. The men respected and secretly perhaps admired his easy-going outlook. He never worried about anything very much, including his own safety. In the end, of course, he fell prey to the good life and that woman Cleopatra. I haven't seen him for years. They tell me he has grown indolent and self-indulgent in her company.

The next day Caesar set up his command post on high ground with a good view over the whole area. We watched as the legions deployed to their new positions and the work of digging the trenches began. At the same time foraging parties were sent far and wide in search of provisions for both men and horses. The foraging occupied a large number of legionaries and Vercingetorix was not slow to observe that at any given time the fortifications were undermanned. He sent out sorties from the town to make simultaneous attacks at different points as the legionaries worked. So far

266

as I can remember we had about forty-five thousand men at Alesia and in addition there were the units of Gallic and German cavalry. The lines of fortification were so long however that it was difficult to defend these against sudden attack. Caesar therefore decided that we would construct traps in front of the two ditches and rampart to slow down the advance of any assault. To this end the legionaries dug five more trenches just beyond the flooded trench. Into each of these new trenches, which were five feet deep, were fastened the trunks of trees whose branches had been sharpened to present an entanglement of wooden daggers to any would-be attacker. Beyond this we dug rows of pits in quincunx formation. From each pit there projected a few inches above the ground a sharp wooden spike, hardened by fire and surrounded by brush and twigs to disguise its presence and the pits themselves. We called these lilies after their resemblance to the flower when viewed from the ramparts. Beyond the lilies we sank blocks of wood into the ground. Each block had attached to it an iron hook and these were strewn thickly over a wide area. The effect of the new hazards was to make it possible for a relatively small number of men to hold the lines of fortification until reinforcements arrived.

One night before our fortifications were complete Vercingetorix sent away all his cavalry. We captured a few and brought them in for questioning. Caesar had one or two of them crucified on a hilltop where they could be seen from the besieged town. This persuaded other prisoners to tell us that they had instructions to ride to all parts of Gaul with a message from their commander asking the chiefs of the allies to muster a relieving army. On hearing this we lost no time in constructing an outer line of defences similar to those around the town itself. The length of these fortifications was about fourteen miles, inside which lay our camps and redoubts. In anticipation of the arrival of the relieving army Caesar instructed each man to provide himself with supplies of corn and fodder to last a month.

About two weeks after the siege had begun I was observing the scene from our command post when I saw the gates of the town open. Hundreds of people emerged onto the eastern slopes of the hill where the Gallic camp had been before the soldiers had withdrawn behind the walls of Alesia itself. These people wandered aimlessly about on the hillside. Some made their way down towards our lines. I called for my horse and rode down to the ramparts. I climbed up one of the towers where a couple of legionaries were keeping watch over the stretch of ground, now lined with trenches and traps, lying between us and the flooded inner trench. On the far side lingered about twenty or thirty people, all either very old men or women and children. There were no men of fighting age among them.

One of the legionaries told me that they had been shouting and gesturing towards our fortifications. From what we could understand it was evident that they wished to hand themselves over to us. We guessed that Vercingetorix was probably running short of food and had decided to throw out of the town all the non-combatants and thereby preserve his supplies for the fighting men. Caesar gave orders that under no circumstances were the people of the town to be allowed through our lines or to be fed. Before the order had been circulated one soldier of the eighth was discovered throwing bread to a woman and her child. He was tied to a wooden frame and given fifteen lashes for breach of discipline.

Once they discovered that our soldiers would offer no assistance many of the women climbed up to the walls of the town and implored the Gauls to let them back in. Most of those ejected were actually citizens of Alesia who now found themselves trapped and left to starve. Caesar knew that the sight of their own womenfolk and children dying would

268

undermine the authority of Vercingetorix over his soldiers. He had no intention of easing this problem for his enemy. As night fell they began to huddle together in groups seeking such shelter as there was on the open slopes of the hillside. Somebody found a spring and we saw fights break out as women and old men fought to get a handful of the water for themselves or their children. Most had plenty of clothing but they were already thin from lack of food. In the dark the sentries could hear the whimpers of hungry and thirsty children until eventually all fell silent. In the morning we saw a number of lifeless figures on the ground, some very small with mothers crouching over them, others of old men who had succumbed to thirst or cold.

During the day that followed there was less movement. Nobody climbed the hill to the walls of the town. Nobody came to our fortifications. Either they had no strength to move or they tried to conserve such energy as they had. Most lay down on the ground, shielding their faces from the sun. I saw one or two women with babies who were trying to suckle from empty breasts. Late in the afternoon there was a shower of rain and we watched as they cupped their hands trying to catch the drops, for they had no bowls or goblets to use. It turned cool and the night brought many more deaths. The hillside became littered with corpses or people who were too weak to move. One or two children stood motionless over the bodies of their mothers hunched up in death. A woman approached the inner trench holding a small child in her arms. She pleaded with the legionaries to take it but they simply stared back at her across the divide, saying nothing. She produced a knife and made a stabbing motion towards the child who seemed to be either asleep or unconscious. She repeated the gesture three or four times in the forlorn hope that the legionaries would have pity on her and take in the baby. At last she realised that it was useless. She let out a scream and plunged the knife into the

269

child's stomach upwards to its heart. Then she laid the bod
on the ground and thrust the knife into her own belly.

Others simply died of exposure or thirst, until one morn
ing we could see no more movement on the hillside. It ha
become a great open grave of rotting corpses, the stench c
which reached our camps when the wind blew.

We continued to strengthen our fortifications. Our cavalr
units were reporting the approach of as many as two hur
dred and fifty thousand men and about eight thousan
horse which had been assembling in the country of th
Aedui. Caesar let it be known that the relieving army was o
its way. This encouraged the legionaries in the digging c
the ditches and construction of ramparts to keep them ou
The vast numbers of the approaching enemy were nc
circulated in order not to lower morale. Caesar believed tha
the troops inside Alesia must be near to starvation and coul
not hold out for much longer. If we could maintain th
pressure, they might crack before the relieving army arrivec
Above all Caesar wanted Vercingetorix, dead or alive. 'If
have Vercingetorix, I have Gaul,' he muttered more tha
once.

Nevertheless, the besieged had shown no sign of surren
der when the Gallic allies finally arrived and pitched cam
on a hill overlooking the plain to the west of the town. Tha
night as I looked out at their watchfires it reminded me o
the eve of the battle of Tigranocerta. Not since that grea
triumph under Lucullus had I seen so many enemy assem
bled to challenge a Roman army, one that was now threa
ened not only from the front but from Vercingetorix as wel
in the rear. When the besieged had seen the arrival of thei
allies a great shout had gone up from the town in antic
pation of their deliverance.

'We shall have a hot few days, my friend,' said Caesar
placing a hand on my shoulder and looking out with m
across the plain. 'But I am confident we can defeat the allies

he legionaries are well rested, the fortifications are good nd though they outnumber us many times, the Gauls will ever cooperate well enough to be able to deploy that umber of men effectively.'

'Suppose they sit down and attempt to starve us out, just s we are starving out Vercingetorix?'

'If necessary, we will break out and march away. Our avalry can defeat theirs and they will not dare to attack the egions in open battle. They have been beaten too often to elish that idea. Too many Gauls have felt this slide into heir guts.' He tapped the shortsword at his side. 'Let's get ome sleep. Tomorrow and the following days will be long nes.'

As Caesar had predicted, the fighting over the next days as fierce. The Gauls deployed a large force of cavalry on he plain in which light armed infantry were mingled with nany archers. When our own cavalry attacked they were at rst thrown into confusion by the slingshot and arrows of he enemy. At length however, our German cavalry re-ormed, charged and put the enemy to rout. The battle was atched from the surrounding hills by us and the Gauls like. Each army cheered on its own side and it felt as hough we were back in the Circus Maximus at Rome atching gladiators, except that this was a contest between housands, not hundreds.

One night the Gauls launched from the plain a great ssault upon our western fortifications. At the same time the orces of Vercingetorix rallied out of the town and threw arth and fascines into the inner ditch, clambered across nd pressed hard at our fortifications. Now the traps that we ad laid came into their own. In the darkness the attackers ecame entangled in the branches of the trees, they impaled hemselves on the 'lilies' as they fell into the pits and got aught on the hooks which were scattered everywhere. The egionaries in the towers threw down burning torches on the

271

attackers which both injured them and lit the scene. As the
Gauls struggled to free themselves our men threw heavy
spears at easy targets. Meanwhile Marcus Antonius was strug
gling to hold the outer line against determined and
repeated assaults from the enemy. They came on in wave
after wave at the rampart, scrambling over fallen comrade
impaled on the tree branches and grappling hand to hand
with the legionaries. In the darkness and confusion some o
the enemy got through our lines, but they were not enough
and Gaius Trebonius soon cut them down with a flank attack
from a redoubt manned by two cohorts of the twelfth legion

The battle raged on until dawn when quite suddenly the
enemy fell back. Seeing this the men commanded by Vercin
getorix became discouraged and retreated to the town
Antonius and Trebonius did not let their men rest. Immedi
ately they were put to work to repair the damaged fortifica
tions and to clear out trenches where the Gauls had filled
them. Caesar then addressed the cohorts which had taken
part in the battle, congratulating them on their victory and
distributing medallions and torcs for bravery.

A few days later came the climax. The Gauls had observed
the unfavourable position of our defences to the north o
the town where the great sweep of the hill had made i
impossible to include it within the fortifications. We had
been obliged to pitch our camp on a slope which favoured
the attackers from outside. Having observed this, a relative
of Vercingetorix, a certain Vercassivellaunus, had led a force
of about sixty thousand men around the hill during the
night and concealed them ready to attack on the following
day. So concerned was Caesar about the vulnerability of the
position that he had garrisoned the camp with two full
legions under the command of experienced men, Gaius
Reginus and Gaius Rebilus. The enemy assault was launched
with the greatest ferocity. Our men struggled to hold the

ine as the attackers had the advantage not only of the slope out also numbers. They flung earth and fascines over the litches and traps. As fast as our men could strike down hose storming the ramparts they were replaced by others. The Gauls advanced with shields above their heads in wave fter wave. The legionaries began to tire and run short of veapons. Titus Labienus moved up with six cohorts to elieve the defenders and was able to stabilise the situation. Meanwhile, however, attacks were launched upon our lines t every point where the enemy perceived them to be veakest. Simultaneously Vercingetorix sent his men in every lirection where they could lend support from the inside nd engage the troops defending the siege lines. The whole rmy was fighting to keep Vercingetorix in and the Gallic llies out.

Caesar sensed that this was the final roll of the dice by the enemy. From our command post high above the valley he ssued orders via gallopers who rode away helter-skelter lown the hill to deliver instructions to cohorts or cavalry to nove this way or that, wherever the pressure seemed great-st. Then, wearing his scarlet cloak and as usual without a nelmet so that the legionaries might recognise him at a listance, he set off round the lines with his staff. We rode rom redoubt to redoubt, from camp to camp, up to the ines, past troops waiting for orders to manoeuvre, through ield stations where the wounded and dying were being reated. Sometimes we stopped to talk to legates, tribunes or centurions as they gave their reports. Occasionally a galloper vould arrive and Caesar would listen intently while he spoke, hen issue sharp orders. The pressure on the fortifications vas intense for the Gauls were throwing everything at us, not hesitating to sacrifice any number of men. The noise of vattle came from both sides, the dull clang of metal on netal, the screams of the wounded and the shouted orders.

Fires burnt everywhere and smoke drifted across the land scape, horses reared and legionaries ran to man the ram parts and towers as another attack came in.

Near the palisades you could hear the slap of catapult fired down by legionaries stationed on the platforms of the towers and the thump of spears and arrows hitting the timber of the fortifications, the shafts quivering under the force of the impact. The veterans went about their business with calm efficiency, waiting for the enemy to close within throwing distance before loosing off their javelins, making sure that each front line man was kept supplied with missiles never looking back to see what was happening behind them only to the front to watch the enemy. There was hardly any talking and no shouting. Each man knew his task. Only the centurions barked the occasional order.

The newly recruited legions from Cisalpine Gaul were less assured. Many had never fought at such close quarter before. Some were alarmed by the sounds of battle behind them, wondering if their comrades were protecting their backs. The centurions had to work harder with these younger soldiers, cajoling and encouraging them, occasion ally administering a sharp blow with their vinestick to any man who was slow about his business. In some places where the attackers had actually reached the breastwork on top of the rampart the legionaries had drawn their shortsword and were skewering Gauls as they came through broken palisades. Then men would move up swiftly with lengths of timber to repair the breach while others covered them with volleys of javelins or arrows. There was no respite. The Gauls seemed to have infinite supplies of men who sought desper ately to scale or break down the defences, despite the pressure of thousands of their comrades lying dead or wounded.

Through all this chaos, confusion, smoke and noise Caesar sat his horse. In between listening to reports and

274

despatching gallopers with orders, he found time to encourage his men, praising acts of bravery, hailing centurions he knew by name. Often as we reached a redoubt or a tower along the line of fortifications the men raised a cheer at the sight of his familiar cloak. Such was his reputation for invincibility by this time that the soldiers knew that so long as he led them the day would be theirs, however hard the fight.

Towards the middle of the afternoon a message arrived from Labienus defending the camp on the hillside. The Gauls were sending in one attack after another and he doubted the capacity of his troops to resist for much longer. He had managed to obtain some reinforcements of infantry from nearby redoubts. Now he asked for more and some cavalry to take the enemy in the rear. Caesar collected four cohorts and set off with these and a few horse. He ordered me to follow as quickly as possible with more cavalry which I assembled from units supporting Marcus Antonius in the plain. We picked our way as quickly as we could over ground strewn with tents, lengths of timber, artillery, forges for beating metal, supplies of corn and forage, field stations, wagons and all the other impedimenta of war. At a gate designed for the purpose we passed through our outer fortifications and put on speed for the hill. There we saw Caesar and Labienus with their cohorts already in the thick of it. I gathered my force of cavalry, perhaps two thousand strong, and we charged down the slope strung out in a line, galloping towards the backs of the Gauls. The men held their stabbing spears parallel with the ground, shouting encouragement to one another as we closed. I braced myself for the impact, feeling a mixture of exhilaration and fear. I picked out a target, a man wearing a blue cloak and a dark-coloured helmet. The Gauls saw us coming and realised that they were under attack from the rear as well from Caesar's men who had drawn their swords and were fighting hand to hand on the ramparts. At our headlong approach the enemy panicked and began to flee in all directions. My men slewed their horses round in pursuit, stabbing Gauls in the back as they ran away or trampling over them and then skewering them to the ground. Caesar and Labienus sent their legionaries after the fugitives and there was a general slaughter, which would have been greater if our infantry had not been so exhausted by the fighting which had gone before. In the confusion I lost my Gaul with the blue cloak but my sword was not idle. I had cut down several of the enemy before my horse went lame and I was obliged to dismount.

Very few escaped. Vercassivellaunus himself was captured together with many of the enemy's standards. The besieged in the town, seeing what had happened, recalled their troops from the entrenchments and retreated to their fortress. By midnight our cavalry had caught up with the allied army which had fled from their camps on seeing this latest defeat for their forces. Many were captured or killed; the rest got away and dispersed to their homes in various parts of Gaul. Our victory was complete.

The following day a deputation from the besieged town was let through the lines. The envoys confirmed that Vercingetorix wished to surrender and place himself at Caesar's disposal. Caesar gave orders that the commander-in-chief and his principal lieutenants be brought before him. A platform was set up in front of our headquarters. Seats were placed upon it for Caesar and the generals, with a canopy erected over the whole. The legions paraded in front of the camp on either side of a stretch of open ground leading up to the praetorian gate outside which the platform had been placed. After a short interval Vercingetorix and about a dozen of his chieftains emerged on horseback from the gates of Alesia and rode down the hill, through our fortifications and up onto the roadway lined by legionaries who stood watching silently. As they breasted the roadway they were joined by a squadron of our German cavalry who rode on each side and behind the Gauls. When they had reached a point about three hundred paces from the platform the leader of the German cavalry motioned to the Gauls to stop. He spoke to Vercingetorix who alone dismounted from his horse and began to walk towards us. He wore a heavy cloak of fur but no helmet or other armour. His long hair hung limply and uncombed over his shoulders. I thought that I detected a slight limp which he was trying to disguise and once he stumbled as he walked up the slope. When he came closer I could see that his face had lost the bloom of youth that I remembered from only a few years before. Now his features were drawn and emaciated, his eyes a little blood-shot and he had assumed a skeletal appearance. In front of the platform he paused, unbuckled his sword belt and then laid the sword itself on the ground in front of Caesar as a token of surrender. It was longer than a Roman sword with a leather-bound hilt round which a golden snake was entwined. The crosspiece was encrusted with jewels. After Caesar's murder, Calpurnia gave it to me and it hangs still on the wall of the atrium here at Baiae.

Caesar motioned Vercingetorix forward and asked him if he had instructed all his forces to surrender. Vercingetorix then confirmed that all forces under his command had orders to surrender but that he could not speak for the rest of Gaul. 'I am surprised,' said Caesar, 'that you have allowed yourself to come before me alive. A Roman general in your position would have fallen upon his sword.'

'That,' said Vercingetorix with a hint of anger in his voice, 'would be the easy escape. I prefer to be scourged and crucified by you as a punishment for the suffering which I have brought upon my people. In that way I can atone a little for my failure to throw off the Roman yoke from my country.'

'You are much mistaken,' replied Caesar, 'if you suppose

that I am going to have you executed here and now. You will wait to die until after I have celebrated the conquest of long-haired Gaul with a great triumph in Rome. There you will be led in the procession, shackled to the back of a chariot so that the people can see you. Afterwards you will be taken down into the Tullianum prison and strangled. Meanwhile I shall take good care that you live and have plenty of time to repent of your rebellion.'

So Vercingetorix was placed in an iron cage on a wagon and taken from place to place as we moved about the country. Eventually he was sent with other prisoners to Italy and held there for display at Caesar's triumph six years later. The soldiers of his army were distributed as slaves among the legionaries, one being allotted to each man, apart from some from the tribes of the Aedui and Arverni whom Caesar hoped to use to regain the allegiance of those people.

Chapter XVI

51 BC

The following year, the consulship of Marcus Marcellus and Sulpicius Rufus, witnessed an incident which I shall never forget. In the far south-west of Gaul lay a town called Uxellodunum. It was situated on top of a hill surrounded by precipitous cliffs at the base of which ran a great river encircling the hill on three sides. After a bloody siege we forced some rebels, who had holed up in the fortress, to surrender, by cutting off a spring which supplied the town with water. The number of rebels was not significant, but Caesar was conscious that his command in Gaul was about to expire and it was imperative that the whole country be reduced to submission before his final departure. He decided to make an example of them.

The legionaries were ordered to go into the fortress and to bring every single man down unharmed to the plain beside the river where one of our camps lay. The prisoners were then shackled in groups of ten, surrounded by armed legionaries so that there was no possibility of escape. They had been stripped of their arms and for the most part wore only short-sleeved tunics for the weather was warm. I estimated their numbers at about two thousand. They watched as a row of tree stumps was set up. Behind stood the army's field surgeons and their assistants who tore strips of cloth into lengths of about a man's arm. A low moan went through the mass of shackled Gauls as they realised that some kind of mutilation was about to take place. I saw many men visibly shaking with fear, some fell to the ground in a faint while most stood with heads bowed awaiting their fate. Then the first groups were ordered to shuffle forward towards the row of tree stumps beside each of which stood a man with a heavy axe. Next to each group stood legionaries with drawn swords. One by one the Gauls were unshackled and shoved forward to the tree stumps. There they were forced to their knees and ordered at sword point to place their hands together upon the surface of the stump. The axes rose and fell as each man in turn had his hands cut off at the wrist. Sometimes both hands were severed at one blow, at others it took two or more strikes. After each amputation was completed the man was lifted to his feet and propelled to a table where the stumps of his arms were bound with the cloth that the surgeons had prepared. He was then sent on his way. At intervals the axemen were relieved and replaced by others with fresh arms.

I have taken part in many battles, I have witnessed many executions and with my sword I have killed many men. I have watched thousands of bloated corpses floating down the Rhine like so many dead fish. I was present at the execution of the Catilinarian conspirators in the Tullianum and I have watched as men were scourged and then crucified. I am used to the sight of blood and death; no one who has served in a Roman army could be otherwise. I had never seen anything such as took place that sunny morning by the banks of the river. In no time the tree stumps were dripping with blood as it spurted from the severed wrists of the prisoners, some of whom either died or fainted under the blows of the axes. One or two refused to place their hands on the tree stumps or were so hysterical with fear that they lost all control of themselves. They were either stabbed in the side as they knelt or their hands were forced down onto the wood now impregnated with gore. Many collapsed and died after their stumps had been bound. Most staggered away to where their womenfolk and children were waiting for them. The latter's screams and wailing filled the air as the men emerged through the line of legionaries surrounding them. When the butchery was over the ground was strewn with hundreds of hands; the soil itself was soggy with blood.

So ended the siege of Uxellodunum. Even the hardiest of the veterans had been subdued by the spectacle, but it had the effect which Caesar desired. All Gaul soon knew what had happened and not for many years afterwards did they seek to question the might of Rome. It was an act of the greatest barbarity. Caesar knew this. For the most part he had displayed mercy to his defeated opponents during the long years of campaigning and he showed this quality again during the civil war. On this occasion he judged correctly that his actions would subdue the sporadic rebellions which had broken out even after the defeat of Vercingetorix at Alesia. His ambition was not to be thwarted by a bunch of vagabonds and rebels in an isolated fortress. He never gave them a further thought.

In the days that followed the legionaries were unusually quiet. Caesar had ordered a rest after the forced marches and fierce fighting which accompanied the reduction of Uxellodunum. Nevertheless the usual bustle of the camp obtained. Men crouched over smouldering cooking fires, horses cantered down the principal street and out through the gates to seek forage. Everywhere one heard the beating of metal as the smiths worked the forges to repair armour or make spearheads. One or two groups were playing at dice on the ground. Others simply lounged in the sun. Caesar was dictating correspondence to Balbus in Rome where the political situation was again deteriorating and would soon engage our time. I felt an urge to escape for a few hours from the company of others. Camp life is lived close to one's fellow soldiers. There is no room for privacy. For a short while I wanted to be alone; perhaps the events of the previous week had caused me a subconscious distress which I sought to alleviate by removing myself from its context.

I called for my horse and rode off into the open country. It was a beautiful fresh morning such as I had experienced often back at my beloved Baiae. I took no particular direction, simply letting the horse canter or walk almost as he liked. For a mile or two we followed the course of the great river which flowed past Uxellodunum. We travelled upstream passing between lines of cliffs and hills covered in woods. Above us I could see buzzards, hawks and the occasional eagle, soaring and floating in the warm air as they sought the thermal currents which would carry them effortlessly higher. We came to a little tributary of the river. There was no means of crossing so I turned to follow it into a narrow valley lined with oaks and bushes of pink flowering cistus and yellow broom. Occasionally I caught the scent of thyme when the horse's hooves crushed it underfoot. The ground rose gently and we slowed to walking pace. The horse lingered to crop the lush grass by the stream. A short distance ahead I saw a pool with a sunny bank on which I could sit for a while. But I stopped short. Someone had preceded me. I could make out the figure of a woman who was squatting by the water, cupping her hands and taking sips. As I watched a small child came from behind some bushes down the bank and sat by the woman.

I slipped off my horse, judging that I would be less threatening on foot, and began to walk slowly towards the pair who had not seen me. Even now I can remember the frisson of delight that ran through me when I first caught sight of this woman, so utterly unexpected. As I came nearer I could see that she was slim with almost white hair hanging down her back. The child was a boy whom I judged to be about five or six years old. As they finished drinking, the woman rose to her feet. I saw that she was tall with a dress that reached to her ankles. She wore a shawl that was held by a clasp at the shoulder. Seeing me, she immediately grabbed hold of the boy's hand in a gesture of protection but made no attempt to run away. I raised my arm in what I hoped was a friendly manner and smiled. As I came closer the boy crept round the back of his mother's legs and clung to the folds of her dress. She did not move, watching me warily out of the bluest eyes that I had ever seen. Her face had a classical beauty with a pale skin which contrasted sharply with the blue eyes and the pinkness of her lips. About her there was an aristocratic air which resembled that of the great patrician ladies of Rome, except that she was younger and the white hair gave her a Germanic appearance. She reminded me of Domitia when we were young. I let go the reins of the horse who put his head down to munch the grass. I moved a little nearer, still smiling and trying to appear friendly. The sight of this woman had aroused in me feelings which I had not experienced since I had had my fling with Fulvia before we went to Spain. I felt an intense desire to make contact. I spoke a few words in Latin which she did not understand. I took a step forward and suddenly she spat at me. It was so unexpected that I let out a little laugh. Evidently she thought that I was about to rape her. To try to show that this was not my intention I sat down on the grass. The little boy came out from behind his mother's legs and watched me for a moment. I could see that he was fascinated by the dagger which was fastened to my sword belt. The sheath was of leather encased in silver latticing. The handle was of polished ivory on top of which sat a lion's head carved also in silver. I took off the belt and laid it on the ground. The boy slipped his mother's hand and came uncertainly forward. I motioned to him and smiled again, inviting him to touch the belt and the weapon. He stroked the handle with his forefinger and then gave a little cry of delight as he saw the lion's head. I doubt that he knew what it was; perhaps he thought that it was a wolf's head. It seemed to please him all the same.

Then I remembered that in my saddlebag my body slaves had placed some cakes made of flour and sweetened with honey. Leaving the boy playing with my sword belt while his mother watched, I walked over to the horse and unbuckled the bag. Still the woman did not move. I had wondered whether there might be other people nearby, yet the place seemed deserted. I sat down again and opened the bag to pull out the cakes. Looking at the woman I gestured to her asking for permission to offer one to the child. For a moment her face softened from the mixture of fear and sullenness which it had assumed. I took this to be consent and handed the cake to the boy. He clasped it with both hands and ate it greedily. I could tell that he was hungry and gave him two more. I looked up at the slim figure with pale hair. She stood motionless, almost like a Greek statue. Her firm breasts showed beneath the worn dress. I sensed rather than saw the long legs which ended in a pair of open sandals tied with thongs. Where had this beautiful woman come from? What in the name of the gods was she doing here alone with a small child? I could not ask her and she could not tell me. I held up a cake and smiled, but she did not react. I knew that if I got up and walked towards her she would probably back away and perhaps spit at me again. I tapped the boy on the shoulder pointing to his mother, then I handed him the cake and pushed him gently towards her. He understood, walked the few steps over to her and placed the cake in her hand. For a moment I thought she would not eat, perhaps even throw the cake into the stream. She looked uncertain. Was she wrestling with her con- science? Could she eat something proffered by a Roman soldier? Then suddenly her hand went to her mouth and the cake was gone. I beckoned to the boy again and gave him another to take to his mother. This time she ate it without hesitation. The trace of a smile came over her face and she inclined her head slightly in what I took to be a gesture of thanks.

There was no more food left in the bag. I cast about for something to detain this woman with whom I longed to communicate yet could not. The horse had wandered down to the stream where he was drinking. I led him back to where I had left the child playing with the sword belt. I pointed to the back of the horse. Would he like to sit on it? He looked at his mother and said something. She replied with one word and a little nod. I picked up the boy and placed him in the saddle. With one hand I steadied the child while with the other I held the reins. We stood there for a few moments as he chattered and laughed with excitement. He began to bounce up and down in the saddle, simulating a rider whose horse was galloping. Then, to my surprise, his mother walked over to us. She held out her hand, clearly asking me to give her the reins, which I did. She placed them in the small boy's hands, talking to him as she did so. She gave the horse a gentle pat on the side of the head and began to lead him very slowly round in a circle. I could see that she was familiar with horses and that the animal understood this. As she led the horse she gave the occasional instruction to the boy, telling him how to sit in the saddle and how to manipulate the reins. When it was over she lifted the child down and I clapped my hands. It sounded a little strange but it was another piece of contact between us. All her movements were graceful, though I noticed that her hands, in contrast to the smooth beauty of her face, were roughened with work, yet without the coarse strength of a peasant woman's fingers. I felt intrigued and attracted to this strange and beautiful figure. I wanted to touch her and to hold her, to stroke the long hair and to feel her body against mine. I wanted to do what any man

285

would do who had been kept from the company of women for so long.

For a little time I played with the boy by the stream while his mother watched. I showed him how to feel under the banks for the fish hiding there. As we paddled in the water I noticed that the woman had sat down on the grass, tucking her knees up under her chin. She had relaxed and even laughed when I took a tumble on a slippery stone and almost went headlong in the water. I pointed to my chest and said 'Lucius,' a couple of times. The boy soon understood and when I pointed to him he said he was called Orgetorix. This set me thinking about the invasion of Gaul by the Helvetii some six years previously. Hundreds of thousands of those people had set off from their Alpine homes and begun a migration westwards in search of better land and pasture. Their movement had threatened the borders of the province. Caesar had ordered them to turn back. When they refused we had pursued them across the river Saône and fought the first great battle in Gaul to defeat them. The Helvetii were then instructed to return to their own country and to rebuild the farms and homesteads which they had destroyed before leaving. I remembered that one of their chieftains had been called Orgetorix. Could this woman and her son be Helvetians, not Gauls? Their appearance suggested that this might be so.

The valley was beginning to fill with shadows. Only the tops of the wooded hills above us were still lit by the sun. I could see no form of habitation. The valley seemed deserted and I wondered where this mother and her son were sleeping. I could offer them no protection. Perhaps there was a man somewhere. Perhaps at any moment he would appear and resume possession of this woman whom I longed to have. I lifted the boy out of the stream where we had been making a dam of stones and clods of earth and led him back to his mother. Smiling I showed them both the saddlebag and by a series of gestures indicated that I would return the following day with more food. I went over to the horse and pulled off the cloth which lay under the saddle. It was not much but I hoped that it might be something in which the boy could wrap himself at night. I had no cloak, otherwise I could have left that. I gave the woman the cloth. She smiled and said something which I could not understand. It was the first time in that afternoon that she had spoken to me. I climbed back on to my horse, gave a wave and said goodbye though I knew they did not understand. When we had gone a few hundred paces I turned in the saddle and looked back up the valley. They were still standing as I had left them. I waved again and Orgetorix waved back with one hand as he held his mother's in the other.

I cannot remember anything of the ride back to the camp. When I reached my tent I ordered a little food and spent the evening by myself. I lay on my couch with a goblet and a flagon of wine. The images of the day flitted before me. It had been a day so different from anything I had experienced in the previous six or seven years. A day without soldiers, without the clamour of a military camp, without the bawdy jokes of the legionaries, without the screams of a wounded man, without bloodshed. I remembered the old days in Rome, playing in the courtyard with my brother where we used to spend hours throwing and catching a little leather ball, as older men do after the baths. Sometimes my father would take us down to the Forum and we would watch the lawyers making their speeches in the open air to the juries of equestrians or senators. A consul accompanied by his lictors might come past on his way to the Senate House. We might go into the Campus Martius to watch the tribes voting in the elections for the magistrates. If we were lucky we would go to the Circus Maximus to see the chariot races. Then there was the villa at Baiae; running in the woods, trapping thrushes, throwing our little wooden spears

287

at anything that moved, rarely hitting. We clambered about on the rocks, swimming and jumping in and out of the sea, lying panting and naked in the sun until we were ready to start again, just as my brother's sons had done in that glorious summer we had spent together there. The day by the stream had reminded me of all this. In my mind's eye I saw that beautiful woman, at first so silent and sullen, holding her son's hand, fearful of the violence to which this Roman soldier would subject her. The slow realisation that it would not happen. I longed for the following day to come, when I would ride out again to find her. Yet I did not want the night to end. The expectation of seeing her again elated me, but I feared even more the thought that she had not understood or even if she had, that she would not be there. The wine at last had its effect and I fell into a heavy sleep.

In the morning I made enquiries about slaves who had been taken prisoner in the campaign against the Helvetii and found that there were several in the service of the eighth legion. I had six or seven of them brought before me and selected one who had learnt passable Latin while with the army. He seemed intelligent and one of the military tribunes, Sergius Flaccus, told me that the man was reliable and that he intended to take him into his own household when the campaign was over. With the slave, whose name was Acco, I set off again for the wooded valley. I had brought with me this time a lot more food together with one of the legionaries' tents and some clothing. The sun shone from a cloudless sky and it was not long before we reached the stream which led up into the valley. I ordered the slave to wait and advanced towards the pool by myself, leading my horse as I had done the day before. When I reached the spot where I had begun building the little dam with Orgeto-rix I sat down. There was nobody there. I heard the occasional call of a bird from the woods above me, otherwise there was silence. I felt sick with disappointment. Surely they had understood me when I said I would come back? They had probably returned to a village nearby where the woman lived with her family. It was ridiculous to suppose that she would have been by herself in that isolated and uninhabited place. I thought of getting back on my horse and going in search of them. But it would have been useless in such a vast area covered with woods and in a territory which I did not know. For want of something to do, I slipped off the bank into the pool of water and carried on building the dam. Mechanically I carried stones from the bank and put them in place. It provided a link with the events of the previous day which I wanted to revive, but the fun had gone out of it and I sat down again on the bank, wondering whether I should return to the camp. In the distance down the valley I could see the slave sitting by his horse. I felt a little foolish.

Suddenly there was a plop in the water in front of me. I thought it was a small fish rising. Then I saw a pebble fly past my shoulder and splash into the pool. I turned to see Orgetorix standing a few paces behind me. He laughed at my surprise and threw another stone into the water. The shyness of the previous day was gone. He turned and called out something. From the shadow of the trees his mother emerged into the sunlight. She came steadily towards us, her blond hair floating off her shoulders as she walked with her hands held loosely together in front of her. Though her dress was old and worn it could not disguise the supple ease with which she held herself. I could not take my eyes away. Forgetting, I said, 'Hello, I am so pleased to see you and Orgetorix again.' She looked uncertain but smiled and inclined her head a little. I motioned to her to sit down and then walked over to my horse and fetched the saddlebag. This time there was no hesitation. Both ate the bread, meat and fruit which I had brought. I suspected that they had not eaten since the previous day.

Judging that she would now be relaxed and leaving Orgetorix to play with my dagger again, I stood up and waved to Acco who led his horse to where we sat. I was apprehensive that they would not understand each other. He came from a tribe called the Tulingi in Helvetia and to my delight she understood immediately when he addressed her. My guess had been correct.

Through the slave I learnt that the woman's name was Ala. She was the daughter of the Helvetian chieftain called Orgetorix after whom she had named her son. Her husband, a prince of the Boii tribe called Amniorix had perished in the great battle near Bibracte. Ala and a number of other women had hidden under a wagon during the fighting. Afterwards they had escaped to the west with a few of their menfolk and continued the migration across Gaul while the remainder of their tribes had returned to Helvetia under Caesar's orders. Very soon Ala had found herself pregnant though I was not clear whether this was by her husband Amniorix or some other man. The group of about a hundred had carried on until eventually they came to Uxellodunum where the inhabitants, the Cadurci, had allowed them to settle. There Ala had brought up Orgetorix, helped by the other members of her tribe who considered it their duty to come to the aid of the daughter of their old chieftain, for she had no husband and no man was of sufficient rank to marry her.

When Caninius had begun the siege of the town Ala had resolved to make her escape before it was too late. None of the other women would accompany her. One night therefore, taking with her as much food as she could carry, she had herself let through the gates and with Orgetorix at her side had stolen away through the incomplete siege works. It had been her plan to return to the town once the siege was over and to resume her life there. Then she had heard of the mutilation of all the men and the destruction of the town itself. I asked what she proposed to do now. She replied that she hoped to make her way back through Gaul and return to her native land. I pointed out that to do this with a young child, without food and without means of transport, through territory that held many dangers for an unescorted woman was almost impossible. She replied that she understood this well enough, but that it was as dangerous to remain where she was as to travel. I asked her if she would allow me to help her.

'Why should I accept help from a Roman? You have killed thousands of my tribe. My husband and my father died under the blades of your shortswords. You stopped us from migrating to western Gaul, simply because your general Caesar wished to expand the Roman province.'

'I cannot deny that what you say is true,' I replied. 'But you have a young son. Do you not owe it to him to accept what help you can get? When he returns to Helvetia he will assume his rightful position among your people. He cannot do that here where his future will be as a mere wandering herdsman. You too are in the greatest danger. I am offering you safety and food until we return to Italy. At that time you will be free to leave and go back to your homeland.'

She made no reply for a moment but then said something to Acco. For a few minutes they spoke together until I asked what was passing between them. Acco explained that she had asked how he was treated. He had told her that he was a slave to Sergius Flaccus, that he was treated well and hoped one day to go to Rome where he would work for the family.

Ala turned back to me and asked, 'Am I to be your slave then?' I said that I did not want her to be a slave, that I wanted her and Orgetorix to remain with me as long as they wished. She turned to the boy and spoke to him. I guessed that she was asking him what he thought of the idea. He looked over towards me and I could tell that he wanted to come. She smiled at him and then spoke to Acco. She told him that she agreed to my proposal provided that it was clearly understood that she could leave whenever she wished. So the tent and the clothing were never needed. Ala demonstrated again that she had no difficulty with a horse. She sat astride the one which Acco had ridden and I saw immediately that she was an experienced rider, a strange thing to me, for Roman women would never have such an accomplishment. Orgetorix sat in front of her while Acco walked behind as we rode back to the camp.

Ala never went back to Helvetia. As I had hoped, she became part of my household on campaign and when I returned to Rome to my house on the Quirinal she came with me. By that time we had become lovers and though we have never married, there has been no other woman in my life since that day outside Uxellodunum. Being intelligent she soon learned Latin and it was not long before she was remonstrating in a mild way at the bad accent and language which Orgetorix picked up from the legionaries. They were very good with him, making him a miniature sword, shield and helmet in which he strutted about camp. When he was old enough he went to Helvetia but stayed only a year. He had grown into a Roman and could not adapt to the ways of a country where he had never lived. Now he is my factor on the estate at Baiae and I shall leave it to him in my will.

As events turned out Ala and I spent very little time at the house in Rome. After Pharsalus we came to live quietly here so that I could recover from my wounds and I have never felt any urge to return to the City. Now that Caesar and so many of my friends are dead, it would not seem the same. Gaius Matius still has his house there. Sometimes he comes down to Baiae to stay and we reminisce. He says the young ones have the most wild and extravagant parties, but the old aristocrats, those who are left, are a boring lot. Octavius decides everything so there is nothing to discuss.

Chapter XVII

51–49 BC

The year drew on. Most of long-haired Gaul was quiet and Caesar was beginning to think about placing the legions in winter quarters before making his usual journey to Cisalpine Gaul to attend to civil matters there. One evening, after all the other officers had retired, we started to talk about the political situation in Rome and his future. His enemies in the city were many. The old conservatives like Cato, Bibulus, Scipio and the rest were anxious to bring him before the courts to answer for the illegal acts which they alleged he had committed during his consulship. Once his command in Gaul terminated and he became a private citizen he would be open to prosecution. Even now the consul M. Claudius Marcellus was agitating for his replacement and the disbanding of his army. The previous day a letter had arrived from Balbus in Rome reporting that a meeting of the Senate had been held on the twenty-ninth of September at which various motions had been passed. The consuls for the following year were instructed to bring up the question of Caesar's command on the first of March, consider the question of demobilising the army of Gaul and decide on the new provincial governor.

'Why is discussion being postponed until the first of March next year?' I asked.

'Pompeius and I agreed at Lucca that the question of my command would not be considered before that date and that was implied in the Lex Licinia Pompeia, passed during his consulship with Crassus the following year. Pompeius is sufficiently vain not to allow his authority to be questioned and has always told the Senate that that is the position. He would look weak if he went back on his word.'

'Didn't the tribune Caelius Rufus get a law passed last year after Alesia which allows you to stand for the consulship without going to Rome? Surely you could simply hang onto your command until you have been voted in to a new consulship and then return to Rome as a magistrate immune from prosecution?'

'That's a possibility,' agreed Caesar, 'but there are a number of problems. Up until now I have had tribunes under my influence who have been able to veto motions of the Senate, just as four of them did at the meeting last week. Next year there will be no tribunes who will act on my instructions, especially now that Marcus Antonius has failed in his bid to be elected. What's more, there are a couple of laws which Pompeius passed during his consulship last year which do not help. If you recall, it is now possible for the Senate to appoint a new governor to a province with immediate effect instead of his going to it after having served his year of office in Rome. Theoretically, therefore, the Senate could appoint a replacement for me on the first of March next year. Even though Caelius' law allows me to stand for election in my absence I am still in difficulty because ten years have to elapse between consulships, which means that I would have to wait until the following year before I could even be a candidate. Meanwhile I would be a private citizen open to prosecution.'

'Surely Pompeius would support you in the interval. After all, he was your son-in-law and you made a bargain at Lucca.'

'I think Pompeius is being pressurised by the old conservatives to side against me. Don't forget that he is now married to Cornelia, Metellus Scipio's daughter. Scipio is no friend of mine. According to Balbus, Pompeius likes to think of himself as the first citizen of the State to whom everybody, including me, should defer. He also passed a law last year which requires every candidate in the elections for the city magistrates to hand in his nomination papers in person. You can't tell me that that wasn't aimed at making things difficult for me.'

'But that's directly contrary to the law passed by the tribunes saying that you could stand for the consulship in absentia,' I said.

'Of course, and in fact Pompeius added a clause to the law after it had been passed and engraved on the bronze tablets to say that it didn't apply to me. He also wrote to me at the time saying that it had never been his intention to embarrass me. I wish I could believe him. In any event, even a consul can't just change a law by adding a clause after it has been passed by the people. His rider is invalid. All the lawyers in the Senate will argue that the law as originally drawn requires me to attend personally in Rome to hand in my nomination. I think Pompeius knows this perfectly well.'

'So somehow you need to retain your immunity from prosecution until you can enter your next consulship.'

'Exactly. I also need a little time to organise my election campaign. I am sending large sums of money to the city and I am confident that Balbus and Oppius can organise things for me to make sure that I win when the time comes. In the meantime I have somehow to prevent Cato and his friends from depriving me of my command. I have eleven legions here, Lucius, but ironically what I need is one man, a sturdy tribune who will interpose his veto when necessary on the motions of my enemies in the Senate.' He paused and we sipped at our wine in silence. I heard the bugle sound to signal the beginning of the second watch.

At length Caesar spoke again. 'I would like you to go to Rome. Perhaps you could take your new woman with you.

Go and see Balbus. Letters are all very well but the situation is fluid. There is no substitute for personal contact. We are bound to be out of touch with the pulse of things at this distance. I need to find out whether there are people whom we can influence. If I can resolve this politically it would be better . . .' He let the words trail off in the night air, leaving some unspoken thought. I looked over towards him as he lay against the back of the couch. He stared straight ahead of him, his mouth was closed with the lips very slightly turned down. The expression was one of absolute implacability. In that moment I knew that he would achieve the transition from commander of the army of Gaul to a second consulship either by political means or by military force; in either case nothing would stop it.

Within a few days I was on my way to Rome with a small squadron of cavalry. It was necessary that I should reach the city in the shortest possible time. I therefore left Ala and Orgetorix to follow in a covered carriage with a handful of slaves and an escort. Through the mountains we rode down to the Via Aemilia and then by the Via Cassia to the city which we entered fourteen days after leaving camp. It was eight years since I had been in Rome and as I turned into the Via Flaminia and crossed the Milvian Bridge I felt almost a stranger. Before reaching the Campus Martius I swung uphill to my house on the Quirinal where the slaves were lighting the oil lamps and closing the shutters against the chill autumnal air. Before bed I sent a message to Balbus that I would see him first thing in the morning.

I awoke to hear a cock crowing instead of the sound of a bugle. A slave sponged me down with fine olive oil before bringing my cloak lined with silk from the orient and trimmed with the fur of a bear caught in the mountains north of Cilicia. As I walked down the hill towards the Forum a cold wind blew at my back, sending a few leaves scuttering along the wheel ruts. The sun touched the roof of the Temple of Jupiter on the top of the Capitol. I caught the smell of cooking and on an impulse turned into one of the taverns which fronted the street. Inside in the half light I made out the innkeeper who shuffled forward and cleared a few crumbs from a table where I sat down on a rough bench. At first I thought I was the only customer. Then the snores from a corner alerted me to the presence of an old man slumped over another table, his stick firmly clenched in his right hand. His gaping mouth revealed two rotten teeth. On the earthen floor a hen pecked at whatever scraps the customers of the previous evening had dropped. Occasionally a snort from the sleeping man caused the bird to squawk and flap her wings momentarily before resuming her search. A bowl of stew in which floated chunks of rabbit and wild pig was placed in front of me together with some coarse bread. My sense of smell had not let me down. It tasted excellent. Outside I could hear two other customers talking as they leaned against the counter over a charcoal fire. I listened to the creak of carts and the calls of the street vendors making their way to the markets on the crossroads.

I carried on down the hill catching sight of the great theatre which Pompeius had erected in the Campus Martius. It was faced with marble in sharp contrast to the brick buildings around it. The walls shone like a pearl in the pale morning light and I glimpsed a lake on which floated a sumptuously decorated barge. Pompeius had done well for himself while we had been away.

Soon I was entering the north end of the Forum, past the ruins of the Senate House which they were beginning to rebuild after the funeral pyre for Clodius had destroyed it. I was just about to turn under the arch of Janus into the Argiletum when I saw Domitus Ahenobarbus with a retinue of clients. He was processing down the Via Sacra in the direction of the House of the Vestals. With a sudden pang I remembered Domitia lying in the house close by, slowly

297

dying, all those summers ago. How different would my life have been if she had only lived? Perhaps now I would be an ex-consul or praetor waiting to see which way the two big cats would jump, wondering which side I should be on, like so many in the city.

Domitius did not see me and I hurried on down the Argiletum until I reached Balbus' office which was behind a bookshop. An entrance lay at the rear by which men might come and go without being observed. Balbus was his usual effusive and garrulous self. He had grown fat since I last saw him and a long girdle held his tunic in place round a considerable paunch. His hair was still dark but now he sported a grey beard and with his aquiline nose he had a piratical air about him. Oppius sat quietly in his chair, clean shaven with closely cropped hair, very much the Roman knight, while Balbus regaled me with the latest scandal and other news. Caesar had chosen wisely in selecting these two to run his office in Rome. Oppius was discreet, yet well informed and well connected. Balbus moved in the *demi monde* of the city's society, knowing who slept with whom, who needed money and who could be manipulated for political ends. He was quick-witted, sharp to detect a weakness in others and totally unscrupulous. Yet at the same time he was excellent company. A ready if somewhat crude wit endeared him to women out of whom he would wheedle the information which he needed to serve his master in Gaul. I asked him to tell me how things were.

'Well they couldn't be much worse at the moment. As you know we have four tribunes this year who can be relied upon to veto any undesirable motions in the Senate. But the bunch elected for next year are a load of tossers.' I caught Oppius wincing at this expression. 'Most of them are too weak-minded to stand up to people like Cato and Scipio even if we could bribe them, and in any event they are anti Caesar to a man. What's worse, you've probably heard, is that Gaius Marcellus is one of the consuls for next year. He can't stand Caesar's guts ever since Caesar tried to get his grandniece Octavia to leave Marcellus for Pompeius. I think that Gaius Marcellus will push for Caesar's replacement in Gaul even harder than Marcus Marcellus has done this year'.

'The only tribune with any strength of character is Curio,' remarked Oppius.

'Yes, and he's more anti-Caesar than the rest of them put together,' cried Balbus.

'Didn't I hear that he got married to Clodius' widow, Fulvia?' I asked.

'Indeed he has,' replied Oppius.

'One of the randiest women in Rome. They say that when she's finished with Curio she summons a couple of strong young slaves to satisfy her.'

'Where do you get these appalling snippets of information from, Balbus?'

'Ah, it's just a question of mixing in the right company. Anyway, you do know Curio's extremely heavily in debt, don't you? When his mad old father, Scribonius, died Curio put on some really spectacular funeral games. You know the sort of thing, five hundred panthers and dozens of elephants slugging it out. Not content with that, he had to build this ridiculous revolving theatre.'

'I suspect it cost him quite a lot to get himself elected a tribune,' put in Oppius. 'It was only a chance vacancy that arose because somebody died. He had to organise his campaign fairly quickly and that always costs more in bribes.'

'So how much do you think he's in debt?' I asked.

'Nobody knows exactly,' said Balbus. 'I've asked around and done a few calculations. My guess is that he owes about six million sesterces and I don't think he's got the means to repay it. His father mortgaged the family estate in Campania after some business venture failed and I think it's been seized by the creditors.'

'Fulvia won't like that. She's used to the high life or wa when I knew her,' I remarked. 'I wonder why she marrie him.'

'Because he's got a cock about a foot long, I shoul think,' said Balbus, producing another wince from Oppius.

The latter turned to me and said, 'Lucius, am I not righ in thinking that Fulvia always got on well with Caesar? seem to remember that they saw quite a lot of each othe before he left for Gaul. She was fond of him because h supported Clodius and got him out of a few scrapes especially when Caesar refused to give evidence at his tria for gate-crashing the festival of the Good Goddess.'

Balbus as usual was quick to grasp the point. 'Do yo think it's worth having a go at bribing Curio through Fulvia?'

'Caesar needs a tribune and would pay a lot of money fo one who would defy the Senate,' I said. 'Perhaps I shoul write her a note and see if we can have a little talk.'

So it was that a slave was summoned and despatched wit a message to Fulvia that I would like to call on her. As w waited for the reply Balbus continued to chatter about th political situation in the city. 'The only good thing whic has happened recently is Cicero going off to be governor o Cilicia. At least we haven't got him bleating all the tim about his time as consul or telling everybody that we mus get back to the old ways of the Republic.'

'He writes quite often to Caesar,' I said.

'I'm not surprised,' rejoined Balbus. 'He writes to every body else, usually in praise of himself. What on earth doe he write to Caesar about?'

'Grammar and style, mostly. He has read Caesar's *Commen taries* on the campaign in Gaul and he writes to him t discuss and compare their respective methods of composi tion. I think Caesar is quite flattered because Cicero is ver complimentary and Caesar himself thinks that Cicero is th best writer of prose and poetry that we have ever produced

They keep off politics, that way they don't fall out. But tell me about Pompeius. He rarely communicates with Caesar and never says anything of substance.'

'It's hard to know what game he is playing. Basically, I think he is a constitutionalist whose natural instinct is to side with the old conservative elements in the Senate. At the same time he wants to be considered the first citizen of the State, to whom everybody else including the Senate should listen. You won't have seen his great new theatre in the Campus Martius.'

I said that I had seen it that morning in the distance.

'Well, it's really a gigantic monument to himself. Next to the theatre there is a debating chamber for the Senate and just outside in the entrance hall he's had a larger than life statue of himself erected. He's got a house there as well.'

'It all sounds very grand,' I said. 'Is he getting even more vain?'

'Possibly, but deep down despite all his success, I think he lacks confidence. He seems to be swayed this way and that, depending on who is talking to him. Sometimes he speaks out quite strongly about Caesar giving up his command in Gaul and the next moment he says it can't even be discussed until next March. I think he's hoping the whole thing will resolve itself in some way that can't be foreseen yet. I reckon he's also a bit worried about Caesar's legions. Of course he renewed his governorship of both Spanish provinces for a further five years, you know. So he has his legions there and plenty of veterans in Italy. But the fact remains they are not fit and trained like Caesar's are. I suspect that Pompeius understands this in a way that the old fogeys in the Senate don't.'

'There has been talk of sending either Pompeius or Caesar to Syria to counter the threat from Parthia. After Carrhae anything might happen there,' said Oppius.

'I don't think that's a goer for either of them,' Balbus

went on. 'To start with, the Senate will never let Pompeius out of their sight while Caesar is lurking on the other side of the Alps with ten or eleven legions, and there would be uproar if anybody tried to introduce a bill to give Caesar another command.'

At that moment the slave reappeared bearing a note from Fulvia. 'Lucius,' she wrote, 'how delightful to hear from you. I thought you were away conquering barbarians in Gaul. Is Caesar with you, I do hope so? Either way, come at once. It will be good to talk about old times.'

'Well,' said Balbus, 'it sounds as if you're in there. You do seem to have a way with women named Fulvia.' He gave me a wink and Oppius looked at him disapprovingly.

I had no idea where Fulvia lived but Oppius said it was a house on the Capitoline not far from the Temple of Concord. I instructed the slave to wait for me at the bottom of the Clivus Argentarius and I would then follow him at a discreet distance. I left the office by the rear entrance and pulled the hood of my cloak up around my face. The wind was bitter and in any event I had no wish to be seen more than was necessary. The slave led the way up the steps and soon we turned off to a street at the side of the temple where a fine mansion rose on the hillside.

I found Fulvia playing with a small monkey which she was teasing with a ball tied to a piece of cord dangled from a stick. Squatting on the floor nearby was an olive-skinned youth aged about seventeen years and wearing only a tiny loincloth. He appeared to be Egyptian and was a most handsome young man. Fulvia herself wore a green dress tied with a ribbon under her breasts which accentuated them even more than I remembered. Her lips were painted bright red and her hair was dressed in plaits around the top of her head like a crown. She looked a tart, but a very alluring one.

At my entrance she thrust the monkey into the hands of the youth and, dancing forward, clasped me round the waist

302

lanting a large kiss on my lips. I was a little startled but
managed to respond appropriately. I had not known her
well. She had knocked around with a fairly raffish lot before
marrying Clodius.

'My, your skin's a lot harder than I remember,' she said,
stroking my arm. 'Don't you boys look after yourselves in
camp?'

'Well, you're just as beautiful as ever,' I blurted. But not,
I thought to myself, as beautiful as the other Fulvia I used to
know.

'Liar,' she cried laughing and patted me on the hand
before motioning me to a couch. She went over to the boy
who was still holding the monkey, stroked his hair and
brought the monkey back to sit on her lap. 'Isn't he
gorgeous?'

'Do you mean the monkey or the boy?' I asked.

'The boy, silly; my cousin Decimus sent him as a present
from the slave market. I picked him from ten he sent up for
inspection. He's only young but he's learning fast.' She gave
a funny smile. I thought back to what Balbus had said. Still,
he could be a lot worse off. Being Fulvia's toy boy was better
than the galleys or sharing the bed of some dirty old senator.

'Anyway, what brings you here? I'm sorry that Gaius isn't
with you. How is he?'

She was making it clear that her interest in me was a good
deal less than her interest in Caesar. I told her that he was
in fine fettle and how sorry he was to hear of Clodius' death,
which was at least partly true. He had lost a useful ally when
Milo's thugs struck him down.

Fulvia's face clouded for a moment. She had been genuinely in love with Clodius. 'The people were wonderful, you
know. They carried him up the Via Appia to our house on
the Palatine. I washed his body and showed it to the crowds
who had gathered outside. They were so angry that their
champion had been murdered. I don't quite know how it

happened but suddenly a bunch of them surged forward and carried his body off to the Rostra and laid it there. I was upset until I realised that it was because they held him in such great affection. Afterwards of course it all got out of hand. They made a funeral pyre from the benches in the Senate – what a mess. They've only just started rebuilding. The mob stoned Milo's house as well. He's in exile now in Massilia – if you and Gaius are ever in that area, you might get one of your legionaries to run him through.'

I wasn't sure how to take this suggestion but said that would mention it to Caesar, on the basis that one good turn might deserve another, a thought which I kept to myself.

We sat in silence for a moment. I decided to broach the subject of my visit.

'I hear you're happily married to Curio now. That must be a comfort to you. He's been elected one of the tribunes for next year, hasn't he?'

Her face brightened a little. 'Well, my dear, a girl can't be long without a husband these days. Of course I had to lend him some money to put up for the tribunate, but he's worth it. So young and vigorous. I had to catch him before anybody else did.'

I suspected that it had taken Fulvia about as long to net Curio as a wolf to catch a stray lamb. Instead I said, 'He's lucky to have married somebody as beautiful and wealthy as you.'

'Not that wealthy, dear,' she replied sharply. 'Of course Publius left a bit but I'm keeping my hands on most of that. You never know what a girl might need in her old age. Curio will have to sort out his own problems.'

'I wasn't aware that he had any problems,' I lied. Fulvia hesitated as if wondering whether she should say anything.

'Well, it's common knowledge in the city that he's heavily in debt. The other day a moneylender appeared at the house asking to speak to me. I didn't see him of course and

304

ad him sent packing. Some dreadful little Armenian who
laims he's owed about a million sesterces and interest on
op.'

'Oh,' I said, 'but that's not such an enormous amount.'
ulvia gave a little laugh and I thought I caught a suppressed
ob in her voice.

'No, a million sesterces isn't, but eight million is.' The
olour had gone from her face. She was suddenly a very
ifferent person from the one who had greeted me with all
he banter and flirtation of old. She looked rather pathetic,
troking the monkey for a little comfort.

'Does that boy understand Latin?' I asked, indicating the
outh who still squatted on the floor.

'Ye gods, Lucius, I didn't get him to talk to.' She got up
nd surrendered the monkey once more, running her hand
own the boy's thigh as she did so. 'No, doesn't understand
word. Why?'

'I think I could help Curio with his debts in return for a
ttle political assistance.' In a few sentences I explained
aesar's need of a tribune who could stand up to the Senate
nd block his recall from Gaul until he was able to enter
pon another consulship.

'You know I should like to help Gaius and we could
ertainly do with the money.' I could see that the idea
ppealed to her and of course it was not bribery, just helping
ut an old friend.

Naturally I agreed, making it clear that the whole thing
nust remain secret until it was necessary for Curio to declare
imself in the Senate or elsewhere. We parted with the
greement that Fulvia would speak to Curio and that if he
ere interested he would send a message to arrange a
neeting.

The next few days were occupied in further discussions
ith Balbus and Oppius. The other consul for the following
ear was Lucius Aemilius Paullus, a member of an ancient

305

patrician family whose basilica ran along the north-east side of the Forum. In recent years it had fallen into disrepair and Aemilius was anxious to restore it, but lacked the funds to do so. Balbus saw his chance and arranged to advance instalments as the work progressed, payable so long as Aemilius did nothing to assist Gaius Marcellus during their year of office.

For some days I heard nothing from Curio, receiving only a note from Fulvia confirming that she had spoken to him. I was beginning to lose hope until late one afternoon soon after dusk a message arrived saying that he would call on me that evening. I bathed and dined with Ala before sending her to her chamber. I ordered the slaves to lay out some good sweetmeats and some Opimian wine.

I had never met Curio before. Balbus however had told me that he liked a good deal to drink and only the best quality. He arrived in a closed litter borne by four slaves with just one torch bearer. All were instantly dismissed with orders that he would send for them when he was ready. It was evident that he did not wish his visit to my house to be observed, from which I took encouragement. If he had not meant to strike a deal he would not have taken such trouble to ensure that our meeting remained secret.

During the previous week Balbus had caused a rumour to circulate that Curio had come into some money from an inheritance, knowing that this would reach the ears of his creditors who in turn would see an opportunity to press for payment. He seemed a little truculent and I observed that he twisted the fold of his toga in his hand as he spoke. He was a man of considerable stature, over six feet in height with black hair which covered his head in tight curls. He had strong features with a pale skin and grey eyes. His voice was that of a man of education and good breeding. I had placed a flagon of wine by his couch where he could easily reach it. Though he made no comment of approval I sensed

306

hat he was agreeably surprised by the quality of the Opinian and helped himself to it liberally, ignoring the food. We exchanged a few pleasantries. I deliberately avoided introducing the subject of Caesar. If the man was interested in a deal he would raise the matter soon enough.

Eventually he said in a slightly aggressive tone, 'So Caesar wants my help next year, does he? That seems rather odd of someone who once tried to get me prosecuted for being involved in a conspiracy to murder Pompeius. Why in the name of Jupiter should I support Caesar? What's that man ever done for me?'

'I don't think that your support is essential by any means,' I replied. 'Nevertheless, Caesar would prefer to resolve the question of his command in Gaul and his future by political means. You could be of assistance in the process.'

'If I do what Caesar wants I will be putting my life in danger. There are plenty of people in high places who want to see an end of him. The consuls next year will be against him and none of my fellow tribunes will support me. I will be very exposed. Caesar's legions in Gaul won't prevent my being stabbed in the back in Rome.'

'I appreciate that it will require courage on your part. But you will not be alone. Caesar has much support among the common people and they tell me that you too have a great popular following in the city. No doubt you can gather around you a bunch of minders who will see you come to no harm. Balbus will ensure that it is worth their while to protect you. Milo and Clodius survived for long enough.'

'Yes and look what happened to Clodius,' he took another slug of wine and gazed at the marble floor.

I let him ruminate for a moment and then said, 'Do you really have an alternative? It's common knowledge that you owe several million sesterces. It will be very difficult for you to survive politically unless you can repay the money – Caesar is offering you the chance to do that.'

307

'Caesar, Caesar!' he shouted in a flash of temper. 'Why should I side with him? Who says he can overcome the whole of the Roman State? He's nothing but another jumped-up general who thinks that beating up a few barbarians in Gaul entitles him to rule the world. What about Pompeius and his legions? They might want a say in the matter, you know.'

'So you think that Pompeius would win if it came down to a fight? If you think that, then clearly it would be unwise to throw in your lot on the side of Caesar. But what makes you so sure Pompeius would win?'

'Well,' said Curio, 'he has six legions in Spain to start with. Then there are his veterans in Italy. Pompeius says that he has only to stamp his foot, as he puts it, and men will come running to his standards. The people will not want to see another Sulla marching on the city with all the bloodshed of proscriptions. They will support Pompeius and the constitution.'

'Do you think they'll be strong enough to withstand ten legions of veterans led by a brilliant general? Pompeius may be a very good leader but I don't believe he has the military genius of Caesar. Pompeius would be in command of veterans hauled out of retirement, long past their best fighting days, and raw recruits. What chance have such men against hardened legionaries with up to eight years of experience in Gaul?'

'Who says that Caesar's men will follow him and take up arms against the State?' riposted Curio.

'Experience indicates that legionaries will follow the man who pays them best,' said I. There was a long silence and Curio shook his head. Eventually he said that he was not convinced, that he could not bring himself suddenly to support a man whom up until then he had vilified many times in public. I reminded him that the offer of help for his debts was there if he chose to take it up, but that Caesar would not wait indefinitely. There the conversation ended and Curio sent a message to summon his litter. I was disappointed, feeling that I had conducted the interview badly and that I should have persuaded him to come over to our side. Perhaps he had arrived with the intention of doing a deal, as I had suspected. In some way I had antagonised him so that he had refused in spite of himself.

Whatever the truth of the matter, I received a note from Fulvia the following evening saying how distressed she was at the outcome of our meeting and that she intended to speak again to Curio, 'to make him see sense'. Balbus was convinced that their extravagant lifestyles made both of them desperate for money and that Fulvia would succeed where I had failed. He proved to be correct. At a meeting in the office off the Argiletum a few days later Curio agreed that in return for an advance of two million sesterces there and then and further payments when he entered office, he would support Caesar in the Senate and the people's assembly. For now the agreement was to remain secret. Caesar had his tribune and the tribune had his money, provided he danced to his master's tune.

That night I slept with Ala knowing that it would be some time before we saw each other again. With a sense of foreboding I mounted my horse at first light and began the journey north back to Gaul. It seemed to me that there were two great fleets at large upon the seas. One was captained by a man who had a sense of his destiny and an unshakable ambition to fulfil it. The other fleet had a captain who was uncertain how to proceed, but a crew which was determined to propel him on a collision course with the enemy. In between the fleets lay a little fishing boat, the remains of the Republic, in which Cicero stood at the helm, isolated and helpless to control the converging ships.

In Gaul I reported to Caesar on the turning of Curio and we waited for the meeting of the Senate which duly took place on the first of March. The new consul, Gaius Marcellus, raised the question of the Gallic provinces in accordance with the motions passed the previous September. To his surprise, but not to ours, he received no support from his colleague Aemilius Paullus who was more interested in watching the restoration of his family's basilica. It was Curio however who turned heads when he rose to propose that Caesar should give up his command in Gaul at the same time as Pompeius gave up his command in Spain. This idea had been hatched in advance in correspondence between our headquarters in Ravenna and Balbus in Rome. Balbus himself, reporting to Caesar afterwards in his letters, said that Pompeius had been caught off balance by this proposal especially as many senators had welcomed it, seeing it as a possible means of averting a struggle between the two great generals.

Pompeius had counter-proposed that Caesar should resign his command later in the year, on the thirteenth of November. Apparently his idea was that Caesar could stand in absentia for the consulship, using the dispensation granted to him under the law brought in by the tribunes. Having been elected in July he would then resign his command in November, leaving him with only a few weeks to wait outside the city before entering upon the consulship. When we received news of this proposal Caesar immediately sent a despatch back to Balbus instructing Curio to reject it. It was too late to be organising an election campaign and in addition there was the ten-year rule to overcome. More importantly, Caesar was no longer prepared to acknowledge that Pompeius controlled his destiny. He also noted that Pompeius would retain his command in Spain. Balbus therefore told Curio to repeat his demand that both men should resign simultaneously, sensing that there were echoes of support in some quarters. Even M. Marcellus had indicated that this might form the basis of a compromise. In the end however, the conservative elements refused to negotiate and Curio interposed his veto on the motions against his paymaster.

Not long after this Caesar received a letter from the Senate requiring him to release one of his legions which was to be sent to Syria to cover the perceived threat from Parthia. Pompeius was required to do the same, but then came a note from the latter saying that he proposed to send the legion which he had earlier lent to Caesar. Caesar became increasingly convinced that his rival was determined not to let him enter upon another consulship without first resigning his command and exposing himself to political annihilation.

'Very well,' he said, as he showed me the letter, 'the Senate shall have their two legions. I cannot choose the one return to Pompeius but the other is at my disposal. Let them have the fifteenth, it's the most recently recruited and has seen little action. Before we send it to Italy I shall extract the experienced centurions and return them to their original legions. They can have what I have recruited, not what have trained.'

So the fifteenth was paraded before Caesar. He spoke at length to their commanding officers, praising their conduct hitherto and apologising that he was obliged to release them by order of the Senate. Then he gave to the legionaries a whole year's pay in advance and reminded them of their oath of loyalty to him. Many wept openly at being parted from their leader as they set off on the march to Italy. Later we heard that neither legion had been sent to the East; instead they had been placed in barracks at Capua. Caesar's suspicions of Pompeius' motives increased.

It was quiet in Gaul during the summer. Caesar decided to hold a review of the army in the territory of the Treveri. The thirteenth had been sent to Aquileia in Cisalpine Gaul to replace the fifteenth, but the remaining eight legions were all present. Caesar addressed his generals, testing the feeling of the troops and warning them of the struggle that might be coming. All of them were staunch in their backing for their commander-in-chief, including Titus Labienus, of whom Caesar spoke to me privately one evening.

'He is a fine general, Lucius, one of the best I have. But he does not mix well with the others. He feels uncomfortable among the young aristocrats from the city. He couldn't stand Antonius when he was here. I once heard Trebonius mocking his country accent over dinner. He rose from the ranks and despises young men who come in as legates and effortlessly assume command of a legion.'

'He comes from Picenum, doesn't he?'

'Yes, I believe his father was a factor or something of the sort on the estates of Pompeius Strabo. If it came to war with the son I think he would go over to the other side. He must be watched carefully from now on.'

Caesar summoned Ventidius. Although it was still summer and this sort of work was normally reserved for winter quarters, he ordered him to go round the legions with Mamurra and ensure that every man was equipped properly to go on campaign at a moment's notice. The armourers were to put to work on making more spearheads and swords. Most importantly, Ventidius arranged for supplies of new boots. To maintain the fitness of the troops Caesar led them on a series of route marches. The men readily took part in these for they had learned over the years the importance of speed over the ground, of Caesar's legendary swiftness which caught so many opponents off guard when he appeared where he was least expected. Having satisfied himself that the army was in the best possible state for war if it came, he sent four of the legions to winter in the territory of the Belgae under the command of Trebonius; four remained in the territory of the Aedui. We then set out for Ravenna, 'to await events', as Caesar put it ominously. On the way a letter arrived from Balbus announcing that Pompeius had fallen sick during the summer with the recurrence of some illness which he had picked up during his campaigns in the east. The city was in a ferment, praying to the gods for his recovery. Sacrifices were offered each day in the temple of Venus with which he had crowned his new theatre complex in the Campus Martius. Pompeius himself had retired to his villa in the Alban Hills where he was convalescing. Meanwhile Hortensius, one of the conservative old guard, had died and Marcus Antonius had been elected to the vacancy in the augurate left by his death. It was hardly important, but had infuriated Domitius Ahenobarbus who had assumed that he would succeed to this priesthood. Much more significant from Caesar's point of view was the news that Antonius had been successful this time in getting himself elected to the tribunate. He would be able to carry on where Curio left off when his year of office expired.

The doors of the temple of Janus might be closed, but they were beginning to creak. Balbus reported that the conservatives in the Senate were hardening in their attitude and Pompeius was showing more resolve now that he had recovered from his illness. He had been much encouraged by the expressions of support received as he lay on his sickbed and believed that the whole State was behind him. In the Senate and from the Rostra many were making speeches calling for Caesar to resign. A meeting of the Senate was scheduled for the first of December. Caesar gave orders for the thirteenth to move down from Aquileia towards Ravenna. In Gaul Trebonius marched his four legions southwards from the territory of the Belgae. The other four legions were instructed to be ready to move south west to block any move by the Pompeian legions in Spain. A fresh letter came from Balbus to Caesar waiting in Ravenna. We were told that Gaius Marcellus would again move that Caesar lay down his command forthwith. Within hours another horseman rode into headquarters – it was Curio himself to report on the proceedings. I remember that it was a very cold day with flurries of snow. Ice covered the water troughs for the horses and the soldiers hurried about, wrapped tightly in their cloaks. The sky had the colour of dark lead – daylight never established itself. The hooves of the horses clanged on the hard earth flattened by the continual passage of men and animals down the principal roads of the camp. Curio had ridden from Rome virtually without stopping. The words tumbled from his mouth as he sought to relay his urgent news. Caesar held up his hand.

'Give me the despatches from Balbus. I will read those first while you get some food and a change from those damp clothes. Then we will listen to your report.' Curio handed over the leather pouch and went to do as he was bidden.

'I think I know what Curio will tell us. I am more interested to know how Balbus assesses the military situation,' he said, turning to me.

From Balbus we learned that the consuls had entrusted to Pompeius the task of defending the state against the attack coming from Caesar. Evidently the movement of the thirteenth from Aquileia to Ravenna had been interpreted as an invasion, though of course the troops had not left the province of Cisalpine Gaul. As we had expected, Pompeius had taken command of the two legions which had been released from the army of Gaul and was now levying troops of his own. According to Balbus some had already appeared in the city. It was rumoured, with what justification we could not discover, that morale in Caesar's army was low and that the legionaries would not follow him in an invasion of Italy. Many of the leading men in the State, both senators and members of the equestrian order, were panicking, while the core of diehards in the Senate remained firm for war. 'They will not let Pompeius wriggle out of this. They mean to make him fight,' wrote Balbus. 'Nevertheless,' he continued,

314

'there is a state of unpreparedness here of which a bold and swift stroke on your part could take great advantage. The Senate may be ready; the army is not.'

Caesar smiled on reading these words. 'I do believe,' he said 'that Cornelius Balbus grasps the situation well.' He summoned a secretary and dictated despatches to the legions in Gaul, ordering them to deploy southwards without delay. Whatever the report by Curio might tell us of the proceedings in the Senate, it was clear that we were moving towards war.

Before he returned to Rome, Curio told us that in the Senate on the first of December the house had passed a motion calling on Caesar to resign, followed by a further motion that Pompeius need not resign his command in Spain. Curio himself had then again put a motion that both men should lay down their commands simultaneously. No fewer than three hundred and seventy senators had gathered on his side of the chamber to support this, with only twenty-two against. Marcellus had thereupon dismissed the Senate and gone with a party of diehards to see Pompeius in his villa outside Rome and asked him to 'save the Republic'.

During the days which followed Caesar kept his own counsel. I could tell that he was brooding over the question of whether or not to invade Italy. Despite the fact that he could, when he deemed it expedient, be ruthless to the point of extreme cruelty, as he had demonstrated at Uxellodunum, he also dreaded the thought of Roman citizens killing Roman citizens. He remembered the proscriptions of Sulla and the social wars when he was a child. He knew that he had the most powerful army in the world at his back. He had contributed immense wealth to the state through the tribute and taxes now flowing in from Gaul. Beautiful new buildings were springing up in the Forum, paid for by him. Surely the old conservatives would see reason. Was it too much to ask for a second consulship after all his services to the state? Had not the vote in the Senate on Curio's motion indicated that they wanted a compromise?

One evening Aulus Hirtius and I were enjoying a fine dish of asparagus, olives and oysters in his house at headquarters. I always looked forward to dinner with Aulus who was well read, amusing and an excellent cook in his own right. For two or three years he had been running the office through which all the correspondence to Rome passed. We were dining alone, savouring some good wine which he had recently received from his estate in Campania. It must have been growing late when a slave appeared to say that Caesar was at the door and wished to speak with us. Aulus immediately offered to have dinner prepared for him but Caesar declined, picking only at a few figs which lay in a dish near his couch. At this time he was eating very sparingly and had no interest in food. Yet he had extraordinary energy, which enabled him to dictate or write straight through the night without any noticeable effect the following day.

'Aulus,' he asked, 'would you be prepared to go to Rome tomorrow? I feel that we must make a last effort for peace. I do not think it is a job for a soldier, such as Lucius; that would create the wrong impression. I have in mind putting a further compromise to try to avoid war and it is better conveyed by a man of letters like yourself. I want you to go to Balbus and then see anybody of influence who can relay your message to the right quarters. Tell them that if necessary I would be prepared to accept a compromise under which I would retain the provinces of Illyricum and Cisalpine Gaul with just two legions, until I entered upon my consulship. Between you and me, I could be persuaded to keep just one of the provinces and one legion, but this is a position of last resort which you must only put forward if it is the sole means of avoiding war.'

I do not think Caesar ever regarded the mission of Hirtius

316

likely to succeed. Indeed he told me that if this proposal were rejected he would feel that he had done everything in his power to resolve the problem politically. In the event, ulus stayed only two nights in Rome, where the reception to his message was hostile. Somebody told me years later that Cicero was attracted by the idea. However, he had only just landed in Italy from Cilicia and did not even reach Rome until the turn of the year. Meanwhile Pompeius had indicated that he could not accept the latest terms which Caesar offered, so Hirtius returned empty-handed.

On the tenth of December Marcus Antonius took office as a tribune. We learned later that without Caesar's knowledge he had made a highly belligerent speech criticising Pompeius. Not unnaturally, Pompeius assumed that the views expressed by Antonius were those of his master. It was probably too late anyway. Balbus wrote saying that Pompeius was already telling everybody openly that war was now inevitable. Antonius had also called for the two legions by then stationed in Apulia for the winter to be sent to Syria as originally decreed. We were not surprised to hear that the consuls had ignored his request.

Despite all this, Caesar took one last step to try to avert hostilities. He summoned Curio again from Rome and handed to him a letter written in his own hand. He had taken some trouble to compose it the previous evening. Briefly he recited his achievements in Gaul and the benefits they had brought to the Republic. He then repeated what Curio had proposed many times previously, that he would resign his command if only Pompeius would do the same. He made it clear that he could not resign, for reasons which the Senate well understood, without the protection of the army of Gaul or the consulship. He asked the Senate whether this was so unreasonable. He left unspoken the consequences of their refusal to come to a compromise.

Within an hour of his arrival in Ravenna, Curio was on a

317

fresh horse and galloping southwards to be back in Rome in time for the meeting scheduled for the first of January. On that day at first light the two new consuls, Lentulus Crus and Claudius Marcellus, as tradition required, mounted the Capitol and there sacrificed to Jupiter. Shortly afterwards the Senate met. Metellus Scipio moved that Caesar lay down his command by a fixed date or be declared a public enemy. The mood in the house was grim and determined. Cato, implacable as ever, and Domitius, as stupid as ever, voiced their support with many others. Marcus Antonius tried to read out Caesar's letter but was shouted down. Lentulus stated that he was not prepared to negotiate. Surprisingly M. Marcellus suggested that further discussions might be held once the levies of troops had taken place. Another man, a certain Calidus, proposed that Pompeius should go to Spain although it was not clear what this would achieve. The house might have been wise to consider favourably the motion of M. Marcellus which would have given further time to Pompeius to prepare for war. In the event he was made to withdraw. Scipio's motion was then put to the vote and passed by a large majority. Marcus Antonius, supported by a fellow tribune, Quintus Cassius, thereupon interposed his veto and the meeting broke up in disarray.

When the courier arrived from Rome with the report from Balbus on the meeting, Caesar took it into his room and remained by himself for a few minutes while he read it. He emerged and called his officers round him. He told us that he was deeply shocked by the Senate's continued rejection of his offer, but his voice was calm and I do not think that he was surprised by the result.

'There are many sensible men who believe that my offer to resign in conjunction with Pompeius was a reasonable solution to this problem. Look at the vote on Curio's motion when the house met on the first of December. Unfortunately a few diehard conservatives led by Cato, the Claudii Marcelli and others of that ilk are seeking at all costs to preserve their position and privileges at the expense of the welfare of the State. It is a tragedy that Pompeius has not the strength of character to withstand them. Now I am forced into the position of choosing between my political death and exile to some distant island, or fighting for what I believe to be justly due to me, namely a second consulship to continue with the reforms instigated when I first held that office nine years ago. I choose to fight.'

Many of the legates and tribunes gathered round shouted their support, saying that it was an affront to Caesar's dignity that he should be treated so badly after all the benefits he had conferred upon the state. He thanked them for their loyalty and asked them to be ready to act swiftly upon his orders.

Balbus had written that the city was filling up with troops levied by Pompeius. It would be necessary to move our forces into position quickly. Caesar therefore wrote to the legates commanding legions VIII and XII, instructing them to advance with all possible speed to join him. In addition we had twenty-two cohorts which had not yet been formed into legions as they had only recently been recruited in Cisalpine Gaul. These units were instructed to travel by forced marches towards the frontier with Italy. The messages were encoded and then translated into Greek, for we had found over the years in Gaul that it was important to maintain secure communications between headquarters and commanders in the field. Horsemen were despatched with the orders and two hours later the same messages were sent by other riders in case the first should be intercepted. Around the camp and in the town of Ravenna many ears were cocked to pick up intelligence about our plans. The camp awoke from the comparative inertia of winter quarters as the thirteenth prepared to move. Men assembled their arms and entrenching tools, gallopers rode up and down

319

the streets of the camp with orders, centurions shouted instructions and the legionaries assembled in their maniples and cohorts. Carts creaked as weapons and stores were loaded. There was the occasional flurry of snow or sleet but nobody noticed the weather now. We were intent upon the business of mobilising for war.

Later in the day Caesar told me that he had received a letter from Cicero in Rome, saying that he was desperately trying to persuade the consuls to accept his offer via Hirtius to keep one province and a legion until he could be elected consul. Nobody would listen. Apparently Cicero was considered to be out of touch with what had gone before because he had only just reached the City, having travelled up from Formiae where he had had conversations with Pompeius. Caesar wrote back a curt note saying that it was too late.

The night passed restlessly. I lay in my bed at headquarters wondering what the future held. Shortly after midnight I rose and dictated a letter to Ala, telling her to go to Baiae and wait for me there. With the bugle announcing the end of the fourth watch I emerged to find light snow was falling. I hurried down to the office where Hirtius was already looking at messages from the commanders of the legions and a letter from Balbus. Balbus reported that at a further meeting of the Senate held on the seventh of January the ultimate decree of emergency had been passed and the magistrates had been instructed to take all steps necessary to save the State. As if to emphasise that there was no way back from the precipice, they had appointed some ex-praetor to take over from Caesar as governor of Cisalpine Gaul. As a final insult, Domitius Ahenobarbus was to supercede him in Narbonese Gaul.

When Caesar read this he grinned and remarked that at least one man would be happy in this miserable situation;

Domitius had coveted Narbonese Gaul for many years. 'But he will not smile for long,' he added, 'soon we shall see to what a pretty pass those obstinate and stupid wretches have brought the State. They have read in my despatches and commentaries how legions led by Caesar fight. Now they shall feel the sharpness of our swords at first hand. Lucius, I want you to take the thirteenth this afternoon just before the light fails and advance to the frontier. It is marked by a little stream called the Rubicon. Wait for me there. I have to attend a dinner in Ravenna this evening. It is best that I go to it and do not arouse any suspicion that we are on the move.'

And so it was that that afternoon, the ninth of January in the consulship of L. Cornelius Lentulus Crus and C. Claudius Marcellus, I took the first step in the war that was to bring about the final downfall of the Roman Republic. I halted the thirteenth in some woods about a mile short of the stream. It was still daylight and the sky had cleared a little. In the west the sun was sinking, casting long shadows as I rode up to look at the little stream marking the frontier between Cisalpine Gaul and Italy. It was barely twenty paces wide – the legionaries would be able to wade across without getting their tunics wet. While the light lasted I ordered some men to build two stone causeways between the banks, so that the carts would be able to cross easily. As I watched them the sun's rays played upon the water and the occasional flash of silver betrayed the presence of small fish. One man suddenly tossed an eel out onto the bank where it slithered about until a legionary decapitated it and slung it in his pouch for supper. The men joked as they worked. Most were oblivious to the difference between one side of the stream and the other. For those who had been recruited during the long years in Gaul, Italy meant little. Others knew that a Roman general could not cross the frontier into Italy

321

without surrendering his imperium and that to do otherwise was an act of aggression against the State. One bank of the stream signified peace, the other, war.

Once darkness had fallen I brought the legion out of the woods onto the open ground. It grew cold and the legionaries fetched wood for their fires as we waited for the order to advance. The sky stayed reasonably clear but a mist rolled in from the direction of the sea. It hung a few feet above the ground so that once I saw a squadron of horsemen canter past me with only the riders' heads and the heads of their mounts visible, while the lower parts were hidden by the mist. The men chattered round their fires, most of them cooking something while they could. I sensed they were restless – they wanted to go. Many asked me when Caesar would come; I must have said 'soon' a hundred times. I felt the tension myself. We had all fought against barbarians before, now we might have to face another legion, perhaps a legion led by Pompeius. Were we as good as we believed ourselves to be? Was our cause right? Ought I to be invading Italy as part of a rebellious army? Was this not Sulla all over again? I was not a politician. Long ago I had set my face against a political career, accepting the advice of my father that I was not cut out for it. I was a soldier of Rome. Could it be right to be marching against Rome? These and many other questions I asked myself as we waited. Yet I knew that I was helplessly bound up with events which were set upon an ineluctable course of which I was part. If there had to be a fight, it was best to be on the winning side. If I knew nothing else, I knew that Caesar was a winner. We had been together for too long. Right or wrong, there could be no going back now.

The moon rose slowly and with it the mist began to clear. In the trees behind us the frost glittered in the pale light. There was a clatter of hooves and Caesar in his distinctive red cloak jumped down from his horse, waved away his escort and sat down beside me.

322

'It's later than I meant to be. I had to stay talking to a few women and look as if I had nothing else on my mind. Are we ready?' I said that the men were all set and eager to go.

'Very well, but first I think we should propitiate the gods. The men will approve even if we don't believe in it. I have had some of the older horses in the stables at headquarters gathered up and brought here. It's an old custom to release horses when you are about to embark on a great enterprise.'

So saying, he gave orders for them to be paraded in front of the legion, where many men were holding torches aloft at the front of the ranks and in the spaces between the cohorts, lined up ready to advance. At a given signal the stable lads let go the horses and cracked whips to encourage them. Under the light of the moon these black shadows galloped off in every direction, some even cantered across the fateful stream. The men gave a cheer and some trumpets sounded. They knew now that their mission had the blessing of the gods. Caesar, mounted on his horse, raised his hand and pointed southwards. The standard bearers moved forwards with their silver eagles gleaming in the light of the torches. The leading cohorts of the thirteenth entered the waters of the Rubicon and clambered out on the other side. We were at war.

Chapter XVIII

49–48 BC

Our advance southwards was rapid as Caesar had intended it to be. At Asculum the twelfth came up with us from Gaul and we were joined soon afterwards by the eighth near Corfinium. Pompeius had been caught off guard, not thinking that we would dare to invade Italy with such a small force. He retreated rapidly, first into Campania and then into Apulia, instructing all to follow him. At Corfinium however we found Ahenobarbus, who attempted to resist. Our legions soon threw up earthworks round the town and in a short time we had forced him to surrender. His troops came over to our side most willingly and Caesar spared his opponent his life, though I would have had him executed. This arrogant and stupid man had opposed Caesar at every step. There would have been no mercy if the roles had been reversed. How cruel the gods had been to let this miserable wretch live and to take away the life of his beautiful sister who had meant so much to me.

Caesar's policy of clemency was effective. Towns willingly opened their gates to us, giving us corn and supplies when they realised that Caesar would not allow the troops to pillage. At Rome the common people came out onto the streets to welcome us. The vast majority of senators and other men of consequence had abandoned the city and hurried to Brundisium where Pompeius lay encamped. We advanced by forced marches and laid siege to the port but could not prevent Pompeius from embarking his army and sailing away across the Adriatic.

Many believed that Pompeius had been wrong to abandon Italy; Caesar did not agree. 'He knows his troops were not ready to do battle against seasoned legionaries like ours. He will take his army into Greece and train it to fight. He has a great fleet with which to command the sea. He will be able to recruit more men and build more ships from his resources in Asia. There they regard him almost as a god. He can exact tribute from the provinces to pay for his army and his fleet. At the same time he can blockade Italy and try to cut off our supplies of corn from Egypt and Africa. It is a good strategy.'

'But you have Italy,' I said, 'and that is the greatest prize. In the end Pompeius will have to come back to fight you.'

'No, we shall take the fight to him. The legions are tired after their long marches. I shall let them winter here in Apulia. Then, when we have assembled a fleet we can cross the sea and bring Pompeius to battle. Meanwhile we need to secure Corsica, Sardinia and Spain.'

'What about Sicily? Cato commands there, doesn't he?'

'There is nothing much to oppose us on the island. I shall send Curio. From there he should be able to move on Africa and that would certainly help with grain supplies. You and I will go to Spain and deal with Pompeius' legions there. He has five and some decent cavalry under Afranius. Our legions in Gaul have already advanced to Narbo. They should be too experienced for troops who have done little but sit in the sun.'

'Once we have secured the West then do we move against Pompeius in the East?'

'We have no alternative,' said Caesar. 'We cannot follow Pompeius until we have transports assembled at Brundisium. At the same time we must either defeat or persuade the Spanish legions to defect to us. Otherwise Pompeius may seek to move them by sea to strengthen his position in the east, on the basis that he can recover Spain once he has defeated me.'

Before we left Brundisium I sought out my brother's estate outside the town. To my dismay I found that his whole family had departed with Pompeius across the Adriatic. A freedman left in charge of the house told me that Pompeius had requested the use of his master's ships for the transport of men and stores. Publius had felt bound to cooperate. He owed an obligation to Pompeius who had given him the opportunity to start his business at the end of the campaign against the pirates. The estate was magnificent, with over two hundred slaves employed in the production of oil and wine. The stables accommodated fifty or more horses which had all gone to serve in Pompeius' cavalry. The house was richly decorated with gold and ivory from the Orient. Wherever you looked you saw plates, goblets, and flagons of chased silver. Marble statues of Athena and Venus stood in the atrium and the rooms were pervaded with the fragrance of myrrh, cinnamon and tarragon. By a stream in the gardens Pan carved in stone played his pipes which sounded when the breeze rustled another set of metal ones hanging in the tamarisk tree above. The walls were hung with silks on which were curious designs and depictions of people of some race which I had never seen before. The freedman told me that they were bought from merchants on camels who came from distant lands in the East, far beyond where Alexander the Great had marched. Publius had prospered and I was saddened that I had missed him. It was at least ten years since we had met.

We soon accomplished the submission of the Pompeian legions in Spain and on the way back Massilia, which had declared for Pompeius, was besieged and surrendered to us. There was no sign of Milo, otherwise I might have fulfilled Fulvia's request to finish him. Our only reverse came in

Africa where Curio was too impetuous and got himself killed. Poor Fulvia; she married Marcus Antonius later and had two sons by him. I heard recently that she had died of a broken heart in Greece when Antonius wrote that he was abandoning her for Cleopatra.

By the time of the winter solstice we were back at Brundisium, ready to embark troops and cross the sea to Epirus. This however was not without its difficulties. Apart from the danger of a winter crossing, we knew that Caesar's old enemy and consular colleague Marcus Bibulus was waiting on the other side with a large fleet. He patrolled the coast with orders to intercept our transports and destroy them. Our vessels could only accommodate about fifteen thousand legionaries and a handful of cavalry. Marcus Antonius was left behind with four legions and the rest of the cavalry. The plan was that he should follow in the empty boats when they returned to Brundisium after landing us.

The men were nervous as we set sail. The overloaded boats sat low in the water. The horses whinnied continuously at the movement of the deck under their legs. This was unsettling. We hoped to approach the enemy coast silently under cover of darkness, so as not to arouse the attention of Bibulus and his fleet. Despite the dangers, the crossing went smoothly. The sea remained calm and the galleys propelled us swiftly across the Adriatic. A clear sky enabled us to steer by the stars. Keeping to the north of Corcyra, where we thought Bibulus had his base, we were able to run ashore soon after dawn at a place called Palaeste. It was the fifth of January and Caesar had been consul with Publius Servilius for five days.

We turned the ships round immediately to fetch the remaining forces from Brundisium. This time however we were not so lucky. Bibulus must have got wind of our landing and intercepted the fleet shortly after it set sail. He burnt thirty transports and their crews as well. Only a few made it back to Italy. Meanwhile we set about establishing ourselves in Epirus and making it difficult for Bibulus to get fresh water to his ships by denying them access to the shore. This was so successful that Bibulus and his lieutenant Libo sought a meeting at Oricum, a port further up the coast from Palaeste, to discuss terms. Caesar had hoped that he might be able to negotiate a settlement with Pompeius through a man called Vibullius, who was a friend of both of them. It soon became clear, however, that Libo only wanted a truce for his boats. This was of no interest to us.

The winter months passed. We heard that Bibulus had died of exposure and that Libo had sailed with a fleet to Brundisium to blockade the harbour and prevent Antonius from sailing. Antonius however employed tactics similar to those which we had used against Bibulus and drove Libo off by denying him fresh water. Nevertheless, Antonius had still not succeeded in crossing to join us and meanwhile Pompeius was advancing from Macedonia and Candavia with a large army. Caesar was determined to avoid battle until Antonius arrived. At last we received a message that he had landed away to the north at Nymphaeum. He had brought three legions of veterans, one of recruits and about eight hundred cavalry. Our scouts reported that Pompeius had changed the direction of his march and was aiming to intercept Antonius before he could join us. We could only prevent this by forced marches to enable us to get close enough to Antonius so that Pompeius would be caught between us, if he persisted in the same line of advance. Caesar sent gallopers to Antonius urging him to make all speed southwards. For two days our legions, travelling with only the kit essential to fight if necessary and leaving the baggage wagons with a small escort, jogged across rough country. It was hard going but Caesar urged the men on, saying that their lives and those of the legionaries with Antonius depended on it. At last, towards evening of the

328

second day, a galloper came in saying that Pompeius' army had halted and pitched camp somewhere off the Egnatian Way. He must have realised that if he had continued to move westwards he could have found himself trapped.

The following morning the standards of Antonius' legions came into view and we joined forces north of Dyrrachium. That night over dinner he and his legate, Fufius Calenus, told us how their ships had been spotted from the shore as they coasted northwards seeking a place to land. A fleet had been sent to intercept but had been unable to catch them because of a contrary wind which had turned into a storm and wrecked the Pompeian galleys on a promontory off Lissus. Caesar said that the fact that we had succeeded in getting the army across the Adriatic in winter against a hostile fleet was a good omen. It showed that the gods favoured our cause. Over the next few weeks I began to have my doubts, for next came the campaign at Dyrrachium and the first clash between the two big cats. All that had gone before was only preliminary skirmishing. The decisive phase of the war was upon us. Gaius Julius Caesar and Gnaeus Pompeius, to whom Sulla had given the title 'the Great', had come face to face. The world waited on the outcome.

Chapter XIX

48 BC

Having failed in his attempt to intercept Antonius, Pompeius continued to the coast and pitched camp at a place called Petra, just south of his main supply base at Dyrrachium. It was clear that he was in no hurry to fight. He could obtain supplies by sea and we knew that he had laid in a good store of corn. Our supply position was much more difficult, as Pompeius well knew. We had little corn and it was too early in the year for there to be any available in the fields. Nevertheless we managed to site our own camp some two miles north of that of Pompeius, thereby cutting off his land route to Dyrrachium.

Next Pompeius fortified an area stretching southwards from his camp for about six or seven miles towards a small river called the Lesnikia and extending inland for between a mile and two miles. Here he could graze his horses within his lines or send foraging parties further afield. In contrast we were cut off from Italy by his fleet which continued to patrol off the coast.

Caesar called a meeting of his legates and some of the senior military tribunes. It was clear, he said, that the strategy of the Pompeians was to secure their own supplies and avoid battle. There was little food to be had locally with which to feed our army and the Pompeians would watch and wait for their opportunity to strike when we had been weakened by famine and disease. The enemy's plan, however, had not

aken account of the army of Gaul. He reminded us of how
e had encircled Alesia and starved Vercingetorix into sub-
aission. The same could be done here. There was a ring of
ills round Petra upon which we would construct forts,
oining them together with a rampart to run from our camp
own to a point south of the River Lesnikia. Once this
ortification was complete Pompeius would be confined to
is own entrenchments. This would help us to restrict the
razing for his cavalry and enable ours to forage safely
ehind our own lines. Furthermore, we could cut off the
upply of fresh water to the Pompeians by damming and
locking the streams running down to the coast from the
ills.

So the legions began to construct the forts and ramparts
vhich stretched for a distance of nearly seventeen miles. It
vas grim work, for the Pompeians did not stand idly by.
hey continually attacked our legionaries with every kind of
nissile, including javelins, darts, arrows and shot from Cre-
an slingers. Our men stuck to their task with great courage.
hey made themselves patches of wadding and leather hides
o ward off the missiles, but many lost an eye. Indeed I saw
wo men lose both eyes in one day. One of them, without
aying a word, knelt down, placed the hilt of his shortsword
n the ground with the blade pointing upwards and then
hrust himself onto it to put an end to his suffering. Every
tight shields which had been pierced in several places had
o be repaired. Caesar was in the thick of it, riding from one
ort to the next, encouraging the men constructing the
amparts and at the same time marshalling the cohorts
vhich were defending them from the missiles of the Pom-
eians. Despite the lethal rain of arrows the veterans from
Gaul took pride in demonstrating their speed and efficiency
n constructing the forts and the connecting rampart. Their
odies were almost as brown as Numidian slaves from Africa,
he result of years of exposure to the sun and the ingrained

dirt of camp life. The Pompeians shouted insults at them, saying that they looked like monkeys, but they retreated quickly enough when a cohort from the ninth or tenth legion gave them the charge. Sometimes messages were attached to arrows. A centurion showed me one which said, 'Why do you fight for the Queen of Bithynia?' He scrawled back, 'Because I prefer to be on the winning side.' Occasionally too, men found themselves in contact with others from the same area of Italy; then the insults became more bitter and the exchange of javelins and arrows sharper.

Caesar praised the men for their steadfastness and the speed with which the earthworks were completed. Of course, he understood perfectly well that the position was quite different from Alesia. Pompeius had a ready source of supplies from the sea and could leave at any time with his ships. Nevertheless, Caesar also knew that the eyes of Asia were watching the progress of the war. The image of Pompeius would be dented by the sight of his being besieged and encircled by an army less powerful than his own. It sent out a signal that Caesar had the upper hand, that we were in control. It was important to show the provinces and client kingdoms of the East that Pompeius was not invincible. If they thought that he was losing they might be slower to come forward with supplies of ships, troops and money.

In truth our position was precarious in many ways. We were desperately short of food, though we had a little meat which was obtained from local towns. To replace the lack of corn the legionaries ate a root which grew naturally in the area. It was called chara and could be chopped up and mixed with milk to make something a little like bread. This became the staple diet for a few weeks, for the root was everywhere. The Pompeians, who had plenty of corn, used to taunt our men saying that they would soon starve. Then ours would throw loaves made from chara at the Pompeian lines, telling them that this showed how hungry Caesar's army was. Ever so, the strange and restricted diet affected our health. Men fell sick and had to be withdrawn from the rampart.

One morning a galloper rode in from Lissus with the news that the son of Pompeius, also called Gnaeus, had succeeded in burning thirty of our transport ships which Marcus Antonius had left there so as to be available if we should need them to pursue the enemy back to Italy. Caesar was undismayed, pointing out that if we could beat the Pompeians on land his fleet would be irrelevant. Of more significance was the report that Metellus Scipio, who had been appointed governor of Syria at the meeting of the Senate on the seventh of January the previous year, was advancing with two legions through Macedonia. It was imperative that Scipio be held in check. Though we could ill spare them it was decided to send the eleventh and twelfth under the command of Cnaeus Domitius Calvinus to oppose him. Domitius was an experienced general who was confident that he could defeat Scipio in a straight fight. As he said to me before leaving, 'Scipio has only one military virtue, his name. For the rest, he is nothing but a vicious and corrupt slug.' Remembering my experience with Scipio when I was aedile, I said that I hoped Domitius would bring back his opponent in several pieces for us to share out. Nevertheless Caesar was anxious at the threat posed by Scipio who could easily disrupt our attempts to secure a supply of corn from the towns in Thessaly and Aetolia. He therefore ordered Domitius to advance rapidly with a view to halting Scipio as far away to the east as possible. Reports came in daily that the two armies were closing on each other. Then Scipio, true to character, turned away to the south where he had spotted an easier opponent. In the plains of Thessaly south of the river Haliacmon lay a legion of new recruits, the twenty-seventh, which Caesar had sent here under the command of Cassius Longinus to try to secure a supply of corn. Scipio saw his chance; one legion of new recruits was a lot more attractive a target than two legions of the army of Gaul. Longinus knew that his men were no match for Scipio's force which included cavalry, and retreated hastily into the mountains. In his anxiety to catch his prey, Scipio abandoned his baggage at a camp on the river and pursued Longinus in light order. On hearing this Domitius immediately advanced towards the baggage camp which was held only by a few cohorts. This forced Scipio to turn about and hurry back to the camp on the river. Here over a period of several days Domitius attempted to bring Scipio to battle. A little skirmishing took place without any general engagement. Scipio would not come out to fight. Caesar sent orders to Domitius to keep in contact with the enemy and try to prevent any further advance in our direction.

At Dyrrachium the position was stalemate. We were worried about the disease running through the legions. Despite this, morale remained high. Deserters were coming over to our lines and reporting that there was a serious shortage of fresh water in the Pompeian camp. Our damming of the streams was beginning to bite. Fodder for their horses was also in short supply. Pompeius had large numbers of cavalry for which forage had to be brought in by sea. One evening Caesar called his staff together and warned us to expect a breakout by the enemy. 'As the weather gets warmer and drier their situation will become more desperate. We must be vigilant. I am sure that Pompeius will make a move soon.' Caesar was relying upon intelligence which we were gleaning from the Pompeian deserters. Unfortunately there were also men crossing from our lines to the enemy and providing information about our fortifications. These men were not legionaries whom nothing would induce to betray Caesar, but cavalrymen recruited in Gaul from the tribe of the Allobroges. These traitors told Pom-

334

eius that there was a gap in our lines about a mile to the
outh of the river Lesnikia.

It happened in this way. Just up from the seashore we had
onstructed a rampart and ditch which were part of the lines
encircling the enemy and led to the camp of the ninth
region situated about two miles further inland. About half a
mile further south we had constructed another rampart
running parallel with the one forming part of the inner ring
of fortifications. The purpose of this second rampart was to
enable the legions to defend the position if Pompeius
should seek to outflank us by landing boats beyond the
southern extremity of our fortifications. Unfortunately, however, the legionaries had not had time to build a cross wall
between the two ramparts on the seaward side. It was this
piece of information which we believe the Allobroges com-
municated to Pompeius.

On the day of the battle I had set out from our camp at
the northern end of our lines. It was a beautiful morning in
July and I intended to exercise my horse with a ride over
the hills round Petra. Over to my right I glimpsed the waters
of the Adriatic. The air was fresh and the sun was not yet
hot, for it was still very early in the day. As I cantered along
I could see the sentries on the ramparts, sometimes above
me, sometimes below. In front of them stood palisades and
leather screens supported on stout wooden frames to give
protection from arrows and slingshot. At regular intervals
were the forts where a cohort or two might be concentrated,
ready to move to any point under threat. I came to a fort
which was manned by men from the first and second cohorts
of the eighth. I stopped to chat with Titus Seguntius who
was an old friend from the days in Gaul and had been with
me on the terrace at Avaricum. He was standing with a
couple of legionaries on the rampart itself and asked me to
step up the ladder. He pointed with his centurion's stick

335

and said, 'Look over there, sir, what do you see?' I looked but saw nothing and said so. 'Precisely, sir. There don't seem to be enough of those Pompeian rats about this morning.' I looked again and saw what he meant. The usual movement of men going about the daily life of camp was absent. The Pompeian lines appeared a little deserted apart from a few sentries patrolling their entrenchments. 'I don't like it, sir. They're up to something. Do you think they're sailing away?' I agreed that it seemed strange and suggested that he should send a report back to headquarters. I bad Titus good day and rode on with a more alert eye.

I had not gone far before I became aware of a great hubbub coming from somewhere near the shore away to the south. I slapped the withers of my horse and we galloped towards what I had already sensed was trouble. Just before reached our last fort, which was situated a little way north of the Via Egnatia and the camp of the ninth, I looked down to see that the Pompeians had landed on the seashore near the end of the parallel ramparts. Our legionaries had been camping out on the beach preparatory to constructing the cross wall to connect them. Now it was too late. The Pompeians were swarming up the beach and into the gap which was like a road leading between the two fortifications to the camp. Our men had been caught completely off guard and some were not even armed. The Pompeians, by contrast, were fully armed and had wicker coverings on their helmets as additional protection from arrows and javelins. I dug my heels into my horse and galloped down to the camp where found a young quaestor, Lentulus Marcellinus, in command He was frantically ordering cohorts to advance to the assistance of their beleaguered comrades. Men rushed through the gate buckling on armour and putting on helmets as they ran forward. I ordered Marcellinus to make smoke signal immediately to request assistance from Marcus Antonius who lay with several cohorts at one of our forts about a mile way. We sent two gallopers northwards to inform Caesar and then rode out with a handful of cavalry to try to stem the tide of panic which had engulfed our men.

The situation which met our eyes was the most chaotic I had ever witnessed. The Pompeians were pursuing our men who were making little effort to resist, partly because they had only stones and entrenching tools with which to fight, having left their weapons in camp. This human river flowing back towards the camp was met by the cohorts which Marcellinus had rushed forward, who were ill prepared themselves and not properly marshalled. The result was that they too were infected by the general panic. The centurions and the standard bearers fought desperately to restore order. I rode round slapping fleeing men on the back with the flat of my sword, urging them to turn and fight, showing them that the eagle of the ninth was in danger of being captured, the greatest possible humiliation that could befall any legion. Some did turn to face the enemy, others were so panic stricken that nothing could stop them. I broke my sword on the helmet of a Pompeian. It had served me ever since I had first joined the army of Lucullus in Pontus and I was sad to lose it. I shouted to a soldier to give me his and continued to hack at anything within reach. Gradually we managed to bring the relieving cohorts through the swirling mass of confusion caused by men stumbling over one another in their anxiety to escape from the sword thrusts of the Pompeian legionaries. The cohorts deployed in three ranks between the two ramparts to slow the enemy's advance. Now we were being attacked from the flank as well where the Pompeians had come up on the outside of each rampart and then sought to assault us from the side and even from the rear. We were retreating steadily and sustaining heavy casualties. I saw a friend of mine, an equestrian from Puteoli called Aulus Granius, thrown from his horse with a sword thrust through his guts. There was nothing I could do. The enemy had almost reached the Egnatian Way beyond which the camp lay virtually undefended. Just as I and those around me believed that we were about to die, a great shout went up behind us. I turned to see Marcus Antonius with several cohorts coming at the double down from the high ground behind the camp. The sight of these reinforcements not only encouraged our men, it also caused the Pompeians to check their advance. Within a few minutes we had stabilised the situation and then forced the Pompeians back towards the seashore as the fresh cohorts came into the front line. Nevertheless, the Pompeians had scored a considerable victory. In addition to killing a large number of legionaries and centurions from the ninth, they had also established a camp outside the southern rampart which they now proceeded to fortify.

Caesar arrived not long after the fighting had ended. Many of the surviving centurions came to him in the camp saying that the legionaries wanted to be punished for having failed him. They asked that the usual penalty in such circumstances be meted out, namely that the soldiers should draw lots and that every tenth man should be executed. Caesar spoke to the men, telling them that they were no different now from the soldiers who had served him faithfully and bravely throughout the campaigns in Gaul. They had lost a battle but they had not lost a war. They would have a chance to redeem themselves. Meanwhile he had no intention of adding to the losses of the day by executing every tenth man. He ordered them to gather the bodies of their comrades and give them an honourable burial.

Worse was to follow a few days later. There was an old camp of ours lying between the northern rampart and the river. Our scouts reported that a Pompeian legion had occupied the place and Caesar resolved to try to retake it with a force of thirty-three cohorts including men from the ninth. I did not take part in the attack which at first was successful. Pompeius, however, withdrew five legions from work on fortifying his new camp and was able to drive our men out of their position. It was a second defeat for us in the space of a few days. Pompeius had broken the blockade. He could now obtain fresh water and fodder for his horses without having to rely upon supplies by sea.

That night Caesar called a council of war at the camp of the ninth. Marcus Antonius, Fabius, Publius Sulla, Gaius Volusenus, Hirtius and I were present. Caesar started by saying that we would have to rethink our strategy. The blockade was broken and there was no purpose in remaining where we were. Indeed we were lucky to have survived at all. 'Today the Pompeians would have won complete victory if they had had a commander who still knew how to be a winner. But he has lost his confidence; he did not press home the advantage when he had us on the run.' Marcus Antonius suggested that there were too many senators and other generals to whom Pompeius listened when he would be better to follow his own judgement.

'What would you do now, Marcus, if you were in Pompeius' position?' asked Caesar.

'I think I would put it about that Caesar had sustained a great defeat at Dyrrachium, to impress the eastern provinces. Then I would take ship and embark all my forces and return to Italy. I would leave nothing behind. Having reached Italy, I would hold elections to appoint consuls, praetors and other magistrates. I would use my fleet to maintain control of the sea and secure supplies to Rome and Italy, which is after all what we are fighting about. The army would be used to regain control of the western provinces and keep the boundaries of Italy itself secure. In this way I would re-establish the authority of the Republic. It would have the appearance of legitimacy and you would appear as a failed rebel and outlaw. You could of course invade Italy, which would necessitate building a new fleet or a long march through Illyricum. The legions are tired and some of the men are sick. They might not be willing to embark on such an arduous campaign.'

Caesar nodded. 'Militarily, I think that your advice to Pompeius would be sound, but I am not convinced that is what he will do. What do you think, Fabius?'

'I think like Antonius that Pompeius' best strategy is to return to Italy. Why risk a battle here when you can get most of what you want simply by sailing back across the sea?'

'And your position, Lucius?' Caesar turned to me.

'I agree with the others that Pompeius would do best to return to Italy, and yet there are reasons to suppose that is not what he will do,' I said. 'For one thing he would have to abandon Scipio and his two legions. For another, I believe that there are many senators with Pompeius who will try to influence him into fighting a decisive battle with you, particularly after the events of the past few days. People like Ahenobarbus, Spinther and Cato desire your defeat at all costs. They will see this as the opportunity to seize victory. There are others who have an interest in prosecuting the war which provides them with a chance to recoup their fortunes from the confiscated estates of the defeated. Peace will not help them to do this. Pompeius also knows that by going back to Italy he does not solve the problem. You have followed him once across the Adriatic; you might do so again. Italy has a long coastline. It would be impossible to guard it against invasion. But in the end it will be his sense of honour and vanity that will persuade him to try to defeat you one way or another here in Greece. He has been chased out of Italy and cooped up in Dyrrachium. Your victories in Gaul have demonstrated to the world that Pompeius is no longer the first man in Rome. While he does not necessarily seek power, Pompeius desires the respect and admiration of his fellow men. Only by defeating you can he regain these

340

ings. So, while I agree it is the right strategy, I do not think Pompeius will return to Italy yet.'

'I am inclined to agree with you, Lucius, though Pompeius may well prove us wrong. What we would least like him to do is to embark for Italy, as this would deprive us, certainly in the short term, of the opportunity to bring him to battle. He has more infantry than us and a lot more cavalry, but I still believe that our Gallic veterans will fight better than his men.'

'Would it not be our best chance of bringing about a decisive battle if we were to retreat from here?' It was Hirtius who spoke now. 'This would give the impression that we were frightened after the recent defeats and encourage Pompeius to pursue us. We might then get the opportunity to fight on ground of our own choosing.'

'I am sure,' said Caesar, 'that we have to retreat in any event. The corn is beginning to ripen in the fields. If we move inland it should be possible to improve our supply position, both from the towns of Thessaly and Epirus and from the open land where our men and horses will find more to eat. I should also like to get our wounded away from here and leave them at Apollonia. This will be better for them and enable us to march at greater speed. We need too to join forces again with Domitius. There is a danger that if we move south towards Thessaly where there is food, Pompeius may strike east and try to catch Domitius before he can link up with us. I am convinced that Pompeius will stay in Greece, but I suspect that he may seek to avoid battle and hope that the towns and cities will close their gates to us, having decided that Pompeius is the more likely victor. He will operate on the basis that our men will melt away through desertion brought about by hunger and disease. This is what we must prevent. Tomorrow we shall prepare discreetly to strike camp and move off in light order at dawn

341

the next day, having sent the baggage in advance at nightfall tomorrow. In that way we should be able to get well ahead of Pompeius, on the assumption that he chooses to follow; I firmly believe that he will.'

Afterwards Caesar told me that his former trusted legate Labienus, who had, as suspected, defected to Pompeius, had executed in cold blood all the prisoners taken from us in the recent battles. He had first addressed them in sneering terms, asking what sort of veterans ran away in the face of the enemy. The ninth had witnessed the deed from their rampart in front of which the prisoners were paraded. Other troops further up the lines were unaware of what had happened. 'I suspect he did it to prove his newly found loyalty to Pompeius,' said Caesar. 'If I ever catch him, I will have him dragged through the streets of Rome and beaten before he is thrown from the Tarpeian Rock like some common criminal.'

The following day Caesar spoke to all the military tribunes. He explained to them his concerns for the health of the men and the need to obtain a corn supply. The harvest was now ripening in the plains of Thessaly away to the south. This is where we would march with all speed, hoping that Pompeius would follow and give us the opportunity to defeat him in a fair fight. Caesar did not mention that the morale of some of the legionaries had been shaken by the success of Pompeius in breaking the blockade. He was anxious to buy some time and let this heal the shame of legion IX.

That night the baggage train stole away after dark, travelling south along the Egnatian Way towards Asparagium and Apollonia with only one legion for an escort. We strove to ensure that nothing unusual was observed from the Pompeian lines and then in the morning before dawn the army marched out of camp in light order. We left two legions to patrol the ramparts until the last moment so that it was some hours before the Pompeians realised we had gone

Sure enough, our scouts soon reported that Pompeius had set off in pursuit. His cavalry rode hard and came up with our rearguard on the River Genusus. We beat them off easily enough. The enemy infantry, however, proved no match for our veterans in their speed of march. The army of Gaul showed why Caesar had such a reputation for swiftness. Even though some were sick and others wounded we could comfortably outstrip our pursuers. Caesar was worried that this would persuade Pompeius to abandon the chase and turn east to attack Domitius. We sent urgent messages via horsemen, warning him that Pompeius might be approaching. No reply was received and we suspected that our messengers were being intercepted and killed. A rumour reached us that Domitius had been seen heading towards Heraclia in search of corn for his men. He was advancing straight towards the lion's jaws. Pompeius veered off towards Macedonia, presumably to join up with Scipio, or did he know that Domitius lay in front of him? Caesar paced up and down, angry that he could not establish contact with his general who might at any moment be confronted by an overwhelmingly larger force.

Fortunately, though we did not know it at the time, Domitius' advance scouts had fallen in with some Gallic cavalry who had deserted from our side to Pompeius during the siege at Dyrrachium. The Gauls boasted to their erstwhile colleagues of their great victory on the coast and that Pompeius was now marching inland to dispose of the remnants of Caesar's army. In the nick of time Domitius was alerted to the situation and turned south. Marching with all speed he crossed the Haliacmon to meet us at Aeginium in Thessaly. For the previous four days Caesar had been brooding and silent. He felt he had been incompetent and lost control. It was only his legendary luck which had delivered Domitius back to us unscathed. His spirits were buoyed up by the realisation that this luck, this peculiar genius to escape from tight situations, had not deserted him. When Domitius jumped down from his horse and advanced to greet his commander-in-chief, Caesar clasped him round the waist and did a little jig in celebration. That night Caesar spoke of his confidence that Pompeius could be defeated if we could only get him to fight.

'On the basis that you always do what your opponent least wants you to do, Pompeius has made a mistake. He has followed us instead of returning to Italy. Let us hope that he gives us the chance to make him pay for it.'

We marched through Thessaly, putting to the sword the inhabitants of any town which refused to open its gates to us and supply us with corn. Caesar was determined to put the whole of Greece on notice that the army of Gaul had not been defeated and must still be obeyed.

We pitched camp in a plain where the corn was ripening in the fields. It was high summer and the men basked in the sun. Nearby ran a river called the Enipeus. Water and forage were plentiful. Caesar had skilfully repaired the damage of Dyrrachium. The men had recovered from the sickness which had struck down so many. Now they were anxious again to prove themselves. They were fit, they were rested and they were ready. Near a village called Pharsalus we waited. The scouts told us that Pompeius, with Scipio who had joined him from Larissa, was approaching from the north.

Two days passed. Late one afternoon we saw a cloud of dust on the horizon as thousands of horsemen cantered along the road from Larissa. Soon the legionary standards of the Pompeian army appeared, coming on towards our camp in the plain. Then the column swung westwards across country behind two small hills. It re-emerged heading for a larger hill lying about three miles to the north-west of our position. We watched as the Pompeian legionaries began to fortify a camp on the slopes of the hill whose southern

344

pect ran down to the river. While the infantry were
ngaged in their entrenchments the cavalry came out onto
he plain seeking fodder for the horses. I watched with Gaius
olusenus, the commander of our force, which was only
bout one thousand strong. He estimated the Pompeian
orse at about seven thousand and reported this figure to
aesar who looked thoughtful and thanked Volusenus for
is advice. During the next few days he trained lightly armed
nfantrymen to fight among our cavalry, to try to compensate
or our inferior numbers. We had learned something of this
echnique from the Germans during the campaigns in Gaul.

Each morning Pompeius led his legions out onto the
purs of the hill where he was encamped, trying to tempt us
o fight on unfavourable ground. Caesar would have none
f it and said that if necessary we would march off again and
et Pompeius tire out his men in pursuing us. Caesar
elieved that his veterans could outmarch the enemy and
he opportunity might come to turn upon them suddenly
nd do battle on terrain where their cavalry would be least
ffective.

One evening when it was virtually dark and both armies
ad retired to their respective camps for the night, a curious
hing happened. A lone horseman rode up to the praetorian
ate and shouted to one of our sentries on the rampart, 'Be
eady, tomorrow Pompeius will offer battle.' Then without
nother word he turned away into the darkness. The legion-
ry, an experienced man from legion VIII, immediately
eported it to his centurion, who relayed it to the tribune,
who in turn informed Caesar. Caesar did not attach too
much importance to the incident at first. We had already
decided that the following morning we would strike camp
and march away. He must have changed his mind because
later, after our meeting had broken up, he took me with
him to see the sentry. The night was warm and sultry. We
could hear the men murmuring in their tents as we walked

down the lines to the gate. A few cooking fires continued to smoulder. Men were still squatting round them, talking quietly before turning in. Somewhere a horse whinnied in the quarter occupied by the cavalry. At the praetorian gate were several guards, their faces illuminated by the burning brands stuck in the ground or the slope of the rampart. The senior centurion of the cohort on duty came forward and saluted his commander.

'Septimius, what is this report that I've received of a solitary horseman? Can you take me to the sentry in question, I should like a word with him.' We clambered up onto the rampart where other sentries stood aside, offering respectful greetings to Caesar whom they all immediately recognised, even in the dark. Septimius led us about a couple of hundred paces along the battlement to a small guardhouse built into the base of the rampart. Inside were two or three legionaries off duty until the beginning of the third watch. Septimius roused a man who was dozing on a wooden bed. He came quickly to his senses and sprang to his feet on seeing Caesar standing in the doorway.

'Now, Publius Crastinus, tell me exactly what you saw and heard,' said Caesar, who had taken the trouble to get the man's name from Septimius. At first he spoke nervously, having never before been in the presence of his commander-in-chief. The latter soon won his confidence by asking for a hand up the ladder onto the rampart where we viewed the position at which Crastinus had been on watch when the horseman appeared. It was clear that Crastinus was a sensible man and that he was telling the truth. What was more, it transpired that the horseman had also said something like, 'I am a friend of Caesar, though he does not know it,' before warning that Pompeius would fight in the morning. Crastinus had asked the man for his name, but he would not give it, saying only that he was under an old obligation to Caesar and now he was repaying it.

346

We walked back to Caesar's tent and he summoned the legion commanders. He warned them to be ready in the morning. We would prepare to strike camp as planned but the men must be ready to fight at short notice. Then he dismissed them. He said he could not sleep and asked me to accompany him as he intended to go the rounds of the ramparts.

We made our way towards the porta decumana on the opposite side of the camp. Caesar said nothing. He seemed to be oblivious of his surroundings and I did not presume to break the silence. We clambered up onto the rampart and stood for a little while staring out over the plain. The sky was clear, myriads of stars looked down upon us. Behind us the legionaries slept. Only the sentries paced up and down, from one guardhouse to the next. Sometimes the silhouette of a helmet or an oval shield appeared, lit up against the night sky by the light of a brand. A soft breeze got up and I sensed rather than saw the corn rippling like the waters of a lake out on the plain in front of me.

Eventually Caesar began to speak, almost more to himself than to me. 'I hope I am ready. Tomorrow will decide whether it is I or Pompeius who will rule the world. I did not want it like this. I do not want to kill Roman citizens. They have forced me into it. If only there were some other way.' He fell silent. I knew that he was weeping and I placed my hand on his shoulder. After a moment we resumed our patrol, stopping every now and then to talk to startled sentries who were unaccustomed to seeing their commander-in-chief at such a time. Caesar recognised a man who had been wounded at the siege of Gergovia, an old legionary from Novum Comum called Sextus Mucius. We reminisced for a few minutes and then Caesar said, almost casually, 'We may fight tomorrow, Sextus. I think Pompeius will offer battle. Are you ready for that?'

'You've never let us down yet, sir. I think the men are

ready and they're just as loyal to you as they have ever been. If we get the opportunity we'll show those soft Pompeians how a real army fights. I can't do as much as I used to, my leg won't let me, but I can still throw a javelin and parry and thrust with a sword. You awarded me these at Gergovia, sir.' He pointed proudly to two torcs suspended from his shoulder straps.

'Yes indeed, I remember well, Sextus. You fought bravely and skilfully that day. If it had not been for your rallying the men around you who were panicking as they fell back down the slope from the walls of the town, we should have suffered even heavier casualties.'

'We learned a lesson that day, sir. We did not listen to the trumpet ordering us to retreat.'

'That may be, Sextus, but perhaps I was to blame as well. It's usually the general's fault if his soldiers find themselves in a position they cannot hold.' Caesar paused and then said, 'Do you think our legions will fight against their fellow citizens? It is one thing to besiege the enemy and another to kill in a pitched battle. Suppose you were to come face to face with men whom you know from Novum Comum. It is quite possible. Ahenobarbus, for example, has estates there where men will have been recruited.'

'Sir, those Pompeians did not treat us as fellow citizens at Dyrrachium. They shouted insults at us, called us monkeys and much worse than that. You have spared the lives of many since this war started. I was at Corfinium when the enemy were dumbfounded by your clemency. Then I saw Labienus kill all those prisoners from our legion. How could he behave like that after what we had been through together in Gaul? Pompeius and his men have insulted your honour by their behaviour. Our men will fight all right. We are devoted to you, sir, and I believe we shall make you proud of us tomorrow.'

Caesar clasped the veteran's arm and we bade him goodnight. We resumed our walk along the rampart to a point where we could see the lights of the Pompeian camp up on the hill above us. The guard changed and there was some shouting as the sentries exchanged passwords. Then all was silence again. The stars hung motionless in the sky above us. Nothing stirred the night air. It was as if time itself had stopped. Caesar sensed my thoughts for he turned to me and said, 'It would be as well, wouldn't it, if the hours would cease their passing. But no man, not even Caesar or Pompeius can do that. Tomorrow will come and the gods will decide how it will end.'

'You are Caesar,' I said. 'I believe in your destiny. The gods have decreed that you will rule the world. I have known that since we first went together to Spain. But let us help destiny by getting some sleep. We shall have to be alert if we fight in the morning.'

Caesar laughed, 'Sound, practical advice, Lucius. We must not tempt Nemesis to step in where you say that Tyche has decided.'

We had almost reached Caesar's headquarters when a bright light appeared in the sky to the south. It seemed to pass over our camp and then bury itself in a blaze of fire in the Pompeian camp on the hill. The guards outside Caesar's tent looked up and asked him what it meant. 'It means,' said Caesar, 'that tomorrow we shall move from this camp to that of Pompeius and enter it as victors. The gods have decreed it, provided we fight bravely. We shall be guided by the sure hand of my ancestor, the goddess Venus. She will be our password in the morning.'

In my own tent I lay awake. The wooden bed beneath me creaked as I tossed and turned. It was too hot to sleep. My mind was full of confused thoughts. Could it be right for a Roman army to be confronting another Roman army, for citizens to be cutting one another to pieces? Were not the legionaries on both sides merely naïve tools to further the

349

ambition of one man and the vanity of the other? Even if Caesar were justified in protecting himself against his enemies, what right had he to expose all these men to death for the sake of his own life? Tomorrow we might be defeated. Pompeius was still a highly competent general as he had demonstrated at Dyrrachium. He had more infantry than Caesar and a much larger force of cavalry. Were the veterans of Gaul too old and too tired to withstand yet another battle? After all, it was not disorganised barbarians who faced us now, but the disciplined ranks of other Roman legions. What about me? I had survived many battles and tight situations. Would I die tomorrow? More importantly, would I die bravely by a thrust in my chest and not in my back? Was there a man asleep on that hill whose destiny it was to despatch me? Where did he come from? Perhaps from Praeneste or Asculum, from Mutina or the city itself? I could not rid myself of a foreboding about the morrow, of a sensation of horror which I had never before experienced on the eve of battle. I called for my bearer and got him to bring me some wine mixed with a little water. He brought a sponge too and wiped the sweat from my face and chest. I must have fallen asleep.

I heard no trumpet at the end of the watch. Then my bearer was shaking me, reminding me that I was to be with Caesar at first light. Others were already there when I arrived. Caesar, as usual before a battle, was clear and calm. First he said that the legions must continue to appear to be packing up to move off. Carts must be loaded and the horses hitched to them. At the same time the legionaries were to don their armour and be ready to march out in battle order if Pompeius showed signs of offering to fight. The scouts were out watching intently for any indication of this. Then he turned to the disposition of our troops. On the left flank our position would be secured by the River Enipeus which had steep banks, making it difficult for the enemy to outflank us with either infantry or cavalry. Marcus Antonius was to command on this wing with the remains of legion IX, and legion VIII to reinforce it. Cnaeus Domitius Calvinus would hold the centre with approximately eighty cohorts. On the exposed right flank the cavalry would screen legion X to be commanded by Publius Cornelius Sulla, the nephew of the dictator. How ironic that Caesar's favourite legion should be in the charge of a man so closely related to an enemy. I realised that in this battle brother would be opposed to brother and sons would fight their fathers.

As Caesar was speaking we heard the sound of horses' hooves outside the tent, a hurried exchange of passwords and then two scouts entered. The enemy were emerging through the main gate of their camp and appeared to be coming lower down the slopes of the hill than had been the case on previous days. It looked as if the lone horseman of the previous night had spoken the truth. The day of reckoning had come.

We hurried out into the daylight. The red flag over Caesar's tent hung limply. The air of the young morning was fresh and the sun shone out of another cloudless sky. It would not be long before it was burning down upon us. Excitement and anticipation animated the troops. Outside Caesar's headquarters the purple tunic was displayed, the traditional sign for battle. Orders were shouted and the men abandoned all pretence of striking camp. They began to don their mail shirts; some had segmented plate armour to strap on. Javelins were issued from the central stockpile and the heavy catapults were hoisted onto carts ready for deployment. Units began to move out of the camp gates and assume their battle formations. The veterans worked purposefully and deliberately. They had done this many times before. There was no panic or rushing. They took the covers off their shields, thrust on their helmets, helped each other to adjust armour and then stood ready in their ranks, waiting

351

for the order to deploy. The standard bearers held the silver eagles aloft, many of them decorated with their individual badges and pennants.

I went to my tent and found my father's sword which I had always kept with me. I had taken to using it since breaking my own at Dyrrachium. My bearer helped with my breastplate which portrayed Hercules battling with the Nemean lion. My horse was brought and I rode out to join Caesar at his command post on a small rise in the plain. About a mile away the Pompeian forces were deploying. Over to our right we could see two legions which the scouts told us were numbers I and XV, the very same which Caesar had been ordered by the Senate to surrender for duty in Syria. 'If our cavalry can hold theirs, then the tenth should cut a fine swathe through that lot,' muttered Sulla.

By the river we saw a legion which Cicero had commanded as governor in Cilicia. In the centre we recognised Scipio's standard with the legions he had brought from Syria. Between these legionaries were stationed many other cohorts, some of which appeared to be Italian troops while others were allies from the provinces of the east and Spain. They were drawn up on the flat land of the plain and the lowest slopes of the hill behind them. A sea of helmets and the tips of javelins shimmered in the heat. Officers were riding between the legions and the blocks of cohorts, no doubt shouting orders or exhorting the men to fight well.

Caesar surveyed the scene intently, watching our men deploy to their battle positions and the enemy's manoeuvres. He caught the arm of Marcus Antonius and pointed, saying, 'I think Labienus is up to one of his old tricks. Have a look over there.' I followed his arm towards the extreme left wing of the Pompeian front. On a spur of the hill not far from the enemy camp cavalry were concentrating. This was understandable. The river would protect their right wing from a cavalry charge just as our left wing would also be covered.

We saw too that archers and slingers were being moved across towards the cavalry, leaving only the heavy infantry in the centre.

'I have seen this tactic before,' said Caesar, 'in Gaul when we were fighting against the Eburones. Labienus used his cavalry to roll up the flank of the enemy who had too little cavalry of their own to resist it. He knows that we have only about a thousand horse and that they cannot defend our legions for long against a determined flank attack. We must organise a welcoming party. I think we need about four thousand infantry with two or three javelins each. Lucius,' he had turned in his saddle and was speaking to me, 'take a cohort from the third rank of each of the legions except the tenth, and make up any shortfall from the men stationed in the centre behind Domitius. I want a force of eight cohorts deployed behind the tenth to form a fourth line. Keep the men well back and out of sight. Tell them to lie down in the grass where they can't be seen. As soon as you have them in position send a galloper for me and I will give them their orders.'

I set off for the river, intending to work my way along our lines towards the right wing. At the rear of each legion I summoned the senior centurion and ordered him to detail a cohort to follow me at the double. With the assistance of three tribunes I soon had my force mustered. As luck would have it, about two or three hundred paces behind the tenth's third line there was a piece of fairly low-lying ground. It was probably the course of a dried-up stream leading down to the river Enipeus. Into this I led the men and ordered them to lie down and remain still until they received further instruction. Caesar appeared immediately, having seen that the new line was in position. As usual he had removed his helmet so that the legionaries might recognise him. He sent for the centurions who gathered round his horse. He joked with them for a minute or two, pretending that they had been withdrawn from the line because they were too old to fight. 'Well sir,' said one, 'you had better jump down from that horse and join us.'

Then Caesar spoke seriously. 'You are to wait here concealed from the enemy. I believe that Pompeius' cavalry will charge at our cavalry which will be screening our right flank. Gaius Volusenus is a brave man and a fine leader, but his cavalry will be forced to give way by sheer weight of numbers. At this point you are to charge out as the enemy horse engage the flank of our infantry. Order your men not to throw their javelins. Instead, tell them to use them as spears to jab up into the bellies of the horses and the faces of their riders. If your men can do this I believe the enemy will turn and flee. Many of them are pretty young aristocrats who prefer the salons of Rome to a battlefield in Thessaly. They will not want their faces scarred by our ruffians. Lead your men bravely when the time comes and you will turn the day in our favour.'

I jumped off my horse and lay down at the top of the bank where I could see forward to Caesar's command post. A red flag would be hoisted when he wanted us to join battle. The grass about me was quite long. A bee settled on a flower nearby, another joined it. The sun warmed my back and the humming of the bees reminded me of sitting in my garden at Baiae. Somewhere out of sight behind me I could hear my horse munching grass. I thought of my father and touched the sword at my side. It had not been used in action by me. I wondered how many men he had killed with it. Perhaps it had killed for the last time. Perhaps I would perish before I could land a blow. I was not frightened. I felt a certain detachment. At the same time I was curious to see how we would fight against legions trained like us. Pompeius had a larger force than ours, but all depended on how you deployed it. I looked up, searching for signs of movement.

354

either army stirred. Perhaps both commanders were reluctant to give the order to attack their fellow citizens. I caught sight of Caesar. He was riding a large black horse and wearing his familiar red cloak even though the day was hot. Every now and then he paused in front of a legion. I guessed he was talking to them and bandying jokes as he always did before action. The men of legions VIII and IX shouted and waved their javelins as he moved away from them. Domitius Calvinus joined him in front of the cohorts in the centre, raising his right arm in salute. The legionaries chanted Caesar! Caesar! Caesar!' and a flock of crows which had settled to feed took off in fright.

The sun rose higher in the sky without any sign from either army. I began to grow uncomfortable in my breastplate. I could feel the sweat running down my chest. I took a swig from my water skin. How different it was from the cloudy and cold weather in which we had sometimes fought in Gaul. My mind wandered to Ala. Was she safe at Baiae? What would happen to her if we lost this battle?

A galloper arrived from Caesar. He proposed to advance and provoke the battle since Pompeius showed no inclination to move. I was to manoeuvre with my force behind the tenth so as to be ready to charge if the enemy cavalry came on as anticipated. I sent an order down the line accordingly, telling the men to remain concealed until we started to advance. In a few minutes I could see the front lines of the legions begin to march steadily towards the enemy. Then the second and third lines followed. A great wave of men was rolling over the plain towards the Pompeian army which stood still in their ranks. Our small force of cavalry under Volusenus circled round the right flank of the tenth where Caesar rode near the front line. I felt a surge of elation and confidence at the sight of our legions advancing behind their eagles in strict formation. A man helped me onto my horse and I shouted orders to the centurions to bring the men up out of the old riverbed and keep a steady distance behind the tenth.

The gap between the armies was closing, yet still the Pompeians did not move. When the front lines were within javelin distance the air suddenly filled with them, as men from each army launched their weapons. Our legionaries charged and became locked with the enemy in a sword fight in the centre ground. From where I was, perhaps a thousand paces back, I could hear the clang of sword and shield or armour, but no screaming from the dying or wounded. The fighting was intense as Roman citizen met Roman citizen. Like gladiators they did their butchery in silence and asked no quarter.

My eye, however, was on the enemy cavalry. They were coming down the hill at a trot, with spears held aloft and fine banners fluttering from poles. Many sported coloured coats on the backs of their horses and their helmets glinted reflecting the rays of the sun. I estimated them at several thousand. As they spilled out onto the level plain they swung round in a cloud of dust and moments later emerged from it, galloping towards our right flank. Bravely, Volusenus set his men to face the foe. They were a thin line in comparison to the thundering wall of horses and men bearing down upon them.

The tenth had stopped advancing when the front lines in the centre joined battle. I had already ordered my men to lie down again in the grass. We were a few hundred paces to the rear. The Pompeian cavalry was closing quickly, soon would come the screams and whinnying of horses as they careered into our forces. I searched for the signal from Caesar. Surely we must move now. Seconds later the first wave of the enemy were in amongst Volusenus' squadrons. There was chaos as men and horses clashed. Spears flew, riders fell and were trampled underfoot, horses reared

Another wave of Pompeian cavalry charged in. They had penetrated our own cavalry screen and were attacking the infantry. I saw Caesar's flag raised to order our attack. He had waited until the initial impetus of the enemy charge had been absorbed. The men leapt to their feet and ran at the enemy cavalry, some of whom were beginning to circle round to the rear of the tenth. I rode with the front line, urging the legionaries on and drawing my sword as we closed. Hearing our shouts some of the Pompeians swung round in their saddles, caught unawares by a line of infantry they had not seen. In a moment we were among them. The legionaries were pent up after the long wait. I could see fury in their eyes as they thrust upwards with their spears. Some pushed their shields up their left arms and used both hands to jab into the faces of the enemy. Others pulled at the legs of the riders, bringing them to the ground and then pinning them to the earth where they writhed like eels. They stabbed the bellies of horses causing them to rear up and throw their hapless passengers. The enemy were so many that they could not manoeuvre or bring any impetus to bear upon us. Our legionaries ran nimbly between the horses, dodging the thrusts from above. The Pompeians flailed about them with their swords which our men could outreach with their spears. I saw a young cavalryman lifted clean off his horse by the thrust of a spear which went in at his throat and emerged through the top of his head. Fear gripped his companions. They had not seen fighting like this before. To the army of Gaul it was all in a day's bloody work. First in twos and threes, then in larger numbers, the enemy turned tail and fled.

I spotted an officer trying to regroup a squadron of Pompeians and mount a charge. I sensed danger. I shouted to the men nearest to me and set my horse towards the squadron. It was almost a battle within a battle. With two or three men running at my side and several others behind me

357

we rode into the Pompeians. I made for my target, the captain rallying his men. He was shouting and gesticulating to his companions, encouraging them to turn and fight. I do not think he saw me until the last moment. My horse crashed over a fallen man who screamed in agony. The officer half turned in his saddle as I caught his eye. I swung my sword and slashed him on the neck between his helmet and his body armour. Blood spurted from the wound and he fell from his horse. My own mount lost his footing and I felt a terrible pain in my right arm as something struck it. My horse rolled over onto my leg, crushing my foot. For a moment I was conscious before passing out.

I have no notion of how long I lay there. It must have been for some time. When I came to, I found myself being carried in a litter by four legionaries. Their jerky movements caused me to shout out in agony. A shooting pain ran through my left foot and my right arm I saw had been bandaged. There was a dull red stain where the blood had seeped through. It stung as though somebody was holding a flame to it. My head ached and I felt a lump at the back where it rested on a cloak or something similar. One of the legionaries apologised for the discomfort they were causing me. 'Don't worry, sir, we'll soon have you up at the field station.'

The soldier's words alerted me, even in my confused state. Why 'up at the field station'?

'We found one up in the enemy camp, sir, on the hill. We got orders to use it. It was much better equipped than ours.'

So we had won the day. I felt no sense of elation or relief. My leg and arm hurt so much. I lay there as the men panted and grunted up the hill, stumbling and tripping over the rough ground but never dropping me. With every lurch another stab went through my leg. I had to clench my teeth to prevent myself from crying out. At last we reached the Pompeian camp and I was carried into a surgeon's tent. He

was a man I knew from the siege at Avaricum, experienced
and skilful in dealing with wounds. He took off the bandage
on my forearm to reveal a deep sword cut which had
penetrated to the bone and broken it. He stitched the skin
together, telling me I was lucky that somebody had band-
ged it quickly or I would have bled to death. He applied a
new bandage and then a splint to keep the arm straight. He
could do nothing for my foot. Bones had been crushed
under the weight of the horse. He could not mend them. In
time they would fuse. I would always walk with a limp and it
would probably be painful. He gave me a potion to relieve
the agony a little. As I lay there a soldier put a small leather
pouch by my side. He told me that he had found it next to
me when they picked me up after the battle and assumed it
was mine. I had no energy to contradict him.

There was a stir at the entrance to the tent. Before he was
leaning over me, I knew Caesar had arrived. He took my left
hand and squeezed it gently. 'Lucius, I'm so relieved. They
told me you were dead. Then I heard that you had been
brought in.' Marcus Antonius stood beside him, his great
mane of hair matted with sweat. Apparently the charge of
the fourth line had turned the battle. The enemy cavalry
had fled in the face of the onslaught and left their own
legions exposed. Our men had gone on to massacre the
archers and slingers abandoned by the enemy's retreat.
Then the third line, which had not previously been engaged,
had advanced upon the Pompeian left wing with support
from the cohorts in the centre. Our fresh troops were too
much for the Pompeians who gave ground steadily. Seeing
that the day would be his, Caesar had sent heralds forward
inviting the Italian forces in the enemy ranks to stop fighting
and ordering our own men to concentrate their attacks
upon allied formations. Many Italians had only too readily
laid down their weapons against fellow citizens, causing the
allies to lose heart and flee from the field. Having secured

359

victory in the plain the camp of Pompeius had been stormed without difficulty.

Much of this I listened to in a blur. The potion which the surgeon had given me had made me drowsy. I heard Caesar give orders that I was to be carried to the headquarters of Pompeius where he had now set up his own command post. The fresh air and the pain in my leg restored me to full consciousness and I looked around in amazement at the tent from which Pompeius had fled only a few hours previously. It resembled more the villa of a rich nobleman than the headquarters of a general. Inside were tables and couches laid out for a feast to celebrate their anticipated victory. Silver plates and goblets gleamed everywhere. The walls of the tent were hung with silks and swags of flowers. Mounds of fruit and sweetmeats lay ready to be served by slaves while great flagons of wine stood by the couches. In one corner were stacked branches of palm trees ready to fan the victors as they indulged themselves. Bunches of grapes hung from trellises decorated with trails of ivy. Wooden pillars painted with acanthus leaves supported the roof. The air was thick with the scent of roses which floated in bowls upon the tables.

Into this scene my litter was borne and placed upon a couch next to one where Caesar reclined. Opposite me lay Domitius and Publius Sulla. Everyone was most solicitous for my welfare and congratulated me upon my part in the battle. Caesar, who as usual ate little himself, kept feeding with me little slices of roasted thrush and sips of watered wine, saying that Pompeius was a poor host for not serving his guests, but that at least he kept a good table. As legates came forward to report to him he paid me great compliments, saying that nobody had done more to win the battle. If my wounds had not been so painful I should indeed have been a happy man at that moment.

Towards the end of the afternoon Caesar left, saying that

he intended to pursue the remnants of the Pompeian army who were retreating towards Larissa. It was warm inside the tent, though some of the side walls had been taken down to let in the air. The wine and the potions had eased the pain so that I fell into a sleep. When I awoke it was dark outside and oil lamps glowed on the tables. Nearby sat two servants who had been deputed by Caesar to attend to any wants that I might have. A few other officers lay on couches like me, but most had left, probably with the four legions which Caesar had taken with him. The air was sultry and still. I felt thirsty and called for some water which a slave brought to me in a goblet. I took it in my left hand and spilt some down my chest. The slave wiped it away with a towel as I gave him back the goblet. I let my arm drop back to my side. In so doing I felt the little pouch which the legionary had left with me when they brought me to the surgeon's tent. I rubbed it idly with my fingers. There was something inside like a coin, and yet it did not feel quite right. I told the slave to bring over a lamp and saw that it was a small leather purse held closed by a drawstring. With only my left hand I could not open it and asked the slave to do it for me. He untied the pouch and took from it a ring. At first I could make nothing out in the dim light of the lamp and told the slave to hold it closer. Then I saw clearly a ring that I had seen before, many, many times. It was a ring that I had known as a child and as a young man, a ring that was part of my family. It was a signet ring which had belonged to one of my ancestors, Marcus Valerius Cotta, who had been consul not long after the defeat of Hannibal by Scipio at Zama. I held it in my fingers and stared at it in horror. There could be no mistake. There was no other ring like it. It was large, too large to be worn comfortably upon a finger. On the face of it appeared in relief the she-wolf suckling Romulus and Remus, while round the edge I recognised the letters M. V. COT. COS, Marcus Valerius Cotta, Consul. It

361

was a signet ring which had been handed down through the generations of our family, from father to son. It was the ring which my father, on the day he died, had handed to my brother to keep. Publius had always carried it with him, ever since that terrible day.

My fingers began to tremble, causing me to drop the ring on the fresh turf which lined the floor of the tent. The slave bent to pick it up and hand it back to me. I motioned it away and asked him to replace it in the purse. He stood uncertainly beside my couch. I felt sick with fear. What had I done? How could that ring have been found lying beside me when I had never worn it nor seen it for so many years? Had I killed my own brother? Surely the gods would not punish me so much on one day. As I lay in that gloomy tent I tried to visualise the man whom I had struck in the neck. We had both been wearing helmets. I had seen his face only fleetingly at an angle from behind. I could not have known. I could not have known. Another voice in my head said, 'Surely you should have recognised your own brother. What have you done? What have you done?'

I told the slave to fetch four bearers and some torches. I ordered the bearers to carry me down the hill to the battlefield. Three other men in front carried the torches which flickered and smoked in the night air. The bearers had difficulty picking their way in the dark. They frequently stumbled and once one fell, tumbling me out of the litter onto some stones. I shouted at them in my agony as they cursed and lifted me back again. If the journey up the hill had been savagely painful, this was a descent into hell. We reached the level ground. One or two shadowy figures moved silently among the corpses, probably stripping bodies of valuables. They darted away at our approach. There was a stench of putrefying flesh and every now and then a groan from some dying man, who, if he were unfortunate enough to survive to daylight, would be finished with a sword through the throat to spare him further suffering. The legs of dead horses stuck out at monstrous angles. Broken swords and spears littered the ground. Occasionally a spent arrow snapped under the feet of the bearers as they struggled forward. Over all this presided the moon which cast a macabre light upon the hideous product of a summer's day.

I directed the bearers towards the part of the battlefield where the Pompeian cavalry had charged. It was not too difficult to find, for the number of dead horses distinguished it from the main clash between the infantry. Nevertheless it covered a large area and I had no recollection of where I had fallen from my horse. In the dark we peered down with the aid of the torches at the corpses strewn about the ground. I began to grow anxious. Suppose that my brother, if it was he whom I had struck, were still alive. He might die before we could find him. I ordered the bearers to stop and the men carrying the brands to move a little distance from me. I looked round in the moonlight trying to spot some feature which might jog my memory and lead us to the right area of the field. I thought I saw the gully in which I had concealed the men before the battle. Taking our direction from that, we moved to where the dead horses and cavalry-men lay even more thickly on the ground. I recognised the body of one of the legionaries who had run beside my horse towards the enemy squadron. He lay transfixed to the ground by a spear which had struck him in the stomach. I knew that we were close to the spot. The bearers carried me in turn to three or four other corpses. None bore any resemblance to Publius when their helmets were removed. I began to feel a twinge of hope. Perhaps there was some other explanation for the ring. Perhaps he had been rescued and carried away for treatment to his wound.

I ordered the bearers to walk round in an ever-widening circle, so that we should not miss any part of the ground. After a few minutes of this a man carrying one of the brands

called us over to a small dip in the ground where a dea
horse was lying. At first I could see only a blue saddlecloth
Then I made out the body of a man partly covered wher
the horse had fallen on him. A great dread seized me in th
stomach. I sensed that this was what I had been looking fo
and hoping not to find. The bearers put me down and ease
the carcass of the horse away from the body. The man wa
lying on his back with one leg tucked awkwardly up unde
his buttocks. I could see the wound at his neck and a dar
patch on the grass beside it. I cannot say why, but even ii
that dim light I knew it was Publius. I asked one of th
bearers to unstrap his helmet and ease it from his head.
saw his white face staring unseeingly up at me. The bearer
stood back, in a shadowy circle around us. I forced myself t
look at the body of my brother whom I had killed with m
father's sword.

One of the bearers went down to the river to fetch som
water. I had my litter placed next to the body and washe
the blood away. It hurt to move my right arm while I did i
and I lay back gasping and sweating when I had finished.
asked the bearers to leave, ordering them to return at daw
with some wood for a pyre. They covered me with two cloak
and I lay there in the dark next to Publius. I reached ou
with my left hand to clasp his arm. It felt very cold an
clammy, but I held onto it. I thought of my mother and m
father and asked them to forgive me. I fell asleep.

In the morning the soldiers came back and made a pyr
on which they placed Publius' body. I gave them my father'
sword which was laid beside him. I could not bear to touc
it and knew in any case that I would never use it again
Before they set light to the wood I asked the soldiers to lif
me into a standing position. Two of them propped me u
between them as I watched the flames consume the corpse
Afterwards the ashes were gathered in a casket to take bac
to his widow and his sons.

Chapter XX

They took me back to Apollonia where I rested for a few weeks. I learnt while I was there that Publius' wife, Sempronia, was in Athens where she had been awaiting the outcome of the campaign. With the aid of a scribe I wrote a letter telling her what had happened. She would know already of her husband's death, but not the circumstances. I held nothing back. I felt a little relief at setting it all down. As I dictated the words, I wondered what would have happened had either of us recognised the other in time. I knew that there would have been no death that day and that Sempronia would understand this. Caesar had already promised that the estate at Brundisium would not be forfeit, that Sempronia could return there immediately with young Publius and Valerius. I made arrangements for this and then took ship myself from Oricum to return to Baiae, landing at Puteoli some three months after the battle. I had decided not to disembark at Brundisium which would have obliged me to make the final part of the journey over land along the bumpy road through Apulia.

Soon after I reached Baiae I received a letter from Sempronia. In it she told me that Publius had only fought at Pharsalus because he believed that I had been killed at Dyrrachium during the breakout by Pompeius and the rout of the ninth. A rumour had gone round that I was among the dead and this was confirmed by someone unnamed who said that he had recognised my body lying by one of the ramparts. Knowing this, Publius had asked if he might fight with the cavalry. He had believed that for all his faults Pompeius stood for the preservation of the constitution and the Republic. He had wanted to avenge himself upon those whom he considered were responsible for my death.

My injuries prevented me from taking any further part in the civil war. In any event I had no stomach for it. After the victory at Thapsus, Caesar held a great triumph in Rome where he was careful to make it clear that the celebration was for the campaigns against the Gauls and other barbarians, not against Roman citizens. He asked me to take part and even offered me a consulship whenever I liked. For a moment I was tempted, then the shadow of my brother called me back. Perhaps I should have enjoyed seeing old friends, watching as the legionaries marched through the streets of the city singing bawdy songs, mostly about the sexual activities of their general. Caesar, decked out in purple tunic and toga, would be riding in a golden chariot up the Via Sacra to the Capitol to sacrifice to Jupiter, the wreath of victory on his head and an ivory sceptre in his hand. Behind would walk the shackled prisoners, including Vercingetorix preserved all these years to be strangled in the Tullianum afterwards. There was to be a mock sea battle on the flooded Campus Martius. The feasting and drinking would last for several days. There would be gladiator shows and many strange and exotic wild beasts would die in the arena, until at last even the common people of Rome were satiated with food, drink and blood. I had lost my appetite for all of this. I preferred the peace and tranquillity of Baiae.

I live here quietly now with Ala. Sempronia and the two boys, I call them that but of course they are long since grown men with their own families, come occasionally to visit me. We can talk quite happily of the old days. Perhaps the terrible events of Pharsalus have drawn us close

366

together. We are reassured by the comfort which each offers to the other.

When I heard the news of Caesar's murder I wondered whether they might come for me too. I was not frightened. I have seen too much of it to be fearful of death. Once or twice after Pharsalus I contemplated suicide. It would have been an easy escape from the pain which my wounds were causing me. It would provide some expiation for what had happened that day. And yet I knew that it would also be a weak and feeble thing to do. I owed a duty to Ala, to Sempronia and her two sons. To kill myself would have been to give up, to abrogate responsibility. If my wounds hurt, that was a penance, and but a small one for all the suffering that I had caused. I must live with it.

Sometimes I lie awake at night and the horror of Uxello-dunum comes back to me. I see the men kneeling in front of the chopping blocks. I hear their women screaming and the children whimpering at the sight of their mangled fathers and brothers. I shout out and Ala comes from her room to lie beside me. Then I can stop shaking, perhaps even go back to sleep. She never asks what has upset me. She says nothing. After a few moments she lays her arm across my chest and gently clasps my shoulder, drawing me to her. I do not know how a man makes himself happy; perhaps it is by making others happy. I have tried to make Ala happy since we met that day in Gaul. When I see the smile upon that beautiful, now faded face, I take pleasure again in my life. I can forget the violence and the suffering inflicted upon others. She is my redemption. When the balance sheet is drawn up, there will be something on the credit side.

My leg hurts often. I walk with a stick and rarely go down to the stream to watch the kingfishers flashing in the woody sunlight by the pool. I prefer to sit up on the terrace looking out over the Tyrrhenian Sea. I sit with my memories. I have learnt to accept them. I was a soldier in an army so strong that not only did it dominate the world, it destroyed the republic which gave birth to it. We could not know this at the time. We were fighting to extend the empire, to bring tribute to the greatest city in the world and to fulfil the ambitions of a few powerful men. We thought ourselves free because we could destroy anything that opposed us. Like many others I became immensely rich and endowed with all the material possessions that a man could want. I paid no attention to humanity and even less to the rights of others. There was no time for that. It is only now that I have come to understand that men are more important than possessions, that freedom is more important than power. We have conquered many lands and tribes, yet no Roman is a better man for that. Now we too have lost our freedom. We are at the mercy of a single ruler, a king in all but name. Octavius may or may not be a good man. Who will come after him? I shall never know. Will tyranny emerge from the funeral pyre of the Republic?

The sun is sinking slowly towards the horizon. The scent of the roses on the terrace is carried on the gentlest zephyr. Ajax stirs and rests his head again upon the sandal of my good foot. I see Ala smile as she sets a cup of wine down by my side. The warm sea begins to welcome to its bosom the golden orb of dying sun and an old soldier watches and waits for his turn to come.